HEIR OF SUN & MOON

THE FIVE REALMS   BOOK ONE

JENESSA REN

Book Cover by Marcia Godfrey @plusinfinityart

Chapter Illustrations by Athena Bliss @chaotictired

Map by Lindsey Staton @honeyy.fae

Editing by Brea Lamb and Allie Crain

First edition 2023

Paperback ISBN: 979-8-9891050-0-7

Hardcover ISBN: 979-8-9891050-1-4

To anyone who thinks it's too late to follow your dreams...
This book is proof that it isn't.

Contents

Trigger Warnings

This story contains depictions of:

Physical abuse (man hitting a woman)

Mental, verbal, and emotional abuse

Depression

Suicide ideation

Talk of self-harm

Sexually explicit scenes

Insinuation of incest

Vulgar language

Adult content

Each topic has been approached sensitively and written with the utmost respect and care, but should any of these topics be triggering for you, please do not read.

Your mental health matters.

-Jenessa

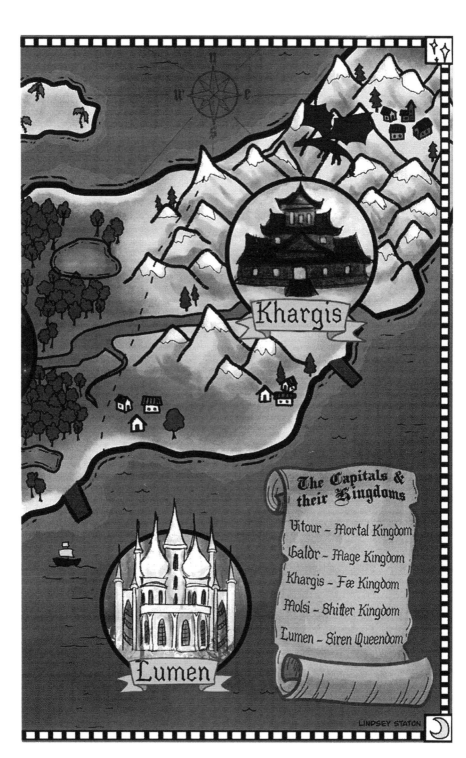

Khargis

Lumen

The Capitals &
their Kingdoms

Vitour – Mortal Kingdom

Galdr – Mage Kingdom

Khargis – Fæ Kingdom

Molsi – Shifter Kingdom

Lumen – Siren Queendom

LINDSEY STATON

Pronunciation Guide

Names:

Rhea Maxwell (Ray-uh Max-well)
Bella (Bell-uh)
Dolian Maxwell (Doal-ee-an Max-well)
Alexi (Al-ex-ee)
Flynn (Flinn)
Tienne (Tee-en-nay)
Erica (Eric-uh)
Xander (Xan-der)
Bahira Daxel (Bah-heer-uh Dax-ehl)
Sadryn Daxel (Say-drin Dax-ehl)
Alexandria Daxel (Alex-an-dree-uh Dax-ehl)
Nox Daxel (Nox Dax-ehl)
Daje Keria (Dah-jay Kare-ee-uh)
Haylee (Hay-lee)
Kallin Keria (Kall-en Kare-ee-uh)
Arav (Ar-ov)
Hadrik (Had-rick)
Osiris (Oh-sigh-ris)
Starla (Star-lah)
Cassius (Cass-ee-us)

Aria (Are-ee-uh)
Allegra (All-egg-ruh)
Lyre (Lie-ruh)

Places:
Olymazi (Ole-mah-zee): World
Vitour (Vi-toor): Capital of the Mortal Kingdom
Galdr (Gal-dahr): Capital of the Mage Kingdom
Celatum (Sell-uh-tum): Small town on the outskirts of the Mortal Kingdom

Prologue

I T IS QUITE THE predicament I have found myself in. I wince as sweat drips down my brow and a burning sensation courses through my body at the massive loss of my magic.

"It's too late isn't it, Father?" Solana asks solemnly at my side, her green eyes shining brightly. I nod from where I kneel, looking up to her with pursed lips.

"It is." I sigh as I drop my head, brows furrowing in concentration. "I've given too much."

My obsession with other worlds—with exploring what lay beyond my own realm—had led to this. As the being in charge of Void and Time, a god as some mortals have called me, I had used my magic frequently to walk within the cosmos. An insatiable hunger to learn and see and *experience* how others lived propelled me to go farther and farther.

Every time I returned to my home world, I was left feeling stagnant, like rain water collecting in a forgotten urn. The politics of life there and the daily responsibilities I held were meek in comparison to what I was discovering lie beyond. I loved my family, of course; my wife was my moon and sun and every twinkling star in the sky. She understood the restlessness I felt though, the curiosity that burned within me, particularly when it came to observing the mortals.

When Solana, my oldest daughter by marriage, showed the same curiosity, I brought her with me to explore. Drawing my magic from the black spaces between planets and stars and galaxies, we moved through voids of time to see new worlds. During our travels, we came upon a planet named Damatus. It was full of mortals who brimmed with life and a curiosity that rivaled my own. Solana and I glamored our bodies to look mortal and visited them often, watching how they interacted and found beauty in a life that was so different from what we knew.

What no one on the planet could see, however, was that their world was beginning to die. The core of it lost more of its brilliance with every visit we made. This visit was no exception. When we had reached Damatus earlier today, I noticed that the planet had started to fracture, its destruction looming in the not-so-distant future. And with it, the death of every being that resided on it.

"There must be something we can do," Solana pleaded, her eyes limning with silver as she looked out at the many mortals gathered in the city center. Children ran past, their smiles wide as they chased each other. I pretended I didn't see the way Solana's eyes lingered longingly on a nearby male, or man I supposed. She thought she was being clever at hiding her relationship with him, but much like her mother, she didn't conceal her emotions all that well.

Truthfully, there *was* something I could do, but it would require an immense amount of my magic to do it. I wasn't sure I would be able to save everyone even if I did act, but the look of anguish on Solana's face moved me. As a long-lived being who generally wasn't motivated beyond my own desires, I had to recognize that this might be a sign. Perhaps these mortals didn't deserve death merely because they were on the planet at the wrong time. Or perhaps I just loved my daughter.

"Let us try then," I replied calmly, chuckling at the widening of her eyes and the smile on her face. So like her mother, capable of feeling emotions far beyond what other *gods* like myself were accustomed to. I had never tested the abilities of my magic this far before, but I was a being that drew my gifts from the vastness of space and the essence of measure. Surely I could save these beings and bring them somewhere better.

Drawing in as much magic from the surrounding cosmos as I could summon, I began to walk between planets, my sights set on a world I had visited millennia prior and my magic taking as many mortals as I could carry. If memory served me correctly, the planet was only home to animals but would be a hospitable place for all kinds of life. It could be a new beginning for a people whose impending deaths were premature.

Time moved slowly at first as the coldness of space and infinite worlds blanketed me. I found the lull soothing as my magic pulled and pushed within. Then came a rush as Time and Void caught up, stars and galaxies surrounded me in colorful blurs before I landed on the new planet, Solana by my side. I carefully brought the mortals into the atmosphere but held them above as I caught my breath. The continent we stood upon was large, but as I looked around, I wondered if it was big enough for the amount of life I had brought with me.

"There are too many for this land, aren't there?" Solana asked, gazing out at the thick lining of trees just beyond the beach where we stood. When I answered with only a slight nod, she looked at me with a frown. "It used too much of your magic to get them here." Not a question, but a statement of observation.

I felt weaker than I ever had, and it alarmed me. "I have never done anything like this before, but I am not sure I could move them to a new planet." *Or bring us back home.*

Her frown grew deeper as though she heard my thoughts. Solana surveyed the ocean and then the jagged snow-covered mountains in the distance. "It is quite beautiful here," she whispered before she brought her attention back to me. "What do we do?" Though Solana was an adult, her voice sounded so small and unsure, like she was but a child looking to her father for advice. It, again, tugged at my heart.

"If I help them adapt to this world, I do not think we can make it back ho—"

"I know," she said softly, reaching out to hold my hand, "and I'm sorry to have asked you to do this."

"Daughter, you asked nothing of me that I wasn't already willing to do"—I squeeze her hand gently—"for you and for them..." I trailed off as an uncomfortable tightness clenched around my throat.

Solana understood what I couldn't voice, her face relaxing as her eyes glistened. "Then let us make this place and these mortals truly represent that which we love most."

And so the beings of this new planet came to be.

On one side of the continent, among the rolling hills of grass, wild-flowers, and sparse forests, I placed the first group of mortals. They were already curious and clever, so I kept them as they were, for that was the characteristic that drew me most to them. These mortals had lived together in Damatus, so I followed the same pattern as I began bringing more down onto the planet.

In the center of the continent now lived beings that included the man Solana loved. To honor her connection with him, she gave them a sprinkling of her celestial magic. I infused an inclination towards peace into their souls, making it an intrinsic part of who they were. Mages, they would be called, because of their ability to manipulate magic in its purest form.

On the other side of the continent, I created what we had called fae on our home world, giving them pointed ears similar to my own. I had noticed dragons that lived in the high mountainous terrains that would be their new home, so I gave them the ability to bond with the winged beasts.

Upon a large island to the south of the continent, I gave the mortals now there the ability to shift into any of the various animals that lived on this planet. Animals to me had always represented bravery and tenacity, which were personality traits and magical gifts of some of the gods I was leaving behind on my own world.

Finally, to honor my youngest daughter—the one I would never see again—I created an all-female race that could live in the sea. Their dark skin and ringlet hair made in her likeness, while their beautiful, powerful voices and fierce femininity rivaled that of my wife.

For each of these kingdoms, I gave them everything they would need to begin anew here. I then wiped away only the memories of the old world that the beings had come from. Magic, like all things, required balance—a price to be paid for its usage. I had saved many lives and had formed entirely new beings, but I had done so at my own expense. Even the magic I had given to this world would have a price of its own, unique to each group of life; for no gift was ever truly free. My magic now lived in the continent and in the peoples, and I knew now with certainty that I did not have a way to bring Solana and I back to our own home.

Coming back to the present moment, I look down at the ground, sweat dripping from my face onto the sand as I repeat, "I have given too much."

"It's alright," she whispers, her fingers finding my jaw and lifting my head back up to look at her. In the breeze blowing in from the ocean, her light blonde hair flutters behind her.

"I am happy to live here with them." To stay among the newly created beings and the man, now turned mage, that she loved.

"Then you shall rule here among them," I say, wrapping my hand around hers. The darkness of my skin was in such contrast with the lighter complexion of hers—though both glowed brilliantly under this planet's sun.

"I will rule over the mages and show them how to wield their new-found magic." She speaks the words with a grim finality as she turns to look back out over the thickly connected trees. "But we will let the other kingdoms find rulers of their own."

"So it shall be," I respond with a smile. A few quiet moments pass, just the sound of the waves and chattering of birds in the distance. A beautiful world indeed. "I cannot stay in this form on this planet. My body has grown too weak," I say finally, watching her face to gauge her reaction.

Though she knew this was a possibility, she is unable to hide her sadness fully.

Solana's lips tip up slightly, her grin tight as she asks, "Will I still be able to talk with you?"

I nod, sitting back on my heels. That burning sensation intensifies in my body as I accumulate the last of my remaining magic to prepare for my final act. "Use your magic, and you can meet me in a space between this world and Eternity." I pause, closing my eyes and taking in the sounds of this planet for the last time. "Name this world Olymazi for it means—"

"All together," she interjects with a pleased look on her face. "Yes, I think that fits rather well." Her chin dips for a moment before she takes a deep breath, her eyes red-rimmed when they meet mine again. "I will miss you, even with the ability to speak to you." A single tear rolls down her cheek, her love for me reflected in her glassy gaze. "Thank you, Father. For everything you have done, both on this world and beyond. I love you."

My eyes shut briefly as I let her words settle into me, easing the weight of my final moments.

"I love you too, Solana. May you always be happy and loved here." With a final squeeze, our hands separate for the last time. I pour my magic into the land, merging my body with the continent before my consciousness joins with the Aethers. My final breath is a plea of forgiveness to my youngest daughter and wife back on my home world.

"Forgive me, my loves. Until we meet again."

Chapter One

RHEA

MY EYES SHOOT OPEN as I sit up, gasping for air and swiping the hair away from my sweaty forehead. The silvery light of the moon reflects off the wood floor around me, illuminating the loft and beyond as my heart pumps wildly in my chest. It was just a nightmare.

"He's not here," I whisper as I force the memories down, my shaking hands gripping the blankets tightly. *He's not here.*

A whimper sounds to my left, coming from the bunched up comforter at my waist. Peeling the bedding back, I look down at Bella, my eyes meeting her big round golden ones. She inches out from under the warmth of the blanket to rest her head on my thigh, my fingers rustling the fluffy fur of her back as I take a deep breath. I don't usually remember my dreams, like my own subconscious doesn't want me to grasp them, but I *always* remember my nightmares. As if living them wasn't bad enough, the memories haunt me while I'm asleep as well.

Shivering at the thought, I shake my head slightly and look down into the living area below. From the loft space where my bed is, I have a partial view of the tower, excluding the library beneath me. The gray stone walls that surround me suck in any of the light offered by the moon, leaving eerie dark shadows in their wake. Sighing, I flip my pillow over—the coolness of the fabric seeping into my neck—as I lay back down and I close my eyes.

The tightness in my chest persists, tears forming despite my willing them to stop. Frustrated, I turn on my side and gaze out the window to my right. The floor-to-ceiling glass gives me a perfect view of the sparkling silver stars in the pitch black night sky and their reflection on the calm waters of the lake below. When I was a little girl, I used to pretend that each flickering light was waving hello to me, their presence offering comfort when I often felt so alone. Even now, though I'm an adult, I still imagine it.

The bed shifts as Bella moves around my feet to come lay in front of me, her body nearly as long as mine. I bring an arm around her as she nuzzles into my chest, her pointed ears partially blocking my view of the sky. The white of her fur glows from the moonlight streaming in through the window, so stark against the otherwise dark room. Despite the anxiety coiling inside me, my tired eyes crinkle as my cheeks lift into a smile. Bella's presence alone calms me enough to abate some of my terror. But I know that sleep won't come for me again tonight.

After her breaths turn even and a soft snore fills the otherwise-quiet room, I gently slide off the bed. Grabbing a long match out of the glass jar on my night table, I strike it and light the candle nestled in its bronze holder. My hair is a tangled, sweaty mess, but I find a ribbon on my white vanity long enough to tie it back away from my face. I'm in desperate need of a haircut again, but Alexi—my guard and only mortal contact besides the king—was so nervous the handful of times he did it in the past that he wasn't eager to try again. No matter how much I told him the trims always looked fine.

I stare at my reflection in the mirror, the taper candle just barely casting enough light to see the normally bright green of my eyes. Tonight, they hold fear in them, the dark circles beneath reminding me that this is the third night in a row of losing sleep. My complexion looks somewhat paler than normal, and even my heart-shaped lips lack their normal fullness, looking more dehydrated and dull. I sigh, but it isn't like I have to worry about anyone seeing me like this.

Reaching for the candle holder, I move down the wide metal spiraling staircase to the bottom level. My thin white night dress sticks to me as a breeze from a small window near the balcony cools my sweaty skin, goosebumps breaking out across my body.

Alexi would tell me optimistically to call this place my home, as if saying it enough would convince myself that it's true. I suppose to a degree it is. What is a home, if not the place you dwell all day and night? But something feels wrong calling this confinement a word as comforting as that. My books describe a home as warm and inviting. Filled with love and happiness, friends and family. Looking around, I can't imagine a colder, more lonely place.

The lower level houses the living area with a sink in the corner. A small black couch is pushed up against the outer wall. The couch faces another wall—the library on the other side—that goes up about ten feet before turning into a black metal railing that frames the loft. A worn white tea table is set in front of the couch, and the green armchair Alexi prefers is off to the side near the glass doors that lead out to a white stone balcony. The entirety of the tower, all the way up to the pointed roof, is made of the same large gray circular stones. The only exception are the floors, both on the lower level and the loft upstairs, which are a light wood.

As a teenager, I begged Alexi to bring me plants and flowers whenever he could. I needed more color—more *life*—in this tower than just Bella and I. The monotony of all those gray stones nearly drove me insane. He was able to bring in a few arastera plants that I now have potted in the corner near the balcony. Their large bright green leaves shaped like wide stars provide that break against the gray. When he can, he'll bring me fresh drangyeas from the castle gardens—the tiny blue and purple petals of my favorite flower brightening up my bedroom and freshening the sometimes-stale air.

When I reach the bottom of the steps, I turn left and enter under an arched door frame into the library. The red and gold of a formerly plush runner guides my steps into the room, my familiarity with the space allowing me to move as though my eyes were closed. There was a time when I thought I would never—ever—get close to reading all the books here. The sheer magnitude of having nearly an entire room lined with them overwhelmed me. Now I'm starting to wonder how many years of reading I have left before I've consumed them all. It can't be many more.

Do books count as friends? If so, then I have hundreds—no, more than a thousand—of those. Snorting to myself at the thought, I continue into the room that still takes my breath away after all these years. Almost every wall of the crescent-shaped library is lined with books and tomes, the finely-crafted dark brown shelves reaching far over my head. A window seat, inset into the stone beneath an arched window, is the only one in the tower that allows me to see a little bit of the main castle and the capital city of Vitour that lies beyond it.

The little flame of my candle dances with the slight breeze reaching into the room as I walk, casting a moving shadow on the furthest wall. I drag my fingers across the many colored leather spines gracing the shelves, knowing them like the back of my hand. Even in pure darkness, I could find exactly what I'm looking for. The worn down wood flooring creaks with each step I take, reminding me of the age of this room.

This tower.

This *existence*.

There. My fingers, stiff from the night air, pull out the book I want. I could close the window letting the chill in, but the truth is just having that small space open to the outside makes the inside of the tower feel less suffocating. Setting the candle down on the stone edge of the window sill, I crawl onto the cushion of the bench seat. The velvet is teal in color and lined with pillows on either side in dark green, yellow, and blue. Spreading a cream-colored blanket over my legs, I lay the book down on top. My fingers trace over the foiled title, the combination of the subtle moonlight and the small candle flame reflecting off the gold embossing. *The Little Sun*. A small smile tilts my lips, nostalgia washing over me as I begin to read.

Once upon a time, there was a little sun who was sad and lonely.
"At least the Moon has the Stars," she whispered, "yet I have no one."
Years and years passed and the sun grew more sorrowful.
"I just want someone to talk to so I am not so alone."
"You are not alone, little Sun," said a voice that spoke all around her, feminine and sweet.
"Who are you?" the little sun asked.
"I am a friend. I have always been here, but you have been too sad to truly notice."
"But I cannot see you now," the sun cried.
"Almost, little Sun. When you hover over the horizon, look to the east."
Anticipation filled the little sun. Finally, she had someone to call a friend.
When she floated over the horizon, the little sun looked east as the voice suggested. At first she saw nothing, but then, a circle of silver light grew in the distance.
"Is that you?" the sun whispered in awe.
"It is, my little Sun."
"But you are the Moon. I did not think we could ever be out at the same time."
"I've always been here, little Sun, waiting for you to notice me," the moon said softly.
"You glow so beautifully."
"It is because of you. Your light makes me shine. Just like it makes every-thing around you brighter."
The little sun sighed.

"Sometimes I do not feel like I make anything shine," the sun lamented.

"My little Sun, you bring balance to the Night. This world would not exist if not for you." The sun could sense the radiant truth in those words.

"Do I truly make you gleam?" the little sun wondered.

"Your light is the only thing that does."

The little sun felt happy that she had helped make something look so lovely.

"We don't get much time together, but look to the east, little Sun, and when we're both in the Middle, between Day and Night, I will be here with you. You are never alone."

"Forever?" the little sun asked.

"Forever," the moon answered.

Closing the book, a shaky exhale leaves my lips as a single tear slides down my cheek. I lean my head back against the cold stone wall, finding the moon in the sky—a shining beacon amongst the black—surrounded by all its tiny friends that sparkle like diamonds.

"At least the moon has the stars," I whisper before holding my breath. I know the moon won't answer, but that doesn't stop the flutter of hope that blossoms in my gut every time I utter those words. Hope that a lovely voice will beckon to me, telling me I'm not alone. I sometimes imagine my mother answering although I wouldn't know her voice if she did—she, along with my father, died the very night I was born. When I'm met with the silence I expect, my eyes drop back down to the book, sadness weighing on my bones.

As if she was summoned by my emotions, I hear Bella's giant paws pad down the metal stairs in search of me. When she enters the room, her eyes scan mine in question. I don't know if animals are supposed to be this expressive, this intuitive, but Bella always has been. I shrug a shoulder, the corners of my mouth lifting up in a smile that doesn't quite make it to my eyes. Bella huffs out a noise that sounds suspiciously like a sigh and walks closer to nudge me with her nose, a silent plea to make room for her on the bench. Her warmth seeps into me as she climbs up and curls her body next to mine. I cuddle into her, keeping my gaze on the moon. "The moon may have the stars, but at least I have you," I say quietly, giving Bella one more scratch behind her pointed ears. Her eyes close, and soon her breathing is deeper, sleep finding her easily. *How lucky.*

I watch the sun rise from my balcony, reveling in its golden rays as they pour over my skin. Breathing deeply, my eyes fall shut as I catch the scent of the freshly blooming flowers below. It's spring in the Mortal Kingdom, and while the days are beginning to warm up to a comfortable temperature, mornings and evenings are still quite chilly. Wrapping the blanket around my shoulders more tightly, I urge the wind to dry my post-bath hair more quickly.

My tower is set apart from the main castle, a long stone bridge just out of my line of sight is the only thing connecting the two. It was an old watch tower that not only housed the occasional guard, but also, at one point, weapons and other things that Alexi told me about, which I then promptly forgot.

My attention shifts back over to the dark blue lake, a few boats dotting the otherwise calm water. I imagine the people in them to be fishing or even just enjoying a day off in the sun—none the wiser that the princess they believe is hiding by choice is actually locked up against her will. Would they even help me if they knew the truth?

Bang! Bang! Bang! The knocking puts a halt to my anxious thoughts. I run barefoot across the bottom level, my light blue day dress fluttering around my ankles as I fling the old wooden door open until it smacks into the stone wall. Alexi startles, nearly dropping the large wooden box in his hands, before he shakes his head and murmurs under his breath about how I'll be the cause of his death. I bite down on my lower lip to stop my laugh from bubbling out and sweep my arm majestically in front of me to beckon him inside. He grumbles again before stepping through the doorway and into the main living area, the boots of his King's Guard uniform clicking on the worn panels. He's dressed—as he usually is—in uniform black; the only exception being the gold cuirass covering his chest and back as well as the gold sword sheathed at his waist.

At one time, there was a rug in the middle of this space, plush and light gray in color. The memory makes my shoulders tense. My throat constricts as my hands fist, an array of images playing out in my mind: a nearly lifeless body, blood pooling out on the rug, Alexi's pale face, my cries echoing out— *No*. I force the memory of that night down, down, down until my hands relax. Interlacing them in front of me, the thumb from one hand runs along the crescent shapes my nails made digging into the palm of my other hand. My smile wobbles faintly before I force it back in place.

Alexi has been with me since I was around eight years old—an imposing presence that used to frighten me as a child but I have now come to rely on for the comfort of companionship. He is the closest thing I've ever had to a parent. Illuminated by the light of the sun, I frown as I study his profile. He looks tired, the purple bags under his eyes visible even with his tanned skin.

"I cannot stay long, Little One." His voice is low, as if he's worried someone will hear—even this high up surrounded by stone. Despite that, the nickname he's called me since I was a child eases some of my concern.

"Is everything okay?" I ask, coming to kneel on the floor next to the box Alexi set down. Twice a month, I get a fresh supply of food as well as toiletries brought to me. Sometimes I even get something special, like papers and quilled pens with tiny pots of ink. My most favorite surprises, though, are desserts.

"The Cruel Death has spread. More than twenty men in the guard alone died last week, an additional hundred or so residents from the capital as well," he says in a grave voice. "We are short a few bodies in the guard until more apprentices finish their training. The king will be addressing the kingdom later this morning, and all the King's Guardsmen are required to attend."

"That sounds *almost* as much fun as attempting to train a fox to dance so that you don't go insane due to lack of entertainment," I snark as I look over my shoulder at him and smirk, watching as he rolls his brown eyes.

I don't mean to be callous; the Cruel Death is awful, and from what Alexi has told me, the way it kills is horrific. One day you could be healthy as an ox, going about your daily business, and the next you've aged ten years and started to waste away. Within a few days, you're nothing but a skeleton, your soul gone to the Afterlife. It has been this way for a long time, and no one has been able to figure out how to stop it or slow it down.

"You were able to train the fox to use the toilet; I have no doubt you could train her to dance if you really wanted to," he insists, fighting his own grin.

"You'll have to let me know what His Majesty has to say about it all. I'm sure he'll use the opportunity to drone on about how *only he* has the capability to keep our realm safe and finally end the Cruel Death." I mimic the king's voice, remembering what Alexi had told me he said at the last kingdom address he made. He doesn't care about keeping anyone safe; he only cares about having power over them—at least if his treatment of me is any indication. Alexi sighs but says nothing.

My attention goes back to the items in front of me as I pull each one out of the box: dried meat for Bella and I, apples, bread, nuts, and fresh peas. A familiar scent hits the air, my eyes widening as I squeal, pushing my honey blonde hair behind my ears and turning towards Alexi. I gasp, asking, "Is that what I think it is?" There is no hiding the excited tremble of my voice because Alexi has brought me a surprise.

Chapter Two

RHEA

I DON'T WAIT FOR him to answer as I grab—and then promptly toss—each remaining item out of the box until I get to the bottom, where the delectable scent is coming from. Alexi squats down next to me, chuckling quietly as he picks up the items I've dumped and begins to sort them. I gently lift the small box out like it might disappear if I move too gruffly. A sweet lemon scent surrounds me, and I can't help the happy sigh that releases as I inhale deeply.

"I'm sorry it isn't more. I had to sneak a slice while Emelia wasn't looking," he says while making a neat pile of my forgotten items on the floor. Emelia, the castle baker, makes the most delicious desserts, but she, apparently, doesn't like sharing them with anyone outside of the current royal family. Which is ironic given that I *am* technically part of the royal family. Or maybe she just doesn't like sharing them with Alexi.

"Don't ever apologize for bringing me even a *crumb* of this treat. I swear it is sent from the gods themselves," I beam. He smiles at my dramatics as I pull out the parchment-wrapped dessert from the box and carefully lay it on my lap.

The sun hits the yellow loaf slice as I unwrap it, making the white icing glisten. My mouth waters in response. *I will not cry happy tears about eating lemon loaf.* I should cut this into pieces to make it last, since I have no idea when I will get more, but my restraint snaps as I take a large bite. I let out a comically loud groan as the flavors dance along my taste buds. It's tantalizingly sweet and sour, perfectly balanced in every way. Mere seconds pass before the slice is completely gone and I'm licking my fingers clean of any evidence. Bella finally makes her way over, sniffing at my crumbs before turning towards me with what looks like a frown on her pointed face. "Don't look at me like that. I don't think foxes are supposed to eat lemon loaf, anyway."

She huffs in response and then walks to Alexi, her fluffy snow-white tail wagging happily from side to side. Bella's head comes up to Alexi's waist, the height just right for him to rest his hand between her ears and scratch without bending over. My eyes trace over him, noting the tense lines of his face and shoulders. I would consider him a handsome man, objectively speaking. His salt-and-pepper hair is shorter around the back and sides, while somewhat longer on the top. In the years that I've known him, I've never seen his square jaw as anything but clean-shaven. But it has always been Alexi's eyes that have held my attention the most with their expression—kind and compassionate whenever they look at me. Except for now. Now they just look tired and sad.

Alexi eyes me carefully, taking a deep breath before he says, "I'm afraid I have some bad news. You won't see me again until the next supply drop-off." His voice is tentative, a note of pain laced within it that causes the high from my treat to immediately vanish.

"You can't come back even once before then?" I ask, my breath quickening as I scan his eyes. "I'm in need of another haircut, and your skills are truly the best." I mean for the words to come out playful and sarcastic, but my voice cracks at the end, giving away my desperation.

Alexi's eyes soften further as he reaches out a hand to pull me up. When his silence goes on longer, unease settles like a rock in my stomach. He flattens his lips together like he's trying to stop the words he has to say from leaving his mouth.

"I was informed by another guard that word has traveled about me leaving my post some nights," he answers, taking another steadying breath. "I'm unaware if the king knows, but I fear for your safety if he finds out I've been coming here. I don't want him to..." He trails off, clenching his jaw as he turns his gaze out towards the balcony.

A ringing starts in my ears at his words. Going forward, he will only stop by to drop off my supplies—once every two weeks—and if he's already being watched, he won't even be able to extend those visits. My stomach drops and my knees wobble as everything around me blurs. *This can't be happening.*

Alexi is so careful—beyond careful—about when, and how long, he visits me. He always waits until the night is darkest and shadows are cast across the base of the tower door, so to the unsuspecting eye, it looks like there might be someone standing there. From what he's said, no one is allowed to even cross the long bridge that leads from the castle to my tower unless they go through a group of guards stationed on that side first. He never stays more than an hour at most, but that hour... that hour is *everything.* An hour where I hear someone else's voice for a change. An hour where I can talk to someone and have them actually respond. When, for once in my twenty-one years of being alive, I'm not completely alone. If not for that single hour a few times a week, I never would have learned how to play cards or how to spell my own name or even how to do basic math. Alexi has taught me all those things and more, in one hour increments, in the dead of night, for *years.*

My lips part slightly as my breathing increases, my chest rising and falling rapidly as if I'm sprinting. And in my head, I am. I'm sprinting towards an existence where I'm free. Free of this prison. Free of the king. Just, *free*. My hands shove into my hair, nails scraping my scalp as I tug the strands taut until I feel like I might pull them all out. There is no stopping the stinging of my eyes as my feet propel me to pace the length of the living area. A scream builds in the base of my throat, constricting the air from reaching my lungs.

I can't do this. I can't do this. I can't—

"Breathe, Little One." Alexi's hands find my shoulders, halting my movements. My head hangs low, unable to lift under the crushing weight of the loneliness and despair that sits heavy on me. He guides me to sit on the small black couch, his warm hand holding my own. "I'm sorry. I know this is hard, but we do not want the king to have more attention on you than he already does. I cannot be the reason he decides to punish you."

My face turns up to him, watching as his eyes go far away in a memory. I was young—barely fifteen—the first time the king laid his hands on me. I had made the mistake of asking about my parents—my father in particular—and had woken up on the floor with a pounding headache and a sore jaw. Alexi had come over shortly after the king left, and I'll never forget the look on his face as he rushed to where I had lain on the ground. Studying the lost expression he wears now—the furrowing of his brows and clenching of his jaw—I know he's back in that moment again. My heart hurts knowing that he feels any responsibility at all. I don't blame him for anything the king has done to me—how could I? If he attempts to step in, he'll be killed, and the king will just put someone else in his place. Someone who probably won't care if my hair needs a cut or if Bella—who isn't even supposed to be in this tower—is fed. Someone who won't sneak me treats just because he knows it's the one highlight I have in this monotonous existence.

"I hate to leave you," he says quietly, "but I have already been here longer than necessary to anyone watching." I nod my head because what else can I do? Desperation creeps in on the edges of my mind like an ominous cloud, threatening to consume any tiny amount of joy I might have dared to store in there. "Rhea..." His words trail off as he slides off the couch, kneeling on one knee before me. "You will be okay. I know it doesn't seem like it right now, but you were meant for so much more than this. I will figure out a way to help you. Do you understand?"

I turn his palm up, showcasing the white line that scars his skin. The blood oath he was forced to make by the king prevents him, and all other members of the King's Guard, from helping me escape this tower. If he breaks the oath in any way, the magic will demand a price—the payment will be his life. It isn't that I haven't thought about leaving on my own either; I have. It's just that, in addition to having nowhere to go, the king has also spread the lie that I'm *choosing* to be in this tower, still grieving over the loss of my parents. Would anyone help me if I told them I was an escaping princess? Would they even believe me?

Sometimes, when my sadness and hopelessness are too much to bear, I like to imagine I'm watching a form of myself who is happy. It's something I've learned to do to cope with the overwhelming loneliness. I'll see myself standing in a field of wildflowers, my head tilting back as the sun warms my face. My long hair flows freely and my green eyes sparkle with life. I'll watch as my toes grip lush grass and my fingertips delicately graze white and yellow petals. With a few slow and calculated breaths, I pretend I'm calm and carefree, just like that vision I've dreamed up. And when my eyes meet Alexi's, when the worry starts to ease from his face, I know I've done a convincing job.

He raises an eyebrow, waiting for confirmation that I heard him. A forced exasperated sigh leaves my mouth as I even out my features further, willing myself to feel nothing and placing a mask over my face. It's the mask of a woman pretending she isn't locked in a tower, tortured by her uncle and left alone to rot.

"Yes, *dad,* I heard you." The sarcasm is thick enough to distract him from looking too deeply at me, but I hope the soft smile I give him lets him know that I'm not using the title as a joke. He's the closest thing to a father I've ever had. We stare at each other for a single moment, one of us with a genuine look of happiness and the other trying with everything in her power to make it ten more seconds before falling apart. Finally, clearing his throat as he stands, Alexi lets go of my hand.

"Bella, make sure she stays out of trouble," he says with a wink to the fox. She yawns in response and lays her head back down on her paws. I follow him to the door, grabbing the box from where it was left on the floor. He steps out onto the stone platform that leads to the spiral stairs of the tower and turns, reaching out as I hand it to him. "I meant what I said. We will figure something out. I promise." His word choice is careful, making sure he doesn't accidentally invoke his blood oath.

It takes every muscle in my face to force a smile, but as soon as he heads towards the stairs and I close the door behind him, the act drops. I count to ten in my head to give Alexi time to get far enough away. The crushing weight of misery settles over my body. It starts with a single tear, its warmth rolling over my cheek and dripping onto the floor. More tears join that one until I don't even notice them anymore. Bella whines, her wet nose nudging my hand, but I'm too lost in the tsunami of my sorrow and fear to stop. Each crest of the wave is a force that pushes me deeper into the depths of my despair.

Crest. *Sadness.*

Crest. *Anguish.*

Crest. *Alone.*

Alone. Alone. Alone.

Everything hurts, and I just want it to stop. I drop to my knees, pain searing up my legs and back, but I don't care. I don't even care that Bella is frantic now, nosing at my legs to get me to notice her. I just want it to stop.

I—

I just want *me* to stop.

Lowering fully to the ground, I lay on my side and hug my knees into my chest. Cold and dark exhaustion bleeds into the edges of my body. Unable to fight the allure of sleep any longer, my eyes start to flutter shut. Briefly, I watch Bella as she stands frozen, only her head swinging side to side as her wide eyes take in something beyond my vision. Darkness and shadows wrap around me until I am finally—blissfully—numb.

The sun is nearly set, the sky aflame in orange and pink, by the time I open my eyes again. My tongue is thick as it sticks to the roof of my mouth. The cold of the wood floor feels good against my pounding head, but even if I wanted to, I can't move. My body is exhausted and heavy, like a lead weight sinking into the ground.

The tickling of fur against my legs lets me know that Bella is here with me. Forcing all my strength into my right arm, I uncurl it and slowly reach back until I feel the whiskers on her nose. She moves, coming to stand right in front of me as she lifts one of her front paws up before putting it back down again. She does this over and over until I understand she is trying to get me to sit up. I don't want to, content to lay here in my misery until I fade away forever, but Bella is insistent. So, with a deep breath, I slowly slide my hands up by my shoulders, my palms pushing into the creaking wood floors. My head swirls as I come up to sit, the throbbing there only outdone by the heavy beats of my heart.

"Now what?" I whisper to her. Bella steps forward, sorrow and sympathy reflecting in her acutely expressive eyes. She brings the top of her head to my chest, and instinctively, I wrap my arms around her massive body, hugging her tightly as I cry—shocked that I still have tears left to shed.

Time moves slowly, how I imagine it feels to wade through waist-high mud, though I've never actually felt mud before. What a silly thing to realize. When the sun is gone from the sky and the moon casts its light into the room, I finally stand up. Bella stays by my side as I head upstairs cautiously, the cold metal of each step shocking the soles of my feet. Dizziness partially obscures my vision, my head pounding to the beat of my heart.

Crawling onto the bed, I don't even bother getting under the comforter as I lay on my side. I prefer the cold and the way it cradles me, desensitizing me enough to rest. Tucking an arm under my head, my eyes close with a tormented sigh. Bella joins me, her body curling in front of mine.

"The moon may have the stars, but at least I have you," I whisper, my free arm wrapping around her as I force myself back to sleep.

Chapter Three

Rhea

A SMALL JASMINE FLOWER floats on the water, the ripples of my movements in the tub sending it twirling delicately across my body. I awoke this morning feeling a bit better, though still somehow exhausted. The sun has already crested over the horizon, brightening and warming up the interior of my tower through the windows and balcony doors.

Examining my body this morning in my vanity mirror before my bath, there were no bruises or marks from where I fell to my knees yesterday after

Alexi left. Any body aches or head pain I had was gone as well. A bone deep tiredness that bled from my broken heart and soul was the only thing that lingered. The water in the stone tub starts to cool, my sign that it is time to get out. Sighing, I stand up carefully and grab a clean towel from the basket by the sink.

My bathroom layout, like much of the tower, is simple: a gray stone sink and small counter in between the tub and a toilet. Whoever built this tower was fond of the color gray—or maybe they just wanted to ensure that whoever was here felt constricted all the time. I wrap the fluffy cotton around me and walk to a small wooden trunk near the foot of my bed in the loft. Drawing the top back, I spot my favorite dress. The fabric is light pink with small purple flowers dotting it from top to bottom. Pink ribbon trims the neckline, which scoops low, showing just the top of my cleavage, though it didn't always fit that way.

After dressing and detangling my damp hair, I take the steps down to the main floor to make something to eat for Bella and I. Setting Bella's plate of dried meat on the floor for her, I add some nuts and an apple to my own before heading towards the library. My steps are halted when I spot the potted arastera plant in the corner. The leaves that, I swear, just yesterday morning were a vibrant dark green are now withered completely into shriveled brown husks. When my fingers pinch a dried-out leaf, it pulls off easily, crumbling in my hand. Brows furrowed, I try to remember the last time I watered the plant. It couldn't have been longer than last week judging by how the soil still looks dark and not dried out... but perhaps I'm wrong.

I give it one last glance over before stepping into the library. Setting the plate down on the teal bench of the window seat, I scan the many books lining the walls of the room, trying to choose which one would be the best distraction. Bella walks in, tail wagging as she looks around the room too, like she's also trying to choose.

"Which book should we read, Bells? You pick," I offer, taking a bite of the apple.

She doesn't hesitate to start searching for a book, scanning them as if she's actually reading the titles, before stopping in front of one in particular. Her wet nose leaves a little mark on its dark-colored spine. Chuckling, I move to see the choice she's made. Sliding the black book from the tightly packed shelf, I flip it over to read the cover, the silver foiling of the title reflecting the daylight. *The History Of The Five Realms*. I lower the book and look at her.

"Really?" I ask, raising a brow. Bella turns and trots over to the bench, stepping up and taking a seat on her hind legs. Her head tilts to the side, the mortal movement making me smile.

I've read many books on the realms that surround us, my favorites among them the ones that detail the beings who dwell in each. Unfortunately, I know this book in particular is very dry. Today I was hoping for lighter subject material. Narrowing my eyes at her, we engage in a staring contest... which I promptly lose.

"Fine," I concede, walking back to her and taking my own seat. "Although if I'm being honest, I would much rather read a book about how a princess seduces a muscular and handsome knight." Bella huffs and then lays down fully, her front paws dangling off of the bench.

The book's spine cracks lightly as I open it, a familiar scent reaching my nose—one of matured leather and paper. Alexi always complains about how this room smells, as if the scent of old books is somehow offensive to him.

A map that details the main Continent, which three of the five kingdoms dwell on, is drawn on the first page. The Continent runs east to west, with the Mortal Kingdom on the west side, the Fae Kingdom on the east side, and the Mage Kingdom centered in the middle. The Mortal Kingdom is depicted with meadows and fields, as well as a large lake near the capital and a half heavily wooded area near the border. The trees extend into the entirety of the Mage Kingdom before expanding partially into the Fae Kingdom. The rest of the Fae Kingdom is mountainous, their capital located right in the middle of them.

"Here is where we are, Bells," I say pointing to where Vitour, the Mortal Kingdom's capital city, is marked on the map. "And down here is the Shifter Kingdom." I drag my finger to the large island drawn to the south of the Mortal Kingdom.

"The Siren Queendom's underwater capital is to the south of the Fae Kingdom, though they have small cities built all throughout the ocean that surround the Continent," I continue, my finger tapping on the open waters where an "X" marks their capital, Lumen. Turning the page again, it goes into detail on the history of The War Of Five Kingdoms.

"The War Of Five Kingdoms of the world Olymazi began after a failed attempt at a marriage alliance between the Siren Queendom and the Mortal Kingdom. Siren Queen Zola Malika suggested a union with her eldest daughter, Amari Malika, and the eldest son of Aron Maxwell, the Mortal King." I pause and look over to Bella, whose eyes are starting to look a little droopy. Smirking, I continue skimming.

"The alliance would have gifted some of the mortal land of the Continent to the sirens while giving the mortals access to the siren legion at will. The deal became null when Queen Zola initiated an attack on King Aron during their meeting."

When I check Bella again, she's fully asleep and faintly snoring. Smiling, I snuggle further into the velvety cushions of the bench and skip ahead in the book to where it talks about the Spell. The tome says that even after weeks of watching the Mortal Kingdom—who had enlisted the help of those from the shifter isle—and the Siren Queendom battle each other, the Mage Kingdom had remained neutral in the fight. However, when the fae rode their dragons down from the mountains, determined to ravage and conquer the distracted realms, they were forced to act. It was at this point that the ruler of the Mage Kingdom cast a spell that separated the beings and sent them all back into their own realms—and kept them there.

In the years after it was cast, there had apparently been a lot of trial and error as the beings tested the Spell to see what exactly had been done and what the limitations of the Spell were. From what I've read, whenever someone from the other kingdoms passes over their border and into another, they lose the magical ability specific to them forever. If a mortal does it, they lose their youth immediately. I wonder if the mages felt any semblance of remorse that it was one of their own that separated the world so completely.

The king had told me that it was the mages who had snuck into the castle the night I was born and murdered my parents. He said they were on their way to murder me before he intervened and stopped them. But, it didn't make sense, even with what little information I had read about the Spell, mages, and their inclination to be more pacifistic. As I grew older, he repeated this story over and over again, saying the tower was the only way I could stay safe until I was old enough for him to protect me in a different way. I wasn't sure what he meant by that but something internal questioned his words and their truth. Shaking my head, I set the book down and slide off the bench, walking over to my favorite collection of romance novels.

Humming to myself, I search the titles, reminiscing on what each book is about and which ones have the more *provocative* scenes. I have learned quite a lot about sex and romance through reading, not that it matters when I will never leave the tower and experience those things for myself. The bench is warm from the sunlight streaming in through the window when I return to lay down, crossing one leg over the other and resting my chosen novel against the front of my thighs. Bella eventually awakens from her nap, stretching her legs before looking over at me. She eyes the book I'm now reading and lets out what feels like a yip of disagreement.

"Bells, you're the one who fell asleep at your own book choice. There is no reason I should be doomed to the same fate." I give her a pointed look, pretending to be stern when her supposed indignation just makes me want to laugh. She hops off the bench, her nails clicking on the wood floor as she leaves. "Wait! Don't go, Bella! I can read this one out loud to you too." I frantically turn to a random page and start shouting, "The knight slowly lifted her dress overhead, baring her breasts to the cold air." I laugh as Bella keeps walking away. When she's out of sight, I chuckle again, turning to look out at what I can see of the castle outside the window.

Tall turrets dot the exterior every few hundred feet, the tops reaching high into the bright blue sky. The entire exterior, like my tower, is made of the same round gray stone—truly, was no other building material available when they built this estate? Dark green vines, dotted with small pink flowers, grow up the walls—different from the jasmine that travels along my tower. I imagine they are clamoring to get out of the castle's shadows and into the sunlight. I can relate.

In the distance, to the right of the castle—more directly in line with my point of view—is Vitour. Alexi has described what life is like in the capital, how merchants line the streets selling goods such as clothing, jewelry, small weapons, and delicacies. He's told me that seamstresses, taverns, blacksmiths, and apothecaries are among some of the more popular shops. I wonder if the air is rich with the scent of spices I've only ever read about or what it's like to have the noises of so many people in one spot play in your ear. I fantasize about how women my age find love in the capital. Was it at those taverns?

Despite the daunting reality of my life in confinement, hope remains within me, a reminder that I have the ability to imagine something better. That I can pretend. And so I do. I pretend that today I walk to those markets. The warmth of the sunshine turns my light-toned skin pink while my hair glistens like gold. I imagine introducing myself to the people of Vitour and partaking in everything the city has to offer.

"The princess grieves no more!" they would exclaim, though I wouldn't correct them on the lies of that assumption. I'd shake their hands and hug my people because that's who they are. My father was the king of these lands, my mother his queen. And I would be happy to be with them, to indulge in the day-to-day of being free to do as I please, where I please, and with whomever I please. I would shop at all the merchant stalls, buying new dresses and shoes without a second thought. I would visit a salon and have my hair properly trimmed.

It's easy to have hope when I pretend. Hope for a love that could heal the way I've grown up. Hope for friends that would link arms with me as we shop, smiling and laughing freely. Even hope for a family that could grow beyond just Alexi and Bella. I would simply hope.

Chapter Four

RHEA

THE DAYS BLUR TOGETHER in a continuous stream of repetition—each day the same as the one before it: wake up with the sun, clean something, practice my exercises at Alexi's behest, bathe, eat, read. Repeat. Repeat. Repeat.

I woke up this morning to the drizzling of rain outside, the gray of the skies matching the dreary stones surrounding me. The sun is hidden behind thick dark clouds, and for some inexplicable reason, tightly wound dread builds inside me. Moving around my tower, I run through my daily checklist of duties to keep busy: sweeping floors, dusting shelves, re-organizing my books by color today instead of alphabetically.

It is late in the afternoon when the reason for the heavy foreboding feeling is finally revealed. Sitting on my couch in the near dark—just the light of a few candles burning to combat the gloomy thunderclouds—I try to sew a small rip in one of my dresses. Bella is laying at my feet when suddenly her head shoots up, her ears going erect as she turns to look towards the door. There is only one person she reacts that way for. *No. No. No.* I fight to keep my breathing steady, laying the dress and sewing needle down on the tea table in front of me.

"Bella, you need to go hide. Now."

She hesitates, her eyes heavy with apprehension. The hackles on her back rise, and her tail goes straight as she comes to stand in front of me defensively. But the king never comes alone. Bella is a large fox, but she couldn't take them all on, and I'm not willing to even let her attempt it. If something happens to her, I might as well turn a sword on myself.

"Now, Bella. *Please*," I beg. Seconds pass, and I can hear the king's steps—slow and methodical—nearing. Bella finally concedes and bolts up the staircase to hide under the bed. She barely rounds the corner of the loft when the door opens and King Dolian walks in followed by his five most-trusted guards.

Unlike how Alexi only wears his weapon and cuirass, these guards dress head-to-toe in golden metal, the Mortal Kingdom's sigil of a roaring lion head engraved on their chests. They stand at attention and block the door like I'd actually try to escape if they didn't. My gaze clashes with one of the guards—his dark eyes wrinkling around the corners for a moment as he takes me in. He's new, I realize, someone I've never seen with the king before. His shoulder-length wavy black hair starkly stands out against his armor. No emotion betrays his face as he stares at me, leaving me feeling oddly exposed. None of the other guards look at me like he does.

The king steps in front of me, drawing my eyes to his. Locked in place under his harsh gaze, my body can't move. My breath catches in my throat, and I quickly clasp my hands together behind me to hide their trembling.

I refuse to cower before him this time, but there is no denying the icy fear that is coursing through my veins. He is dressed in his usual kingly uniform—a black button-up dress shirt neatly tucked into tan breeches. It's offset by an embroidered blue and gold vest that fits snugly across his chest. Shiny black riding boots without a single scuff click on the wood floors as he nears me. Outwardly, he looks every bit the regal king he presents himself to be. You would have to dig deeper, beyond the façade, to see the true evil that I know lurks beneath.

My posture is rigid as the king runs his gaze over me from top to bottom, his hazel eyes leering while a malicious smile widens his mouth. I shiver under his attention, making his smile grow even wider—the white of his teeth glowing against the shadows of his face. It is horrifying and everything my nightmares are made of.

He is everything my nightmares are made of.

"Do you no longer bow before your king, Rhea?" he chides.

The hair on my arms rises at the sound. My body trembles as I lower down into a curtsy, gaze falling to the floor as I will my face to appear calm. He tuts in disapproval, walking around me slowly and appraising my bent form. I cast my eyes further down as my legs shake, my toes trying and failing to grip onto the wood floor for balance.

The king comes to stand before me, hooking a finger under my chin to make me look up. His face transforms with a sneer, and I am immobile, pinned under the venom in his eyes. Releasing me, the king winds his hand back so quickly that I can't brace myself for what is to come. *Crack.* My head is thrown to the side with the force of his slap as my knees buckle and I fall to the ground. I hold my breath and pry my watery eyes open, a copper taste filling my mouth.

"Stand. Up."

My jaw clenches at the anger in his voice as I push through the burning sensation in my legs and come back up to stand. Any hope I had that this would be a more mild visit vanishes. His moods are always wild and unpredictable. Sometimes he comes in and just sits with me, talking as if we've always been close, as if we are actually family. But today the king is angry and I am meant to be a release for that fury. My eyes find a chipped stone on the wall behind him, and I focus on it, allowing everything else around me to blur.

"Do you have any idea what it is like running a kingdom? To have the people of this realm rely on you to make the right decisions?" he questions, voice deep with rage. I know it's rhetorical, but my surprise at the absurdity of his words nearly allows a scoff to leave my mouth. Nearly. His hand reaches out to play with a strand of my hair, twisting it between his fingers. "Of course you don't," he continues, tone full of disdain. "My father used to say I had to earn my title. I was not sure what he meant until that fateful night on the Summer Solstice."

His hand shoots out suddenly and grabs on to my jaw, his thumb and fingers running up my cheeks as he squeezes—making my lips pucker. Forcing me to look at him again, my shoulders creep towards my ears in response while I watch his eyes burn with an unmatched fury. But there is something else there too. With one hand locked on my jaw, his other slowly tucks my hair behind my ear on one side, the tender and gentle movement contrasting the anger radiating off of him. He drags a knuckle from my temple all the way down my cheek and neck to my shoulder, making my skin feel as if it's crawling under his touch.

The king's warm breath caresses over my forehead as he leans in to give me a kiss there. I've had years of practice not reacting to his touches, but it's still a battle to not try to yank away from him. Sometimes I wonder if King Dolian Maxwell, my uncle by blood, sees me as something... other than his niece. The thought chills me to my bones.

"You look more and more like her every time I visit," he murmurs, his eyes wistful as he studies me. My stomach clenches uncomfortably at the longing in his voice. "Nothing to say today? I have a hard time believing you are finally being obedient," he remarks, releasing his grip on my jaw, but not moving to back away. He just stares intently at me like he's gearing up to do *something*.

"Well," I respond automatically, "what would you like me to say?"

When his eyes narrow into slits and his body becomes tense, I know I've said the wrong thing. I start to apologize, but my plea is cut short when he brutally wraps his hand around my neck and forces me backwards until

I slam into the stone wall. Tears well in my eyes from the pain—from the fear of what's to come. His lips lift in a snarl as he looms over me. My hands grasp onto his wrist tightly as I try to pry his grip from my neck, but I'm not strong enough. His hand tightens further until I start to see stars.

"Do you think you are clever?" he asks through gritted teeth, a scrutinizing look flashing over his features. "Your father thought he was clever too, and look how that ended for him."

Each word is like a blade slicing under my skin. I wince at the clear disdain in his voice when he speaks of his brother. Warm tears slide down my cheeks, endless words and emotions I can't voice held in each drop. A familiar sensation low in my stomach starts to build within me, its humming making my fingers tingle. I first felt it years ago and it has only continued to make itself known in the time that has passed. Mostly, it appears when the king is preparing to punish me, but he must never know what I can do. So I focus on squashing it down within me, gritting my teeth as I push and push to snuff the feeling out.

The king steps quickly to the side, using his grip on my neck to throw me ruthlessly to the ground. My knees hit the floor first, swiftly followed by my hands. Sharp pain lances through my limbs, traveling to my hips and shoulders.

"You just can't help yourself, can you? You must like it when I have to punish you." He steps closer, grabbing a handful of my hair and yanking my head back, forcing me to look at him. A guttural scream leaves my throat from the pain of his grip. He leans in close as he squats down in front of me, his lips a mere inch away from my own. "I will do this until every trace of *him* is gone," he whispers. His other hand—closed into a fist—connects with my side. Air pushes out of my lungs as another shriek leaves me, my vision beginning to swirl. "We will do this until you are worthy of your title, Rhea." His fist pounds into my side again and again, my ribs aching with a pain so fierce I feel it in my toes. "Until *you* are worthy," he grits out again, the back of his hand finding my cheek. The ring he wears on his middle finger slices into my lip, blood dribbling from my mouth and onto my dress.

When he is satisfied with the damage he's caused, he lets go of my hair, and my body falls to the floor. The king stands, reaching into his pocket and coming out with a white handkerchief embroidered with his initials in gold. Calmly, he wipes my blood off of his hand, deliberately making sure there is no trace left. Like it never happened.

"I will make you different, Rhea," he vows. "You *will* be different."

My head is heavy as I hear him and his guards walk out the door, slamming it shut behind them. Darkness blurs my vision, sucking me into a void until I feel nothing at all.

Cool air caresses my cheek, tickling my eyelashes as my consciousness starts to awaken. My body feels weightless, like I'm floating on water—the smell of jasmine wafting in the wind surrounding me. In the recesses of my mind, warning bells start to go off, but the breeze and the scent, combined with a vague feeling of being insubstantial, makes my concern fade away. The last thing I can remember is falling to the ground from the king's clutches. I should feel the hard floors beneath me. Bella should be nuzzling my face to try and wake me. My body should be in pain, bruises blooming and soreness settling in bone deep. But I feel none of that.

"Open your eyes, Rhea."

A soft feminine voice surrounds me, somehow familiar, yet it's not a voice I know by heart. It takes a concentrated effort to pry open my eyes. When they finally obey, I blink multiple times to try and make my surroundings come into focus. With each blink however, the image doesn't change or sharpen—the area around me stays formless, lacking definition. There is a sky above me—no, around me—dotted with flickering stars. The sheer number of them changing the normally black night into one that glows silver. How did I get outside? I lift my hand in front of me to see if my body is really here or if I'm some sort of ghost. Maybe the king has punished me too hard, and now my soul is heading to the Afterlife.

"You are not dead, Rhea." The soothing lilt of the woman's voice is closer than before, but I still cannot see who it is.

Scanning the space above me, I notice swirls in shades of blue, red, purple, and green. Each color slowly spinning, illuminated even more by the stars. Gods, there must be millions of them. Confusion continues to build inside of me, and I'm not entirely convinced I didn't die. What is this place?

"The colors are other galaxies. Different worlds and beings and gods who dwell in them."

Who is that? My mind whirls as the feminine voice chuckles in response; the sound itself is even otherworldly.

"I'm afraid I cannot tell you who I am. And as for where you are, they call this place the Middle."

My head tilts to the side, processing what the woman said. The Middle. "I've never heard of such a place. Is it within the five realms? Wait, how did I leave my tower?"

There is no way I escaped, not on my own, which means someone has removed me. Since Alexi is bound by his blood oath to never let me leave, that means it must have been the king. But I had heard him leave the tower before succumbing to the darkness, so it couldn't have been him. Uncertainty turns to panic at the thought that I'm somewhere unknown. My eyes dart back and forth trying to understand where this place is and how I came to be here.

"Do not panic. You have not left the tower." Her voice is all around me now.

"That doesn't make sense," I blurt as I try sitting up, but it's like my body is not my own. I can't move with any fluidity.

"We don't have much time together, but I wanted to visit you here—to let you know you aren't alone." Her words give me pause, my heart pounding in my chest and mouth struggling to find my reply. Despite the chaos of my thoughts colliding with each other, I manage to finally speak.

"Who are you?"

"I am many things," she answers, amusement tinkling her tone.

This must be why I never remember my dreams—this one is extremely odd. I try once again to tilt my head around but still can't find who is speaking to me.

"When the stars try to lead you away from the false king, follow them. Look to the east for the answers you seek."

"What?" The word comes out as a squeak, my heart beating fast and loud in my ears.

"Trust the stars over the ancient trees." Her voice starts to fade away as my eyelids flutter closed. *"Look to the east."*

A growing heaviness invades my bones, like each layer of my body is being stitched back together. It feels like I'm falling through the night sky and back into Olymazi, the wind whipping through my hair and lashing against my cheek harshly. Each second that passes is another weight that presses down on me.

I keep falling, the stars swirling around me faster and faster and faster until—

My eyes fly open as I suck in a long breath. Feeling returns to my fingers and toes—a tingling sensation that slowly moves up my legs and arms to my head. I swear I can feel each separate hair follicle on my scalp. I expect to wake on the balcony, outside in the elements and under the night sky. That this was all some half dream where I straddled the line between being awake and not. Instead, I'm staring up at the rafters of my tower from the floor on the lower level—right where I remember falling before the darkness swallowed me. Bella is by my side, her golden eyes burning with emotion.

Slowly, I move to sit, leaning on the tea table for support. My hand cradles my forehead, my body tense like I truly did just come back into it from the Afterlife. While I'm happy that it wasn't a nightmare, the odd dream leaves me feeling off-kilter. Still, I remember every word that the ethereal woman said. Perhaps it is a sign that I am losing my sanity, but I find that my gut instinct is to listen to her. The words rattle around in my head as I stay seated on the floor and try to decipher their meaning.

Trust the stars over the ancient trees to guide me away from the false king. And look to the east for the answers I seek.

Chapter Five

BAHIRA

A BREEZE BLOWS IN through the open doorway, the humidity of the spring day likely making my thick curly brown hair a frizzy mess. Standing behind the old wooden table that holds memories of all my experiments—both successful and failed—I place two small glass bottles containing the dead leaves of the pirang tree in front of me. Squatting down until I'm at eye level, I reach blindly to the left for the container of water that Hadrik, a mage that sits on my father's council, infused with his raw magic. Of course, I nearly knock it over and have to hold my breath as I watch it wobble from side to side, liquid sloshing, before settling back down. *Shit, that was close.*

Councilman Hadrik is my father's oldest friend and one of the biggest supporters of my research outside of my family. While everyone in the kingdom agrees that magic is declining, no one else seems to be actively working towards finding out why. It's like there is a sense of complacency because it has been happening for so long.

I've always had a curious mind, constantly putting my nose in a book or looking down the eyepiece of a magnifier—the magnified instrument used for my experiments—trying to find the answers to questions that plagued me. My curiosity has led to a better understanding of nearly everything in the world around me, with the exception of one—what is happening to our magic and how to stop it.

Grabbing my tray of hourglasses, I flip them over to begin a count-down while I lift the infused water and pour it into one of the bottles of dead leaves. The hourglass tray is something I custom made for myself to keep track of elapsed time during my experiments. Between two planks of wood are ten hourglasses, each one a different measurement of time starting with one minute and continuing up to ten.

A soft, light green glow emanates from the bottle of decayed foliage, briefly blinding me before winking out. The oval-shaped leaves in the bottle turn vibrant green, growing in size while roots and new buds sprout. Hadriks' more powerful magic works to help bring life and new growth back into the remnants of the plant within a minute. As I expected.

In our kingdom, mages come into their magic at around eight years of age and participate in a Flame Ceremony to demonstrate how strong their prospective magic is. During the ceremony, a drop of their blood is given to the Cauldron of Vires, and a flame rises in response, the size of it indicating how powerful the child's magic has the potential to be. In centuries past, it wasn't uncommon to see a flame more than six feet tall, but magic seems to have been in more abundance then. Over the past many decades, the magic manifesting in both young and old mages has been weakening, and recently—for the first time in our history—a mage was born without magic. A fact that I am, unfortunately, very intimate with.

Sighing, I reach for the container on my right filled with the water infused by one of the younger mages. The wielder is a twelve year old girl named Alba who has just mastered infusing her magic into an element like water. This task is something that used to be learned within weeks of turning eight and starting your training. Now, along with the magic being less powerful, it takes much longer for children to learn to wield their magic in what were previously simple ways.

When the one minute hourglass finishes, I pour the infused water into the second bottle of pirang leaves. I expect at least a small amount of magic light to emit from the bottle, but nothing more than a minuscule spark of blue—the color of Alba's magic—twinkles before my eyes. I watch as the leaves slowly rehydrate and expand, turning from a dull, dead brown to a light green, but do not sprout roots or grow buds.

Then after five minutes have passed, the leaves at the top of the bottle holding Alba's magic begin to shrivel back down to brown. I stand up tall as I stretch out my back before untying my apron. I turn to the faucet in the basin built into a black stone countertop, wetting my hands before sliding them down my face. A ragged breath leaves me as frustration at our kingdom's predicament, at *my own* predicament, weighs heavily on my mind.

When it was revealed that I had no magic, I made them do the test again. *Five* times. Five drops of blood. Each with the same result: no flame growing over the cauldron—not even a tiny spark of light. I allowed myself to wallow in sadness for a long time—not even wanting to be around anyone casting magic. Which proved quite difficult considering I am the only one who doesn't have any, a fact I wish I had an explanation for. Eventually, I decided that maybe this perceived weakness was actually a test.

I am inquisitive by nature, always trying to dig deeper and see things from every perspective. Who better to try and figure out why our magic was draining, why mages were weakening, than the person with no magic to speak of? With each year that passed, I spent more and more time reading, researching, and experimenting on everything and anything that might give me a clue as to why it was happening. *Something* is making it so mage magic is growing weaker overall, and I intend to be the one to find out why it's happening and fix it. *I have to.* Because figuring that out is the only way to find my own magic.

Footsteps outside the threshold of my workshop draw my attention. My gaze lifts, a small smile curving my lips when Daje—one of my oldest friends—walks in. He smiles back at me, his blue eyes piercing in the sunlight streaming through the windows.

"Working hard, Bahira?" he asks, his voice teasing. I smile faintly in response, though my shoulders tense imperceptibly. Lately, Daje has made passing remarks about how I need to "relax about the magic stuff." What he doesn't understand, what a lot of the people around me don't understand, is that I can't just stop. If I forgo my research, I will be a princess of the Mage Kingdom—a realm known for its skill in wielding raw magic—who is magicless. That is something I just can't accept.

"Clearly," I joke, my hand motioning to the two glass jars. A knot forms in my throat when I see the jar that contained Alba's magic has already reverted the rest of the leaves back to a shriveled brown, the magic within the bottle depleted quickly. Meanwhile, the jar containing the leaves of Councilman Hadrik has stopped blooming new roots but remains alive and vibrant in color. I know the difference is significant, I just haven't figured out how yet.

Daje takes a step forward until his hip is leaning against the edge of the table. He reaches out and tucks a wayward strand of curly hair behind my ear, his gaze lingering on it before bouncing to mine. The movement is intimate—too much so—forcing me to avert my gaze and clear my throat.

"To what do I owe this visit? Are you *finally* here to help me for once?"

Daje smirks, taking my slight rejection with ease, as he straightens back up and clasps his hands behind him. The movement makes his broad chest strain against his light blue tunic, and I really can see why women obsess over him. His dark brown hair is cut close to his head, his clean-shaven jawline sharp despite the more oval shape of his face. It's his eyes that make him such a popular commodity though—the light blue of them stark against his tanned skin. He's also one of the only men that I have to physically look up to; as a taller woman, most of the men my age are at eye level or below.

"I'm afraid not. I was sent to retrieve you by your father," he says casually, walking over to the small desk that I share with our friend Haylee. My body turns as I follow him with my eyes and process what he's said, my hands flattening out on the wooden table in front of me.

"Is something wrong? Is it Nox?" The words come out of me so quickly that they are almost incomprehensible.

Daje shakes his head as he looks at me, his features easing when he takes in my panicked expression. "Your father didn't say, but he didn't appear overly concerned."

I blow out a breath at that and nod my head, following Daje out of the workshop. Three stone steps lead away from the little room built into the wide trunk of an albero tree. While I've never been to any of the other kingdoms, I can't imagine that they are as beautiful as this one. Even in the daytime, sunlight only reaches the ground through the small gaps within the dense treetops, creating a near-permanent sort of twilight. Nestled deeply within the forest, many of our dwellings and shops are built into the ancient albero trees themselves. Their massive trunks are so large and tall that as many as two stories can be built into them without disrupting its own growth and life, though mages do infuse some magic into the tree to help.

Separate from the albero trees, pirang and banya trees grow in abundance. Their wild, intertwining limbs and thick canopies provide the forest with not only shade and protection from the elements, but they also shield attacks from other kingdoms. Not that attacks could happen, with the Spell that was cast two-hundred years ago still in place. The Spell sent beings back to their own kingdoms and ensured that they couldn't leave unless they gave up their magic, a process that I had read was extremely painful and resulted in loss of life within a week. In the mortals' case, crossing borders meant giving up decades of their lives until they, too, were days away from death.

There is one exception to the consequences of the Spell that no other kingdom is aware of. It's a tightly guarded secret, one that my ancestors decided should be kept during the aftermath of the Spell's casting. Mages can walk through the magical borders without repercussion. It isn't exactly known how or *why* that is the case—perhaps it's because of the queen of Void Magic who originally cast it—but this loophole has been kept quiet for two centuries. Despite our ability to walk into the other realms without consequence, it's very rare for any mage to actually leave. It has become apparent over time that even if the Spell weren't in place, we are not exactly welcome in other kingdoms. Past foreign rulers felt that the mage queen, Lucia, made a horrible mistake and was too hurried in her decision to end the war happening at the time. They blamed all mages and made sure it was known that we were not wanted in their lands. So our people remain content here—surrounded by the trees and the safety they provide. If I'm being honest, it sounds utterly boring to find fulfillment in just merely existing, but I suppose I'm a bit of an anomaly that way.

Daje and I continue on the trail of moss-covered gray stones that weave through the forest and straight to the palace—though *palace* is too fancy a word for the warm and loving place Nox and I grew up in. I drink in the greenery around us, an abundance of color and fragrance everywhere I look. Flowers in every shade and variety grow around homes and even on top of them. Wild gardens and fruit bushes dot the land in each direction. The people here relish being surrounded by so much vegetation, by so much life.

After a few minutes, we finally reach the white stone steps that lead up to the palace. Nodding to the guards as we pass, we take the numerous steps two at a time—playfully racing each other until we reach the top. Built squarely in the middle of four of the largest albero trees in the kingdom, the three-story estate somehow manages to camouflage into the dense forest around it. A wrap-around balcony lines both the lower and upper levels, the structure made from a combination of white and black stones and wood. Each floor has arching windows every few feet, allowing what sunlight shines through the forest to pour into the palace. Green vines with small white flowers wrap around each of the balcony beams, adding not only to structural stability but the efficacy of concealment as well. Small spelled flames in glass orbs hang every few feet all around the palace, illuminating the structure with a buttery glow.

I push the large wooden double doors of the palace open, the mage sigil of an albero tree under the stars carved delicately into them. Our sandals scuff slightly on the black stone floors as we walk, and I realize I never asked Daje where I was supposed to meet my father.

"He is in the council room." Daje's voice echoes faintly off of all the stone that not only lines the floor but makes up the walls as well.

"How did you know what I was thinking?" I gape, turning to look at where he walks beside me.

"Ah, that is a secret I'll never tell," he taunts with a wink. When I narrow my eyes at him, he laughs heartily until we're a few steps away from the council room. "The secret is that you said it out loud."

I roll my eyes in response, bumping him with my shoulder as I step forward to open the door, but Daje does it first. I plaster on a small smile as I pass him, but a part of me wishes he wasn't so *chivalrous*. I'll never be the type of woman that preens over such acts, but Daje—despite being my oldest friend—believes I might find those things attractive. And for all that I care about him, I just can't *make* myself feel for him in the same way he so obviously feels for me. Even if he's never actually confessed those feelings.

Inside the council room, a long wooden table sits in the middle, the natural edge of it curving like the waves of the ocean. Around it are twelve chairs—one at the head of the table where my father sits, five on either side of him where the council members sit, and one at the end where my mother sits when she attends meetings. Two massive chandeliers of glowing flame are evenly spaced above, casting the room with enough light to make out the intricate details carved into the wood.

My father's gray eyes meet mine, a copycat to the color of my own. A symbol of the pure mage blood flowing through our veins, which makes the fact that I was born with zero magic even more gutting. When my older brother Nox dropped his blood into the Cauldron of Vires, the flame that grew was the largest our realm had seen in at least two centuries. He not only has an abundance of magic, but he can wield it more easily without growing as tired as the other mages his age, and even some that are older.

My hopes were high when it was time for my own ceremony two years later, and I couldn't wait to join Nox in all the different magic classes of the mage schools. There was a small part of me that thought maybe I'd have even more magic than him. Not because I thought it was a competition, but because I've always felt like I was different. Like I was made for *more*. I suppose the gods had a good laugh at that. I'm the princess of the Mage Kingdom who comes from two powerful parents, yet I am also the first mage in history to be born without magic.

I'll never forget the look on my father's face when not even a spark grew from the cauldron after my blood dropped in. He wasn't upset or even angry, as I worried he might be. It was pity that filled the depths of his gaze as he realized his daughter was magicless. When the crowd gaped in confusion after my fifth attempt at drawing any sort of ember, my parents and brother hugged me tightly and promised it would be okay.

As king and queen, they created a special curriculum for me to continue my studies like normal. As if *I* were normal. And I quickly realized that if I couldn't wield magic, then I would sharpen every other possible tool at my disposal. While the mage children my age played with their magic and learned summoning and infusing, I spent my time reading as much as possible about all topics and sparring with our instructor, Dilan. Being a princess didn't stop other kids from bullying me about being magicless, though. So I hardened myself until I no longer cared about the opinions of others that weren't close to me. I became formidable in every other way that I could. As I got older, and the jabs became harsher, I refused to let it affect me.

Then the offers for marriage started flowing in. I overheard my father talking with my mother about how unusual it was to have so many non-nobility ask to wed a princess, and I knew it was because they viewed me as less for what I lacked. It was even brought up in the council by some of the older members that perhaps I should be "encouraged" to marry the strongest magic wielder of eligible age, though my father quickly and furiously shut that down.

It's not that I don't want to marry eventually or that I even care if I marry someone who is of nobility or not. I simply want to have the freedom to focus on what I view as my most important task—finding my magic and fixing it as a whole for the kingdom. I want my freedom to explore while also knowing I have somewhere to anchor a home to. I want to be challenged and forced to look at things from new perspectives without my intelligence being questioned. I crave someone who doesn't want to dull all my jagged edges, but instead sharpens them with their own. Not in competition, but in mutual understanding and respect. There is nothing wrong with settling down, but I was never made to settle. Certainly not with anyone who can't let me be who I am supposed to be.

Shaking my head lightly to clear my thoughts, I walk to my father's right, leaning in to kiss the top of his head. His long black hair is tied back, stark against the light gray color of his tunic.

"How is my darling daughter today?" my father asks, his eyes coltish as he takes me in.

"I'm well, where is everyone else? Is Nox okay?" I inquire with a gesture to the empty seats around the table.

"Yes, your brother is fine. I received a letter from him this morning." I relax my shoulders at my father's response, nearly sighing in relief. "This isn't a council issue," he says, his lips sliding into a teasing smile. "I called you here because I received another offer for your hand in marriage." My loud, irritated groan fills the space as he laughs. Daje stands on the opposite side of the table from me, chuckling as well, though I notice it doesn't quite hold his usual levity.

"Please tell me that I did not leave in the middle of my experiments only to find out that some random man in the capital thinks himself *my savior* for being willing to marry me. *Oh look at the poor magicless princess; surely she must need a man to save her from her own existence.*" My hands gesture wildly as I continue my mocking of whichever idiot assumes I want to be tied down simply because the magic in my blood is somehow blocked.

"I thought you might react this way, but I still had to tell you nonetheless."

"You couldn't possibly wait for our dinner tonight?" I snark, my hands resting on my hips.

My father's smile widens as he shrugs. "I was bored and needed some entertainment."

I scoff and flip him my middle finger, which he heartily laughs at. We eventually fall into chatting about the man who asked for my hand as well as the updates with Nox. Daje, as the son of—and advisor to—one of my father's oldest and most-trusted council members, is able to listen to the details that not many outside these walls know of. To them, Nox is out exploring our kingdom, enjoying some freedom before he steps into the role of heir apparent. But the truth of his absence is much more frightening. I've only seen my brother a handful of times in recent years because of the mission he is on for my father—for our kingdom.

When the council members start to filter in for their daily meeting, I give my father a hug and leave, Daje quick on my heels. "So what would it take for a marriage proposal to be accepted by the incomparable Bahira?" he asks in a joking tone, but I've known Daje for far too long to not hear the genuine interest hidden there.

Shit, I knew this was coming. My shoulders tense, knowing that he would propose to me this very moment if he thought there was a chance I'd say yes. So I deflect the only way I can that won't hurt his feelings—with sarcasm.

"Hmm, well obviously I'm looking for someone wealthy," I start, a forced dreamy look in my eyes. Despite the underlying seriousness lining his features, he can't help the small curve of his lips. "And of course, I need someone super powerful, like the *most* powerful." Daje rolls his eyes.

"Be serious, Bahira," he grumbles. "This is, what, your twelfth marriage offer this year alone? I'm just curious why you haven't accepted any of them."

I sigh. Daje is many things: funny, altruistic, an exceptional swordsman, but a talented liar he is not. He wants to know the things that would make me agree to *his* proposal. My heart cracks a little at the thought.

"I don't want someone to marry me because they think they're doing me a favor. Most of the men proposing are ones that never would have normally if I could render magic," I answer, keeping my gaze forward.

He scoffs, hands clasping behind his back as we pass some guards and walk up the stone steps to the third floor, where my bedroom is.

"Since when has someone's station in the kingdom mattered to you?" he grills me, causing frustration to prickle my skin. "Because they aren't the most powerful mages, you automatically refuse them?" He keeps his face neutral when I peer at him, but I don't miss the judgment in his tone.

"Don't twist my words, Daje. What I am saying is that I want someone to choose me because they *love* me as I am. Not in spite of me being magicless, and not out of some sense of imaginary duty to the kingdom."

We reach the top of the stairs and round the corner in silence before stopping in front of my bedroom door. Purple and green vines wrap along the arched door frame, a blue petalum flower—the fragrance subtle and sweet—permanently bloomed in the center at the very top. When I was born, my father knew this room would be mine so he spelled the lush, long flat petals of the flower to stay open and redolent. I turn the handle to the door, intent on ending this conversation, when Daje stops me with a gentle hand on my shoulder.

"Bahira, you know there *are* men in this kingdom that care for you as you are. Ones that don't give a shit about you not having magic," he says, voice low and gravelly, but I hear the words he isn't speaking—*I'm right here*.

Daje would be a fine partner, one that would care for me and treat me well. It probably makes me an idiot, but I can't force myself to long for him the way he does for me. I wish I could, it would make things so much simpler, but he doesn't challenge me in any way—he doesn't stoke the fires of curiosity and discovery. On paper, we should fit together perfectly in some respects, but in spirit, we couldn't be more opposite. He's a good, kind man, and that's enough for most. Unfortunately, I'm not most.

When I don't respond, he removes his hand with a small sigh. "Just... think about it, Bahira."

I look at him over my shoulder and smile faintly, not wanting to hurt his feelings but unable to give him hope for something more—unable to be what he wants me to be. He waits for a few seconds before turning and walking back down the hallway to the stairs. Exhaling, I enter the rest of the way into my room, gently shutting the door behind me. Leaning against it, I survey my personal space with a contented sigh. It might be my favorite spot in this realm—excluding the library. In the center of the room, a large circular emerald green rug covers the dark wood floors. They contrast with the creams and whites of the stacked stone walls. Potted plants of all varieties local to our kingdom fill each corner with little pieces of life. Across from me, a wall with three windows and a set of glass doors, which lead to the veranda, let the trickling daylight in.

There are still a few hours before the sun goes down and I'm to have family dinner, so I quickly get undressed and start a bath, the water steaming hot by the time the tub is filled. While soaking, I reminisce on my experiment from earlier. I've tried infusing water with many different strengths of raw magic. My hands are calloused from the many flowers and leaves I've plucked to see how they interact with the magic-infused water. One hundred and sixty two attempts to break this damn curse, disease—whatever this is—in our kingdom to free up our magic and return it to what it used to be. And each try has been a failure.

Cursing under my breath, I finish washing and drain the tub, reaching for a towel hanging on the wall next to me. I wrap the soft blue cotton around me and lean against the counter while I wait for the mirror to defog. My fingers drum on the glittering gray stone as I think about what I could possibly test next. The potency of Hadrik's older magic gives new life to the plants, whereas the younger mage's magic only temporarily feeds it. I have even tried combining mage magics in the past with no discernable difference in the outcome, but maybe I need to switch up the medium. Maybe water isn't working as the correct conduit for the raw magic.

When the mirror clears, I stare at my gray eyes and blow out a breath. I know I'm reaching a point where others might tell me to give up, but I've always been a stubborn woman. My father likes to joke that I was born with enough moxie to lead two kingdoms. I just know—a feeling that can't be explained—that I was made to do this. Why else would I be cursed with no magic of my own?

Chapter Six

BAHIRA

THE LOW MURMUR OF voices intensifies the closer I get to the throne room. The early morning sun is barely peeking through the thick canopy of trees, just enough to trickle in and dot the shiny black stone floors with little globes of golden light. It is a public forum day, a day where anyone can come and voice their concerns with my father, King Sadryn Daxel. Most of the time it is simple things, like a neighborly dispute over sheep or cows grazing on someone else's property. Sometimes merchants will come and say they need more materials to set up their stands in different parts of the kingdom.

My father believes in always putting the people of the kingdom first. *"What is the loss of the price of wood to us when it will mean so much to the one who needs it—when it will support their family for years to come?" he had said.* And he is right; those requests are easy ones for him and the council to approve because they better everyone overall. The harder ones come from those who don't understand why their magic is failing. While few and far between, the complacency of living in a peaceful kingdom is enough to nullify most concerns. And we are a peaceful kingdom. A part of me wonders if that knowledge gives us a false sense of security. Hell, it's why Nox left four years ago—he had the same thought.

Outside, I can hear the chirping of the various birds through the open windows as I round the final corner and walk through the guarded double doors to the throne room. On the dais, my parents sit on their thrones made of twisted ancient banya trees, spelled vines and flowers woven throughout and in permanent bloom. An orderly line forms at the base of the dais and leads out through a second set of double doors on the other side of the room. My father signals the first mage to approach, and he climbs the stairs of the dais, stopping directly before my parents. I know there are a few council members who scoff at the fact that my parents allow the common public to approach so closely, who believe they should instead keep that pretend barrier up between royals and non-royals. It is idiotic to me. The people know who their king and queen are.

My father smiles warmly when he spots me before his attention shifts back to the young man speaking in front of him. I take my place leaning against a white stone wall, the picture hanging behind me a painting of one of the Mage Kingdom's past rulers. It depicts the queen of Void Magic standing on the dais in this room and looking out at the mages dancing. The Autumnal Ball transforms this space into a sea of oranges, reds, golds, and greens. Yet it is the queen who steals the attention of the audience, shining as if she is the sun.

"Bored enough to attend today, Bahira?" Daje asks under his breath, coming to stand next to me.

I smirk as I look him over, his light blue shirt and gray training shorts stained with grass and dirt. "Too lazy to bathe before walking into the palace?" I counter with a raised brow.

"I just finished sparring. I was coming to see if you wanted to have lunch together, before I remembered it was public forum day."

"Hmm, worked up an appetite getting your ass kicked?" I tease quietly, looking pointedly at his soil-marked clothing.

Daje snorts, the sound louder than he intended and drawing the attention of a few people, including my mother. He mouths *sorry* to her, stepping closer to the wall as if he can be absorbed into it. Her responding smile is mischievous as she shakes her head in pretend disapproval, flicking her curly brown hair—twin to mine—over her shoulder and turning back to the mage in front of her.

"I didn't get my ass *totally* kicked," Daje whispers as he leans in closer. "I managed to get Arin in the balls, not once, but twice."

This time it's me who lets out a totally inappropriate laugh that I try, and fail, to turn into a cough. The room falls silent, the stares of the other mages heavy on me as I pinch my lips together. When my father clears his throat and they all look back to the dais, I elbow Daje in his side. He chuckles quietly before turning and facing the thrones. A woman who looks to be in her third decade of life is talking, her hands gesturing wildly in front of her. I take note of her haggard appearance, her clothes rumpled and her hair gathered messily on her head.

"—he's been missing for three days. It isn't like him to just disappear like this," she cries, wiping her cheek.

My mother leans forward in her throne, holding the woman's hand between her own. "We will send out some men to look for him. Perhaps he was injured and is just in need of assistance." Though my mother is doing her best to sound convincing, I can see her worry etched in the way the corners of her mouth tense. The woman doesn't look reassured, but she nods her head all the same and thanks my parents before leaving the room, wiping her tears as she goes.

"That was odd," Daje comments.

I nod. There are wild animals in the less populated parts of the kingdom that could definitely take down a mage: panthers, mountain lions, bears—any number of them could attack, rare as it would be. There's even a chance he could have walked too close to the beach and got lured in by a siren's song. Again, it's rare but not out of the realm of possibility, I suppose.

A man walks up next, his black hair perfectly pulled back into a low ponytail. His clothes are nicely pressed, no wrinkles or dishevelment like the woman before him. He bows in front of my parents before beginning to speak.

Daje nudges me in the arm. "Come on, let's go get some food."

I start to follow him out of the room when I hear the tail end of the man's sentence to my parents. "—near the border. I want to know what you can do to help there? Loss of magic is worsening more quickly than here in the capital." I stop in my tracks, turning to look over at the mage. My father's face is a careful mask of consideration.

"I understand your unease, and as you are surely aware, this is an issue beyond what even a king can fix." My mother nods next to him, looking sympathetic. "Though, our princess has been working on finding a solution." My father's eyes flick to mine as he gives me a soft smile.

A knot of emotion works its way up my throat at him publicly acknowledging my work. It's quickly shoved back down by the look on the man's face as his eyes roam over me dismissively. "Yes, yet it would appear she has been unsuccessful. Perhaps one *with* magic might want to be tasked with taking over?"

Subtle. I return his slight scowl with a sarcastically sweet smile of my own.

"You think it is a good decision to question the intelligence of your princess in front of her parents, sir?" My head snaps to Daje as he folds his arms over his chest.

"Of course not," the man replies smoothly, "but why not bring in more minds? Why not let someone else try?"

"I have offered everything at our kingdom's disposal to anyone who is willing to help. There have been few who have taken up the offer," my father chides. His voice is even, but there is no mistaking the undercurrent of power that radiates from him.

"Let's go," Daje rumbles under his breath as his fingers close around my elbow.

A spark of irritation flares through me at the touch, at his assumption that leaving is what I want to do, but I bite it down. I don't hear the man's response as we walk through the doors and I remove my elbow from his grasp. We silently move to the kitchen to request lunch, my long green skirt swishing with my determined steps. My flats tap on the stone with each movement as I fight to cool the anger slowly boiling up.

"Are you okay?" he asks, his hands clasped behind his back, spine straight as he walks next to me. No, he is partially *ahead* of me. Like he is trying to place himself in front of me to protect me from some invisible enemy—something he's done our whole lives. I *know* it comes from a place of fondness, of friendship— *Fuck.* I recognize there is more there too, but I push that knowledge out of my mind.

"Of course," I answer, purposely lengthening my stride so I'm back to walking in line with him. "You, of all people, know that I am not bothered by the words of others regarding my lack of magic."

"You don't *seem* like you're not bothered," he counters, looking down at me from the corners of his eyes.

"Oh I'm bothered, but not by what that man said." The swinging wooden door to the kitchen comes into view and I stop, placing a hand on Daje's forearm. "We aren't children anymore, Daje," I start, sharper than I intend. Blowing out a breath, I remove my hand from his arm. "I don't need you to step in for me."

"Call it a force of habit then," he says, taking a small step towards me. "It's like second nature for me now."

"But it shouldn't be," I counter, staring at him before shaking my head. "I don't need you to save me, not like that." It's something I've told him before, that the need for him to step in and protect me from all manner of things he views as threats isn't what *I* need anymore, that I don't *want* that from him.

"But if I want to?" he asks, reaching out to tuck a strand of hair behind my ear.

"Daje, it only helps *you* in those moments. It makes *me* appear weak. Please, do not step in like that again," I warn, my voice low.

"I doubt anything could make you appear weak, Bahira."

Sometimes I feel like I'm talking in circles with him. Can he not see that despite the façade I put up, despite the healthy dose of bravado, there's still a part of me that feels small and insignificant when someone points out how I'm different? That it *hurts more* when he steps in than it does when strangers speak poorly of me, because he is supposed to *know* me.

"Enough talk, let's eat," he gestures towards the door.

Even though I'd definitely like to continue this conversation, to truly get him to see what I'm trying to say, I don't want to fight with him. So I nod my head and join him for lunch. We let the kitchen know our orders and then head to a small dining area outside on the lowest level balcony. Just enough sunlight bathes the table and chairs that they are warm when we sit. I let out a sigh as I tilt my head back and close my eyes—just letting myself soak in the sun's heat.

"What are your plans for the rest of the day?" he asks.

"Heading back to my workshop," I answer, bringing my head forward again. "I need to check some things—" My voice halts at the look on his face. "What?"

"Your workshop *again*?" he mutters, a near-annoyed flair to his voice.

My eyes narrow as I cock my head to the side. "Yes, it's where I like to get work done, as you may recall."

"It's just that I thought after yesterday maybe you'd want a break." His voice falters, but he keeps his gaze steady on me. His eyes catch in the light, gleaming like sapphires.

"What are you talking about?" I question, genuinely puzzled by his response.

"I could tell by the look on your face yesterday that the experiment didn't go as planned," he says carefully, slowly. Like he's bracing for a fight.

Good.

"Which is all the more reason I need to go back today, to prepare for my next one," I snap. My frustration rises as I draw my brows together. "What is it you're really trying to say?"

"You're not happy doing them anymore," he replies, leaning forward to rest his forearms on the table in front of us. "Why don't you take a break?"

"I don't want to take a break," I fire back. "You say you don't see me as happy, but then are you really looking? Doing these experiments, trying to find a solution to this problem that doesn't *just* affect me, *that* is what makes me happy."

"No," he counters, the word dragged out by his deep voice, "it's what makes you obsessed. I can tell the difference in you after one of your experiments fails. Do you truly believe it isn't obvious to anyone paying attention the way you beat yourself up over it?"

I scoff, but there's an annoying truth to his words. I never realized he had been watching me so closely. I hadn't thought he'd have this observation ready to attack me with as soon as he needed it. It makes me feel cornered, and like a trapped wild animal, I lash out.

"At least I am trying to do something *useful*, Daje. Can you say the same?" I forcefully push my chair back and stand, stepping back from the table. "Some of us may be content to play the roles given to us by our fathers, but I would rather work towards something that would actually make a difference in people's lives," I seethe, unfairly reminding Daje how his father created an advisor position just for him.

My chest tightens at the look on his face. He may have hurt my feelings with his blunt words, but I purposely sliced at him with a sharpened tongue. Neither of us speaks for a moment before I turn and leave, walking around the porch, down the stairs, and onto one of the many stone paths that lead away from the palace. My hands tighten into fists at my side, each word spoken between us on repeat in my head. I walk and walk, not really paying attention to where I'm going, until the pathway opens up into Galdr's central shopping square. The sheer number of people here makes crossing the wide road tedious, but I finally make it to one of the many taverns.

The bar is built into an albero tree, with two windows and a swinging door on the front. Pushing through, I let my eyes adjust to the slightly darker space. Spelled flames in small orbs hang every other foot in a zigzag pattern on the ceiling. Patrons fill every table and chair spread throughout the establishment, loud music from a small band vibrating the tree bark walls. It smells of incense and sweat and like mead has been spilled on every surface in this place. Yet like a moth drawn to the small flames above me, I make my bad day worse by heading to the bar and taking a seat next to a man that I absolutely *loathe*.

"Hello, Bahira," he purrs the moment he realizes I'm next to him. "Interesting seeing you here. Last time I checked, it wasn't a library."

I don't bother hiding my annoyance or the eye roll that comes with it. "Gosston, interesting to see you look relatively clean today," I counter, ordering a drink from the bartender. "I didn't realize you knew what bathing was." My eyes take in his appearance, his stark flowing white tunic and black trousers. Curly black hair falls to his shoulders, the strands untamed except for where he has them tucked behind his ear.

He snorts, not hiding his irritation with me either. We sit in silence, both drinking our pints of mead, though I go through mine much faster. When I've ordered the fourth one, Gosston speaks again.

"Tough day?" he inquires, sounding alarmingly sincere.

"You could say that." I turn to look at him. Under the light of the spelled flames, his lighter olive complexion takes on a yellow hue, making the purple circles under his eyes stand out more drastically.

"What about you?" I ask because I'm already three drinks in and clearly not thinking well.

"You could say that," he repeats with a small tilt of his lips. He signals the bartender over, and before I know it he's handing me a shot of some kind of liquor. "Here's to bad days," he salutes, clinking his glass to mine and downing his shot. I do the same, and we each turn back to our meads.

I wake up the next morning to the sound of Gosston snoring and the pounding headache of deep regret.

Chapter Seven

RHEA

The morning after the king visits me, I expect to be somewhat bruised and sore, especially on my face and ribs, but my body shows *no* signs of the beating it took. All I feel is a slight headache. I have noticed my healing after punishments from my uncle is becoming more accelerated. But even now, looking over my skin in the vanity mirror, I'm still surprised to not see even a hint of a fading bruise. I take one last look at my complete lack of injury before I go downstairs.

Since I awoke, that odd dream and what the ethereal woman spoke to me has replayed in my mind. *Trust the stars over the ancient trees to guide me from the false king. And look to the east for the answers I seek.* What could that possibly mean? Sitting at a small table, I write the words down so that I don't forget them. Something about them feels significant, though I can't exactly pinpoint why.

Later, I rest in the library, getting lost in book after book to keep my mind off of... well, everything. How would I spend my days if I had not been born a princess to parents who were murdered? If I had not then been thrust into a tower by my cruel uncle and kept here against my will, guarded by men who are sworn through magic and blood to keep me here? Would I still spend much of my time in a library pondering the history of our realms and the intricacies of blood oaths? It is an interesting thing in and of itself—*magic* in the Mortal Kingdom. It supposedly comes from the Continent, though all the history books I've read have never explained how that came to be or why mortals can only access it by giving up their blood.

My attention goes back to the current book in my lap. In the story, the protagonist is in love with her best friend, but she doesn't believe she is good enough for him. So she goes on an adventure through her world to try her hand at becoming different versions of herself in an attempt to be something she thinks he could love. However the best friend confesses he adored her as she was. He didn't want to change her; he just wanted *her.* Is it possible that this kind of love exists outside of stories? The thought that, if I ever get to leave this tower, there might be someone who isn't put off by my lack of social, personal, and relationship skills weighs heavily on my mind. It is nice to daydream that there might be someone out there that would like me for me, despite how broken I know I am.

When the sun starts to dip, coaxing the moon out of its hiding place, I light a candle so I can finish my book, reading to the very last page and then blowing it out. Bella is already asleep upstairs; she had popped her head into the library a few times before returning to the balcony to soak up the remaining sun. It is something she has loved to do for as long as she has been here. While I am so grateful to have her in my life, helping save me from truly being alone, I can't stop the seedling of guilt I feel for the years she's been with me—a wild fox trapped in a small, stone cage. It was that thinking that had led me to beg Alexi to free her, to let her out of the tower all those years ago.

The night Bella nearly died is something that will forever be burned into my memory; not only because it was horrific, but also because it was the first time that I realized I was *different*. That I wasn't just a mortal, but instead I had something *other* flowing in my veins. Something that shouldn't be there, that didn't make sense. And on that night, I had called upon it somehow. Swallowing anxiously, I move upstairs to draw a bath and relax before bed, lighting some candles in the bathroom for light. Once the hot water fills the tub, steam swirling and twisting above it, I slide into the water and close my eyes. Despite the way my muscles relax in the bath, flashes of that night—when things both changed and didn't—begin to play in my mind, one after another.

When I was seventeen, Alexi told me he had spotted her on the castle grounds one night, skulking through the garden trying to hide within the flowers. He grabbed a bow and arrow, intent on hunting the white fox down, but the minute he had met her gaze through the various blooms, he felt she was different. Something in his gut told him not to kill her, and he listened. When he lowered his bow and dropped down on one knee, Bella had slowly made her way to him. She was docile—keen even—and that night he brought her to me.

I named her Bella after a favorite book character, whose name in the story meant "hope." I was so ecstatic, so beyond happy to have another living being here with me, so hopeful for a future without that constant void of loneliness. Alexi had tempered my excitement by warning me not to let the king see her, that my uncle would take her away or, more likely, kill her if he knew she was here.

For a few days, I did nothing but relish in having this new being here with me. I talked to Bella as if she were mortal and could understand what I was saying. All that was missing was her ability to speak back to me, but even then, she always had a way of communicating.

Despite the joy of having a friend, I felt guilty keeping a wild animal confined with me. I questioned if, when she stared out of the tower windows, it was longing she was feeling. If, when she laid out on the balcony in the sun, she missed frolicking in the woods. If she hated being trapped here as much as I did. Her energy even seemed to deplete with each day that passed. It hadn't taken long to convince myself, but I felt deep down that she would be better off not stuck in this prison alongside me. That she should be able to return to her true home. So I told Alexi he needed to set her free.

At first, he had been hesitant to take her from me, having seen the change her company had brought me even in just a few short days. But I was adamant. I didn't want to deny Bella her true nature, to have her suffer the same fate I had been given, just because I was lonely. I didn't want to be her captor.

Bella fought him at first, refusing to follow him through the door. But when she walked up to me, her nose bumping against my thigh, I ignored her. I held back sobs, as it broke my heart to hear her whine and try again and again to get my attention, but it was for the best. She deserved to be free.

Alexi finally managed to sneak her out in the dead of night, promising me that he would lead her away from the palace grounds.

I had never before cried as much as I did that first night without her. The tower felt lifeless to me, as though every bit of joy, excitement, and contentment I had managed to find in her presence had been completely sucked out. I slept through the entire next day, the hours blurring together. It was just before nightfall, the last bit of sunlight streaming through the windows setting the tower aglow in gold, when a loud banging on the door startled me. Then I heard Alexi's voice. "Little One, it's me."

I was not prepared for what would greet me when I opened it. Alexi was panting, his face red from exertion and his salt and pepper hair curling at his temple with sweat. When my attention fell to what he was holding—to the blood smeared across his armor—my confusion turned to growing horror. In his arms was a shaking bundle of white fur streaked with deep crimson.

"Bella," I gasped, reaching out to touch her. Her blood dripped steadily, quickly staining the stone floor beneath Alexi's feet.

"She's been shot with an arrow. I brought her here to see if I can stop the bleeding." He rushed past me, laying Bella on the gray rug taking up most of the floor in the living area. Bella whined as Alexi carefully removed his forearms from beneath her body. He quickly unbuckled his armor, tossing his blood-streaked breast plate to the side, as I closed the door and knelt beside him.

He moved his hands to where the arrow was protruding from Bella's side and separated the fur around it, assessing the wound. My hands trembled in my lap, a humming sensation building in me that I had never experienced before. It felt like the warmth of the sun, a bright light just waiting to be called upon. It was a strange bone-deep knowing but I couldn't quantify what it was that I knew.

"I think I can pull the arrow out and stop the bleeding. Can you go get some towels, soap, and a bowl of water to clean the wound with?" Alexi spoke calmly, assuring me with the evenness of his tone as I gathered the requested supplies.

Coming back to his side, he instructed me on what to do once he pulled the arrow out. Kneeling on the floor, I scooted closer to Bella and leaned down, whispering quietly into her ear, "This is going to hurt for just a second, but then we're going to fix you. I'm so sorry for making you leave, for causing your pain."

Bella slowly laid her paw on my knee, the movement shaky as if she used all the energy she could muster. I placed my hands on her to hold her steady as Alexi counted to three and then began to slowly pull the arrow out, the muscles in his arms tensing with the careful movement. A howl reverberated off the walls, piercing through my nerves as Bella vocalized her pain, and I wondered if it could be heard well into the city of Vitour.

It felt like it took years, but with one final small tug by Alexi, the arrow was removed. I quickly placed a towel over her wound and applied pressure, my heart racing in my chest. A minute passed before Alexi gently moved me aside and replaced the now blood-soaked towel with a fresh one, his hands holding it in place. But the bleeding didn't stop. Bella's breaths started to become slower and more irregular, her heart beating at a new, labored pace. One of death.

"No. No. No. We pulled the arrow out. Why is she still bleeding so much?" I cried to Alexi. He slowly lifted his hands from her, wiping them on a clean towel as blood continued to leak out. My bottom lip trembled, my hands rushing to replace his, applying pressure.

He whispered remorsefully, "Rhea, it must have hit an artery. I'm so sorry." I felt his hand settle on my shoulder and squeeze, but I just shook my head. This couldn't be happening. I couldn't lose her. Not like this. "I think—"

"Don't!" I hissed through my teeth, my jaw clenching so hard I thought they might break. "Don't you dare say it."

Tears spilled from my eyes, blurring everything around me. I leaned down, my hands still applying pressure to Bella's wound as my forehead came to her furry temple. Her eyes were closed, and her jaw had grown slack, but her chest still rose and fell. Though the pauses were growing longer between each strained movement.

"Please hang on," I begged, my chest heaving with a sob. My hair fell around my face and Bella's, as if it was a curtain that we could wrap ourselves in to shield everything else out. Alexi removed his hand from my shoulder but stayed kneeling next to me.

"You can't leave me," I whispered to Bella. "You have to live. Please, you have to live."

That warm feeling in my belly stirred again, causing me to gasp and jerk back upright. It traveled up my torso, passing my chest and shoulders until I felt it pouring down my arms, a tingling following in its wake. It was calling on me to use it, to wield it, but I didn't understand how. This feeling was speaking to me in a foreign language that I couldn't interpret. All I knew was that I couldn't give up on Bella. She didn't deserve this and it was my fault that she was in this position.

"You will live. You will live." I repeated the words. The sensation that moved through me halted like it was waiting for permission or directions. I couldn't make sense of it, but I knew we were running out of time. So I closed my eyes and gave my body over to that feeling, to that light I imagined was burning inside of me—not burning to cause pain, but burning with life. A few seconds went by before I felt the warmth gathering in the palms of my *hands. I kept my eyes squeezed shut, afraid that opening them would cause me to lose whatever this connection was.*

"Gods." Alexi's voice was a shocked whisper, but I didn't stop.

I imagined the luminescence pouring into Bella's wound and healing it completely. I pictured it restoring her blood loss and making her whole. I saw in my mind her muscles and veins coming back together—becoming one again.

"Rhea." It was a silvery, ethereal murmur on the wind, but I paid it no mind. I couldn't. Not with the humming in my body, the warmth flowing through me.

"Rhea," Alexi said, his voice different from the one I'd heard a moment ago.

His hands landed on my shoulders, but I tried to shake him off. He couldn't *stop me from doing this. I* had *to do this.*

"I'm not trying to stop you, Little One. I want you to open your eyes."

Open my eyes? I felt his thumbs sweeping back and forth on my shoulders, and the movement calmed some of the frenzy I felt.

"Open them, Rhea."

My eyes obeyed and immediately focused on Bella. The white light I had imagined inside me was shining brightly from my palms and onto her—into her. My gaze slowly traveled up to Bella's head, and when I saw her eyes were open, I nearly crumpled with relief.

"Can you stop... this?" I heard the hesitation in Alexi's voice. The fear.

"I don't know how," I muttered, still confused about what had actually happened. My eyes were wide as I looked at him, sweat beading down my neck.

"Try to take slower breaths, like when we do our mind cleansers," Alexi said, his eyes betraying the attempted calm of his voice. "Bella is alive. She isn't bleeding anymore."

I let my shoulders steadily relax, let my mind release all of the worry that I had held there and replace it with relief instead. My gaze moved to hers as Alexi's words pierced through the haze I was in. Bella was alive. Somehow, she was alive because I had done something to save her. Time lost all meaning as we sat there, no one moving beyond the rising and falling of our chests.

Slowly, the bright light faded from me. Alexi tentatively slid his hands under mine, removing them from Bella's fur. He laid them on top of my lap, squeezing our blood-covered hands together. Bella was sleeping peacefully. Her breathing was normal and healthy, and she was whole again. I watched her for a few seconds before turning to look over at Alexi. His normally tanned skin was wan, his gaze lost as he stared down at where he was still holding my hands.

"What was that?" I whispered, slowly lifting them from his hold. I examined my palms, checking to see if they looked any different now, but they appeared as they always had.

"Magic," Alexi answered, his brows drawn up on his forehead in surprise. "You have magic."

Chapter Eight

RHEA

MY EYES FLING OPEN from the knocking on the door. After my bath, I had gone to bed reliving that night with Bella, my heart pounding in my chest at the memories, at how close I came to losing her. Sliding out from the comforter, my feet hit the cold wood floor as I adjust my dark blue nightdress. My fingers comb through my hair as I start down the stairs, fairly certain of who is on the other side of the door.

A smile breaks out across my face when I open it. He's removed his armor, only wearing the all-black trousers, boots, and tunic—leaving him looking more relaxed. I start to wonder if he knows the king visited recently, but when I see Alexi trail his eyes over my face in an assessing way, I get my answer. I don't move—other than to place my hands on my hips—letting him see that I am healed and okay.

"What are you doing here," I ask, chewing on my bottom lip nervously. "Aren't you worried about being caught?"

"Don't worry, Little One. I think one night is alright." His eyes soften as he looks at me before he holds up a familiar deck and a small white bag of something that smells delicious. "Are you ready to beat an old man at cards?" He winks at me as he steps into the tower, walking directly over to the tea table. Sliding his green armchair over, Alexi begins to shuffle and deal out the cards while I grab some pillar candles to light. Setting a few around the table, I strike a match and light each one until their glow illuminates the darkness of the space between us.

"So," I drag out, glancing above the cards in my hand, "how is life in the King's Guard lately?" My brow raises sarcastically in question while Alexi snorts in response. I lay my first card down onto the table.

"The same as it always is. Training and guarding." His dry tone makes a small laugh burst from me. "Speaking of training," he hints, returning an arched brow of his own, "have you been exercising?"

"Yes, of course. Every morning," I drawl, giving him a fake bored expression which he smiles widely at. Alexi had been worried that my sedentary lifestyle of reading all day would make my bones weak, or something to that effect, so he taught me some of the basic exercises they teach guard apprentices when they enter training.

"Good," he says simply as he leans forward to lay his card down.

I can't help but beam at him, my hands nearly shaking from the delight and relief his visit brings. Still, a small part of me worries that the king will somehow know he is gone from his post. I work to keep the anxiousness from showing on my face. However, Alexi misses nothing, and after his turn laying down his next card, he attempts to distract me.

"Win this hand, and I'll show you what's in the bag. Win the next hand, and you can have all of the treats in there." His eyebrows raise slightly, baiting me to accept. The light of the moon mixed with the low light of the candle flame makes his dark brown eyes sparkle, giving him a mischievous look. Despite the fact that he has always fallen into that parental role so easily, it is in moments like these that I find he is more friend than guardian.

I narrow mine in return, attempting to keep my face serious, as I lay my next card down on the table. Back and forth we go until we each come down to our last one. My eyes flick down to the one in my hand and back up to him, a slow smirk spreading before I slap the card down on the pile. Alexi chuckles, laying his down far more gently and accepting his defeat before gathering all the cards back up to shuffle and deal again.

"I am a generous winner and will let you go first this time, despite losing," I joke, but my smile falters when I glance up to see that his expression is more pensive. His eyes appear lost in a memory as he absent-mindedly shuffles his own cards.

"Do you remember when you turned thirteen and I brought you that small gold bracelet?" he asks, sliding his gaze to mine. While Alexi normally brought me special treats for my birthday, that year he had given me the bracelet.

I smile at the memory, nodding. "I do. You were frustrated with me about something, but then you gave me a gift. I remember you held out your hand, a little black pouch nestled in your palm," I say, grinning at his answering chuckle.

"I had been trying to be what you needed while inside I felt like I was coming apart after Alanna's death," he confesses.

My hands slowly place my cards to the table as I stare at him. Even though it's been many years since he lost her, the grief in his voice is unmistakable. Alanna had been Alexi's childhood best friend before becoming his wife, and then she was killed in a tragic accident. From the solemn look in his eyes now, you'd assume it was more recently that he lost her. I wonder if truly loving someone means that even long after they are gone, you never stop mourning them. That they live on in you through memories and dreams.

"You had the worst attitude problem I had ever seen in a child, by the way. You still have it," he teases.

I scoff, reaching my foot under the table to kick his leg. His laugh brightens up his demeanor again, the tension leaving the air as I exhale a little deeper.

"Prior to your birthday that year, I was feeling lost, and I—" He hesitates, taking a breath and holding eye contact before continuing, "I was unsure if I wanted to continue being your guard."

My heart skips at his confession, our card game forgotten temporarily in light of his words. Even though it was years ago and, obviously, he is still here, I can't help the feelings of betrayal and sadness trying to claw their way up my throat.

"I was going to petition the captain of the guard to reassign me." It's barely more than a whisper, yet his regret is weaved thickly through it.

"You were?" I breathe the words out, feeling a slight tremble in my hands as my mind begins to spiral with this new information. Did he ask for a transfer and get denied? Has he wanted to leave this post—leave me—this entire time?

Seeing the panic on my face before I am able to verbalize it, Alexi vehemently shakes his head. "I never ended up asking for it."

"Why?" I breathe.

He sighs, scratching the back of his neck before setting his cards down on the table and leaning forward, completely abandoning any pretense that we will finish this game.

"I was stewing in indecision. I knew that I was a lifeline you didn't have with anyone else and that no other guard would dare go against the king to make sure you had what you needed." I see the pain and guilt in his expression, his eyebrows furrowing together as he rests his elbows on his knees, clasping his hands in the middle. "It wasn't about you in any way. I just— I missed her, and everything about my life here reminded me of her. I wanted to get away, maybe move to one of those small towns on the outskirts of the capital to start somewhere new."

I can't help the small twist of pain in my heart. I came so close to losing him, so close to being even more alone. What if he had left? What if the past almost *nine* years had been spent without him here to visit and teach me things I wouldn't have learned otherwise?

"What changed your mind?" I question, my voice still small.

Seeing the fear and hurt that I am failing to suppress, his expression turns remorseful. "Alanna's voice came into my mind, and I was reminded of something she told me before she passed away."

Over the years, I've only gotten small bits and pieces out of Alexi about his wife and his life outside of being a guard. Most of them are just little facts about their relationship—they were married, she was a seamstress that worked at one of the shops in the capital square, and her death had come as a shock. I didn't know if his desire not to tell me too much about her was to protect me from his sorrow or if he was trying to protect himself from her memories.

"Alanna knew that I often snuck in to visit you. She hated that the king secluded you and then told the kingdom that you had chosen this life because of your grief. She never spoke a word of it to anyone else, but when it was just her and I, she would ask about you," he explains. My breath squeezes out of my chest, an overwhelming feeling of sadness, but also appreciation for her, settling in deep. "Alanna and I were unable to have children, but she always had the softest spot for them. She would tell me over and over again that I needed to be a safe place for you to anchor to, someone that would keep you from harm."

My hands press together as my lip starts to tremble. The thought that this woman, whom I had never met, cared about me at all, let alone this much was overwhelming. She was under no obligation to. Neither was Alexi. They cared because they felt it was right to do so, because they were good people.

"And I failed, Rhea. I fail every time the king comes to your room and I do nothing." He hangs his head low, his gaze moving to the ground by his boots. The air feels heavy with the weight of regret and despair bearing down on me.

"No," I whisper, shaking my head. Then my voice grows firm as I say, "The king would have just killed you if you tried to stop him. He would have killed you without a second thought, and some other guard, one more loyal to him, would have replaced you. You know this."

When my words don't reassure him, I move around the tea table to kneel by him, taking his hands in my own. "Have you ever told anyone, the king or otherwise, about the night Bella almost died?" This is a topic we never talk about, haven't talked about, since the night it happened. Alexi's wariness then made me hesitate to ever bring it up with him again. But with the memory fresh on my mind, I know it's the perfect opportunity to show him that he's wrong.

"Never," he answers firmly.

"Then you haven't failed me. That knowledge in the wrong hands is a death sentence; I have no doubts about that. I can handle the king's visits, but I can't handle your guilt over them." I squeeze his hands more tightly, willing him to understand. "You have made this existence more bearable. You have taught me, guided me"—my breath catches for a moment—"raised me to be something better than I ever could have been on my own." His eyes yield further at my words. "Besides, my body is healing me while I sleep now."

Alexi's brows furrow as he again looks me over, like he is seeing if he can watch the action as it happens. "It's healing you without you trying?" He asks the question quietly as though the magic can hear him, as if it's a separate entity from myself. Maybe it is.

I nod my head, giving his hands one more squeeze of reassurance before standing and walking back to take my seat on the couch. Reaching down, I give Bella's head a little scratch as she resumes her position at my feet.

"You were in the guard at the time my parents were king and queen, did—did they ever seem like they had magic?" I stammer, a blush creeping up my cheeks. It's such a ridiculous thing to ask. If somehow my parents weren't mortal, how did they keep their magic when they crossed through the Spell to come to this kingdom? I know that I got my honey blonde hair, bright green eyes, and creamy complexion from my mother. Is it possible I got magic from her too? And if so, how am I able to *keep it* while living in the Mortal Kingdom?

"As far as I know, they were just mortals. But you know that mages look like us. There are no physical differences, just the presence of magic and a marginally longer life," he answers.

My head tilts in contemplation. "What if the magic came from my father's side? Is there a chance the king has it as well?" I wonder as chills work their way down my neck and back at the thought. The king is terrifyingly powerful enough without adding magic to the mix. Alexi pinches his lips together in thought.

"King Dolian is not the sort of man who would keep something like that hidden if he possessed it. He'd use it to his advantage somehow and would certainly show it off. And if he had their magic flowing in his veins, he definitely wouldn't have made it his mission as king to declare that mages who enter these lands would be killed."

Chewing on the inside of my cheek, I consider what Alexi said. It makes sense. Why would the king encourage his own demise by creating contempt between the Mortal and Mage Kingdoms if he did indeed have magic. I imagine his little *sessions* with me would be quite different if magic were present. Still, I can't dismiss it completely.

"Have you ever tried using it again? Testing it out since that night?"

"No. I'm afraid to. I can sometimes feel it sitting inside me, here." I rub my hand over my lower abdomen. "Like it's letting me know it's there, waiting for me. It gets more... active when the king is near me, but I've been able to keep it from showing."

Alexi leans back, elbows braced on the sides of the armchair and fingers interlaced under his chin. I turn my gaze out to the glass balcony doors, watching as the stars twinkle a bright silver in the sky.

"One more round," he says, leaning forward again to collect our cards and start a new game.

"You just want a do-over since I was winning our current hand," I respond, giggling when he gives me a wry look. He gestures with his chin to the white bag on the table.

"Don't you want to see what's inside? You won the first hand."

"I want to be surprised," I respond as I spread my newly dealt cards in my hand and plan which one I'll lay down first.

"Never thought I'd see the day that Rhea Maxwell would not take an opportunity to see what sugar-filled treat was waiting for her."

I roll my eyes, feigning mock offense. Alexi stands abruptly and walks to the balcony, scanning the sky like he's looking for something.

"What are you doing?" I ask, jumping to my feet as Bella startles awake and comes up to stand by me, both of us now on high alert.

He sighs, running the hand not holding his cards through his hair. "Just checking to see if the stars are falling. It is the only explanation for why you would deny yourself a peek inside that bag." He turns around, an almost boyish grin on his face while my own expression is that of pure shock.

"Gods, don't *do* that Alexi!" I smack him on the arm as he laughs his way back to his chair. Bella lets out a huff and lays back down, as if this whole interaction is nothing but an interruption to her nap. "You're such a jerk," I croak out. I finish the game of cards with another win under my belt, and Alexi slides the bag of treats over to me. Slowly, I open it, anticipation killing me. Alexi is right that I love all things sweet. The scent of cocoa is rich enough to make my mouth water as I look in and see a delicious assortment of chocolates. "Did Emelia make these?"

"No. They are from a confectionary in the capital," he says while cleaning up our cards. I pull out a creamy milk chocolate ball with a delicate white chocolate rose on top. I almost feel bad eating something so beautiful. Taking a bite, I let the candy melt in my mouth, the flavors smoothing over my tongue and making me shut my eyes in delight. It is rich and decadent, with a fruity note bursting through. Alexi laughs at my enjoyment, choosing a chocolate of his own when I extend the bag out to him.

"You know, you're lucky I love you because, as you so *graciously* pointed-ed out, I take my treats very seriously and don't normally share."

His chuckle dances between us, the sound settling some of the sadness I feel about the night soon coming to an end.

"Alanna and I used to visit this confectionary shop on our way home from work every evening. She always gravitated to the more unique flavors of the chocolates. Always willing to try something new," he says quietly.

"What flavors did *you* usually get?" I ask, pouting when I reach into the bag and feel only three more chocolates left.

"Always the same one—chocolate cream."

"I am not surprised by that," I deadpan. Even Bella twitches in agreement. Or she could be asleep, I realize, and having little fox dreams. I lean over and look at her. Yes, definitely having little fox dreams.

When I've popped the last chocolate in my mouth, my heart and belly now content, I walk with Alexi to the door. He opens it and listens carefully to make sure no one else is in the tower. When he is satisfied that the space is empty, he steps onto the platform, turning back to face me. A small torch bathes this part of the tower in a subtle buttery glow, lighting just enough of Alexi's features to show his soft smile.

"The next supply drop-off is in three days. I better not push our luck and try to visit before then."

Nodding, I lean against the doorframe, arms folded in front of me. "I'll be ok. I can handle another three days. Although it would be more entertaining if Bella," I look over my shoulder and yell, "would learn that little jig I've been trying to teach her!" The only sign I get that she's heard me is a tiny wiggle of her ear.

Alexi laughs, the smile widening on his face as he places a hand on my shoulder. "You can handle anything, Little One. You are the strongest person I have ever known." He gives my shoulder a little squeeze before dropping his hand to his side. My eyes glance away from his for a moment as I blink back tears that threaten to spill.

"Aww, thanks, dad," I say, attempting to lighten the mood. "Hopefully, I shall continue to honor you by teaching the fox beast to dance and beating you in card games."

"Such a brat," he answers with a roll of his eyes. He backs up and goes to take a step, but pauses again, almost looking unsure of himself.

"What is it?" I ask, glancing around the platform and at the stairs that lead down the tower. Alexi clears his throat, resting one hand on the hilt of the sword at his belt. I always forget he is armed, as his guard uniform now just feels like an extension of him after nearly thirteen years. His other hand scratches at his jaw.

"The gold bracelet I gave you," he falters, looking at me as I nod. "It was Alanna's."

My head jerks a little at the admission, eyes going wide. "Why would you give that to me? Don't you want it to remember her?" The words come out choked, my emotions overwhelmed by this knowledge. I'm surprised, but honored. So, so honored by his gesture.

"I got it for her as a gift right after we married. It then sat on my dresser in the years after her death—a constant reminder of what I had lost. I couldn't bear to look at it any longer, but I wasn't sure I wanted to part with it either."

Straightening up from the doorframe, my arms uncross, and I reach a hand out for him. He places his in mine, his fingers squeezing around mine lightly.

"The bracelet was important to her, like a physical symbol of our love. I knew that there was only one other person that I could possibly imagine giving this to. Only one person who needed to have something physical to remind them that they were cared for. That they were loved." He looks to the side, taking a deep breath, and then turns his gaze back to me. "I have loved to watch you grow up into an amazing young woman despite your circumstances. To see you have such compassion and kindness when you are shown so little by others." He shakes his head, but he must not realize that anything decent about me is a direct result of him and our one hour visits. He gestures around at the tower. "This place, this *prison,* is not where your journey is to end, Little One."

It takes me far too long to speak, my words jumbled and caught so thickly in my throat that it takes several swallows to clear them. "I know," I whisper as I hold his gaze, silver lining both of our eyes.

With a warm and affectionate smile in place, Alexi squeezes my hand and then lets go. He throws a final wink Bella's way before turning and heading down the stairs. I shut the door and beckon Bella upstairs for bed, stopping in the bathroom to wash my face and brush my teeth. When I've done both, I crawl under the covers, laying on my side to gaze out at the stars through the window.

Alexi's words repeat in my head over and over again. I know a life outside these walls is better than the one I'm currently living, and as I close my eyes, my body drifting into sleep, I have hope that maybe I was meant to do more than rot in a tower.

But hope is a dangerous thing.

Chapter Nine

RHEA

STANDING ON THE BALCONY, the wind rustles through my hair as I close my eyes and lean farther into it. It's a perfect spring day in the Mortal Kingdom, the chill of the morning chased away by the pleasant warmth of the early afternoon sun. Bella lays next to me, basking in it with utter contentment. I open my eyes to take in the view before me.

The dark blue water of the lake in front of my gray tower extends far beyond where my eye can see, sparkling in the sunlight. Only a few boats, distinguishable by their white sails, float in the distance. I take in the various green meadows and rolling hills that are to the left side of the lake, leading up to a thickly wooded forest. Wildflowers bloom in large patches throughout, a kaleidoscope of colors breaking up the sea of verdant land. This is all part of the royal family's estate, with the exception of the lake where it appears anyone is allowed to fish or enjoy the water. Even though I've seen maps of the other kingdoms and where they are in respect to Vitour, I have no idea what that distance realistically looks like.

Is the Mage Kingdom truly just beyond the forest that edges the rolling hills? Could I see the shifter isle from the Mortal Kingdom beaches? How far to the east would I have to travel before I see the rising mountains of the Fae Kingdom? Are they snow-capped all year long or only in the winter months? I think about the beings that neighbor us as well. How powerful are the mages? Many of the books I've read call their magic "raw," but the descriptions never fully explain what that means. Though King Dolian says mages killed my parents, it just doesn't fit with everything I've read about the people as a whole. But can one ever truly know an entire people? Could historians really categorize a whole kingdom as peaceful, when each being in it is so multifaceted themselves? And what about the fae? They have the ability to bond with dragons, does that mean they are as unpredictable and dangerous as those beautiful beasts are rumored to be? I had always loved reading about dragons and often wished I had that particular magic for myself. Could the shifters change into dragons? Or was their fantastical capability to transform limited to less intimidating animals? What of the sirens? What else can they do besides use their song to lure men to procreate with? How did the mechanics of sex underwater *work*?

Though unfamiliar with the physical act myself, all the information I know about it has come from books. I *have* explored myself, taken the time to adequately see how I like to be touched by my own hand. Yet it's hard to imagine what involving another person would be like. What if I eventually leave this tower, meet someone, and they expect me to already know what to do? How to touch them? Gods, how embarrassing is it going to be to explain to someone that, despite being an adult, I've never touched—or been touched by—another person that way? Feeling a blush bloom across my cheeks at the thought, I shake my head and look back out over the water.

At the very least, all the romance books I've read start with the couple kissing, which is something that should be more manageable. I suppose, even if I start off terrible at it, the right person will show me how they like it and I can learn. These thoughts are insignificant, though, because the first thing I'd need to do for any of it to happen is leave this tower. So, for now, I focus back on the wind on my skin and the view from the balcony over the mortal lands.

When the sun starts to dip to the west, I finally get up from where I've been laying on the balcony floor, stretching my arms overhead and side to side. Content from the day in the sun, I brush off the back of my white day dress before deciding to make something to eat.

Food is another thing I think about often, as I have eaten basically the same thing for my entire life. Would I like the foods of the capital? Of other kingdoms if I could visit them? Would Bella even be able to hunt for food after so many years of being hand-fed? Once I have secured my small plate of dried meat, nuts, and an apple, I head to the library and relax onto the bench by the window.

Looking out over the wildflower field beyond the castle and into the capital of Vitour, I notice there are newly placed flags of all colors rising from the shops and blowing in the wind. Though they look like mere colorful dots from this distance, they glow against the sunset sky. The banners signify the peak of spring, a time when the growing season reaches its pinnacle and everything from flowers to vegetables sprout at a faster-than-usual rate. Some books say it's from magic somehow imbued into the land of the Continent. Others say that it happens to be just the right combination of sun, water, and earth to make things grow more efficiently.

I honestly don't know what to believe. Only that one day, I would love to walk in a field of blooming wildflowers or pick fresh fruit right from where it's grown. Such simple mundane wishes, but they're mine. Sighing, I grab the book I had started yesterday and flip it open. I continue reading until night falls fully, before making my way to the washroom to bathe by the light of a small taper candle.

Today was a good day, as much as one can be when in my circumstance. It is the kind of day that makes it easy to pretend that I am someone else. Perhaps I'm still a princess, but I'm just visiting a faraway castle. Not trapped within these walls, but simply a guest able to leave when she wants. With another contented breath, I drain the tub and dry off before dressing for bed. Snuggling up against Bella, I allow my body to relax into the relative peace I feel for once. My mind is blissfully quiet as I let the darkness pull me away.

The tower is quiet, dark. The pitch black is lit up only by the moon and a few winking stars. Wiping a hand down my face, I move to get off the bed when Bella puts a paw on top of my leg over the comforter. My eyes are still half closed when I look at her, but it doesn't take me long to realize something is wrong. She is sitting straight up, completely alert. She whimpers, and my heart drops into my stomach so quickly that I physically have to put my hand over my abdomen.

"Rhea, wake up." His voice. His. Voice. It strikes through the night and directly into my heart like a poisoned arrow. He's found me again in my dreams. Bella whines once more, louder and closer to my ear. "Rhea..." The muffled sounds of footsteps are everywhere.

"Rhea. Get. Up."

I gasp as I sit up, my eyes wide in the near darkness of the tower. Beside me, Bella has buried herself beneath the covers, the shadows cast by the waning moon through the window enough to conceal her. I clutch the comforter to my chest as I watch the king approach me from the stairs.

"I have a surprise for you." His smile, if it can even be called that, sends a chill deep into my bones. "Let's go," he commands, voice clipped as he turns back towards the stairs.

Disoriented, I slowly push the blanket off of me, feeling like I'm not fully conscious. When my feet touch the floor, a chill shocks the remaining haze away. *It isn't a dream. He's inside.* Propelled by my fear, I take one step, then another, following King Dolian down the stairs. The heavy sensation of something sinister has me holding my breath until I reach the bottom. I freeze, my eyes pinned on the man kneeling across the room from me.

"No," I beg, but it's barely a whisper. Something moves in the corner of my eye, the presence of others pushing on me, but I can't look away from him. Even in the dark, with just the little slip of moonlight coming through the glass of the balcony doors, I can see one of his eyes is bruised and swollen. Blood leaks from his nose and mouth, and he's been stripped of his armor and sword. Taking a step to him, my movements are suddenly halted by the king.

"I wouldn't do that, Rhea." His voice slithers down my spine. My shoulders creep up and my hands curl into fists. He steps closer, his presence behind me like a malignant ghost intent on haunting me until I either go insane or die from his malice. A hand gruffly lands on my shoulder, spinning me until I'm facing him. He's too close, his body leaning over me as if he intends to swallow me whole. His fingers trail down my arm, squeezing so tightly at my wrist that I let a whimper slip out. He smiles at the sound. "Do you care about this *guard*?" he taunts, his chin gesturing to Alexi with disdain, as if he is no better than excrement to be scraped off the bottom of a boot. "You are acting as if you do."

It's a struggle to remain calm, to keep my mouth shut and this magic inside of me hidden. I can feel it humming now, near my stomach, and I'm not sure if it wants to be used or is just reassuring me that it's there. I don't know if it's even sentient at all.

King Dolian sneers as he stares at me, his hazel eyes narrowing. Color leeches from my skin, and my chest goes tight with panic. *This can't be happening.* He shoves me to the side, the force causing me to fall to the ground with a loud thud. Alexi grimaces as he reaches out his bloodied arm towards me. The king motions with his hand, and that's when I take notice of the five King's Guardsmen that are also in the room—the others I had felt before.

One guard—the only one who has ever met my gaze—grabs Alexi's hair and gruffly pulls his head back, snapping his face up towards the ceiling. I move to my hands and knees, just a few feet away. Is it possible to discreetly send my magic to him? I discard that thought, however, as I remember how brightly it glowed when I used it on Bella. Can it protect him or just heal him? I'm nearly desperate enough to find out, starting to lift my hand, when my eyes meet Alexi's. He subtly shakes his head at me, willing to sacrifice himself to protect my secret. A scream begins to burn in my throat, only stopped by the sound of movement.

The king walks in front of him, drawing my gaze as he moves with measured steps, as if he has all the time in the world. Looking down his nose at Alexi, he drawls, "When it was reported to me that you had been abandoning your post in the middle of the night, I assumed it was to go to one of the many bars in Vitour. Or perhaps a brothel. You *have* been alone for a long time now."

Alexi's jaw clenches, the only indication that the king has hit a nerve. My uncle's responding grin is like that of a serpent's, pointed and horrific. His shiny black boots tap on the wood as he starts to circle Alexi again. Each step he takes is like a needle pricking into my skin.

"I wanted to give you the benefit of the doubt," he continues, eyes cold. "But I also needed to know for sure, so your punishment would match the crime. After all," the king growls, "you left the most important thing to me vulnerable. So I assigned one of your own, one I trust, to watch you in secret. To follow you and see where you were sneaking off to." He gestures to the guard holding Alexi's hair and prowls around so that he is now behind them. "Nothing to say, Alexi?"

The king pauses his movements as if he actually thinks his question will be answered. In the silence, he sighs dramatically, placing his hands into the pockets of his breeches. The casual calm of his demeanor somehow makes him appear even more terrifying.

"That's alright. I already know where you were going."

My blood runs cold as pure terror slices through my veins. I gasp for air, but my breath isn't coming in fast enough. The king meets my gaze, his brows drawn down and a near-feral look in his eyes.

"You were here, sneaking off to take what doesn't belong to you. To touch what is mine, and mine alone."

I try to deny his accusations, but the words are stuck in my throat, the shock of this moment locking me down. He can't possibly believe Alexi was touching me... like that? Even more, why is he acting as if *he* would have the right to? As if I'm *his* to claim? To *own*?

"I never—" Alexi attempts to speak, but the words die on a grunt when he is kicked brutally in the side by the king. He tries to double over his knees, but the guard holding his hair won't let him move. My heart speeds up even faster, the thumping in my ears sounding like a death march. King Dolian wastes no time delivering another kick to Alexi's back.

"Stop it!" I shout, not caring if it results in me also getting hurt, *wishing* he would hurt me instead. I can't just sit by and watch this. I refuse to let them harm the one person in this kingdom that truly cares about me. Scrambling as fast as I can, I crawl to Alexi. My trembling hands lift towards him, but before I can make contact, King Dolian is shouting at his guards to drag me away. Screaming and kicking, I fight to get out of their grip, but the two men holding me are stronger than I am. They force me to my knees, their hands wrapped around my upper arms so tightly that I know they will bruise.

"Light some torches. I want to make sure she sees this."

Dread tingles down my limbs until I can't feel them. It's such an odd experience, to be so astonishingly terrified that I lose the ability to sense touch. I try again to fight my captors, but I can't. I'm forced to watch as the remaining two guards light torches and hold them on either side of Alexi. The flame illuminates his bronzed skin and the tousled salt and pepper hair that hangs over his forehead. Even beaten and bruised, he still looks like a formidable opponent. However, not even Alexi can fight off five trained men, even with my pitiful help.

The need to go to him is overwhelming, but I try to remind myself that whatever the king does to torture Alexi, I can mend him after. My magic can heal whatever wounds he sustains. I know it. A small flicker of hope lights within me at the knowledge that I can make sure he is alright until I hear the unmistakable whistle of a sword being drawn from its scabbard.

Time stalls, and every sense—every part of me—focuses on the king standing behind Alexi. His lips pull to the left in a half smile that I swear comes from the pits of hell itself. It's pure evil. I want to vomit. I want to squeeze my eyes closed and shut this out like it isn't really happening. *Can my magic stop this?*

"Rhea, let this be a lesson for you. *I* control your life. *I* decide who you are allowed to speak to. *I* am your future." He speaks with a low, taut voice, saying the words through gritted teeth while trapping me with his gaze. The energy in the room shifts, a crescendo building as if in warning of what is to come.

I move my eyes down to meet Alexi's, expecting to see terror on his face, but instead I'm met with calm resignation. And somehow, that is so much worse. I try to scream at him to move—to fight. To do *something* so I don't have to watch what is about to happen.

"It's okay," he whispers, but the words don't comfort me.

This is not okay. Tears roll down my cheeks and drip one by one onto the wood floor.

In the deafening silence, the king makes his last remarks. "I will make sure no one ever tries to take you from me. Everything I have done has been to keep you here, where you're safe," he declares, eyes bearing down on me.

Safe from what? The only person I've ever been in danger from is *him* because I am nothing more than something to possess—a thing to him, not a person. He's never loved me like a family member should. Not like the man he's currently holding captive.

"Look at me." Having zero fight left, I obey. In the glow of the torches at his sides, my uncle doesn't even look mortal; his eyes and smile are illuminated, while shadows cover the rest of his features so that they appear contorted into something monstrous. "This is your fault, Rhea," he says calmly, like it's the most obvious truth. "You allowed this *guard* to pretend he was someone important, and it will cost him his life. Don't ever forget that."

Before I can inhale my next breath, King Dolian plunges the sword through Alexi's back, the tip of the golden steel dripping blood from where it protrudes from his chest. A scream like nothing I've ever heard before pierces the air; its anguish and sorrow causes the guards to cringe as it reverberates off the stone walls. Alexi's eyes are wide as he slowly looks down to where he's been stabbed. The king plants a boot onto his back as he kicks him off the sword, leaving him to fall chest first onto the floor. There is already so much blood, the crimson color pools around Alexi and dots the walls; it splatters across King Dolian's tan breeches and his otherwise pristine boots.

It's like time is moving in slow motion, my body thrashing as I fight to get out of the guards' hold. If I can get to him, I can save him. Finally, I'm shoved to the ground in a painful crash. My screaming stops as I crawl on my hands and knees to reach Alexi. Grunting, I push with all my strength to roll him over, the new position placing his head in my lap as I sit back on my heels.

"Should we take the body, Your Majesty?" asks a muffled voice behind me.

"No. Let him lie there until tomorrow morning." There is a shuffling of footsteps before the door slams, the king and his guards gone. Grim silence settles in as Bella darts down the stairs, coming to a halt and taking in the scene before her. A whine leaves her throat, long and high pitched, as she sinks down to the ground away from the blood still pooling around me.

Alexi's face is pale, his eyes nearly shut as tears flood my own. Leaning forward, I whisper on a shaky breath, "I will heal you."

My left hand cradles Alexi's head as I move my right hand down to his chest, on top of his horrific wound. The warmth of his blood seeping out temporarily distracts me. Even Bella didn't bleed this much. My eyes close, and I try to settle into the warmth coiled near my stomach. My mind feels too full to focus though, too many thoughts and feelings rushing past to silence. I let out a frustrated growl, squeezing my eyes even tighter. In my mind's eye, I visualize my magic at the base of my spine—like glowing white ends of a flame. I reach for the tendrils, but it's like my hands keep swiping through, unable to grasp them.

Suddenly I feel a hand, not quite warm but not quite cold, land on top of my own. I startle, my eyes opening as I look down at Alexi. The tips of his fingers, now pale in color, lay over mine on his chest as he slowly pushes our hands from his gash.

"No," he rasps, blood leaking out of the corners of his mouth while his eyelids droop heavily.

"Alexi, I can fix this. Let me fix this," I beg, trying to close my watery eyes again to focus.

"No," he says a little more forcefully. I blink and stare at him, confused about why he won't let me try. "You can't. He will know." The words are spoken so quietly, barely loud enough for me to hear though I hover over him.

"I don't care. I *can't* lose you. I—"

His other hand, trembling with the effort, slides up to cup the side of my face gently, silencing my words.

"I love you, Little One." A tear rolls down his cheek as he struggles to take a breath, a gurgling sound coming from the movement.

My tears drip faster down my own cheeks as a sob rips from me. "Please," I whisper, trying to slide my hand to his wound again, but his fingers scarcely press down in resistance.

"This is not where your journey ends. Promise me," he gasps, the gurgling sound louder as his lips move but no sound comes out. The hand on my face falls to the ground, grimly splashing the blood that now surrounds us as his eyes flutter closed. My chest heaves as I watch the man who raised me, the guard who protected me, the *father* who loved me, take his last breath. Frantic, I lay both palms flat on his wound as I try to call on that magic to help.

Save him, I beg internally. *Please, save him.* I reach inside of me for that feeling of life that is coiled within, but like before, I can't grasp it. The magic seems to dance away from my touch. "Save him!" I desperately scream out into the room, my hands pushing down more forcefully.

Finally, *finally*, that warmth begins to move up my torso. It's something I can feel, but it can't be seen from the outside. It flows slowly, resisting my call. Like it knows it's too late. My teeth grit together as I force it to move, to get to my palms and flood Alexi with its healing abilities.

When I feel the tingling sensation gather at my hands, I watch as the shimmery white light hovers over him.

Save him. Save him. Save him. Over and over, I command it to heed me.

But nothing happens. Seconds turn to minutes while my entire world crumbles around me. Alexi's chest never rises again; color never returns to his beautiful skin, and his eyes never come back to life.

Chapter Ten

BAHIRA

"COME ON, HAYLEE, ARE YOU even trying?" Drenched in sweat, I bounce on my feet, waiting for my friend to get back into her stance and lift her weapon. Her bright blonde hair is pulled back, her tan skin flushed as she breathes heavily. She's already exhausted, likely from a night spent with Arin and not from our training.

"Bahira, you're more feisty than usual this morning," she pants, her hands on her knees as she rests.

"And you're more tired than usual. What's your point?" I retort as I twirl my spear.

It was a gift from my father when I turned nineteen. "A uniquely perfect weapon for a perfectly unique mind," he had said when he handed it to me. And unique it was: black steel mined from the mountains to the north wraps around the body of the spear—made from the thick bark of the pirang tree—from the leaf-shaped tip on one end to the solid cap gracing the other. Our kingdom's sigil was engraved on the cap, and through it, my father had even spelled the spear to be impenetrable, unable to break or nick when hit with a sword.

Haylee smirks, her pink lips pulling up to the side, as she finally lifts her own sword and returns to the first position. "Maybe the cause of my tiredness could be the solution to your snippy attitude," she quips before attacking, lunging forward as she brings her blade down, the motion fluid and form perfect. I block her attack, metal singing as we clash together.

"I thought you said I was feisty. Now I'm snippy?"

We break apart and begin to circle each other. My muscles tense as I rotate my spear in my hand, the movement as familiar as breathing, while I map out my attack. I've sparred enough times with Haylee that she is keenly aware of how I fight—and how often I like to change things up. Patience has never been her strong suit though, so after a few more seconds of baiting her, she goes on the offensive. Gripping her sword tightly with both hands, she swings from left to right as she advances on me. I parry each of her moves, holding her off. When she glances away for a second, to someone or something behind me, I slide the spear down her sword quickly and jerk my arms as I forcefully snap the body of my spear into her side. Not enough to injure, but enough to sting.

"Haylee, you're distracted," I taunt, lowering my spear beside me as I begin to circle her again. She's a few inches shorter than I am, but what she lacks in height she more than makes up for in fortitude and grit.

"At least I have a reason to be distracted," she hisses. "How long has it been for *you*?" One of the things I like about my friendship with Haylee is that she isn't afraid to be honest with me, including when she makes fun of me. Though, it hasn't been as long as she is assuming since I've been *distracted.* My night with Gosston flutters briefly on the edges of my mind, causing me to shudder before I push the memory away. It has been a few days since our drunken coupling, and thankfully, I haven't seen him since then. I also haven't spoken to Daje since the public forum, where we got into a heated argument.

Haylee spins suddenly, her sword lifting over her head as she faces me. In one swift motion, her blade swings down. I brace my hands on my spear and block her attack, my shoulders straining with the effort. Our weapons cross in front of us as we lean in towards each other in the hopes that the other will give up.

"You've gotten stronger," I state, sweat beading down the sides of my face. Haylee winks, pushing forward as her biceps bulge with the effort of her attack. Stepping back too quickly for her to prepare for, she stumbles before I kick out my left leg and sweep her feet out from under her. Haylee grunts when her back hits the ground, a curse leaving her lips as I stand above her—my spear pointing at her chest.

"I surrender, bitch," she huffs, breathing heavily as she sprawls out on the ground.

Chuckling, I take a seat next to her and stretch my legs out in front of me, carefully laying my spear down at my side. We rest in a small field of pillow grass, named for how incredibly comfy and, well, pillowy it is. The blades are a rich dark green so thick that, as they grow longer, they begin to fold over themselves. It's perfect for training in bare feet and for cushioning your falls.

"Is that any way to address royalty?" I jest, laughing as she groans and punches me in the leg. "Do you want to go another round?"

"I would rather roll around in that mud over there." She points to a small pit on the other side of the field. A sudden sly smile lights up her face as she rolls onto her side. My eyes narrow at her in response, knowing she's about to say something that will likely make me want to hit her again. "You could always spar with Daje," she teases quietly as her eyes dart across the training yard to where he is practicing with Arin.

Both men are shirtless, their muscles gleaming in the sunlight with sweat as they fight with their swords. Even staring at Daje like this, I don't see him as anything other than a friend. There is no urge to trace my fingers down his defined stomach or shoulders. Or to run them through his dark brown hair.

"The man would let you walk all over him. I mean that literally, Bahira. You could actually walk all over him, and he would probably die of happiness. Or maybe just come—"

"Stop," I cut her off, my hand slicing the air with the word. Haylee, like my mother, thinks Daje and I would be a happy couple. And I suppose if platonic cordiality were the only key factor in a relationship, we would be. Daje's friendship has brought me joy and happiness since our childhood. When the children my age joked and taunted me for my lack of magic, he had befriended me and come to my defense. Sighing, my head tilts back and my eyes close. I don't want to think about Daje and the awkward tension between us after our argument, so I focus on my schedule today instead. After training, I need to visit the library to hopefully find some inspiration for my experiments. I don't know how much longer I can test on plants before I need to move on to something else. For the first time since I've started researching, I feel unsure of how to proceed. How can I figure out what is blocking our fucking magic when every experiment I've tried thus far has failed? There *has* to be something I'm missing.

A warm breeze blows across my face, the salty air blending with the scent of the grass around us. Our training grounds are on the south edge of the capital city Galdr, situated close to the ocean, and from here I can hear the rolling of the waves. A small feeling of bitterness roils my stomach at the thought that I've never been able to swim in the blue waters of the sea. Not because of the Spell, but because the sirens patrol all of the waters around the continent, so it's not a risk worth taking. Though their song only works on men, their rumored ruthlessness is not limited to a single sex.

The clashing of distant swords takes me out of my head and back to the sparring going on around me. From self-defense and weapon training to learning how to wield magic, these grounds house it all. Surrounded by a thick ring of twisting pirang trees, the middle field is completely open to the sky above with a few crested hills and small ponds. Lining most of the ring is an obstacle course built into the trees while also incorporating the earth, rocks, and water. Dotted throughout the grounds are pockets of mages grouped together based on their experience level. Together, they will spar with various weapons, learn how to take down and defend themselves against opponents, as well as pick a combat specialty to sharpen. Our instructor, Dilan, often has us rotate to different areas of the grounds to focus on strengthening every aspect of our defense.

There is balance in using what the Continent has provided to train with, both in magic and simply in life. Though I haven't taken any of the magic courses for obvious reasons, I have read the majority of the texts used in teaching them. With that information and Nox's secondhand account, I've learned how important balance is when wielding magic. All magic use has a toll. The cost usually involves extreme focus while wielding it and the need to rest immediately after so that it can slowly replenish. This balance is unique to each person, though when I've watched Nox practice with his, he is able to expend more magic and recover far more quickly than anyone else. I lean back, bringing my elbows to the ground as I bask in the direct sunlight.

"Bahira, do you want to spar with me?" The question comes from a voice so deep that I nearly startle.

Slowly, I lift my head forward, my hair sliding over my shoulders as my eyes open and take in the owner. He is incredibly tall, his broad shoulders easily double my own while his arms are as thick as my thighs. The size of his jaw, which is dusted in dark stubble, has me convinced he could easily chew through stone. He's handsome, but in a harsh sort of way. Curly black hair cut close to his head is the only thing about him that softens his rugged features. I've seen him before, around the training grounds, but only from a distance. He's *much* more impressive up close.

"You know, Bahira was just talking about how she could use a distraction," Haylee practically purrs from my side, winking over at the man.

His dark gaze slowly travels over my body, and I can't help the way my thighs clench together in response. He catches the movement, pupils flaring for a brief second before he recovers. *Oh yes, he definitely wants to be distracted too.* I watch as he holds out his massive hand, brows furrowed in concentration as blue light plucks and manipulates a long blade of pillow grass into the shape of a flower.

"Is that supposed to impress me?" I quip, raising a brow as the pillow grass flower comes to rest on my lap. A brutish smile grows on his face as he steps closer and reaches out his hand to help me up. I'm desperate to erase the thought of Gosston and distract myself from the lack of progress with my work, both of those things he can *definitely* help with. His skin is darker than my own, a rich brown that would absolutely gleam against the white silk of my sheets. I can easily imagine him tangled with me in them. Grabbing my spear, I let him help me up, his large, calloused hand squeezing mine before letting go.

"Maybe a little," he replies with a waggle of his eyebrows. I roll my eyes, falling into step with him as we walk away from the crowded area to find one more secluded to spar in.

"Have fun!" Haylee sings at our backs. I'm not sure if she's watching me, but I raise my arm and give her the middle finger just in case. Based on the laughter that follows, I know she saw.

"You know my name, but I don't know yours," I say, keeping my gaze forward and on the small pockets of sunlight streaming through the trees ahead. Around us, the other mages train, the reverberation of steel weapons and magic zinging in the air.

"My name is Max." *Gods*, his voice is so deep.

"Well, Max, I have a wager for you. If *you* win, you can pick whatever prize you want."

That gets his attention as we stop near the edge of the trees. He pulls his sword from the sheath on his back, the movement flexing every muscle not covered by his white sleeveless tunic.

"And if *you* win?" he counters, angling his body as he steps one foot back and brings his sword into both hands. His thighs strain so tightly against his black trousers, I briefly wonder how they haven't ripped. Mirroring his stance, I lift my own weapon, twirling the spear until it's pointed at him.

"If I win," I say slowly, glancing around to make sure no one is within earshot, "I get to decide where I want your tongue." Then I strike.

Chapter Eleven

BAHIRA

MY MOANS SATURATE THE air in Max's bedroom as I claim my prize for winning our sparring match. After legitimately trying for all of five minutes, Max let me best him with a move he could have easily blocked. With the metal tip of my spear pointed at his neck, he smiled down at me as if he had just become the champion of a kingdom-wide tournament.

Discreetly—at my request—he led me back to his place through the cover of the thick trees surrounding the training grounds. We showered together, but also at my request, we kept our hands to ourselves. I was in no rush to have this moment over before it started. I *needed* this distraction. That didn't stop either of us from eyeing the other intensively before we finally made it to the bedroom.

Thankfully, Max has proven that he is *very* skilled with his tongue. His wide jaw creates the most perfect place for me to sit, my knees on either side of his head. He holds my hips, those large hands fanning across them more gently than I wish they would. The thought causes a shiver to roll down my spine as he continues encouraging me to move faster on top of his mouth. My toes curl from the tingling sensation building at my center. His eyes sear into me as I slowly slide my hands up my stomach in tantalizing motions until I reach my breasts. My pace picks up, Max more than willing to help my hips move, as his tongue continues its assault on my clit. I knead my breasts and pinch and pull on my nipples, giving myself that small bite of pain I crave. With another roll of my hips, my thighs clench together and a wickedly loud moan leaves my lips as I climax. Max holds me in place, his tongue diving into me as he consumes my release like it's a favorite meal he's been denied for too long.

"I need more," I say breathlessly, every nerve ending still buzzing. Max wastes no time picking me up from his face as he sits up, no easy feat considering I am not a small woman. I move to my hands and knees, anticipation coiling within as Max positions himself behind me. Looking at him over my shoulder, I shudder as his eyes devour the part of me he wants to claim. It's like being hunted by a dangerous predator, and at this moment, I am more than willing to be prey.

Lining himself up, he begins to push into me at an agonizingly slow pace, groaning when he can feel how ready for him I am. I force my hips back hard until he is buried to the hilt and I'm stretched around him indecently. A slight prickle of pain quickly gives way to pleasure as we both pause, our breathing ragged.

"Fuck," he curses under his breath.

My hips start moving in small circles in response, and I smirk when he lets out another string of curses. Tension starts building again as he thrusts into me. I throw my head back, my long curly hair tickling me as it fans across my skin. The memory of my night with Gosston pierces my lust-addled brain, and for a moment, I lose my focus and fall out of rhythm. Max, however, is intent on making sure I stay thoroughly distracted and pulls my hips back in time with his next thrust.

"Harder," I command. His pace slows down as he thrusts deeper into me, his grunts meeting my moans like an obscene, forbidden song. Wrapping an arm around my waist, he pulls me up so that my back meets his chest. Gently moving my hair over my shoulder, he then trails a hand over my breast and down my stomach until he reaches between my legs, circling my clit with precision. My back arches as I gasp for air, tilting my hips to get him even deeper.

"*Fuck*. Yes, Bahira." His thrusts start to speed up again, his breathing as staccato as mine.

"Work me harder if you want me to come with you," I urge, my nails digging into his forearm. Max rises to the challenge, hitting me deeper while also moving those deft fingers faster. His other hand moves back and forth between my breasts, mimicking what he saw me do to them earlier. Finally, I'm near the edge again, my orgasm right on the cusp. My inner muscles clench together, and after a few more punishing thrusts, I'm screaming as I fall over that ledge, Max following shortly after with a noise that can only be described as a roar. We're a heaving, sweaty mess on our knees, Max's arms still wrapped around my torso holding me to him. He stills suddenly, the tension in his corded arms making the veins there more pronounced.

"Please tell me you're taking something to prevent pregnancy." The fear in his voice makes me laugh as he slowly begins to pull out behind me.

"Yes, I'm taking the preventative tonic," I confirm, groaning again when he fully slips out.

"Thank the stars above. I'll get a towel." He moves from the bed and into the bathroom as I search the floor for my undergarments. "I didn't think it would be this easy, you know," he says, walking back into the room and handing me a wet towel to clean myself up with as he begins to pull his trousers on.

"You didn't think what would be easy?" I question, my back to him as I grab my own tunic and trousers off the floor, grimacing when I remember how dirty they are from training this morning.

"Bedding you," he responds with an air of nonchalance that makes me grip my clothing tighter.

"And why would you assume it would be easy?" I challenge, pulling the tunic over my head and promptly cursing when it gets snagged on my hair.

"Gosston said all I had to do was invite you to spar, and it would end in fucking." I turn to look at him when I finally get my wretched top on. Max takes in the hard look on my face and cringes before shrugging and adding, "He wasn't wrong."

I roll my eyes and scoff. "Did Gosston also tell you that he lasted all of five thrusts before he came?" I ask, stepping into my pants. Max barks out a laugh, shaking his head.

"No, he conveniently left that out. He did say that you cried after, telling him you wished you had magic."

My hands tying the laces of my trousers falter as anger floods my veins and a vow begins to chant in my mind: I'm going to murder Gosston.

"What else has he been running his mouth about?" I grit out, turning to face Max as my hands go to my hips. He suddenly gets quiet, pinching his lips together as he avoids looking at me. My hands fly up in exasperation. "Really? *Now* you're not going to talk?" I don't know why I'm surprised to hear that Gosston has already spread word of our night together. Though together is hardly the right word considering it was mostly just him drunkenly coming at record speed. Still, thick regret and something that feels an awful lot like shame begins to settle heavily on me.

"I don't want to cause problems," he deflects, his voice becoming higher, as if he's scared of my reaction.

If I weren't already heated with anger, I might have laughed. "It's too late for that," I mumble, lacing up my sandals and heading towards the hallway outside of the room.

"Does this mean I've lost my chance for a repeat sparring session?" he yells after me.

"You never had one."

Without another word, I step out and start my walk home through the forest. The earthy scent of the trees and foliage calms some of the rage in my veins though images of stabbing Gosston with my spear dance in my mind the entire walk home.

After spending my shower wondering how much trouble I would get in if I maimed Gosston, I dress and walk to the library. The late afternoon sun shines through gaps in the canopy above, dotting the gray stone pathway with golden light. While the palace itself is mostly secluded for security, the surrounding area does boast several residential homes. Smoke trails out of a few chimneys as I follow the path lined by the thick foliage. The remnants of a cool spring breeze blow my hair faintly as I walk and nod to mages who pass me. While my distraction with Max had been successful—prior to the Gosston comments—all my previous worries bubble right back up to the surface. I find myself eager to find refuge within the pages of a book and, hopefully, some ideas on what to experiment on next.

My steps quicken when the rectangular two story white building comes into view. While it does have draping vines at its entrance and beautifully carved wood-lined windows, the structure stands out like a white cloud among a green sky. It is made of white dragon stone, like most of the buildings and homes, which is sourced from the Fae Kingdom through trade deals. Their dragon stone is easily carved but extremely durable. In exchange for the building material, we provide the fae with an abundance of fruits and vegetables not easily grown in their own mountainous terrain.

The library is set back a few feet from the main road, a small gray stone pathway lined with varying flowers and bushes guides the way to a large set of arched double doors. A giant yellow galanthus flower permanently blooms at the pinnacle of the arch, the long skinny petals delicately flared open. The wooden door creaks as I pull on it, the familiar aged smell of old paper and leather hitting my nose immediately upon entering. I exhale as I walk in, feeling more calm now than I had since leaving Max's. Memories of all the time I spent here over the years play in my mind. At first, it was to escape all the whispers about how I had no magic, but eventually, I came to crave the exploration and discovery of the knowledge that lines the shelves in this place. The silence found here was an added bonus.

I walk past the front desk where Elisha, an older mage who runs this place, sits. She smiles warmly when she sees me, the gray-blonde hair pinned to the top of her head bobbing as she dips her chin in hello. The first floor has the same white stone as the outside. It lines the walls and ground, though the floor is covered by rugs of dark red and blue that are spread out to muffle the sound of shoes clicking on the hard surface. Dark wooden tables and chairs are placed throughout, and lining the walls in all directions are shelves upon shelves of books. A wooden staircase in the back leads up to the second floor, the middle of which is open to the main level below. A railed walkway wraps all the way around and houses even more books on ancient wood shelves. Windows on both the first and second floors let in whatever light sneaks past the treetops. Spelled flames in glass bowls help make up the difference so that the entire library is cast in a decadent glow. Besides the ruffling sound of pages being turned and a few muffled footsteps, it is expectedly and pleasantly silent. I feel like I can finally take a deep breath here.

After gathering several books from the Magic section, a few that are familiar and some I haven't read yet, I take a seat at a table closest to the bookcases. Sliding a tome to me, the leather crackles as I open it and begin to read the yellowed pages. Anyone in the realm is welcome to check books out, but they are spelled to make sure that they aren't destroyed—accidentally or otherwise.

I'm not sure how much time passes when a familiar female voice says my name.

"Bahira with her nose in a book—that's a sight that will never get old." My mother heads towards me, her gait more like a waltz with the natural grace of her movements. She stops beside me, her hands immediately moving to fuss with my hair. While Nox takes after our father with his wavier black hair, angular jaw, and lightly tan skin, I mirror our mother.

Like her, I have wild and unruly dark brown curls; my skin is more tan than Nox's and my jaw softer. The only trait that our entire family shares is the dark gray of our eyes, signifying that our line has only ever been that of mage blood.

When the realms were easily traversed before the war, it was rare—though not uncommon—to marry someone from a different realm. After the Spell was put into place, however, that changed. I had heard rumors that beings who were of mixed blood may have been sent to a different kingdom than where they were living when the Spell was cast. It all depended on what magic they had, or I suppose, didn't have.

My mother gently tugs on my hair, drawing my attention back to her. "Where did you go, my rose?"

I smile at her term of endearment. It is both her favorite flower and my middle name. "Just contemplating the usual," I answer in a hushed voice, gesturing to the books in front of me.

She smiles, but it doesn't hide the concern lining her features. I start moving to clean up the books, hoping to avoid a conversation I'd rather not have at the moment. When the books are put back in their place—no helpful information gained on this trip—I walk with my mother outside, waving a small goodbye to Elisha. I'm shocked to realize the sun has already set, darkness concealing the forest. Spelled flames illuminate the path as my mother and I start our walk back to the palace. My hands rub the sides of my arms as the still-cool spring night air blankets us.

"You know that you are not any less mage because you do not have magic," my mother affirms in the silence, her hand reaching out to squeeze my arm gently. "Your soul, your very essence—*you*—are what our people are made of. Magic is secondary to the person who wields it." Her voice is dulcet, her words holding her conviction.

A knot of emotion tightens in my throat before I clear it, dropping my hands to my sides as I sigh. "I know I have magic, Mother," I say, looking up at what I can see of the night sky. "There is no reason I shouldn't. Not only do I have pure mage blood in my veins, but I also have two of the most powerful magic wielders as my parents. It does not make sense that I was randomly selected to be punished by not having a gift when Nox was blessed with the most magic we've seen in well over a century." The cadence of my voice changes as my frustration bleeds through.

"It is not a punishment," she counters, tugging on my arm to stop our walk as she turns towards me. Her gray eyes are filled with the kind of unconditional acceptance and love I fear will only ever come from a parent. "You must believe that the gods did not single you out—"

"It's the only thing that makes sense!" I yell, cutting her off and stepping out of her hold. My mothers eyes widen at my outburst, her mouth dropping open slightly. She tries to step closer, but my hands go up defensively. I wish she understood—I wish anyone else understood why what I'm doing is so important to me. I fight back the tears welling in my eyes as I force a deep breath into my tightened chest. "Imagine how incomplete I feel in my own family," I whisper, laying my insecurities bare at her feet. "I just—" I hesitate, my gaze lifting from hers and back to the night sky. "I just want to be whole."

Chapter Twelve

RHEA

I SPEND THE NIGHT cradling Alexi's head in my lap and gently brushing my fingers through his hair. I've lost feeling in my legs and feet from how I'm kneeling. Though in truth, I've lost much more than that. Bella lays on the opposite side of the room, avoiding the pool of blood that eventually stopped spreading out over the wood floors. The thought should make my stomach turn, but I don't feel anything at all. My body, my mind, my emotions—they all shut down. I'm hollow as I repeat the same two words in my mind—*he's gone.*

My shaky fingers then trace along his jaw, the skin there colder than it had been earlier. A small part of me is glad that Alanna is also no longer here in this world. I picture them now in the Afterlife, holding hands and reliving their most fond memories together. The thought is almost enough to bring a semblance of a smile to my face. My head throbs as my swollen eyes take in every detail of Alexi's face, committing it to memory. When the sun begins to rise, the sky glowing a deep orange that floods through the balcony glass doors, I hear footsteps on the stairs outside. Bella quickly makes her way up the stairs on her own, which is good because I'm not sure I can talk right now anyway. The door to my tower opens, and I know it's the guards here to take him away. I keep my gaze on Alexi, not ready to let him go. My fingers curl tightly into my palms as I fight to keep my breathing controlled. They don't deserve to touch him.

"We are here to take the body," a guard states, his voice callous. This is just a job to him—to them all. They don't *care* that the one person I had in this world is gone. And it's all my fault.

"No," I rasp out, the sound like stone scraping against stone.

"Move out of—"

"No!" I scream again, leaning further over Alexi. I hear sighs, even some groans of annoyance, as if none of them can understand why I won't let them take him. I don't know why either. I don't want to have to look at his dead body and be reminded of how my existence is now irrevocably changed. Yet I can't let him go. I can't let this be the last time that I see him. *I can't. I can't. I can't.*

"He's dead," a deep voice says, his boots stepping into my line of sight. "Holding his body hostage won't bring him back." My head tilts up to look at the guard, who I immediately recognize as the one that held Alexi as the king buried his sword into his back. My lips lift in a snarl, a near growl barreling out of me. "Let go," he commands, completely unaffected by my anguish and grief.

Somehow, more tears well in my eyes and slide down my face, like sand falling in an hourglass. I know I have to let him go. I just wish it didn't feel so wrong. Leaning down, I give Alexi's forehead one last kiss, tears dripping onto his face, as I whisper my promise to him, remembering his last words. *This is not where your journey ends. Promise me.* So I do. I promise him that I will escape this tower. No matter what it takes.

The process of carefully removing his head from my lap is slow. Within a few moments, he is gone. Just... gone.

Blood is everywhere. It's caked on my hands and soaked into my night-dress. It surrounds me from where it's pooled out in the living room.

"We will have the maids come in to take care of the blood and clean you, on the king's orders. If you give them trouble, he will come here personally." There is no sympathy or concern in the guard's voice. It's spoken matter-of-factly, as if this was the only outcome one could have expected.

My eyes shift up to look at him. He stares back down, cold and un-yielding. His tan hand rests on the hilt of his sword, while his long, wavy black hair is pulled back from his face. He may not have driven that sword through Alexi himself, but he held Alexi's body still so the king could. When it's clear I'm not going to answer him, the guard huffs a breath and walks to the door, his steps leaving bloody footprints the entire way.

Not long after, the maids appear. When they step into the room, one of them lets out a low curse under her breath before silence descends again, only broken by the clamoring of buckets and mops hitting the floor. I can sense their stares as two maids walk over to me, holding out their hands to help me up. Keeping my head down, I place my hands in theirs and slowly get my feet underneath me, pushing up to stand between them. I wonder what the maids are thinking as they work to clean what remains of Alexi off the floors and walls. Were they told what happened here? My legs nearly give out with each step as circulation slowly moves back to my feet, causing a painful burning sensation to work its way down to them. The maids holding me up are patient, not uttering a single word as I take slow, awkward steps. They move in tandem with me, letting me set the pace as we go. I know my body is moving, and I know my heart is beating. It's all I can hear. Everything else is drowned out in a buzzing haze. When we reach the washroom, one of the maids lets my hand go and starts the bath.

"Do you have any oils you would like us to add?" she asks, her voice somehow reaching me through my daze. I shake my head in response, still not looking up at them. There is a pause before the other maid lets go of my hand and moves to step in front of me. "We have to undress you for the bath, My Lady."

I nod, not waiting for them to help me as I reach for the strap of my night dress. This is the first time since I was a very small child that I have had other people present while I bathed. Maids helped until I was about eight, then they suddenly stopped showing up. I was older when I figured out it was on the order of my uncle. My trembling hand wavers as my gaze finally lifts to look at the maid in front of me. She studies me, taking in my hesitation before realization hits, and her eyes soften.

"We take care of the ladies of the court. You needn't worry about us seeing you in this state, My Lady," she says quietly. After a few moments, I take off the dress and my undergarments and step into the bath. Misty heat curls above the water, signaling its warm temperature, but I don't feel anything. Sinking down, my legs extend out in front of me as my hands grip the edges of the tub. "I am going to have to wash your body first; then we'll put fresh water in and move on to your hair." Her voice is firm but not unkind.

The two maids work in tandem, doing just as they said. When the bath turns red, they drain it and put fresh water in. One wets my hair, then slowly and carefully scrubs it clean. My knees draw into my chest, my arms wrapping around them as I lay my cheek down. I feel them rinse my hair and then start to wash it again. It's unsettling how being cared for in this way manages to ease some of the shock of what I witnessed last night. And I know that I must be in shock because even though Alexi's pale face is all I can picture, even though his cold blood is all I can feel, my thoughts are eerily quiet. My eyes are heavy as exhaustion from being awake all night pushes down on them. I allow them to close, knowing that there isn't much more these maids could do to me that could hurt me further. I've already lost nearly everything.

I know that some time has passed when I come out of the heaviness of sleep still in the bath, the water now cold, to hear the low murmuring of voices nearby. Opening my eyes faintly, I see the forms of three maids now huddled together, one of them gesturing towards me before looking back to the others. Another nods her head and then leaves. The original two who had helped me bathe walk back over, one of them kneeling at the edge of the tub. Now that I am looking at them, I can see that they are a bit older than me, likely somewhere in their third decade. One has blonde hair lighter than mine, and the other's is dark brown.

"My Lady," the blonde one whispers, "let's get you dressed and put to bed." She helps me stand, the now cold water of the tub dripping down my body in little zigzag patterns. Immediately, I'm wrapped in a towel and brought out into the bedroom. "Where are your clothes kept?" she asks, looking around the small space.

My shaky finger points to the trunk at the foot of my bed. As the one with brown hair rifles carefully through my clothing, she shakes her head before grabbing a thin sleeveless pink night dress and white under-garments. They help me get dressed and lead me to the vanity to sit on the small stool. I don't want to see myself in the mirror—don't want to stare at the eyes of the person who led Alexi to his death—so I keep my gaze fixed on the ground.

One maid brushes my hair slowly before braiding it into a single plait and tying it off with a ribbon. I wonder when she learned how to braid hair, who taught her. It's such a simple thing. One that I wish I had been taught.

"Let's get you to bed," one of them says again. The blankets are still rumpled from the night before when *he* barged into my tower. Like a thief in the night, he stole the only person that mattered to me. But he isn't the only one to blame. When I'm tucked into bed with the comforter pulled up to my chin, I close my eyes and *beg* to drift away into oblivion.

"We are sorry for your loss, My Lady. Alexi was known amongst the staff. He was..." She trails off momentarily. My eyes open, vision blurring as I try to focus on the woman with blonde hair. "He was kind when so many are not." Her blue eyes meet mine, and while they are caring, I also see the sadness layered there. The other maid clasps her hands in front of her body as she comes to stand by her companion.

I open my mouth to speak, but a rasping sound is the only thing that comes out. It takes a few times clearing my throat to be able to say anything. "What are your names?"

The blonde woman smiles brightly, gesturing to herself. "I am Erica, and this is Tienne, My Lady."

"Please, call me Rhea. There is no need for titles."

Erica shakes her head in disagreement. "Are you not the daughter of the late King Conrad and Queen Luna?"

Hearing their names spoken out loud for the first time by someone other than Alexi or myself is a shock to my system, like a lightning bolt piercing through fog. King Dolian avoids talking about my parents in general, but he's never given them the respect of mentioning them by name. Pinching my lips together, I dip my chin in agreement.

"Then that makes you worthy enough of the title, My Lady." She smiles again, something she seems to do easily, while Tienne rolls her eyes in a playful manner. I wonder if they are related or if they are just good friends.

What would it be like to have a friend like that? They both dip their chins towards me in goodbye before turning to leave.

"Thank you," I rasp, catching them both mid-step. They look over their shoulders at me simultaneously, but it's Tienne who answers.

"Of course, My Lady. Now rest. The others have cleaned up everything downstairs." With that, they both continue down the stairs and to the door, closing it quietly behind them.

"Bella, are you there?" My words are barely a whisper, my eyes already closing, when I hear her scurry out from under the bed. Without hesitation, she jumps up and lays next to me, her head resting on top of my thigh. I'm conscious for only a few breaths before darkness sweeps in.

"Wake up, Rhea." The familiar female voice wraps around me, goosebumps covering my body in response. My eyes flutter open, easier this time than

the last. There's weightlessness to my body again, as though I'm floating in time and space. Maybe that's what this place is... a spot between worlds. Or—the more likely scenario—it's just a really good dream. "You are not too far off." Her voice startles me as I nearly feel it brush my skin. That sense of familiarity returns at the sound, but I can't pinpoint exactly why.

My eyes stare above, to the night sky that is not quite a night sky. In-numerable stars light the pitch black until it flares silver instead. Those purple, blue, pink, and green galaxies swirl throughout—an endless spinning of worlds that is as jarring as it is beautiful.

"Why am I here?" It's almost as if I can see my voice flutter on a phantom wind to wherever the woman is waiting.

"I wanted to talk with you. I know you were close to him," she replies softly. The sound is ethereal, like the gentle tinkling of bells in the distance.

"You know of Alexi?" I whisper in a jagged voice. I keep my gaze pinned on the celestial bodies above, but my mind replays every single memory of Alexi. Even the earliest ones, when I was just a small child and his presence scared me. I wish I could hug my past self and tell her that Alexi would become the best part of our life. Then a cold feeling settles into me as I'm reminded that he died because he was *so good and kind to me.*

"I do know of him," that sweet voice answers, slicing through a little of the iciness I feel. "You mustn't blame yourself, Rhea; you cannot control what the king does."

"I tried to save him," I whisper. "I could have. But my magic... I couldn't call it up in time."

"You are still learning what it means to have magic. But even if you had full control, it was too late for him. It was his time."

"You don't know that," I gasp. Tiny specks that look like stardust begin to swirl around me, glowing as they brush soothingly against my skin.

"I suppose you are right. Only one being truly knows all," she says softly. Her voice is like moonlight; it shines into the darkest recesses of my mind, but I don't want to see what is hiding there. I wish I could know if Alexi is okay, if he is indeed with Alanna. If they are happy. "You can ask me anything. I will always do my best to answer what I can."

I huff a breath, slightly annoyed that she can hear my thoughts before I've voiced them. The scent of jasmine hits my nose as I close my eyes and prepare to ask a question that I hope I like the answer to.

"Is he with her?"

The woman hums, the vibrations of the sound something I feel deep in my bones. "He is. His mind and soul are with hers in the Afterlife." I can feel her joy seeping out with her next words. "They are happy."

A tear rolls down my cheek, my body tingling with too many emotions, as varying colors of stardust continue to twirl around me. "Good," I finally whisper in response.

"It is not your fault," she laments as tendrils of what looks like pearlescent mist gently caress my cheek.

"Yes it is." A deep sadness robs me of my breath when the stars suddenly start to flicker around me.

"I will talk to you again soon," she says, but her voice barely reaches my ears.

I don't have time to respond before my stomach drops and I'm falling blindly through space again, the stars moving past me so quickly that they are nothing but streaks of light. Heavy sensation returns to my body in waves, as if my bones and muscles and skin are coming back into place layer by excruciatingly heavy layer. My hair snaps against my face wildly as I fall and fall and fall.

Sensation tingles into my fingers and toes as I wiggle them. My eyes flutter open. I roll onto my back with a groan, my head pounding viciously, as I squint at the sunlight pouring in through the window. With each thump of my heart, more sadness sweeps in. I'm still in my tower, very much alive. *And alone.* What I wouldn't give to be anywhere other than here. Warmth tracks down my cheeks as I stare up at the pointed ceiling of the tower. I wish so desperately that I could just disappear, even as I stare at Bella where she lays beside me.

I can't help but feel my life here is a waste. I don't add value to anything. No, all I am—to my very core—is a death sentence. Despite the fact that I've cried more in the last twelve hours than ever before, wetness continues to pool in my eyes. The weight of my guilt is just *so heavy,* and I wish for nothing other than to be crushed by it. I'm tired of crying. I'm tired of being given reasons to cry. I'm just so godsdamn tired. And being awake just reminds me of everything I've lost. So what is the point? When exhaustion—thick and heavy—settles on top of me, I welcome it. Darkness and numbness cover me like granules of sand until I'm completely buried. I don't fight it, and it doesn't take long until I completely succumb.

Time is a blur between waking up briefly for a few moments and forcing myself to fall back to sleep. Though I don't have to do much forcing at all. My mind craves being silenced. Unfortunately, my body and a certain fox are done with me laying in bed. The sun is back in the sky—or is it the same day? I can't be sure. Dizziness rocks me as I force myself up, hitting me like the winds of a powerful storm. *When was the last time I ate?* I should be due for a supply drop-off soon and—

My throat closes, and my lungs squeeze like the invisible hands of a god are around them, draining them of oxygen. I can feel tears welling as my body tenses, preparing itself to let everything out, to release the emotion that has steadily built up over the past however many hours I've been asleep. My eyes squeeze shut, and my fists clench by my sides. Supply drop-off was Alexi's job, and he's gone now. My lip trembles as a pathetic whimper crawls up my throat. It's too easy to succumb to the tidal wave, to drown myself in the tears that are never-ending. How does one continue living when there is no one left to live for? Bella nudges my leg from where she stands at the edge of the bed. Guilt floods over me as I look at her and lean forward, pressing my forehead to hers.

"The moon may have the stars, but at least I have you." It's the truth—a lifeline I need to cling to because as much as I miss Alexi, as much as I know his death is my fault, Bella needs me too. So for today, I am done crying. I can force this pain down until it's nothing more than shadows lurking in the recesses of my mind. I can pretend to be okay for her because she deserves for me to at least *try*. I shake out my hands and head, the movement making it hurt even more, but at least physical pain is better than the emotional agony currently tearing me apart inside.

I will not cry.

I carefully stand from the bed, looking down at the light wood floors. They look so pristine up here. Such a stark contrast from how those same floors had appeared below my blood-soaked knees last night. Will downstairs still bear the memory of Alexi's lifeless form? Will there always be a spot of discoloration from where his body had fallen? *Stop. Stop thinking about that. The maids said downstairs was cleaned up.*

Taking a deep breath—so deep it burns my lungs and expands my chest to the edge of pain—I force my thoughts to quiet. I look down at Bella and her expressive golden irises illuminated by the sunlight pouring in. They hold mine, and I can see the emotions swimming in them: sorrow, concern, sympathy, love. Clearing my throat I attempt to smile at her, though it doesn't quite reach my eyes.

I will not cry.

Still, I can't force myself to go downstairs yet, to see with my own eyes what awaits me there. So I turn and walk over to the large window by my bed instead. The colors of the world beyond this tower are resplendent—blue from the lake and sky, green of every shade from the meadows and faraway trees, and small dots of red, white, purple and yellow from the wildflowers in the distance. It all makes up a stunning tapestry that speaks to how suffering can hide in a world of beauty.

It's a normal day, and yet it isn't. It is life amongst death, and I can't help but feel like I am on the wrong side.

After a few more minutes of mindless gazing at the scenery, I make my way to the washroom. The cold and uniform gray stone that makes up every inch of this prison mirrors the emotions I'm trying so desperately to keep from bursting inside me. Emptiness and desolation and guilt and regret— *Stop it.*

Relieving myself first, I splash cold water from the sink onto my face, closing my eyes as the water drips down onto my night dress. The same one the maids—Tienne and Erica—dressed me in. I need to keep moving, to keep my mind busy, so I don't drown from the sea of misery choking my entire being.

I will not cry today.

Chapter Thirteen

RHEA

ESPITE MY WISHES TO just *not feel,* each step down the spiral stairs to the lower level of my tower makes me break out into a cold sweat—fueled by the terror that threatens to overtake me. When I reach the final two steps, I have to fight to tear my gaze away from my feet. Will the wounds that now stain my soul stain this tower as well?

I will not cry.

With a deep breath, I slowly lift my head up to look out into the living area. The sunlight that pours in from the glass balcony doors brightens every corner; the floors, the walls, the furniture—it's all clean. No evidence exists of what happened here the night before, and I can't tell if that makes me feel better or worse.

As I turn and head to the balcony, intent on clearing the stagnant air that carries a coppery scent, I see a wooden box set on top of the tea table. My brows furrow as I halt where I am, eyes glued to the box in utter confusion. I try to think about what day it is, but I can't clear the heavy fog that swirls in my mind. This must have been dropped off at some point as I slept. It's different from the one Alexi would use for supplies, smaller in size and darker in color. Tentatively, I make my way over to it as my hands tremble faintly, though I'm unsure why.

Get it together, Rhea. Steeling myself after the self-scolding, I flip the lid off of the box and peer inside. Fabrics in colors I've never seen before glimmer in the sunlight. My uncertainty grows as I pinch the cloth on the top between my fingers. They are dresses—gorgeous dresses. Bewilderment gives way to awe as I pull the first one out. The fabric is a stunning shade of green, similar to the sage leaves that I can see growing outside of the tower. White ribbons are gracefully laced throughout the hem of the puffed sleeves and skirt. The fabric is a lightweight cotton and a thin corset is built in at the waist. It is such a unique piece, especially in comparison to the plain dresses I own. Laying it on the table, I pull out the next one. It's a similar style but in a shade of pink that I've never seen before. When I go to reach for the next dress, I notice a small piece of paper tucked into the folds of the fabric. Pulling it out, I carefully unfold the note to read it.

My Lady,

Tienne and I noticed that you needed new dresses. There is a woman at court who is of a similar size and had ordered more dresses than she knew what to do with, so we offered to take them off of her hands. We've also added in some floral bath oils for you. Please do not hesitate to let us know what else you might want or need.

I have left extra papers and a quill with a small pot of ink, should you wish to respond with those requests. Just tuck the note into one of the empty boxes that your guard will bring back with him after supply drop-offs.

The boxes come directly back to us, and we shall make sure no one else knows about or sees the letters. Your new guard will be in later to bring you supplies. It was a pleasure meeting you, though I do wish it was under better circumstances.

Until next time,

Erica

My lips pinch together as I fight to hold fast to my "no crying" rule for today. Slowly, I take out each of the remaining dresses one by one, reveling in the peculiar colors and textures of them. When I've lifted the last one out of the box, I see the oils, papers, and writing supplies. Grabbing one of the little glass vials, I uncork the top and bring it to my nose, sniffing at the robust scent. I do it again with the second vial and recognize the more subtle aroma of lavender right away, as it was the only one Alexi ever brought me. My fingers tighten around the vial, my teeth grinding together at the thought of him. My breaths turn choppy, and I forgo smelling the final vial. Placing the paper and writing supplies on a small table in the library, I then gather the dresses and oils to bring them upstairs. Bella sniffs at the dresses while I lay them on the bed, her eyes moving back and forth as she takes them in.

"Aren't they lovely?" I ask, my voice distant, as I reach down to trail my fingers along one. "Which one should I wear today?"

I've never really cared about how I store my dresses, more than content to let them get wrinkled in the small trunk, but these dresses are far too beautiful to stuff away. In truth, they are far too beautiful for this place and the woman meant to wear them. I decide to store them on the floor in a small space next to my bed, near the window to its right. Carefully, I lay every dress down, stacking them gently one on top of the other except for the unique pink one.

Bathing quickly, I use a few drops of the fragrance from the first vial. When I'm clean, my hair brushed and undergarments on, I hold Bella's chosen dress out in front of me. The pink is deeper, richer than any I've seen before. How did they find the dye for such a vibrant color? This one also has the same puffed sleeve detail and built-in corset as the green one, but the material is even softer than the cotton. It's not quite silk but something in between that feels lush. The skirt of the dress flows down from the corset to the tops of my feet. It's a little long, but the fact that it fits perfectly otherwise is a testament to how good of an eye Erica and Tienne have. Stepping into it, I slowly pull the gown up and reach my hands behind me to work the buttons that line the back.

I've only clasped a few of them when there are two gentle knocks on the door. I freeze, my eyes widening as I look over to Bella. Unbridled fear overrides my thoughts as I try to figure out what to do. Can I ignore the knock? Should I? But my questions are answered for me when I hear the creaking of the door opening. Bella burrows into the blankets on the bed while I quickly press myself into the wall by the railing. My heart pounds harder and harder; it's a rattling in my chest that I'm sure whoever is down there will hear. Footsteps beat steadily on the wood floor as the stranger enters the tower. My curiosity briefly overrides my fear, and I peek around the corner of the wall.

A member of the King's Guard slowly walks around the lower level, eyeing the space like he's looking for something. He's dressed as Alexi often was—not wearing full armor, just enough to cover his chest and back. He wears a thin black tunic underneath, the sleeves rolled up to expose his tan forearms. The uniform trousers of the guards are tucked into his boots—both black in color—and a gold sword is sheathed in black leather at his waist. The sun shines on his dark wavy hair, a few unruly strands hanging over his forehead faintly.

He holds the wooden box I recognize from Alexi's past supply drop-offs. I watch as his gaze travels over every corner, eyeing the balcony and windows before he turns around and takes a step closer to where the library is. *What is he doing?* He sets the box down carefully, resting a hand on the hilt of his sword while he continues to peer into the space below my loft. I hear him mumble something under his breath about it before he takes a small step back. His eyes catch on the staircase as they travel up the stairs and to the loft that houses my bed. And then his gaze meets mine.

"Shit!" he yells, startling me as I yelp and stumble back against the wall. My chest rises and falls rapidly, a slight ringing sounding in my ears. My eyes squeeze shut as I slowly slide down the wall to sit, hugging my knees into my chest. "I didn't mean to scare you. I'm sorry for yelling." I don't respond, unsure of what to say. Is it possible to just pretend I'm not here? Will that make him leave? "Are you alright?" he asks in a softer tone than before.

When I don't answer, an awkward silence fills the room. I swear I can hear an imaginary clock ticking as each moment passes, like a leaky faucet dripping into a basin. Despite my apprehension, my curiosity is piqued again until I find myself standing back up and slowly peering back around the corner of the wall. The guard is still standing near the middle of the room. His eyes locking onto mine as his brows furrow. I'm unsure of what to do besides stand here, half-hidden with blood rushing in my ears. The silence in the tower turns palpable as both of us continue gawking at each other. When it finally becomes too much for me, I ask something semi-obvious with the hope that it gets him to leave faster.

"What are you doing here?" My throat feels scratchy, and my voice comes out more like a rasp.

His eyes roam over what he can see of me, like he's trying to figure out what he is looking at. "I was told to drop off supplies here today," he says hesitantly, breaking eye contact to look back over the room as if checking he is in the right place. If today is supply drop-off day, then that means I did sleep an entire day. "Are you okay?" he asks me again. My attention snags on his hair as I look at him, the sable strands looking nearly iridescent in the sunlight. A line forms on his forehead at my inspection.

"Why do you look so confused?" I counter while ignoring his question.

He shakes his head a little, like what I've said is ridiculous. Sighing, he waves towards me with his right hand. "I wasn't expecting to see anyone up here."

Now it's my turn to draw my eyebrows up in confusion. "Did you think you were dropping off supplies to an empty tower?" I ask, a bit more sarcastically than I mean to. My lips pinch together, and my body moves farther behind the wall as I expect him to get angry like the king would at my attitude. But he doesn't. His gaze is stuck on me, his face open and curious as he watches.

He doesn't seem at all like a regular guard—not that I would exactly know what a regular guard is like. It's just... he isn't like the ones the king keeps close to him. He observes me like he's working out the solution to a puzzle that doesn't quite have all the pieces yet. It doesn't make me uncomfortable. Rather, I'm interested to know what he sees.

"Can you just—" He hesitates, taking a measured step closer, his hands coming to rest on his hips. "Can you come out from behind the wall? I feel like I'm talking to a ghost."

I chew on my lower lip as I consider, quickly glancing to where Bella is. When I look back at him, a dark brow lifts as he tips his head to the side. His lips curl into a small smile that feels like a taunt. My eyes narrow in response, making that baiting smile of his grow bigger. I step in front of the railing haltingly, tucking my hair behind my ears before resting my hands on the black metal.

"Not a ghost," I say quietly as I gesture to myself. "Just a regular girl."

The guard's expression changes the longer he observes me. He looks almost taken aback with his eyes wide and his jaw somewhat slack. It makes me self-conscious enough to look down at myself and smooth a hand over my new dress. Perhaps I said something wrong.

"Not just a regular girl," he finally responds, stepping closer yet again. I lift my head to look at him, the cadence of his voice catching me off guard. That previously stunned look has morphed into something else, something akin to... wonder. My own head tilts to the side in inquiry. "And to answer your previous question"—he swallows roughly—"I was told that you would be hiding in here. That the weight of your grief has turned you into a recluse who shies away from mortal contact of all kinds."

I can't help but retort, "Yes. Well, *His Majesty* does have fun making up lies about me." There are about three seconds where I don't realize what I've said before my hands quickly cover my mouth. Stupid. How can I be so *stupid*? I have no idea who this guard is or how deeply his loyalties lie with the king. Of course he must be loyal; he's in the King's Guard for a reason.

Alexi's disdain for the ruler he was meant to protect and follow above all else came from learning how the king treated me. This guard doesn't know me at all. I open my mouth to backtrack, to feign temporary insanity, but my words are interrupted when I see the look on his face. He's smiling broadly, like I just told him I can make rainbows shoot out of my hands or something equally as insane. I'm once again confused. "Why does your face look like that?" I blurt out before cringing.

He chuckles, the sound rich and captivating, and I find that I can't look away from him. He appears to be a little older than I am, but still somewhere within his second decade. I examine the straightness of his nose and how it looks so perfectly proportioned to the rest of his handsome face. His tanned skin is smooth and his eyes dark, though the exact color I can't quite make out. The angles of his defined jaw are accentuated by the light pouring in. My gaze then travels to his lips and the fullness of them does something to my stomach. It's as though small butterflies have taken up residence there, wings fluttering and tickling every part as they move. I swallow, a hand going to my abdomen to see if I can actually feel that fluttering movement. When I watch those lips move into a smirk at my perusal, I quickly glance away, looking down at my feet and feeling a blush rise to my cheeks at being caught. It's odd to feel something so *light* compared to the other darker emotions I'm buried under.

"If you mean why am I so ruggedly handsome, I'm afraid I was born that way." He gestures with a hand to his face. "But if you mean why I appear confused," he continues, waiting until I lift my head, gazing down at him from under my lashes, "it's because you aren't what I expected."

"I thought you weren't expecting anyone at all?" I can't help but counter.

"You've got me there, My Lady. I *was* expecting someone to be up here. I just wasn't expecting it to be someone like you."

I stay quiet, not exactly sure how to respond to that. I know I don't look like a princess, at least not in the ways one might expect. We stand there in silence, seconds that feel like hours tick by between us as his eyes continue to ensnare mine. The intensity of his stare makes me fidget, my thumbs nervously swiping up and down the metal of the railing. I've never held anyone's gaze like this before, and I've certainly never felt so noticed.

"Aren't you worried about getting in trouble for being up here so long?" The words come out rushed. My nervousness, first for him being here at all and then for him being caught because of it, tickles at my throat. For some reason, I feel myself blushing again and grip onto the railing a little harder.

He shrugs in response, interlacing his fingers behind him as he turns away from me and begins pacing around the room. "What usually happens at supply drop-offs?" His back is to me as he changes the subject and surveys the interior of my tower like he's just remembered where we are.

"It's as it sounds. You drop off my supplies, and then you *leave*," I answer. My head shakes incredulously at having to explain this to him. Did the king, or at the very least the other guards, not give him any instructions other than to be here on a certain day?

"Are you going to come down here and get everything out, or am I to do it?" He looks up at me over his shoulder, that ridiculous smirk still in place.

The butterflies flutter again in response, and it leaves me feeling uneasy because I don't know this man or his intentions. Yet something about him draws me in. The way he looks at me makes me feel like I'm being seen somehow for the first time. It's a peculiar feeling, and one I'm unsure what to do with—am I so sheltered that any attention by a man not acting fatherly like Alexi or cruel like the king disorients me?

Stepping back from the wall, I tentatively make my way to the stairs. Frustrated and lost in my own thoughts, I don't notice that I'm rounding the final spiral of the staircase until I see the guard standing directly in front of me. My steps falter, both startled by his closeness and by the way he's looking at me. His eyes, I notice now, are like dark pools the color of slate; they pin me in place with their intensity. I can better grasp how tall he is as well, our height nearly in alignment even though I am still three steps away from the ground floor. This close to him, I can admit that the beating in my heart is marginally less about fear and more about his handsome features. And truly, he is the most beautiful man I've ever seen.

Despite being mostly hidden by armor, my eyes dance over his large chest and shoulders. My gaze continues down his body, the tan skin of his forearms catching my attention again briefly before I make my way down his torso and legs. Every part of him is solid with muscle, the firmness of his body obvious even through his clothing. It's so at odds with the softness I know of my own. Is it a weird thing to notice it like I have? I shift my eyes back up and immediately regret doing so. His mischievous smile tells me he's caught me staring. Again.

Chapter Fourteen

RHEA

"Are you going to move?" I ask, faking some bravado as I lift a brow. I may have been caught ogling him again, but I refuse on principle alone to allow myself to blush a third time.

As if knowing my thoughts, his smile grows, straight white teeth fully on display, before he steps out of the way. "After you, My Lady. Your box awaits."

His joking tone catches me off guard, momentarily making me pause on the steps before I snap out of it. I grumble a thanks under my breath before moving past him, my new dress making a swishing sound as I walk over to the supplies. Before I can kneel down to start unpacking, the guard clears his throat.

"Your dress is—" He waits as I look over my shoulder at him. "It's not clasped all the way in the back."

Heat flares on my cheeks—damn it, that is three times now I've blushed in front of this man. My hands, shaky from embarrassment, start fumbling with the last few remaining buttons that I can reach. I angle my body so that I'm facing him, trying to hide whatever skin he's already seen. I wonder if this guard is going to tell the others about this interaction. While I may not be a recluse hiding under the covers of my bed, I'm almost positive that normal women in the castle aren't accidentally in the vicinity of men with the back of their dresses undone.

When I start cursing under my breath from trying to loop the same button five times in a row, the guard takes a step towards me, his hand reaching out tentatively before freezing mid-air when my body flinches away on instinct. Engrained memories of a man who puts his hands on me influencing the motion before I even realize what I'm doing.

The guard lowers his arm quickly to his side. "Would you like me to help you with that?" he offers softly.

I quickly decline with a shake of my head, my muscles tensing in anticipation of his exasperation. But he returns that easy smirk to his face, not acting at all bothered by my rejection, as he nods his head and steps back. My fingers finally manage to loop the troublesome button, then the next, as I work as quickly as possible. The guard gives me space—walking around the tower feigning interest in the gray stone walls. Though when he peeks into the library again, that does genuinely catch his attention.

Finally looping the last button, I blow out a breath and kneel next to where the box of supplies is. Packed on top are my normal food items: apples and nuts, dried meats and bread. Underneath are items for my washroom, including some more shampoo, mashed mint leaf paste for my teeth, and soaps.

Memories of my last supply drop off move to the forefront of my mind before I can stop them. I tuck my chin into my chest, keeping my gaze down as the images wash over me. My hair falls on either side of my face like a shield, one I hope will block the guard from seeing it as I wrangle to get myself under control. My eyes squeeze closed, hands holding the edge of the box tightly as I force the memories back into the darkest depths of my mind. It's shocking how quickly sadness can rise to the surface when I'm not actively pushing it down. *There will be no crying today.* The wood creaks beneath my grip, and I hear the guard's boots click, the sound getting closer with each step. I focus on my breathing, on trying to clear out the knot of emotions being shoved down my throat. *No crying.*

Still, the memory of Alexi squatting down next to me, laughing as I devoured the surprise lemon loaf he brought, breaks free. Biting the inside of my cheek until I taste blood, I try to focus on anything else, but with my eyes closed, all I see is the memory. His smile. His eyes. His laughter. It's too much. I gasp, trying to hold a sob back while a warm tear traces down my cheek. I open my eyes, desperate to find anything else to focus on to get my mind off of the despair building up inside me.

Squatting across from me on the balls of his feet, the guard looks at me, concern written on his face. "Are you alright?" he questions. My body tightens as I again jerk back from him. He holds his hands out in front of him in a placating manner. "I'm sorry; I didn't mean to frighten you. I just— What's wrong?"

Is that sympathy in his voice or maybe pity? What he must think of me... Shaking my head, I quickly wipe away the tear before gathering the food off of the floor. I don't want his concern, and I don't want to explain why I'm upset. I just need to be alone, so I can go through the rest of my normal routine and keep my mind occupied.

The guard watches me quietly for a moment before standing and moving a few steps back. My thoughts about him turn inquisitive once more because he isn't put off by my emotions, unlike the other guards who came to get Alexi's body. Why is he acting so nice? Is it a ploy of some kind? And for what reason?

When the last of the items are removed from the box and put away, the quiet tension that stretches between us is noticeable enough that I find myself with the need to squirm. I clear my throat as I look at the guard, signaling that I am done with a gesture to the empty crate. He nods and starts moving, his stride long and unfaltering as he retrieves it with one hand. When he reaches the door, he falters, waiting a few seconds before looking back over his shoulder at me.

"Should you ever need anything, My Lady, do not hesitate to ask."

It's the empathy in his voice that causes my gaze to linger on his face—searching for what, I'm not sure. Before I can discern anything, he opens the door and leaves, shutting it quietly behind him. A breath releases from me as I shake my hands out and try to regain my composure. Interacting with that guard felt different. I realize that I never asked for his name. Then again, he never volunteered it either. I berate myself for going back and forth about this when, in the end, it's inconsequential. This man may have taken over the vacancy left in my guard at Alexi's death, but he could never replace what Alexi was to me.

Realizing my thoughts have started spiraling again, I walk out onto the balcony, the warmth of the sun a welcome distraction. The sky is such a bright blue that it almost hurts to look at it. My eyes squint as I watch birds fly from tree to tree, and I can hear the low humming of bugs in the distance. The lake in front of me gleams with the reflection of the bright spring sun. It's deceptively calm out here. Peaceful even. Not a hint of the locked up princess and her murderous jailor king to be found on these grounds.

I lean my elbows onto the railing, forcing myself to daydream about the world beyond these walls, beyond this tower. I know that there are outposts and smaller towns that line the edge of the Mortal Kingdom from the maps in the books that I have read. Would they be a sufficient distance away from the king? If I left, could I hide out as long as necessary for him to give up his search for me? Is *anywhere* safe? Nerves simmer inside me at the thought of interacting with new people as well. I've been locked up with barely any mortal contact with anyone else for almost twenty-two years. Will I come off as odd? Will the people know who I am and report me to the king? Or will I be a stranger to them, easily able to hide in plain sight? Even if I could get away, is there any running from the guilt embedded within me? Is there any way to escape the sound of the sword piercing Alexi's chest? Or the memory of his blood pooling out around me?

I think back to my exchange with the guard. He didn't mind that I insulted the king. In fact, he appeared to *enjoy* it, if that annoying quirk of his lips was any indication. I huff out a breath at the thought. Alexi never really talked about what the other men were like or if he even had any friends in the King's Guard. He always made sure that our hour together was more about teaching me something or distracting me in some way to get my mind off of how desperately lonely I was. We never talked much about him or his personal life. Until that night where, unbeknownst to us, we played our last game of cards together, had our last laugh, and enjoyed our last moment of contented happiness. That thought—that quick, tiny thought—shatters the weak dam in my mind holding my emotions in check. I feel it start to seep in, like water through a crack in the stone. Like a slow fog rolling over the mountains until it bleeds into the valley below, the feelings of hopelessness, of despair, of unrelenting guilt suffocate me. *I could have saved him.*

My eyes squeeze shut as I grit my teeth together and hold my breath, desperate to stop this assault. I clench my hands into fists, using the pain of my nails digging into my palm to center me, as if I can tangibly force these feelings into a box and lock it, throwing away the key so that they can never escape again. I want to push it out of sight so that I don't have to relive every minute detail that haunts my waking hours. *No crying.* Seconds that feel like the slow drip of honey pass as I shove and shove the feelings down until I sense them fade away. Until I am met with silence.

Gasping for breath, I open my eyes, feeling a sort of wildness about me as I try to clear away the blurriness. My chest heaves with my quickened breaths as I fight for control over myself again. Slowly, my hands relax as my fingertips rest against the warmed stone. A few more breaths later and my heart has stopped hammering against my rib cage. Peering past the edge of the lake, I look to where the meadow of wildflowers grows up to the treeline of the forest. There are so many colors and varieties of plant life that my fingers and toes crave to touch, so I focus on that to anchor me.

I stay in the sun a little longer, feeling my skin turn warm and slightly pink, before I'm ready to head back inside. My breaths are even as I climb the stairs to check on Bella. Her large paws wiggle and jerk on the bed from the little fox dreams she is having. Nuzzling into the soft white fur at her neck, I give her a quick kiss before quietly opening the trunk at the foot of my bed, removing the lone pair of trousers I own and an undershirt that was Alexi's.

When Alexi first wanted to teach me these exercises, I had refused. I didn't see a need to do it. Alexi had persisted, telling me that just because I was locked in a tower didn't mean that I had to be lazy too. I remember scowling and whining in protest the entire time. Looking back now, I am grateful. He gave me something to do when my mind would spiral into despair because of the lonely monotony. He gave my body a reason to get out of bed on days when all I wanted was to sleep it all away. And now... Well, now I can at least have something else to focus on.

Once I'm changed and back downstairs, I push the white tea table out of the way to create some space in the middle of the living area. When I'm sure I won't accidentally hurt myself on a piece of furniture, I sit on the floor and close my eyes. Alexi always started every exercise session with what he called "mind cleansers." He would guide me through a sort of meditation where I would imagine a golden ray of light pouring from the clouds above and onto the crown of my head. As the imagined light flowed over my body, I would focus on relaxing each muscle that was touched right down to my toes. He said it calmed the mind and prepared the body for movement. Today however, it doesn't clear my mind or fill me with relaxing thoughts, it merely helps steady my breathing. Methodically, rhythmically, I move through the different exercises Alexi taught me. Sweat beads on my forehead as I squat and lunge. Once I work through the rest of the leg exercises, I move on to upper body ones. I work the series twice over before I hear Bella coming down the stairs.

"You hungry, Bells?" I pant, moving to grab her some food and fresh water. She eats quickly before settling on the couch and watching as I repeat the exercise sequence over yet again. I push myself harder and harder, until I am sick to my stomach. My body is the only thing I allow myself to focus on; the turmoil that lurks in the corners of my mind stays out of sight temporarily while I move.

I want my mind to be like the prison I live in: a void of silence. When my body feels like it might not be able to make it up the stairs and my long hair is a tangled nest from sweat, I collapse on the floor with a huff. I turn and look out the open doors of the balcony, the sky a dazzling display of purple and twilight blue layers as the sun nears the horizon in the west. I can hardly see the outline of the moon rising in opposition, its silvery color barely set aglow by the sun's setting rays.

I think about how the moon wouldn't be seen if it were not for the sun, how its very visibility is tied to how brightly something else burns. Maybe I'm more like the moon than I realized. Except the *something* that set me aglow was actually a *someone.* Does the fact that they are gone now mean I'm destined to be invisible? To float away in a dark night sky with no one knowing that I'm there? To disappear without a trace, like I never existed to begin with? Then I think, maybe that would not be such a bad thing.

Chapter Fifteen

BAHIRA

A KNOCK AT THE door pulls me from sleep, my eyes slowly opening as I stretch my arms overhead. "Yes?" My voice is gravelly as I call out.

"You have a Flame Ceremony to attend this morning, Your Highness. It is time to get ready."

I groan out a "thank you," rolling to my side on the bed and silently cursing the ancient mages who thought doing these ceremonies right after the sun rose was a good idea.

My father attends every blood ceremony in the kingdom, as the participants must travel to the Temple of Petalum in Galdr. I didn't start attending them until I began investigating what is blocking our magic. Now I try to attend them all to make note of how large the flame is for each of our newest magic users. It's all data to me; the trick is figuring out how to take that data and turn it into something that I can experiment with, something that is tangible.

I lay in bed a little longer, running through different theories and ideas in my head. Once magic is expelled from mages, by infusing water or casting a spell on a physical object, it doesn't seem like it can be used to influence someone else's magic. I have run experiments to see if stronger mage magic can fill in the gaps of a weaker mage's spells. The magic stays completely separate from each other, not absorbing or able to be used outside of its original intended purpose. Admittedly, there isn't a ton known about the origins of mage magic, though many ancient mages have done plenty of their own experimenting on it. So not only am I trying to understand why it's suddenly *not* working as it used to, but I'm also trying to decipher where our magic actually comes from. I *do* know that we have a magical relationship with the land, and that in part, is why mages can manipulate the elements as they can.

Stumbling out of bed, my vision is still blurry as I draw the curtains open in front of the veranda attached to my room. Pushing the wood-encased glass double doors open, I step out into the cool early-morning breeze. Thick green and purple vines wrap around the slats that make up the roof for the outdoor space, creating a natural shade cover. Little flowers—no bigger than my thumb nail—in pink and white dot the vines, their sweet, delicate scent barely a hint in the wind. The dawn's golden rays trickle through the gaps in the thick canopies of the banya and pirang trees that tower above us, their wild limbs intertwined together in a chaotic vision of brown and green. Blue and gold macaws squawk at each other from the branches as they wake from their resting, preparing to take flight for their morning hunts. As much as I want to complain about being up so early, I find it easier instead to take in the beauty of the land. Of my home.

On the way to the bathroom, I stop at the other three windows in my room to open the curtains until all the shadows are chased away from their corners by the light filtering in. I start the shower, and within seconds, steam curls around me as I step in, the hot water raining down from the spout above me. My muscles instantly relax from the heat. Another groan, this one less annoyed, echoes off the tiled stone walls around me.

After I've showered, I braid two front sections of my hair around the crown of my head, leaving the rest of the thick, curly waves down to air dry. Generally for ceremonies, it is expected that the attendees dress a little more formally than the everyday relaxed garb. Moving around my closet, I thumb through the blouses, skirts, and dresses hanging from metal hooks attached to a carved tree branch. Shorts, pants, and undergarments are folded neatly into a wooden dresser tucked into the corner. I choose a flowy white off-the-shoulder blouse to be tucked into a deep plum high-waisted skirt. I add a silver chained girdle belt with attached amethyst stones to complete the look. Stepping in front of the standing mirror in the corner of my room, I smooth out the fabric of the skirt and center the belt as another knock on the door sounds.

My mother's voice comes from the other side. "Bahira, it is time to leave. Are you ready?"

"Yes!" I call back, running to the closet to grab a pair of light brown leather flats. I join her out in the hall when I'm finished, linking arms with her as we head towards the stairs.

"Do you know if it is a little boy or girl whose Flame Ceremony we are attending today?" I ask.

"A girl," my mother responds, her serene voice carrying in the staircase. She gives my arm a little squeeze as we round a corner and see my father standing in the receiving hall in his traditional mage robe. The navy and silver garments are embroidered with the Mage Kingdom sigil of an albero tree under the stars and were made to wear specifically for important events like a Flame Ceremony or a royal council with another king or queen. The crushed velvet material is tailored perfectly to his tall frame, barely brushing the tops of his feet. He holds a staff of wood made from a banya tree, the top adorned with a smooth round piece of black dragon stone.

My father pulls me into a hug, his chin resting on my head affectionately. "Did you sleep well, Daughter?"

I nod, the movement difficult in his embrace. When he releases me, I step back and see Daje standing behind him. Dressed in his finery, the dark green and gold long-sleeved tunic fits impeccably paired with his dark brown trousers. Black boots complete his look, and even I must admit that he fills the outfit out well. Our gazes briefly clash, an apology written in his eyes that I accept with a nod.

My father holds out his hand for my mother with a look of pure adoration. While their marriage was somewhat arranged—my father, then the crown prince, and my mother, the daughter of a former mage on the council—their foundation is built entirely on the love they have for each other. It's the kind of the love that sustains, that encourages and supports. That allows room for challenging each other while knowing that there will always be a safe spot to land. It is such a unique thing, a once in a lifetime kind of love.

We wait in the receiving hall for the rest of the council to join us. When all ten are finally present—eight men and two women—we proceed through the tall wooden double doors leading out to the front of the palace. The woodsy scent of the forest surrounding us permeates the chilled air, my bare shoulders breaking out in goosebumps from the cooler temperature. In groups of two we take the steps down from the palace and out to a gray stone landing where four horse-drawn carriages are waiting. I watch as my parents and two of the oldest councilmen get in one carriage while the remaining eight council members split up equally into two more. Which leaves one left for just Daje and I to ride in. Our carriages are carved from the dense light-colored wood of the albero tree and left open at the top, letting the elements in. When the temperatures dip in the winter or when rain or snow falls from the sky, the carriages can be spelled to keep the occupants dry and warm.

Daje opens the door and extends a hand out to help me up, which I take as I dip my head in thanks and step in. He follows behind, shutting and latching the door before sitting across from me. Settling down on the purple velvet cushion, I look out the glass window to the side as the carriage lurches forward and we make our way to the temple.

It's blissfully silent, my mind once again working through possible experiments and ways I haven't yet tested out magic, when Daje clears his throat. Without turning my head, my eyes dart over to where he is sitting across from me. His booted ankle rests on top of his knee, arms spread out wide over the back of the bench. His face is carefully unreadable, which is unusual for him considering he tends to wear his emotions on his sleeve.

"Something to say, Daje?" I ask with a smirk, returning my gaze to outside the carriage as we move down the bumpy stone pathway. He doesn't immediately respond, the extended silence causing me to narrow my eyes.

"Did you know that there are... rumors about you?"

I slowly turn my head again to look at him, a single brow raised in question. "You will have to be more specific; I'm aware of many rumors about me." Being a magicless mage—and a princess no less—means that my name is often either gossip fodder or in the center of drama about the state of our kingdom. Some feel uneasy that there is a spare heir to the throne that is, in their minds, defective. *Though are they wrong?*

"It has to do with your sleeping habits," he says cautiously. His choice of words brings me out of my thoughts.

"I find it odd that people would make up rumors about how I'm falling or staying asleep," I volley back, grinning wider when he rolls his eyes at me. Teasing Daje is something I enjoy immensely. I'm also hoping it eases some of this tension between us. We haven't spoken since our fight, and I hate it when the silence goes on for too long.

"You know that's not what I mean," he sighs, running a hand over his short hair.

"I do," I relent, forcing my face to relax, "but ignoring it has always been the best course of action. You know that no matter what I say or do, it just feeds into their need to make disparaging remarks about me."

"But are those remarks true?" he asks quietly.

My lips pinch together as I survey him. His interest in my *sleeping habits,* as he called them, can't simply be because he wants to know if

Gosston is speaking truthfully. I know how Daje feels about me, and I know how he feels about sex. The older we've gotten, the more I've begrudgingly recognized that I have never seen Daje even *appear* to court other women. It doesn't mean that he hasn't, by any means, and I never inquire about his sex life, but it's part of the reason I am more discreet with my own. Sure, it's probably not the best look for the royal family if their princess is fucking whoever she pleases openly, but even more so, I don't want to hurt Daje's feelings. Sex for me is purely a release and a way to feel powerful without magic. I don't repeat sex partners because I don't want any attachments forming when my attention is so firmly fixed on other things. Sex for Daje has meaning, especially if it were to happen with me.

"That is none of your business," I finally answer.

He scoffs and shakes his head, turning to look away from me. I've steeled myself against the words and actions of others through many years of practice, but Daje has always had an easier time getting under my shields. It squeezes something inside me when we don't happen to see eye to eye on things.

"I know you still view me as that little girl you first met, crying in a field because the other children called her broken," I say, leaning forward slightly, "but I am not that little girl anymore. I don't need you to protect me from things that aren't actually threats."

"You don't believe tarnishing your reputation with rumors isn't threatening?" he rumbles. "Bahira, if something happens to your brother, or if he simply decides he doesn't want to be king, and you're asked to take the throne, you'll have to deal with these rumors then. The council—"

"Nothing is going to happen with Nox, and I don't give a shit what the council thinks."

"Do you care about what *I* think?" he asks, his voice low and woven with a hint of desperation that fills the space between us.

"Of course I do," I acknowledge, "but, as I mentioned before, details about who I may or may not be fucking are not something you should expect to have access to." Daje bristles, his hand gripping the back of the bench tighter. "And if you interfere, if you try to step in and act like my savior, all it shows everyone else is that I *need* someone to save me.

It confirms what the council, the men who propose marriage, and the gossipers say about me—that I can't do it on my own." The words feel rushed, my heart pounding in my chest as I try to make Daje understand. "I need to prove to these people that I am *just* as capable, *just* as powerful as they are, even without my magic."

He stares at me, his gaze relaying far too much about what he's thinking as the carriage begins to slow down. When we've nearly come to a stop, he leans over the middle threshold, a determined look on his face. "You wouldn't have to prove anything with me."

We stop moving and sit in the uncomfortable, stilted silence for a few moments before a knock rasps on the outside of the door. I move before Daje does, unlatching it and taking the hand offered by the mage outside to step down. Straightening my spine, I roll my shoulders back, catching my mother's eye as Daje steps out of the carriage and joins me by my side. Her eyes bounce between the two of us before a slow, playful smile tilts her lips. Gods help me. My mother believes that Daje will be the man I end up marrying. His glaring devotion to me is already a positive checkmark for him on her imaginary list of positive suitor qualities. What she—or anyone else except maybe my father—doesn't understand is that, while Daje is a great man and friend, I can't force myself to feel more for him. I don't want to be in a relationship just for the sake of being in one.

I yearn to be with someone who challenges me. I want to feel like I'm standing with them at the edge of the cliffs by the ocean, peering over into the turbulent waters below, in those heart-pounding moments before we jump. And I don't feel that with Daje. He is the one who would pull me away from the edge instead of jumping with me because he's more worried about my safety than anything else. And it isn't as if that is a bad thing—a part of me hates that his kindness and devotion isn't enough for me.

I blow out a pained breath, shaking my head faintly as we make our way up the steps. Built from wood and stone, the temple is completely covered in a rainbow of petalum flowers, including the pointed roof. It's a collage of colors that even in the faint twilight of the morning stand out vibrantly in the rich green of the forest. The flowers smell like honey and lemon, the scent of them coating the air for miles. Inside the temple, long trailing heart ivy hangs from the wooden beams running across the ceiling. The thin stems and heart-shaped leaves create a waterfall effect of differing lengths dangling over us as we walk. White stone lines the ground and inner walls, creeping vines of jasmine and wisteria growing along them. Carved wooden benches are set on either side of the center aisle we walk on, leading to three steps and then a dais where the Flame Ceremony is performed.

My mother and father move up the steps and stand near a small table that the Cauldron of Vires sits on. On the other side of the table—opposite of my parents—is a young girl. Her brown hair is tied elegantly in an updo, and an overly frilly pink dress drapes down her small frame and onto the floor. If her slight scowl is any indication, the dress wasn't her choice.

I take my seat in the first row on the right, along with Daje and half of the council; the other half sit in the first row to the left with the girl's parents. At a second glance, I see that the two women sitting there are not actually her parents. They wear the dark purple and black uniform of those who work at the orphanage. My gaze goes back to the girl, noticing how she stands with her spine straight and shoulders rolled back. It's a defensive posture I recognize from myself, a way to appear more confident than you feel.

Low murmurs around me draw me out of my thoughts. Anyone in the kingdom is welcome to attend Flame Ceremonies, and within a few moments, the temple is packed with people. My father begins the ceremony by tapping his staff on the dais three times, silencing the crowd and garnering their attention.

"Welcome! Welcome everyone," he starts, his voice booming and echoing off of the stone. "We come today to honor young Starla as she drops her blood into the Cauldron of Vires as many mages before her have done and as many after her will."

My father steps forward, producing a small silver dagger from the sheath on his hip. The dagger has been passed down from ruler to ruler, its only purpose for use in situations where blood must be drawn. Set in an intricately crafted black stone hilt, an old spell is attached to the dagger, one which makes it painless for whoever is pricked by it. Flame Ceremonies are always performed by the current monarch and before my ancestors took over as rulers—a change that happened after The War Of Five Kingdoms—it had always been the queen of Void Magic. There was only ever one wielder of the powerful magic at a time, always female, and according to our ancient texts, when a descendant of that family line was deemed worthy, the magic would transfer over to them. The only indication that it was time for a transfer of magic was during the Flame Ceremony. When the female descendant dropped her blood into the Cauldron of Vires, the flame would turn blue.

The ancient sigil of the former line of queens is etched into the metal on the front of the cast iron cauldron that the little girl bravely holds her finger over. My father lightly cradles Starla's hand in his, bringing his other hand holding the dagger up and to her finger tip. With a wink, he pricks her finger and turns her hand over the cauldron. Blood slowly wells, and the temple grows quiet in anticipation for that single bead to show what magic the little girl has.

I watch as the fat droplet finally lets go and plummets into the cauldron. A second goes by, then three. My heart beats frantically in my chest as I lean forward from the bench, seeing Daje's head turn to me out of the corner of my eye. Low murmurs begin to resonate in the temple. Then, directly over the cauldron, a small flame sparks.

Chapter Sixteen

RHEA

THE METALLIC SCENT OF blood is finally gone from the tower. I am unsure if it's something I imagined or if it's because I've kept the balcony doors and tower windows open for as long as possible each day. Either way, I am no longer hit with phantom scents of the night my soul fractured irreparably.

It has been three days—or perhaps more—since the guard dropped off the supplies, and our interaction has rattled around in my mind a few times since. So have those weird stomach butterflies. Which is absolutely ridiculous, because what is there even to reminisce about? He's a guard, and he dropped off my supplies. *He's also tall and rather handsome*, but I quickly shake that thought away.

Bella has been glued to my side, her pointed ears always erect as if she is straining to hear a shift in the wind that will indicate my breakdown is looming. Or maybe she's just waiting for Alexi to come back too. I've kept my emotions under lock, deciding to stick with my no crying rule for as long as possible. Shedding those tears will not bring him back. Reducing myself to a sobbing mess will do nothing to help me escape this tower. As if I can barter with my own emotions, I promise myself I can break down once I've left this place with Bella in tow. Once we are safe, far away and hidden so that King Dolian can't find us, then—and only then—will I permit myself to grieve.

To help keep myself unfeeling, I focus on how I will escape. A lot of my supposed plan requires luck, but I owe it to Alexi to try. I don't want to spend any more of my life trapped in this place than I already have, and I can't hold out hope that perhaps the king will eventually just leave me alone. A nagging feeling in my gut tells me that he's kept me in this tower for a reason and I don't want to be here long enough to find out why.

Working backwards, what will I need with me when I escape? Food is the obvious first choice—of course, I'd need something to carry it in. Changes of clothes would be nice, as well, but would take up a lot of room. Somehow, I'd need to get a pair of shoes, as I assume walking barefoot on the grounds and in the surrounding forests is probably not wise. I know I have to go east, partly because of that strange dream-that-isn't-a-dream that replays in my mind, but also because I have no choice but to go that way. Going west just leads to the ocean, and as wonderful as it would be to sail away, I don't exactly have a way to do that. So, that's the beginning of my plan: get supplies—somehow. Get past the guards, both guarding my tower and any that might surround it—somehow. And then go east—that, I know how to do.

Sitting in front of my vanity, I brush my hair harshly, working all of the tangles from my post-bath hair. After sweeping and mopping this morning, I exercised and then soaked in the tub for a long while. The longer my hair gets, the more easily it tangles, and right now—with its length nearly skimming the top of the stool I'm sitting on—I know that it will only get worse if I don't do something about it. I roughly grip the hairbrush as I remember that Alexi was the last—and only—person to cut my hair. The memory of him kneeling behind me, scissors in hand as he kept finding excuses to stall, robs me of my breath. He was meticulous, afraid cutting my hair would be a disaster, but it turned out just fine. My eyes close as I squeeze the wooden handle of the hair brush so tightly I think it might snap. Holding my breath, I count to five until the icy numbness I've grown accustomed to blankets my heart, until all that's left is a shadow of what once was. Exhaling, my eyes open and I continue brushing my hair, tugging at the knots until they are either undone or ripped into the bristles in large clumps.

When I'm finished, I attempt to put my hair into a braid and fail miserably, the twisted strands completely undone by the time I make it down to the living area. Bella follows behind me, trotting delicately down the stairs. Grabbing food and water for us both, I take a seat outside on the balcony. Drawing my knees into my chest, I focus on my breathing. It's the only thing I have control of anymore. The morning sun cradles my body and perfuses my skin with warmth, seeping in almost deep enough to penetrate the frozen fortress I've subconsciously constructed around myself. *Almost.*

The feeling of confinement weighs more heavily on me since Alexi's death. I've always felt imprisoned here, the stones sucking out any sort of contentment or joy I might dare to feel. Although how content can one realistically expect to be when their very life is reduced to repeating the same things over and over again? It's what I imagine free falling off a mountain must be like, except you never actually hit the ground. Your arms and legs flail about, but there is never any chance of finding anchorage. Eventually, you resign yourself to your fate as you tumble through the air forever.

Each year that passes with me still trapped here is like a layer of myself slowly being peeled away. Sometimes they are small insignificant pieces, like when I see the lanterns from the Summer Solstice celebration floating in the sky and realize with a pain in my gut that it's my birthday. Or when I reach for one of the hundreds—no, thousands—of books in the library, only to find I've already read it. Then there are bigger moments, where I know a huge chunk of my soul has been ripped violently from me and shredded in such a way that it can never be replaced. Like when the king first laid his hands on me. Or when I watched Alexi die because of me. These moments have chipped away at me until I'm nothing but a husk of a person, and I'm afraid that even if I somehow escape, I will never know the peace of being whole again. How could I?

As if in response to my thoughts, I feel the warm, humming sensation inside of me stir near my stomach. It has been dormant since that night, and I wonder if it somehow knows I don't want to sense its presence. Can it *feel* my vexation at having the ability to heal but being unable to save Alexi? I don't know if I'm just going crazy or if the magic inside me is actually sentient, but I can sense it there—lying in wait until I'm ready to use it again. My hand flexes in front of me, and I consider pulling that little invisible string that calls my magic up. However, the thought is fleeting, gone before it ever has the chance to settle.

We stay outside a little longer, letting the sun move higher up into the sky before eventually coming back in and settling onto the window seat in the library. Covering my legs with a blanket, I grab the half-read romance novel I started last night and lean back against the sea of pillows stuffed onto one side. With each word, my mind drifts off into a fantasy land and I become that much more insensate to my surroundings.

The living area of the tower sparkles in the dimming light of sunset. Needing to keep my body moving, I start sweeping the floor while Bella watches from her curled up position on the couch.

"You know, it would be nice if you helped every once in a while. Most of what I'm sweeping up is your hair," I tease half-heartedly, placing a hand on my hip as I lean against the broom.

Bella doesn't move for a few seconds, and I'm inclined to believe she's ignoring me when suddenly her head shoots up, ears perked in that way she does for only one person. Our eyes meet as she lets out a small whine, but we both already know what's coming. *Who's* coming. She bolts up the stairs right as the door opens.

King Dolian walks in, his eyes moving right to mine where I stand in the middle of the living area, broom still in hand. His five trusted guards flow in behind him in a flurry of black and gold, three blocking the door and two standing in front of them closer to the king. The guard who took Alexi's body catches my gaze again—his black eyebrow rising as our eyes stay locked before his dart back to the king.

King Dolian slowly looks me over, hands clasping behind his back. Posed like this, he is very much the depiction of regal importance—a benevolent king. His clothes fit him impeccably, and his chestnut hair is coiffed to perfection. Even his dark brown beard is trimmed flawlessly close to his face. But I see a side to him no one else does. Well, except for these guards. He leers at me, too many emotions to decipher flashing through those hazel eyes. His stalking steps towards me are an ominous march, matching the beat of my heart.

When he's close enough that I can see a few of the freckles on his cheeks—the small pigmentations too much like my own for comfort—I freeze. It's then that I remember my mistake. I start to lower into a curtsy, but it's too late. His hand snaps out to grab my arm, the grip so painfully tight that I let out a yelp.

"You will no longer be required to bow before me, Rhea," he says with a tense voice, barely lessening his grip as his thumb moves up and down my arm. "At least, not in *that* way."

I don't know what he means, but the tone of his words cause nausea to churn incessantly in my stomach. I can feel the power of my magic, but something else is there too. It surrounds the warm buzzing that I'm used to feeling with something dark and ancient, like a small spark in the middle of an inky cave. I grit my teeth together, forcing the magic—and whatever that other feeling is—back down.

King Dolian smiles wide, his white teeth showing in a horrifying display that looks more animal than man. He leans over me, my body naturally moving away until my back is straining at a curved angle to keep distance between us. "I have so many plans for you, Rhea," he whispers, his breath touching my forehead.

My stomach plummets, leaving me feeling dizzy and sick. "What do you mean?" I ask with a shaky voice.

The king lets go of my arm jarringly, making me fight to maintain my balance as he steps away. He begins pacing the tower, his hands clasped behind his back once more, as if he needs to restrain himself from acting. On what, I don't know. The atmosphere in the room is vile, a sort of heavy and thick foreboding that suffocates me as I try to wade through it.

"Did you know that word is spreading around the castle—throughout the capital even—about the traitorous bastard?" he asks, far too calmly. I don't answer because he already knows what I will say. No, the king is cruelly taunting me. He halts his pacing to peer out over the balcony, but even with his back to me, I can feel his sickening gaze like a brand. I watch as his knuckles turn white from how tightly he clasps them, my fear rising with every second that passes. "Apparently, a few guards who liked Alexi don't agree with the fact that he was *punished*. They find it unjust that I executed him for stealing something of mine." He pauses, the air around us tightening. "As if that is not enough cause for his head on a stake."

Shock rolls through me as I fight back the urge to vomit at the image of Alexi's kind face rotting on a spike. I had never considered that he would get anything other than a proper burial, one deserving of the man he was.

"Why are you telling me this?" I plead, unable to reconcile this information in a way that doesn't leave me near fainting. King Dolian whips his body around, those hazel eyes alight with something far more sinister than ever before. My fear is replaced with revulsion the longer I look at him, and like the lighting of a candle in a pitch black room, clarity strikes me—I cannot possibly survive whatever future he has planned for me.

"I am trying to make you realize how much I am willing to lose in order to maintain your safety!" His face grows red with his barely tempered fury. I subconsciously step back, feeling my magic hum more strongly. "This is your proof, Rhea! How can you not see all that I do for you? How can you be so *ungrateful* when I am allowing my people to believe I'm the villain, just to ensure you are protected? To guarantee no one touches what is mine!"

"Alexi never touched me—"

"Rhea," he interrupts, scowling at me. "There is only one reason why a man would come to visit you. Don't think me naive!" He approaches me, a predatory gleam in his eye.

I take another step back, shaking my head vehemently as disgust slices through me. "He never—"

"Don't lie to me!" My uncle quickly closes the gap between us and grabs me by my hair, viciously tugging until my chest crashes into his. "Do you expect me to believe," he whispers gratingly, his horrific mouth so terrifyingly close to my face, "that a guard was just leaving his post to *talk* to you? Am I to assume you gave him such alluring *conversation* that it kept him coming back? Do you think I am a fool?"

My eyes squeeze together as I shut down, trying to tunnel deeper into myself to avoid his putrid words.

"Look at me," he whispers, gripping my hair harder when I don't immediately obey. "Look. At. Me." Each unmercifully enunciated word hits me like a knife, gutting my soul until tears blur my eyes as they open and meet his wild gaze. "No one—absolutely *no one*—will *ever* touch you again. Except for me."

"What?" Dread floods my body as my eyes widen. I want to scream. I want to struggle out of his touch and run so far away from here that I end up at the edge of the world. Even *that* might not be far enough.

"When I look at you, I see a second chance, Rhea." His mood is now somber as his heavy gaze drags over every inch of my face. Terror bleeds into my limbs, freezing me in place as a single tear rolls down my cheek. He brings the hand not gripping my hair up to cup my face and wipes the tear away with his thumb. My head jerks away from his touch—I can't help it. All my movement does is enrage him further. His pupils widen, nearly eclipsing the hazel of his irises, as his lip lifts in a snarl. "You will understand soon enough," he claims, trailing his thumb down my cheek again. "But for now, you must be punished for allowing him to touch—"

"He didn't touch me!" I scream, the sound shrill and panicked and far too loud. But I don't care. I can't let him talk about Alexi this way. That man was my *father*. In every sense of the word, he was. He protected me as best as he could. He took care of me when no one else would. He taught me when he had no reason to.

He *loved* me.

He loved *me*.

"You will stop saying that he laid a single hand on me. No one has ever done that except for *you*," I seethe, my vision going red as I lose all rationality. "And I would rather *die* from your hand than hear you speak another vile, untrue thing about Alexi."

King Dolian looks at me, silent for all but a moment before a menacing smile creeps over his face. "You might wish for that but the truth is, my darling," he taunts, his breath warm on my cheek, "you will *never* escape me. You are *mine*."

I try so, so hard to stay strong. To not cower under the weight of his words and actions but when he leans in to kiss my cheek, I can't do it. I struggle, trying everything I can to get away from him, even knowing that it won't matter in the end. It never does. And when his hands alternate their hits—fists and slaps and shoves—I reach out to that imaginary place I can run away to. I picture a free and happy version of myself picking wildflowers in a sun-filled meadow. My bright green eyes aren't tarnished by the ministrations of a madman. My heart isn't broken beyond repair by grief.

When the king leaves me, a battered mess on the ground, the fantasy fades away and I'm once again reminded of the cold reality of my prison.

141

A knock on the door wakes me from sleep the next morning. The sun hasn't fully risen yet, nothing more than a crescent glow emerging above the horizon. My throat feels scratchy and raw; my tongue sticks to the roof of my mouth. I'm willing to bet that my magic has healed any physical mark left by the king on its own while I've slept, but I still have that aching feeling in my bones. In my soul. I suppose the magic can't heal the damage there.

When another round of gentle knocks sounds, I slowly move out of bed, Bella immediately at my side as we warily make our way down the stairs. Her ears twitch as she listens to who is outside. When she doesn't growl or whine, I step up to the door but don't open it.

"Hello?" I say, needing to clear my throat several times after.

"My Lady, I'm here to drop something off for you. It's from Tienne and Erica."

I tense at the familiarity of his voice. "Are you... Are you the guard from the supply drop-off?" I inquire, leaning in closer.

He chuckles, the sound oddly enticing as he answers, "Yes, I am."

I contemplate opening the door for all of one second before I remember that I'm in my night dress and probably still have drool on my face. There is also the fact that I still do not particularly trust this guard—in any fashion. I stand frozen, the silence slowly stretching between us until, I'm sure, he thinks I have left him. Finally, he clears his throat, and I brace for what he'll do or say next.

"Would you like me to leave this out here for you?" he asks matter-of-factly, like he understands why I would hesitate to open the door for him. My magic hums from deep in my stomach, in what feels like approval—or maybe it's those stupid butterflies fluttering again.

"I—I just—" My hand covers my mouth to stop my stammering.

"You don't have to explain. I'm happy to do as you command." He hesitates before adding, "Have a good day, My Lady."

I hear his footsteps trail away from the door and down the stone stairs of the tower. When the echoing of them fades away, I carefully open the door a little and peek through the small crack. Once I'm sure he's gone, I pull it open the rest of the way and find a small wooden box on the stone landing. My brows knit together as I bend to pick it up, the feeling of it light in my hands. The arched wooden door creaks as I close it and walk over to the couch, sliding the lid off of the box. Laying inside is a brand new silver brush, the bristles straight and white and the handle engraved with a floral pattern. Next to the brush is a bundle of new hair ribbons in a variety of colors. While I can't quite find it in me to smile, I do feel a glimmer of happiness at the thoughtful gesture. My current brush is years old and nearly unusable, something they must have noticed when they washed and braided my hair.

Bundling the new items, I make my way upstairs and lay them on my vanity, avoiding my reflection in the mirror. Briefly, I eye the tub in the bathroom, like it's beckoning me to go to it and get ready for the day. But the truth is, I don't want to. The abyss that opened inside of me when I watched that sword move through Alexi's chest is all consuming. It's a pit of inky shadows and ice and regret and guilt—so much guilt. So I crawl back into bed, pull my comforter up to my chin, and allow the darkness to claim me.

Chapter Seventeen

RHEA

BELLA PRACTICALLY FORCES ME out of bed the next morning, her large paws pressing gently on my back. I fight with her for a few minutes, but when it's clear she isn't going to give up, I make myself get up and run a bath. The steaming hot water scalds away some of the turbulent emotions that were rolling through me when I awoke, until all that's left is red skin and welcomed numbness. When I finish, I draw a fresh bath for Bella—much to her dismay. Once we are both clean and I am dressed, I head downstairs to find that I have no appetite. So I place food down for Bella and head out to the balcony.

The aching hollowness inside eases a little when the sun hits me, pushing its warmth down almost to my very core. The magic inside me flutters in response, like it's energized somehow by the golden light. The humming of it settles, and I lean forward against the white stone railing, looking out over the vast expanse of water and land that the Mortal Kingdom sits on.

Time drips on slowly as I find anything I can to distract myself. Most of my temporary comfort comes from reading; the stories of others adventuring across new worlds and fighting their own demons are relatable in a way. Though I now struggle when those characters get their happily ever after at the end. The longer I am stuck here, the longer I am under the king's command, the closer I begin to feel to death. I was never destined to have a happy ending, but I made a promise to Alexi that I would try to escape this hell, even when it hurts to move past him. Even when my mind feels so scrambled that I can't think straight. I have to shove it all down and focus on only one thing: leaving this tower.

I turn and walk back into the living area, staring at the door like it's going to open and show me the way. What happens when I step across that doorway with no intention of coming back? How can I possibly even *hope* to escape when there is a guard standing outside day and night? I allow those worries to linger all day. Technically, by worrying I am feeling something, allowing that single emotion to bubble up from where I have locked it away, but forming an escape plan has to be my priority—even if it scares me. I have to try. I promised him I would.

⁂

The moon and stars dot the midnight sky hours later, flickering and gleaming in their silvery brilliance. I lay in bed—the small flame of the candle barely lighting my book—when a knocking on the door startles me upright. I swing my head to look at Bella, but her relaxed posture tells me that she isn't very concerned about whoever is on the other side of the door.

Tip-toeing out of bed, I make my way downstairs and reach the door right as another set of gentle knocks comes. I look down at my blue nightdress, the gown silky but thick enough not to be see-through. I have a feeling I might know who this is, but I still ask through the door.

"It's the drop-off guard," he answers, "The extremely handsome one." My lips quirk in response, but I make no movement to open the door.

"What are you doing here?" I inquire, my fingers nervously playing with the fabric of my nightdress.

"Another item from Tienne and Erica for you, My Lady." He tentatively adds, "I could leave it out here for you again, if you'd like."

I anxiously chew on my lip, unsure of why I'm even considering answering it—maybe the magic inside me is making me go insane. *Or maybe it's that curiosity again, wanting to see if he's as good-looking as you remember him to be.* I scoff at my own thoughts, deciding that yes, the magic has definitely made me go insane.

Timidly, I turn the handle and open the door. A foreign feeling of anticipation glimmers within me, no bigger than a crumb but somehow making it through my frozen shields. He stands a few feet away from the door, as if knowing somehow that being any closer would make me uncomfortable. I notice he is wearing all black, like that of the guards uniform, but he has no armor or longsword. Our eyes meet, the torch burning behind him still leaving parts of his face in the shadows and yet he is as handsome as I remember. His tanned skin glows under the meager light of the flame, and he's smiling, one that grows the more I stare at him. *Does nothing bother him?*

"Hello." His voice is deep and smooth, like a midnight whisper on the wind.

My heart beats a little faster at the sound of it. I pry my eyes away from his face and bring them to the item he's holding. It's rectangle shaped—like a book—and wrapped in thin white paper. He holds the gift out to me, keeping the distance between us. Slowly, I reach out to grab it, accidentally brushing his fingers with my own. We both momentarily freeze, just a split second where we recognize the contact, before I quickly bring the item to my chest. My gaze drops as I give a hushed "thank you."

"You're welcome," he responds, and despite myself, I can't help but look back up at him. His gaze pierces me in a way that isn't invasive or lascivious but curious and perhaps a little mischievous. My magic wakes up in his presence, humming low in my gut and aching to show him what I can do. I'm not sure if it wants to protect me or show off to him. "Are you okay?" he asks, a subdued firmness to the question. His arms cross in front of his chest—a chest that is exactly at my eye level.

I swallow, the movement oddly difficult as I open my mouth to answer him but then promptly close it. He lowers his head slightly, like he's trying to catch my gaze. *Am I okay?* No, absolutely not, but for reasons this guard will never understand. I step further back into the tower, my hand on the edge of the door.

"Thank you for dropping this off," I manage to finally squeak out.

He pauses, eyes searching mine when I look back up at him before he dips his chin in acknowledgment. "Have a good night then, My Lady." His booted steps echo in the tower as he descends the stairs.

"You too," I whisper through a constricting feeling in my throat. Shaking my head, I close the door and head back upstairs to bed. Bella watches as I climb in, covering myself with the comforter and laying the item—which I'm now sure is a book—down in front of me. I carefully unwrap it and hold it up to get a better look. The silver foil of the title shines in the combined glow of moonlight and flame.

"*The Starry Night Of The Forest*," I read out loud.

A small kernel of excitement, something no bigger than a seed, flares in the anguish inside me. For the first time since Alexi's death, I don't feel all-consuming despair, guilt, sadness, regret, or anger—though each of those emotions lingers in the background. No, that little kernel shines like a single star in a dark night sky as I turn to the first page of the book and start reading.

The tower is pitch black as I stumble my way through it, trying desperately to find a candle to light. The ominous beat of my heart picks up speed, and I feel as though it's composing the symphony of my demise with each step.

I call out for Bella, my arms blindly reaching out in front of me. There is such an absence of light that the darkness feels thick and inky. Suffocating. An evil laugh sounds behind me, the hair on the back of my neck rising in response. I know that voice, its cadence sending terror down my spine and through my body like an icy flood. I freeze, fear cementing my feet to the wood floor.

"Rhea, do you remember what you did?" His oily voice surrounds me from all sides, and my chest rises and falls rapidly as I desperately gasp for air. "He died because of you," he murmurs, closer this time. "You could have saved him. He wanted you to save him."

"No," I whisper, shaking my head as bile fights to crawl up my throat. "He sacrificed himself for me. He wanted to keep me safe."

His laugh is a sound so harsh and horrific that I fall to my knees in terror, hunching over myself.

"Why would he want to die for you, Rhea? Who are you to think that your life is worth more than his?" His voice fades away to nothing more than a disquieting whisper on the wind, his presence vanishing along with it. My body shakes, chest heaving, as the sobs I've tried to hold in start to shred me apart from the inside out.

"Little One." A more gentle voice calls out to me. I lift my head, twisting side to side trying to find Alexi. I want to see that he is happy and whole and safe with his wife. A familiar hand squeezes my shoulder in comfort, new tears forming in my eyes. I go to place my hand on top of his, but then I shriek in pain. His grip is now squeezing so tightly that I wonder if his fingers will pierce through me, like the sword did his chest. "You let me die. You let me die!" he howls over and over, the chant embedding into my very soul as the pain of the truth lashes into me. My hands cover my ears as I scream and scream and scream—

My eyes fly open, my screams still ringing in the air from my nightmare. Bella nuzzles into me, forcing me to wake up further, as my hands dive into her soft fur to help settle me back into reality. I fling the comforter off of me, sweat soaking through my nightdress and still beading down my neck. Fresh tears threaten to fall, but I force them to stop. Those boxes of emotions sitting locked away in my mind rattle, like they are about to break open, but I imagine they are frozen shut and unable to. The rattling stops. My hands curl under my head as I turn to my side, my back to the window and the night sky beyond.

You let me die.

"I know," I answer out loud.

The layer of ice around my heart thickens.

My head is throbbing by the time the sun rises, sleep having eluded me for the rest of the night. Laying on my back, I stare at the ceiling of the tower, the same chant from the nightmare playing in my head.

You let me die.

Emotions I'm trying to deny burn in my throat, their weight bearing down on my chest. My eyes close, and I squeeze my hands into fists.

No more crying.

I imagine another box as I grip onto those feelings that threaten to break free, violently shoving them into it over and over and over again until there is nothing left. That comforting feeling of nothingness coats my mind, now blissfully quiet. My fingers and toes tingle faintly, a frozen vibration that feels like my magic but... not.

With a deep breath, my eyes finally open. Bella's ears perk up, her head lifting from where she lays next to me. I watch as her gaze goes to the door, her eyes narrowing. Panic floods me as I sit up and crawl to the edge of the bed, looking down into the living area.

I hear a slight scraping noise and then, from the crack where the door meets the frame, a small white piece of paper appears. It's pushed through until it flutters to the floor. I look over to Bella, watching as her posture relaxes. Turning back to the door, I stare at the piece of paper on the ground. Intrigue and confusion make me feel like I should move forward but also stay put. Eventually, my curiosity wins and has me getting out of bed and venturing down the stairs. The early morning sunlight barely spills into the room from the balcony and windows, giving just enough light to see by. The white paper is folded twice, the handwriting on it uniform and neat.

MY LADY,

I WAS WALKING THE GARDENS THIS MORNING, AND THIS FLOWER REMINDED ME OF YOUR EYES. I SET IT OUTSIDE THE DOOR.

SINCERELY,

THE "DROP-OFF" GUARD

My lips quirk at his sign-off as I blindly reach for the door. Opening it slowly, I peer out onto the landing before drawing my gaze down to the flower laying on the ground. The delicate petals are a rich green, large and heart-shaped, and they attach to a dark green center with flecks of golden yellow. Bringing it to my nose, I inhale its fragrance, the scent light and fresh. It's beautiful and I... I don't know how to feel about it.

The ice inside of me shifts somewhat as I stare at the gift from the guard. Twirling the stem in my hand, I watch the flower spin, noting how this is the first one I've ever gotten that's not from Alexi. It's the first one since he— The thought dies in my head as I turn towards the stairs and take them back up to the loft. Laying the flower down on my vanity I climb back into bed, hoping sleep comes soon.

My legs curl to the side as I sit on the window bench in the library and watch the rain drip down the glass. Stormy wind blows the trees, the leaves rattling as they move against each other on the current. There is no sunshine today, as the sun hides behind thick dark gray clouds. What is outside of the tower finally reflects what I see inside it every day.

Bella lays at my feet, and I tuck them underneath her for warmth. I watch a raindrop roll down the glass, reminding me of a similar day when I was around eleven.

It was a supply drop-off day, and I sat in this very spot, watching a storm pass through. The clouds were so dark that it looked like the middle of the night despite it being sometime in the afternoon. The wind howled, shaking the windows and balcony doors. I wasn't sure if Alexi would come with the weather being so bad.

Thunder cracked so loudly that I wondered if the tower might fall. I bolted from the window and ran upstairs to crawl under my blankets. I wasn't sure if minutes or hours passed by, but I stayed under the covers, curled in on myself, willing it to stop. In between booms of thunder I thought I heard Alexi's voice, but I was too scared to lift the blankets and check. A few moments passed when I heard booted steps coming up the stairs.

"Little One, are you up here?"

I yanked the blanket off of me, my hair a tangled mess as I forced it away from my face to see him clearly. He was drenched from head to toe, dripping water onto the wood floors.

"I didn't think you would come," I whispered, jumping as another clap of thunder rang out through the air.

Alexi stared at me, his face reassuring as he took in my terrified state. "I brought you a surprise. Come see what it is." He reached a hand out, helping me from the bed. Grabbing a towel from the washroom, he dried himself off as best as he could before we went downstairs together. I knelt down by the supply box, lifting the lid and looking at a cloth-wrapped item on the very top. Carefully, I unfolded the layers until the gift was revealed.

"You brought me a new book!" I exclaimed happily as my fingers traced over the engraved title on the front.

"It was my favorite story when I was a boy," he replied, squatting down next to me and unloading my supplies. "You might find it boring though. There are a lot of fight scenes and dragons."

I laughed and hugged the book into my chest. "I like those things too," I said as I rolled my eyes at him. "Does it have any princesses?"

"It does. Her name is Armina, and she isn't a regular princess," he said, reaching his hand out to take the book from me. He turned and walked to the couch, and I followed—the two of us sitting side-by-side, my legs crossed in front of me.

"What kind of princess is she?" I asked, startling as thunder shook the tower again, my eyes darting to the balcony windows. By the time I looked back, Alexi had already lit the candles that sat on the tea table, illuminating the living space as he opened the book and turned to the first page.

"She is fierce and brave, unafraid to follow her own path. She uses swords and fights boys—"

"She does?" I interrupted, eyes wide as I stared at him. I couldn't imagine a princess using a sword and fighting boys. Maybe because I was a princess and unable to do either. His chuckle drowned out the storm outside, and I relaxed a little more into the couch, scooting an inch closer to his side.

"She even rides a dragon," he said with a wondrous look in his eyes, like he couldn't imagine such a thing. My own awe had matched his, as dragons were my favorite of the creatures I had learned about from other kingdoms.

"Like the fae do," I said, looking at him in excitement. He nodded, a small smile gracing his lips, before he began to read.

I feel a crack in the ice surrounding my heart as the memory recedes in my mind. I imagine reinforcing that frozen wall—layer after layer—coldness seeping in and snuffing everything else out. The boxes in my mind shake as they try to break open, shadows surrounding them in every corner, but I squeeze my eyes shut, not allowing anything to reach the surface. Feeling these things won't change anything. Crying serves no purpose. I have to stay numb. So I do.

The sun has refused to come out for almost an entire week, making it difficult to rouse myself from bed. Today however, I finally bathe and get dressed, washing a reluctant Bella as well. I find that my appetite eludes me these days and I barely have the energy to move. If it weren't for Bella needing to be tended to, I imagine I would stay in bed forever. At least I have my library and the stories and fables that distract me from suffering in reality.

Bella's head pops up from where she's laying next to me on the window seat, her gaze going to the living area. My body tenses, fear that the king is back making nausea burn in my stomach. I hold my breath—waiting for the door to open and his boots to pound across the wood. But he never comes in. I look back at Bella and see her head now resting back over her crossed paws. The last time she reacted like that was when the guard had dropped off the note and flower.

A gut feeling has me moving off the seat and through the library, passing the shelves of books as I make my way to the front door. My steps come to a halt when I see a piece of paper lying on the ground. My fingers twitch at my sides as I slowly step towards the paper, not exactly sure why I'm hesitating. I blow out a breath and finally grab it off the floor, gently unfolding it. A smile threatens when I see the handwriting.

MY LADY,
I MISS THE SUN. DO YOU? I'M NOT MUCH OF AN ARTIST, BUT I DID TRY DRAWING A SUN FOR YOU. YOU CAN TELL ME IT'S BAD; IT WILL ONLY HURT MY FEELINGS SLIGHTLY.
SINCERELY,
THE GUARD WHO IS COLD AND TIRED OF THE RAIN

At the bottom of the note is a crudely drawn sun and three scraggly looking clouds. My lips faintly pull up on one side. Quietly, subtly, within the frozen layers that surround my heart, a tiny fracture appears.

Chapter Eighteen

RHEA

I COULDN'T SLEEP. MY mind was plagued with unwanted memories every time I closed my eyes, so I came out onto the balcony for fresh air. Leaning forward on my elbows, I watch the water of the lake ripple in the wind. The scent of flowers and earthy grass from the rain travel on the breeze, surrounding me with fragrances that I don't know the names of. I'm lost in the headiness of it, eyes closed as I finally start to relax, when there is a knock on the door. I whirl around—the door to my tower directly in my line of sight from where I stand on the balcony. Keeping my steps silent, I slowly walk to the door, my heart curiously pounding.

"Hello?"

"Hello, My Lady," he says. "I have another gift from Tienne and Erica for you." My eyebrows draw up in surprise at the, once again, thoughtful gesture of the two maids. "I'm happy to leave it out here for you, if you'd like," he adds.

I chew on my lip, unsure of what to do. It's not that I exactly *want* to talk with him, but even I must admit that these days of complete isolation are beginning to wear on me. Yes, I have Bella, and I am so grateful she is here, but a part of me yearns to hear another voice. Even if it is just so that I don't only have to hear my own. I'm tired—so, so tired—of this aching, heavy feeling that threatens to pull me under every minute of every day. Maybe talking to this guard can somehow reset my brain so that it doesn't keep haunting me nearly every night.

"Can you," I start and then pause, clearing my throat before trying again. "Can you wait a moment?" I ask awkwardly through the door as I stare down at my nightgown.

"Yes," he answers in a slow drawn-out drawl. Before I can second guess myself, I quickly run up the stairs to change into something more appropriate. I grab one of my more plain dresses, the light blue color and cut of it unremarkable. When I finally come back down, I rush to answer the door but don't see anyone at first. My brows draw in as I stick my head out past the door frame, disappointment at the guard no longer waiting threatening to bring me to tears. Turning my head left, I yelp when I see him leaning against the wall next to the door, his eyes closed and arms folded over his chest. "Shit, I'm sorry," he says, opening his eyes and straightening back up.

My hand goes to my chest, feeling my heart pound against my rib cage. I watch as he slowly moves to close the distance between us, stopping a few steps in front of me.

"Hello." His voice quietly caresses my skin and makes the magic inside me perk up with interest for the first time in a while. Or maybe that's my nerves.

"Were you sleeping?" I ask him, practically gasping while I try to tame the thumping in my chest. He chuckles and shakes his head, his hand running through his hair. Even with the dim lighting of the tower, I can't help but stare at him. My heart never actually calms, but it beats excitedly for a different reason now.

"Just tired," he answers with a grin. "I do have another gift for you though." He holds out his hand, something wrapped in light brown parchment paper resting on his palm. The scent of it is delicious, but I'm uncertain what exactly it is I am smelling. There's an underlying sweetness that I do recognize; it reminds me of apples.

"From Tienne and Erica?" I ask as I take it from him, the bundle still warm.

"Yes. I've apparently become something of an errand boy to them," he says flatly, though the humor that I swear I see in his eyes relays that he doesn't actually mind. He studies me, his gaze roaming my face for a moment. I want to ask what he's searching for—what he sees when he looks at me. Instead, I look down at the ground and notice his boots. They are the same boots Alexi had—the same *all* the guards have. I pry my eyes away from them, emotions thickening in my throat. "Did you like the sun I drew?"

I have to tilt my head back to look into his dark eyes. His hair is styled the same as before, the inky wavy strands rumpled on top with a few of them tumbling over his forehead. A moment passes before I remember he's asked me something. "What?"

His grin widens, and those stupid butterflies come to life again in my stomach. "Did you like the sun? In my note." he repeats, arching a brow. His arms fold over his chest, his dark silhouette outlined with the flame of the torch behind him.

"Was that your first time drawing anything?" I respond, surprised by my own audacity.

His eyes sparkle as he laughs, the sound catching me off guard. His laugh is rich and deep—like his voice—and though it is strange to admit, the sound is like a balm that soothes something deep inside me. "You wound me," he mocks, placing a hand on his chest. "I tried my best."

I snort in response, still holding the bundle in my hand as I inspect it. "If you had not told me it was a sun, I don't think I would have known," I joke as I unwrap it and see there are two small baked items lying in the middle of the parchment paper. They are round and light brown in color, and the smell of them is even more divine now that they are out in the open. "What are—" I begin to ask but then hesitate. Embarrassment burns under my skin at him finding out that I don't know what these are. My eyes flick back to his and, instead of seeing mocking cruelty or even pity like I expect, his face is soft and open.

"They are apple cinnamon muffins," he explains, clasping his hands behind him. My eyes draw down to his broad chest, his muscles flexing with the movement, and I notice he isn't wearing any armor again.

Nodding, I take one of the muffins off of the paper and extend the other out to him. "Do you want one?" I offer, barely above a whisper.

He regards me, head tilting to the side. I wonder then if it's stupid to have done so. Deep and uncompromising sadness creeps into me—a knowing sort of beast that tells me I will never fit in with others, so what's the point in even trying to escape? Dreaming of an existence beyond these stone walls is easy, but as I've often been reminded during my life, reality is all too eager to steal away those fantasies. To shred them apart piece by piece until all that remains is the staggering truth that I could never actually belong anywhere.

My hand begins to withdraw when the guard steps a bit closer.

"I'd love one." He moves to carefully pluck the other muffin from my hand. "Thank you, My Lady." I shift on my feet, something the guard notices before bringing his eyes back up to mine. "I should probably get going," he says, jerking his head towards the stairs. There is an odd feeling of disappointment that flutters through me.

Alone. Alone. Alone.

My eyes start to water, overwhelming feelings of isolation and anguish threaten to burst free from me like a tainted butterfly emerging from its cocoon. I'm transformed by this despair in ways I never thought possible, in ways I can't properly fathom. I nod my head and step back, ready to close the door. This is insanity. I don't even know this guard, and yet some small part of me wants to. Maybe to feel less alone or less insane, I'm not sure.

I miss Alexi so much.

As if he somehow sees the emotional turmoil raging inside of me, the guard clears his throat and draws my attention to him. "Have you ever played noughts and crosses?" he asks quickly. I shake my head and take a deep breath, pushing down those feelings inside of me along with the curiosity that starts to bubble up at his question, until I am— "Would you like to play? I can bring the game tomorrow night and teach you."

My spiraling thoughts freeze at his offer, like a string suddenly pulled taut. I stare at him, trying to figure out if he's being disingenuous. "Why would you do that?" I ask cautiously.

A line forms between his brows as he smirks. "Why wouldn't I do that?" he counters while his dark eyes hold mine.

"Because you are... You're a guard," I argue hesitantly, leaning a shoulder lightly on the door.

"And guards can't play games?"

"Well, of course they can. But what about your post? You aren't supposed to leave," I say.

"I will have already fulfilled my duties for the day," he replies. My eyes narrow at that, a question burning on the tip of my tongue. "One game. If you absolutely despise it—or me—then I won't return," he proposes coolly, shrugging one shoulder up.

It's dangerous, reckless, *stupid* even. But before I can let myself second-guess my response, I nod, tucking my hair behind my ear with my free hand.

"Great!" he grins, the smile appearing effortlessly. "I'll see you tomorrow, then." He steps back, popping the entire small muffin into his mouth as he does so, then spins on his heel and walks down the stairs, a noticeable bounce to his step. I listen as his steps echo down the length of the tower before I step back into the living area and shut the door.

Walking over to the couch, I take a seat and bring the muffin to my mouth for a small bite. Warm and spicy flavors burst onto my tongue—unlike anything I have ever tasted before. It's sweet without being overly so, the texture dense yet fluffy. I hear Bella pad down the stairs, her nose sniffing the air when she reaches the bottom. Holding out a little bite for her in my palm, she carefully licks it up—tail wagging as she does.

I replay the *strange* interaction with the guard in my head. I still don't understand why he wants to spend any amount of time with me in any capacity. Surely he must have other things to do that are more interesting. Or maybe he is just curious. He had said that I wasn't what he expected, so perhaps he just wants to figure out what I am. I'm probably just an oddity to him, a *thing* that doesn't quite belong.

I find myself with a ridiculous nervous energy the next morning, so I work through my chores for the first time in a week. I clean my bed linens and wash the laundry. I dust and sweep and mop until I'm sweating from the exertion. Hunger rumbles in my stomach, so I make a plate of dried fruits, some nuts, and a slice of bread and head outside to the balcony to eat. Only a few wispy white clouds are painted above me, the sun shining brightly in the sky. As soon as I cross into its warmth, some of the tension constantly coiled within me begins to marginally ease.

I'm afraid, however, that if I relax too much, all the things I'm bottling up will rush to the surface with a force so strong that I won't be able to recover. But even spending time outside, one of my favorite places to be, sets off so many memories and moments when *he* was here. My heart is in juxtaposition—I feel both everything and nothing. The aching loss of never seeing Alexi's face again battles with the invading numbness I've come to prefer at the memory of his death. I've always felt some sort of loneliness and sadness because of how I'm forced to exist, but this feeling? It's oppressive—like being trapped in a well and watching water slowly pour in, looking up at the sky and knowing you won't be able to tread water long enough to survive.

I stay outside for a while, looking out to the edge of the forest in the distance. My mind wanders to the guard and the strangeness of him coming over tonight. Do I let him in the tower? What if his intentions are nefarious? I suppose Bella would protect me, but that would be a problem itself. My mind wars internally as I acknowledge that I'm so desperate for mortal interaction that I'm risking not only myself but Bella's safety as well.

Sighing, I grab my plate and bring it inside to wash. Then I sit on the little seat by the window in the library and read until the sky turns from a light blue to a pale lavender. Closing my book, I lay my arms on the ledge and place my head atop them as I watch the horizon fade to pink. When the pitch black of night comes, only lit by the stars and moon gleaming brightly above, I make my way upstairs.

Sitting at my vanity in near darkness, the dancing flames of a candle my only source of light, I brush my hair out until it's silky smooth—admiring my new brush as I do so. Frustration stings within when I tie my hair back into a low ponytail with a hair ribbon. I wish I had been taught to braid my hair; it would be nice to be able to style it differently every once in a while. *Like when a handsome guard is coming over.*

Tightness grips my chest at the thought, and I immediately blush, scared I'm going to look the wrong way in front of him. Or worse, *say* the wrong thing. I don't even know why I agreed to this when the only thing I am capable of is being alone. Setting the brush down, I nervously fidget with my dress. I picked one of the lovely pieces from Tienne and Erica in hopes of feeling more confident. Or maybe less like the truth of what I am—a scared, lonely, and battered girl in a tower. My eyes squeeze shut, and I hold my breath, willing those thoughts that have rushed to the surface back into those boxes in my mind. Four gentle knocks on the door startle me out of my concentration, nearly causing me to topple off the stool.

I look to where Bella is laying on the bed, ears perked but body relaxed. I don't have to tell her to stay, she looks more than comfortable where she is. With my heart inexplicably pounding in my chest, I make my way down from the loft, rounding the three spirals before stepping onto the wood floor. My hand shakes as I step forward and grip the handle of the door. *For the love of the gods, Rhea, calm down.* I blow out a breath at my own command and slowly open the door to the guard.

His eyes immediately ensnare mine—like magnets being drawn together. His mouth is relaxed into a small smile, his body language and posture calm and open. Like he knows I'm nervous being around someone new, so he's making it as easy as he can. But that's a ridiculous thought because why would he do that? He doesn't even know me.

"Hello again," he says, that charming voice setting something small aflutter in me. He's wearing all black again, no sword or armor in sight.

"Hello," I repeat quietly, holding his gaze while I twist my dress nervously in my hand.

His eyes dart down to my hands for a second before he brings them back up to mine. He ponders something for a minute, his fingers flexing around a black bag in his grip. "Is it okay if we play the game on the landing?" he asks politely.

My shoulders ease down from my ears—a position I didn't even realize I was holding. "Okay." My voice is a shaky whisper. I find it annoying and I wish I wasn't showing how off-kilter I feel.

The guard just smiles and steps back to take a seat on the stone landing, leaving plenty of room for me to take my own. I notice that there is a second torch lit on the wall behind him, both casting plenty of amber light as their flames cause our shadows to sway around us. One foot steps beyond the door, and a realization hits me so hard that I freeze where I am, half in and half out. The guard notices immediately, a dark brow lifting in question. My cheeks heat up as I clear my throat and prepare for his ridicule.

"This is my first time stepping out past the door," I confess self-consciously.

The guard stills, halting his set up of the game. "Your first time stepping past the door... ever?" His tone is incredulous. It makes me feel even more humiliated that I'm an adult and have never even *attempted* to walk out onto the landing.

"Maybe this isn't such a good idea," I breathe, bringing my foot back inside. I can't do this, I don't know why I thought I could.

"Wait, I'm sorry, I didn't mean to come off as rude or insensitive. I just assumed..." he says, holding out a hand to stop me. His head shakes before he clears his throat. "I'm sorry."

I force back the knot in my throat. Why does it feel like even the smallest things are too monumental to get through?

"I would still very much like to play, but if I've ruined it and you want to leave, I understand." Several moments pass as I mull over his words and contemplate what to do. I don't want to go back to the quiet tower with only my consuming thoughts for company. Tentatively, I step back out over the threshold and take a seat across from him as he smiles, looking relieved and even delighted. There's a wooden board with nine squares broken up into three rows of three.

"Do you want to be the naughts or crosses?" he asks, holding a pile of pieces in each hand out to me. I lean over to get a better look and point to one of the heaps. "These are the crosses," he tells me as he carefully sets the wooden pieces into my hand. The warmth of his touch brings an intense sort of awareness to where our skin meets. My eyes flick up to his, but he already has his gaze on me. He looks at me like he's discovered something new—something exciting. I quickly bring my hand back to my chest, cradling the pieces that look like their namesake. He holds up his pieces—the naughts—which look like the letter "o." "The point of the game is to try to get three in a row. You can get them by going across," he points with his finger, dragging it from the left to the right side of the board, "or by going vertically or diagonally. You can also block a person from getting a three in a row by laying your piece down to break it up." I nod in understanding, and he gestures with a hand towards me. "Why don't you go first? Lay a piece down anywhere you want on the board."

Contemplating my first move, I twirl the cross piece in my hand. I decide to go for the middle, as it is likely the easiest way to have a few chances at getting three in a row.

"Interesting choice," he says, smiling at me before laying his piece down. He chooses a spot also in the middle row, on my left. I place a cross in my bottom right corner. He blocks my attempt at winning by placing his piece in my top left corner. I'm so focused on trying to find another spot for me to win, that I lay a piece down on the top right corner. He smiles as he lays his piece in the bottom left corner. "I win," he exults.

I narrow my eyes at him and grab my pieces off the board. "I want to try again."

He grins, clearing his pieces off. "Of course. But I will start this time, since I won." He lays his first piece down in the middle.

I jokingly scoff, "That's not very gentlemanly of you." Following his lead, I place my next piece down as well.

"Good thing I never said I was a gentleman," he replies, his voice low and teasing. His pupils flare for a second before he breaks eye contact and lays a second piece down on the board. Back and forth we go in silence, but it's not awkward or heavy. The game ends in a tie, so we start over. We play nearly twenty games before a yawn breaks free from me. He's won six times to my four, the rest of our matches ending in ties.

"I should probably call it a night," he groans, stretching his arms overhead after our next game ends in yet another tie. I yawn again, covering my mouth with my hand while nodding. I hand him the pieces and fold up the board while he puts them back in their bags. When everything is cleaned up, we both stand and dust off our clothing. I take a step back over the threshold, leaning on the door frame as the guard keeps some distance from me.

Clearing my throat, I look up at him through my lashes. "Thank you for teaching me how to play," I say, chewing on my bottom lip. His eyes catch the movement briefly before he glances away and nods.

"You're welcome." He halts, his head tilting and causing some of his dark hair to slide over his forehead. "Would it be ok if I came back?"

His question is genuine, and I'd be lying if I said I didn't feel my heart beat funny because of it. Do I trust him? No, not at all. But is it nice to have someone else here? Is it welcome to have something *different* to break up the repetitive dullness that has me alternating between pretending to be fine and actively forcing myself to be? Is it a relief just to hear a voice other than my own?

"Yes, I would like that," I answer before I can stop myself. I clasp my hands in front of me and glance down in embarrassment before sneaking a look back at him.

"Then I will see you tomorrow," he responds, giving me a parting grin.

I close the door and lean my back against it, a small smile tugging on the corners of my mouth. Drawing my fingers to my lips, I realize that this is the first time I've *wanted* to smile since that horrific night. That darkness inside me falters faintly and a tiny bit of it is replaced with something pure—something reminiscent of happiness.

⚜

"Rhea." The whispered voice tickles my ear as I open my eyes. Icicles—long and pointed—hang from the ceiling above the bed. Shadows dance in the corners of the room—writhing and swirling higher up the tower walls, moving to cage me in. "Rhea, why did you let him die?"

I shake my head at his sickening familiar voice, my hands digging into my hair and scraping my scalp. "I wanted to save him," I whisper, tears dripping onto the blanket. There's silence for a moment, the only sound my heavy breathing.

"But you didn't," he growls, "and he left you knowing that your fate would be with me." His voice slices through my skin, my bones, my soul.

"I wish it had been me."

"It wasn't though, was it?" The shadows move in as the king's oppressive darkness pushes down on me, my body crumbling under its weight. "And now, you are mine. Only mine. Forever."

Gasping for air, I jolt awake. The details of the tower come into focus with the small amount of moonlight shining in through the windows. I push my tangled, sweaty hair away from my face as Bella lifts her head off of my leg. King Dolian's voice lingers in my mind like a terrifying omen of my future. It reminds me that my time here is like sand falling in the middle of an hourglass, except I don't know what will happen when time runs out.

164

Chapter Nineteen

BAHIRA

M<small>Y NAILS DIG INTO</small> the ancient wooden table in the council room, leaving crescent shapes in the surface, as I anxiously wait for the rest of the members to arrive. The soft light from the chandeliers above reflects on the midnight black stone that lines the floor. The breeze blowing in from the open windows is warmer, a sign that the shifting of the seasons from spring to summer is nearing. The earthy scent of the trees surrounding us permeates the otherwise-stagnant air as the birds flitting between them voice their songs.

Footsteps echo off the stone as the last few mage councilmen enter the room and take their seats. Councilman Kallin, Daje's father, takes his seat on my father's left-hand side. Across the table from where I sit, his eyes meet mine briefly, a look of dismissal flashing in them before he turns his attention back to my father. There have been brief moments when I consider marrying Daje just to spite his father. How upset would he be if his son married a magicless girl? Nevermind the fact that I am the fucking *princess* of this realm. I fight the almost-dominating urge to roll my eyes.

Looking at my father—his hands relaxed on the top knee of his crossed legs—I'm reminded again how lucky I am to have been born to parents who care more about the soul than the magic they might possess. With a flick of his wrist, the doors to the council chamber close quietly. Another has copies of Nox's latest letter sent by raven floating to each council member from a stack in the middle. I had almost ripped the original one out of my father's hands to read the newest updates. It turns out that Nox didn't have much to report, and the silence is deafening as the council reads over the sparse correspondence.

Daje's father sighs when he gets to the end, letting his copy drop unceremoniously back onto the table. "There is not much of anything to this letter," he mutters, running a hand over his balding head.

My father nods, ever the regal presence. Even dressed casually as he is now in a plain white long-sleeved tunic and black trousers, there is no denying that King Sadryn was born to rule. His night-black hair is pulled back, his tanned skin taking on a bronzed glow under the golden flame of the chandeliers. Mumbles of how a lack of meaningful information has been common with Nox's letters lately trickle in around the table. While my father's face is a mask of pure calm, those who know him best know his frustration manifests in small movements from his fingers. So when Councilman Arav voices his concern that Nox could be compromised, my father's fingers grip his knee so hard they start to turn white.

"My son loves his kingdom and the people within it more than any-thing," he says in a tight voice.

"I do not mean to question the prince's loyalties, Majesty. I just mean, what if something has happened in which he hasn't been given a choice?" Councilman Arav replies, a sheen of sweat causing his forehead to shine.

Arav is younger for a councilman, which is especially apparent as he is seated next to Daje's father. He was chosen because he is from a smaller town on the very outskirts of our kingdom, near the border with the mortal lands, and the people there love him for how he advocates for them to the king. His blonde hair, blue eyes, and pale skin stand out starkly against most everyone else at this table, but his features represent the mixed-blood population of the town he is from.

"Are you insinuating that the prince may have been found out and captured?" Councilman Hadrik inquires. Hadrik is my parent's closest family friend and like an uncle to me. Growing up, his presence was a common occurrence around the palace, and he never missed an opportunity to indulge my curious mind in whatever unique or unusual questions I would ask of him. His graying-black hair and kind brown eyes stand out against the silver tunic he's wearing as he stares at Arav.

"Nox is the most powerful mage born in the last century, possibly even longer. I do not doubt that if trouble had arisen, he would have found a way to get back to our kingdom," Daje's father adds.

"Councilman Kallin is correct. Nox would protect himself if need be." I hear the assurance in my father's voice—for my benefit, I have no doubt.

"How long do you plan to leave our crown prince in an enemy kingdom?" one of the older councilmen, Osiris, asks from the end of the table.

"We don't know that they are the enemy, only that we felt a heavy burst of magic there and—"

"And that alone should signify that they are up to something!" he says, interrupting my father. "With every day that passes we are risking our future ruler! Do you not think the—"

"Osirus, that is enough. No one could possibly care more about the future ruler of this kingdom than his own father." When my eyes bounce to his, I don't have to look for his tell to know that my father's anger is building.

"And yet, you keep him there," Osiris continues, and I begin to wonder if the man has some sort of separate grievance with his king. None of the council members have ever challenged him like this. "You allow him to try to get close to a ruler who may be hiding magic. Why else would they do that if not to use it against us? Perhaps they are even aware of our ability to pass through the Spell without consequence!" Osirus' pupils widen with each word out of his mouth, an odd sort of panic to his voice.

My father must notice it as well because he leans forward slightly and narrows his eyes at him. "What is it you are more worried about? The fact that something may happen to my son, or the fact that if it does, my daughter will become heir to the throne?"

I stiffen at my mention, but Osirus' panic makes much more sense if my rule is what he truly fears. Nox is eldest, so he does technically have first claim to the throne. But my father has always made it clear to both of us that, much like how a new ruler was chosen before the war, the position should go to whoever is worthy of it. And he determines that worthiness not by the strength of our magic, or if we have any at all, but by our morals—by how we treat others and show our love for the realm. And I know without a shadow of a doubt that both Nox and I care about our kingdom more than anything. It's why he's currently undercover in another realm, and it's why I've dedicated myself to fixing what's blocking our magic. But as far as I'm concerned, Nox can have the throne. He's always been the more serious and ruler-minded sibling. Whereas I have no interest in figuring out how to be politically correct, among other things. A fact that is proven when I open my mouth to defend myself.

"Councilman Osirus, surely you have no qualms about a woman leading our kingdom? As you may recall, rulers were exclusively female before my ancestor was named king." I'm provoking him into speaking out loud what I know he is thinking—what I know a majority of the old men at this table are thinking.

"You are forgetting the very *important* detail that they also had magic. Void Magic no less. And the fact remains that you have no—"

"Enough, Osirus." My father cuts him off, but I've goaded the old councilman too far, he can't help but keep going.

"—us to feel comfortable with the fact that if something happens to Nox, we are left with someone who has no magic of her own to protect the kingdom with. Our history dictates that rulers are chosen by the strength of their magi—"

"Osirus," my father interjects, voice cold and lethal from where he stands, placing his hands on the table. The energy in the room becomes ominous, palpable to every person within it. Nearly all of the men on the council shift uncomfortably in their seats, but the two older female members remain motionless, small smiles curling their lips. "Let's first start with the fact that you are wrong about previous rulers being chosen by their magic. They were chosen when their souls were deemed worthy. *Then* the magic shifted to them from the current ruler, who was *also* chosen because of their worthiness."

The ancient texts we have on Void Magic rulers dictate that when a descendant of the Void line was found worthy, their flame would turn blue during their ceremony. I've always found it odd that the texts left out how that worthiness was determined. The child chosen would have common raw mage magic like everyone else, but when they reached the age of sixteen, the life and death magic of the Void would transfer to them from the current ruler. Together, both would rule, until the next-in-line reached the age of twenty-two and officially took the throne.

"Secondly," my father continues, "I absolutely can—and will—expect you to bow before Bahira, should she ever be named queen. If that is going to be a problem for you, Osirus, then I will have no choice but to remove you from this council."

I keep my posture steady, spine straight and head raised, so that—on the outside—I appear calm and collected. On the inside though, my mind is chaotic from my father's words. He has never, ever threatened anyone on this council before for disagreeing with him. In fact, he's always chosen people that have varying ideas and opinions—a necessity, he claims, to running a well-balanced kingdom.

"The fact of the matter is that my son, your crown prince and Bahira's brother, is in a foreign kingdom to figure out why we felt such a strong presence of magic there and why we continue to feel it in waves now," my father says, pushing back from the table and folding his arms over his chest. His magic, a light purple in color, pulses around him as he looms over everyone else.

"Disregarding everything about your daughter becoming ruler, which is currently a moot point considering Nox is alive," Councilman Kallin says, eyeing Osirus down the length of the table before looking back at his king, "we still should consider the possibility that we may need allies should Nox find something that *could* be used against us. We may need to reveal our long-guarded secret."

My father stares at him for a few seconds before jerking his head in a small nod. "It is something I have been considering already, Councilman Kallin."

My head swings to look at him, the surprise surely showing on my face. The other members start talking in low voices to each other, but my eyes are locked on to my father's. Noting my shock, he leans towards me and speaks in a low voice,

"It will depend on what Nox discovers that is emitting such powerful magic that we can feel it even here. It might be something to bring down the Spell or break through it. And with what Nox has reported regarding the size of their army…" He trails off, shaking his head. "We would not have enough magic to protect us, should they try to attack."

I lean back against my chair soundly, my self-composure crumbling under the weight of what's just been revealed. We are talking about war. A war between realms that shouldn't even be possible. The pressure to figure out what is blocking our magic doubles in an instant.

※※※※※ ※※※※※

After the revelation that war might be a real possibility, I need to get my mind off of everything. I worry daily about Nox being so far from home and surrounded by people who might kill him if they find out who—or *what*—he is. I worry about finding a fix for the declining magic that is our people's very soul. I also selfishly worry about who I will be if I never find my missing magic at all—if I never become whole. But now is not the time for those thoughts.

No, as I climb up the hill that leads to our training grounds, the only thing my mind is focused on is Gosston. The late afternoon sun shines on the open landscape dotted with hills and small ponds. In the distance, younger mages practice wielding their magic. Tree branches and rocks lift into the air, glowing lightly in a variety of colors. Water gleams a muted red as it spins like a cyclone above a pond, a mage nearby standing with his eyes closed and hand extended out. When I crest the top of the hill, the land flattens back out and I see a group of men and women sparring togeth- er. Standing off to the side—his muscled torso gleaming with sweat—is Gosston. He's only a little taller than I am, but he's much wider, his arms and shoulders thick with strength. He already looks fatigued, most likely from sparring most of the day. Pity for him. My steps are sure, my grip on my spear tight, as I stalk to Gosston like a forest tiger hunting a gazelle.

"Hey, Bahira, do you want to spar?" I hear Daje ask a little too loudly as he begins to walk towards me.

"Sorry, Daje," I respond, my voice low. "I already have a sparring part- ner in mind." Daje comes to my side, matching my steps as he follows my line of sight.

"Bahira, don't do this," he warns as his hand stretches out to grip my arm, but I quickly step out of his reach. Ignoring his protests, I continue walking until I'm just a few feet in front of Gosston.

"Hello, Gosston." I twirl my spear until it's in front me, the tip point- ing directly at his heart. "Let's spar."

He gives me an incredulous look before stepping back and releasing a scoff. "I think I'll pass, Bahira," he chides, moving to get around me.

My spear snaps out, the side of it stopping a hair's breadth in front of him. The air crackles with anticipation, like an impending maelstrom of violence while I smirk bitterly at him. "What's the matter? Afraid that I'll beat you in front of all your friends?"

He laughs, though the sound is shaky. "I'm not going to spar with you."

"No, you'll just run your mouth and expect me to not do anything about it," I say, dropping my weapon slowly to my side as I step in front of him. His eyes narrow in my direction, his muscles beginning to tense. "Pick up your sword."

"I'm not sparring with you," he repeats, frustration causing tight lines to form at the corner of his mouth.

"Pick up," I growl the words this time through my teeth, "your sword." More people start gathering around us, forming a semi-circle in the grass. I know I should probably care about creating a spectacle, about how it will look *politically,* but everything around me fades to a blurry haze except for Gosston, whose annoying face is the center of my building fury. He folds his arms over his chest, making no move to unsheathe his weapon.

"Bahira, there are other ways we can let out your frustration," he jeers, licking his lips as he eyes me over with zero regard. "Let me take care of you. You already know it's—"

"Quick?" I interrupt, my eyes and smile daring him to act. "I know it's quick—and terribly unsatisfying. Just like how this little *sparring match* will be."

He scowls, a blush beginning to stain his cheeks. "Fine," he snarls, bending over to unsheathe his sword from where it lays. "I'll spar with you. But just remember, it was your *crazy* ass that asked for this."

Someone—perhaps Haylee—starts cursing under her breath. I have been called many things, but *crazy* is one that perhaps bothers me the most. That one word changes everyone's perception of me and demeans and discredits everything I am working for. It's a cheap way for those who lack the intelligence to see beyond what's right in front of them to try and bring me down. I inhale deeply, honing in on my surroundings to help me focus. I feel the warmth of the sun above and the tickling of the pillow grass beneath my feet.

Challenging someone to fight isn't the mage way of handling disagreements, but when was the last time any of them treated me as mage anyway? I've had to navigate my role in this kingdom as the only one of my *kind*. No, violence certainly isn't the mage way, but it is absolutely *my* way.

Gosston lifts his sword as we begin to circle one another, his face contorting into a confused snarl. "You have to know I was just *joking* when I said you cry about being magicless. It's not like it is a *sensitive subject* or anything."

A shot of rage-fueled adrenaline goes through me with his words. *Of course* he would say it's a joke. That's all it is to him and everyone else who thinks that I'm less than because I am different. They are cruel until they are called out on it. Then suddenly, *I'm* being overly sensitive and dramatic.

"You might want to shut up and focus. I'll even give you an advantage and tell you I'm going to attack first."

His eyes narrow, his anger flaring like I hoped it would. Dilan always told us that letting our emotions get the best of us during a fight would only lead to injury and loss. It doesn't matter how much stronger or taller you are than an opponent, all it takes is one misstep, one break in concentration, to have a sword jabbed into your side. Or a spear. Of course I won't kill him, despite my baser urges to, but I will revel in beating him in front of his friends.

Gosston takes the same measured steps that I do while he taunts me. "You know, I've always felt bad for you. You have all the prestige of a princess born to one of the strongest mage couples in the kingdom. You have a brother whose flame sparked higher than any other in well over a century." He stops, dropping his arms to his side in an attempt to lower my own defenses. "Yet you were born magicless. And all your dedication and *tinkering*," he says with a mocking sneer, "has yielded nothing. The very thing that you've made your life's work has been for nothing. That must be so hard for you. It must be hard knowing that no matter what you do, your fate is to be nothing more than a magicless wife."

The world seems to slow, a loaded pause building in the air, as I stare Gosston directly in the eyes. I inject every ounce of rage that has boiled over into that stare before I lift my lips in a smile that is mostly a baring of teeth. Then I swing. My spear comes down hard and fast, Gosston barely having enough time to lift his sword and block. His eyes widen as he looks at me, almost like he can't believe I'd do what I said I would. *Idiot.* I lift my spear again, before arching it down and to the side. He doesn't have time to block this strike, the force of my swing causing his breath to rush out with a loud grunt from the contact.

"You bitch," he seethes as he lifts his sword and starts to advance towards me. His swings are powerful as he counters, moving left to right and jabbing forward. The clashing of our weapons echoes out into the air, the people around us silent while they watch us go back and forth. I parry every time he comes at me, my agility helping me counter his advances without taking the brunt of his power. When he presses forward again only to have me block and twirl away from him, his eyes flare briefly with panic. "Let's do this without the weapons," he says, chucking his sword to the side.

"You want this to be even more humiliating for you?" I taunt as I watch him shake out his hands.

"You've got a pretty face, *Princess*, are you sure you want it ruined?" My eyes roll in response.

"Bahira, come on. You've proven your point; there's no need to keep fighting," Daje pleads loudly, and though his voice is calm, it has the opposite effect on me.

"Thank you for your input, Daje, it's duly noted," I respond before tossing my spear to the side and stepping closer to Gosston with raised fists. Low murmurs sound around us as we begin to circle each other again. I breathe in deeply, relaxing my shoulders and tuning out anything that isn't the sound of my fast-beating heart.

Gosston moves first, leaning in to snap his fist towards my jaw. I dodge the movement, using his own momentum to tug on his wrist and pull him right into my oncoming fist. His head snaps back, his guard rising before I jab with my other hand. He blocks my fist, but it was nothing more than a distraction. With his arms lifted and his focus so heavily on my hands, it leaves his sides exposed, an opportunity I greedily take advantage of by bringing my knee up forcefully. He bellows at the contact before gritting his teeth and staring at me with an unhinged gleam in his eyes. I move to retreat a step and block his attempt to hit my face. He counters quickly with a hard jab to my ribs, causing me to drop down onto one knee while my breath whooshes out of me.

I can hear a voice in the background hissing my name, but I'm too lost in the blinding anger within me. I will never let someone else determine my own worth. I will never let someone treat me as nothing more than a metaphorical or literal punching bag for their cheap jokes. Only *I* decide what hurts me. Only *I* decide what can be used as a weapon against me.

I jump back up to my feet, swinging my leg out and kicking directly onto the side of his knee. My fist closes the distance between us in an uppercut to his jaw, making his head jerk up. His face flushes with irritation, blood dribbling from the corner of his mouth. Gosston's fatigue begins to show as his next attempt to hit me is weak.

Holding my guard up, I bounce on my toes, planning my next hit when a sudden flash of orange light blinds me. Before I can react, I'm thrown back hard against the ground. The bastard used his magic against me. My ears ring and my head aches as I try to blink through the dazed fog. I move to get up, but Gosston stands at my feet, the orange glow also emitting from his raised hand. He squints with concentration, using nearly all his effort to hold me down with his magic. Orange rings wrap around my wrists and push them above my head, more glowing around my torso to hold me in place. I start to struggle out of his magical grasp on instinct, but I know I can't get out without magic of my own. The best thing I can do is wait until he's too weak to hold me down anymore.

"All your talk and now look at you. *This* is your reality, *Princess*," he says, his teeth showing like a rabid dog. Sweat beads down his temple and his hand begins to shake. It won't be much longer until he'll be too weak to hold me down fully.

"Let her go, Gosston." Daje's voice pierces the violent tension in the air. I watch him step forward, holding his sword in one hand while the other is in a tight fist at his side. The mask of lethal fury on his face is illuminated by the soft yellow glare of his magic surrounding his entire body, like a stunning cloak of sunlight.

"Stop, Daje," I say, wiggling and finding there is a little less resistance holding me down.

"Bahira, I won't stand by and watch this. This asshole—"

"I don't need your help," I grunt, clenching my jaw as I try to roll onto my side.

"Don't be so stubborn," he seethes—actually *seethes*—back at me. Daje has never spoken to me like that, and he briefly draws my concentration away from trying to get to my knees. He walks to Gosston, raising the hand not holding his sword. His yellow magic grows even brighter where it gathers in his palm.

"Daje, *stop*," I breathe, pushing my body harder to free myself.

"Yes, Bahira, let Daje *rescue* you. He's been doing it since we were kids anyway."

"Shut up, Gosston," Daje growls back.

"Daje," I repeat, but the hardened lines of his face tell me he's not listening to anything I'm saying anymore. Gosston's hand falters, the light of his orange magic beginning to flicker.

"Daje! Look at me!" I shout, finally getting to my knees, the magical bindings now loose enough for me to move more easily. Daje's gaze flicks to where I'm kneeling and my eyes bore into his as I command quietly, "Do *not* hit him with your magic."

Gosston's magic starts to fade from his palm, the intense orange now dimmer, barely there. I can feel it lessen its hold on me, and my body becomes my own again. Finally able to stand, I move towards Gosston, but as I am mid-step, Daje lifts the hand holding his yellow magic up.

"No!" I shout, but Gosston is already grunting from Daje's hit. The orange glow from his hand winks out instantly while Daje takes a step forward. Gosston drops to a knee, the people around us either cheering or snickering from where they stand before yellow bindings appear around him and anchor him to the ground. I turn to Daje and shove him—*hard*. He looks at me, eyes wide and full of shock.

"What are you doing?" he shouts, splaying his arms out in frustration. "Gods, are you so afraid of appearing weak that you won't even take protection when it's clearly needed?"

My head snaps back like I've been slapped, my brows rising high on my forehead. I'm rendered speechless, my gaze locked on my best friend. He's slow to hide his shock, as if he's just realized what he's said. His mouth opens to say something, but Gosston interjects.

"She's not worth it, man," he slurs from where he's still kneeling in the grass, "her pussy isn't even that great." My body turns rigid, the crowd around us falling completely silent. Even the trees pause their rustling in the breeze, like they too are waiting to see what happens next. "She's nothing but a fragile, magicless whore."

Before my mind even registers what I'm doing, my feet eat up the space between us.

"Call your magic off!" I yell to Daje, who is still staring in shock at me. "Now, Daje!" Standing in front of Gosston, I watch the yellow bindings holding him down disappear. I wait until his head slowly lifts and his eyes meet mine in a vengeful glare. My voice is low, so that he is the only one who can hear me, when I say, "I may be magicless, but only one of us is weak."

His lips lift in a snarl as I wind my arm back. And when my bloody hand connects with his temple for the final time, his body keeling over into the grass, I remind myself that I may be a princess, but I am nobody's fucking damsel. Turning, I pick up my spear—ignoring Daje's attempts to talk with me—and walk away from the whispering voices on the training grounds.

Chapter Twenty

RHEA

THE GUARD COMES AGAIN the next night, and the next, until a week has passed of him visiting. I want to be embarrassed that I'm just now learning how to play what appear to be children's games, but instead I find myself *confused*. Why does this guard want to spend time with me? The question gets louder in my mind each time we sit across from each other, and as a result, I find it difficult to speak at all around him. He isn't bothered by it though, and the same is true for right now.

I nervously chew on my lip, a move his eyes get drawn to briefly before he turns his attention back to our game. Today, we are playing something called checkers. The board is a pattern of alternating black and white squares, and the pieces are circular and of the same colors. He contemplates his next move, elbow resting on the bent knee in front of him—no armor in sight.

Feeling awkward about the silence, I blurt out the only thing that comes to mind. "Why aren't you wearing any armor?" My cheeks heat, but I keep my gaze on his and hope that the light of the torches behind him aren't bright enough to reveal how flushed I am. "I just mean that if you're the new night guard, shouldn't you be wearing your armor?"

"Actually, I am not the new night guard," he answers with a shake of his head. "I'm the new day guard. The old one got moved to the overnight position."

I frown slightly in confusion. "If you aren't working right now, then why are you here?" He chuckles as he watches me, making my confusion only grow as I wonder what he might find funny about what I said.

"I'm here because I want to be," he replies, a broad smile gleaming back at me. My eyes narrow suspiciously, and his chuckle grows into a rich laugh. Annoyingly, I find that I like the sound. I should interrogate him again on why he's here, or how he is even getting *in* the tower if it's currently being guarded. But that isn't what I ask.

"And are you— Have you been told what happened to the former night guard?" My voice is shaky—not from nerves this time, but from the mention of Alexi. The always-lingering sadness within me rushes to the forefront, mixing with my guilt until I'm overwhelmed and working my lower lip between my teeth once again.

His gaze drops down to my mouth, a slight frown forming the longer he looks. "Yes," he answers hesitantly. "I know he was punished for stealing from the king."

Sharp anger floods my veins as my teeth absentmindedly bite down harder on my lip. *Lies.* Just thinking about how the king painted the false story, that Alexi was the kind of man that would take from others, makes me feel sick to my stomach.

"You might want to stop chewing so harshly on your lip," the guard says with a grimace, cutting into my thoughts.

"What?" I snap, my mind still reeling at the idea that everyone believes Alexi was the type of man who deserved to be punished by death.

"Your lip is bleeding." A concerned look crosses his face as I bring my fingertips to my mouth, wincing when I see the small amount of blood coating them. In my anger, I hadn't felt the tooth break through. "Do you have a cloth and warm water inside?" My brows knit together in confusion, and his mouth twists into a smirk before he answers my unspoken question, "So I can clean up your lip."

"I can do it myself."

"Let me help you," he urges, lithely coming up to stand and extending a hand out to me.

Those four words widen the small fissure in the cold fortress around my heart, turning my breaths sharp as I stare at him. *Let me help you.* Has anyone ever offered that to me before? In any context?

My hesitancy doesn't go unnoticed, and he quips, "Something tells me you don't like having others help you."

I snort at his assumption and reply, "My circumstances haven't really led to many offerings of help to begin with." I gesture around me like he's forgotten that I'm no more than a woman imprisoned.

"I can stay out here and clean it if I make you uncomfortable." His words are excruciatingly gentle, like how you would speak to an injured animal so as not to spook it. I wonder if that's what I am to him.

"You don't make me uncomfortable," I respond, rolling my shoulders back as I tilt my face up. His lips widen into an almost-full smile, and gods help me, my heart lurches at the sight of it. The magic inside me responds as well, curling and coiling in what feels like excitement. I take his hand, allowing him to pull me up and trying to ignore the way his skin feels against mine. I let my hand linger a moment too long in his, or maybe he holds on to it a moment longer than he should, before we let go and I walk through the doorway. He doesn't move to follow, and when I turn back to look at him, I realize he is waiting for permission to. "You can come in," I say quietly. It's an interesting thing, to invite someone into my space for the first time. Alexi was always welcome, but in the beginning, he showed up without me asking him to.

The guard looks around slowly. At what, I'm not sure since the room is mostly empty with the exception of a few plants and pieces of furniture. I leave him there to make my way up the stairs and grab some washcloths. I note Bella on the bed, mostly tucked under the covers with her head just barely peeking out.

"It's okay," I whisper to her as I grab two cloths before I head back down the steps, my bare feet nearly silent on the metal. When I step off the stairs, I bump into the guard, whose dark figure blends almost entirely into the shadows. Only the small amount of moonlight coming in through the balcony doors glints off of his face.

"Whoa," he says, hands coming to grip my elbows gently. "Are you okay?"

My hands grab onto his forearms to steady myself. "I'm sorry, I didn't see you in the dark," I rasp out. It's his touch under my fingers, rather than stumbling into him, that squeezes the air from my lungs.

"Do you not have flame gems?" he inquires.

I cock my head to the side, my hair sliding across my back with the movement.

"What is a flame gem?" Though I can't really see it, I can sense the guard's eyes on me, even in the scant light.

He drops one of his hands from my elbow and uses the other to guide me towards the couch as he asks, "What do you do for light at night?"

"I light candles. Is that not what everyone else does?"

"No," he answers softly, stopping us right in front of the tea table. "In the castle, there are flame gems that go in lamps and chandeliers. The sunlight charges them during the day so that they glow at night. One medium-sized gem would light most of this entire tower."

"Oh." A wave of humiliation rushes over me, followed by one of recognition. I *had* heard about flame gems—in some of the books I'd read. *I didn't believe they were real.*

"The gems are rare to come by nowadays. They were easier to mine before the war and before the Spell was put in place. They come from the mountains of the Fae Kingdom." He speaks tentatively, but I can't help but hear the pity in his voice. I had never really thought about how I might not have the same basic amenities as the castle I'm attached to. I mostly focused on the larger things I wasn't experiencing. Alexi certainly never mentioned anything about what I may be lacking in this tower. "Do you have something we can put water in?" he asks. I nod my head then realize he probably can't see it in the dark.

"Yes, I have a bowl."

"Perfect, can you grab it while I light these candles? I'd prefer to see your face while I work," he adds, his warm fingers finally leaving my arm.

Despite feeling embarrassed, butterflies of a different nature flutter in my stomach. *It's ridiculous to feel this way.* I walk to the sink by the door and fill up a small bowl with water while he works on lighting the pillar candles I have on the tea table. When they are all lit and I take a seat on the couch, I expect the guard to sit next to me. Instead, he gets down on one knee in front of me, taking a cloth and dipping it in the bowl of water I've set on the table.

"Let me know if this hurts," he says softly. He moves to bring the hand not holding the cloth to my face, and I can't help but flinch on instinct, the memory of another's touch sending a burst of fear through my body. "I'm sorry." He holds his hands up in front of him, where I can see them both clearly.

My head dips in embarrassment, and I wish I could explain that it isn't him. It's just the culmination of years of fearing anyone other than Alexi. I've tried so hard to suppress any sort of reaction when the king has his hands on me, but maybe this guard lowers my own shields more than I realized. More than it makes sense for him to.

"Hey, it's okay. Do you want to do it yourself? I can just supervise," he reassures lightly as he holds the cloth out to me, keeping both hands in front of him. I see his head dip as he attempts to pull my eyes back up to look at his face. I should take the cloth; I am more than capable of doing it myself. There's just a part of me that is begging to let him do it. A selfish, guilt-ridden instinct that wants someone to take care of me for once. "What do you want, My Lady?"

My eyes finally lift to meet his. "You can do it," I whisper. His eyes hold mine for a moment, their smoky concentration on me overwhelming. I'm warm and breathless, and it makes exactly *zero* sense.

"Okay." He moves slowly, keeping eye contact with me the entire time as he lifts the cloth up to my face again.

"Is it alright if I hold the side of your face to keep you steady?" he asks. I nod, watching him do exactly that, keeping his touch featherlight as his fingers brush against my cheek. The warm cloth touches my lip as he works to clean the blood off. A gentle tension in the air brackets us, not awkward or strained but sweet and tender—kind.

Despite knowing I'll get caught for it, I can't stop the way I study him. His features are nearly artistic in their beauty. The distinct thought that he is too good-looking to be a guard runs through my mind for a fleeting moment. My fingers unexplainably twitch with the urge to run through his thick, wavy hair. His dark eyes dart up to my own—his nostrils flaring just slightly—and then they look back down at my mouth. But he doesn't stop his unhurried touch.

I have to work to keep my breathing even, taking slow, calculated breaths. I get a hint of something I've never smelled before. It isn't floral, but it reminds me of early autumn mornings when the trees around the castle start changing colors. There is a different aroma in the air at that time of year. Was it the trees? Or the grass? Whatever it is, this guard smells similar.

Needing to fill the silence, I ask a question that I've been curious about when he moves the cloth to dip it back into the water. "Aren't you worried about being caught up here?"

His gaze meets mine again as he shrugs. "Not particularly." He slowly lowers the hand that was cradling my face. The skin there feels cold now in the absence of his touch. "There," he says, placing the wet cloth down and picking up the dry one to dab at my lip. His brows furrow suddenly as he examines the spot.

"What is it?" I bring my own fingers up to touch my bottom lip, noticing the soreness is already gone.

"There should be a mark where the blood was coming from, but I don't—"

"Maybe it wasn't as bad as you thought," I interject, pinching my lips together in an attempt to hide them.

I have no doubt that my magic healed the cut made from my tooth already, and I don't exactly know if I should be in awe of or terrified by the prospect of it working on its own accord so quickly. *And without being noticed.* He simply nods his head and places the dry cloth back on the table. I try to read him, to see if he is wondering why my lip doesn't hold a single mark, but he shows no sign of perplexity. In fact, I'm sure I must look more confused than he does.

"How do you know Tienne and Erica?" he asks, sitting down with his knees bent in front of him and feet flat on the floor. The question catches me by surprise.

"They came to the tower and cleaned me up after Alexi died." There is a significant wobble of my voice when I say his name. I can feel my emotions fighting to get to the surface, trying to break free of those spaces within me where I've allowed them to dwell. With a squeeze of my fists and a deep breath, I am able to push it all down again.

The guard observes me from his place on the floor, face nearly unreadable except for the sympathy reflecting in his eyes. Sounding genuine, he says, "I'm sorry," He doesn't move to adjust his position or fidget; he just looks at me with understanding. "For what happened to him and for what you've had to endure," he continues.

I can feel the tears welling behind my eyes, fortresses inside me shaking from the acknowledgment of what I've been through. I need the conversation to keep moving before I fall apart in front of him. "How do you know them?"

"I guess they have been in charge of putting together your supply boxes for years. Your previous guard—Alexi—was actually pretty adamant that they were the only ones to do it." His words convey reverence, as if knowing just how much it means to me to hear that Alexi trusted them. "When I took over the position, they made it clear that I was to only come

to them with anything you might need. They are intense, but I like them."
He chuckles lightly at the thought of them.

My eyes linger on him, the bewilderment at him being here, talking
with me and taking care of me, bubbles up until I can't help the words
that escape. "Why are you here? Why are you being so nice to me?"

A breeze from the open balcony door blows in, causing shadows cast
by the candle flames to dance on the stone walls.

"Why wouldn't I be nice to you?" he counters, looking genuinely
confused.

"Because no one besides Alexi is nice to me. He was the only one who
cared ab—" I falter, taking a breath. "Can you just please tell me why you're
here?" I'm desperate to understand the reason why this normal man wastes
his evenings with me, ones where he isn't even duty-bound to do so.

"I told you. You weren't what I was expecting," he says like it answers
the question. When I gesture for him to continue, he huffs out a laugh
and adds, "I was intrigued by you that day. You're something of a... myth
around the castle. People know you exist, but the king has done a good job
of making it sound like you've almost gone insane from grief."

Shame slams into me at his words, flattening me like a boulder let loose
from the top of a hill. I'm nothing more than a joke to him and everyone
else in the castle.

"I see," I say through gritted teeth. "You're here to report back to the
others." The anger in me feels dark this time, like a beast waking up from
hibernation. I stand up from the couch and move to the opposite side of
the tea table, away from the guard. My chest lifts and falls as my breathing
starts to pick up. This makes so much more sense. He isn't here because of
kindness or whatever other sweet emotion I thought to conjure up.

"Wait, I didn't— Fuck, I didn't mean it like that." He scrambles to get
the words out, jumping up much more swiftly than I did. Somehow this
makes me even angrier, considering he is so much bigger than I am and
was starting from the floor. He moves to take a step closer, but I counter
by stepping back, nearly moving onto the balcony.

"I think you should go. You have plenty to report back on now. What
with my inability to button my own dresses and my stupidity in not

knowing that flame gems are real. You can even tell everyone how I didn't know how to play children's games!" My eyes water as my hands fist at my sides, nails digging into my palms. I hate feeling this way, like a naive fool. I hate that the first person to give me an ounce of attention was only doing so as a *joke* and that I didn't realize until it was too late.

"Please, you don't understand. I misspoke—"

"Get. Out." The breach he had created near my heart earlier with his caring words and actions frosts back over. I can almost see it, the shadowy ice swirling around inside of me and snuffing out the normally glowing and warm magic there.

The guard opens his mouth again to speak in protest but is interrupted by a deep growl rumbling through the tower. The hairs on the back of my neck stand as I look behind him to where Bella prowls down the stairs. She rounds the final spiral and jumps over the remaining few steps, landing in a crouched position on the ground. Her canines glisten in the moonlight as she snarls at the guard, that deep rumble from her throat so dominant that I swear I feel it rattle my brain.

I do not fear her—never her—but I know it will be messy if she attacks this guard on my behalf. Slowly, I walk towards her, backing the guard up at the same time. Bella stalks around him, mirroring each of his steps with one of her own until she is facing him with me at her side.

"Holy shit, that's a huge fox," he whispers, hands raised in front of him as he freezes in place.

"She will not attack you if you leave," I snap. The guard's wide eyes bounce back and forth between Bella and I before he swallows and begins to back up. Reaching behind him blindly, he opens the door and pauses there. Bella releases another warning growl as my hand rests on the top of her head. The guard surveys Bella again before moving his gaze back over to me.

There isn't as much fear there as I expect. No, my gut says that there looks to be something like amazement in his eyes. That can't be possible, however, because he should only care enough to tell the king that I'm keeping a fox up here. If King Dolian finds out, he will *kill* Bella. Another death will be on my hands, and I will be truly alone this time. When the tears well, I let them fall onto my cheeks, the fear of losing my last friend too much to fight off. I take a step in front of Bella, trying to partially hide her as I clutch onto the fur at her neck. The guard's gaze drops down to what he can see of Bella, his brows drawing in slightly in concentration.

"My Lady, I meant no disrespect to you and I apologize. Your secret," he says as he pointedly brings his eyes back to mine, "is safe with me." With a nod, he steps back onto the landing and closes the door behind him. A chill runs through me as Bella nudges her nose against my leg. My cheeks puff with air before I blow it out, my hands shaky in front of me.

"I've never heard you make that noise before, Bells," I whisper, kneeling down to look at her. Her golden eyes stare back while I wipe the tears from my face and then wrap my arms around her neck. I breathe her in for a moment before I stand and we walk side-by-side back up to the loft.

I snuggle under the covers of my bed, the large window to my right opened to let the night air in. Bella curls into me, her head resting on my thigh. My hand lazily moves back and forth over her soft fur until her breathing grows heavy and small snores fill the silence of the tower. Maybe the caring side of the guard wasn't all an act and that means he won't actually tell the king about Bella. At least, I have the hope that he won't.

"The moon may have the stars, but at least I have you," I whisper before laying my hand flat on her back and closing my eyes.

⚜ ⚜

I awake the next morning to a familiar scraping noise at the door. When it stops, I get out of bed carefully—so as to not disturb Bella—and make my way down the stairs. The sun is just barely cresting over the horizon, the vibrant golden colors of the dawn sky just starting to peek past the midnight blues from the previous night. I retrieve the folded up paper laying on the floor.

MY LADY,

I KNOW THAT YOU DO NOT OWE ME THE CHANCE TO EXPLAIN, BUT I WOULD LIKE TO TRY TO DO SO ANYWAY. I'M SORRY FOR INSINUATING THAT I WAS MERELY VISITING YOU TO FEED SOME INNATE CURIOSITY OR TO BRING GOSSIP BACK TO THE GUARDS. THE TRUTH IS, SINCE THE MOMENT I SAW YOU (MORE APPROPRIATELY, SINCE THE MOMENT YOU STARTLED ME), I HAVE NOT BEEN ABLE TO STOP THINKING ABOUT YOU.

NOT BECAUSE YOU'RE HERE FOR MY ENTERTAINMENT OR ANYONE ELSE'S, BUT BECAUSE—AS I'VE MENTIONED BEFORE—YOU ARE NOTHING LIKE WHAT I EXPECTED, AND I'D BE LYING IF I SAID I WASN'T DYING TO KNOW MORE ABOUT YOU. SO, I OFFER A PROPOSITION: TOMORROW NIGHT I WOULD LIKE TO BRING YOU MY FAVORITE DESSERT FROM VITOUR. IF YOU ARE FEELING GENEROUS ENOUGH TO GIVE ME A SECOND CHANCE, PLACE A NOTE OUTSIDE YOUR DOOR AFTER THE SUN SETS TONIGHT.

PLEASE KNOW THAT I HOLD YOU TO NO OBLIGATION. MY APOLOGY STANDS NO MATTER WHAT YOU DECIDE.

SINCERELY,

FLYNN

Flynn. The guard's name is Flynn. I reread the note an embarrassing number of times before folding it back up and walking to the couch to take a seat, laying the note down in my lap. Is it insane of me to actually think this guard is interested in getting to know me? Or am I falling prey to someone who will take advantage of me the first opportunity that he gets? Am I so hopelessly desperate for a friend that I'm willing to risk everything with a King's Guardsman whose only known attribute is that he's been *nice* to me? My knees draw up on the couch as I hug them to my chest, indecision warring inside me. Then again, his knowledge as a guard could be invaluable to helping me escape. The blood oath prevents him from helping outright, but what if I can get information from him somehow? Maybe pretending to be his friend will be enough to get him to unknowingly help me or give me an opening to do it on my own.

I spend most of the day wondering about what I should do and if I should respond. When the sun starts to set in the sky, I grab a small pot of ink and a quill and set them on the tea table—sitting cross-legged on the floor next to it. I also grab extra paper, as it has been a while since I've written anything and I'm sure I need to practice. My first few attempts are sloppy at best, but eventually, my writing is neat enough to start. Just as the sun is crossing the horizon, with a candle lit next to me for extra light, I write my letter to Flynn.

Dear Flynn,

I accept your offering of treats as well as your apology. Also, I am not your Lady.

Cordially,

Rhea

Chapter Twenty-One

RHEA

C ANDLES ARE LIT ALL around the lower level of the tower the next night as I wait to hear the knocks on the door from the guard. He had dropped a note off this morning claiming he was happy I accepted his groveling and to expect him this evening. Since he already knows about Bella, I don't make her move from her spot on the floor next to the couch. Her head is propped up on her crossed front paws, taking away from the vicious image she had portrayed the last time Flynn was here.

"We need to be nice to him when he comes over. Okay, Bella?" She opens one eye to look at me, the act making me smile. "He might be the key to our escape," I confess in a hushed voice, like I'm worried my secrets will be carried on the wind directly into the king's ear. I'm not taking chances either way.

My nervous energy has me pacing back and forth, the old wood floors creaking with my steps. Anticipation at what I plan to do eats at me. I'm doing what I have to in order to escape, something I know Alexi would be proud of me for. I also remind myself that earning the guard's trust enough to get him talking about where other guards are stationed and their shifts around the tower, as well as the king's schedule, might take time.

There is a part of me that mourns the opportunity to have a real friend for the first time in my life. Though maybe I can still get practice with talking to others and building my social skills, even if it *is* under false pretenses with Flynn. I clear my throat, thinking about how odd it is to refer to him by something other than "the guard."

His knocks on the door pull me from my thoughts as my heart unceremoniously kicks up its beats. Blowing out a breath, I roll my shoulders back and plaster on the best semblance of a smile I can, while knowing on the inside that I am pretending. No, that I am *lying*. And while something small inside of me dies a little at that admission, it's not enough to stop me from doing what I need to.

Pulling the door open, I'm first hit with his scent. That unique crisp aroma that somehow smells like fallen leaves. It knocks me off balance, and just as I'm about to pull myself together again, the door opens the rest of the way. The composure that I worked so hard to craft starts cracking when his face comes into the light, a grin stretching his full lips. His dark eyes gleam with the reflection of the firelight from the torch in the hallway. He lifts a cocky brow as if he somehow knows he's thrown me off course. Both of his hands are behind his back, and I have an indescribable urge to reach around and grab them to see what he's hiding. *Focus.*

"Hello, Rhea," he says, and my body shivers in response. My name on his lips shouldn't be an experience that leaves my knees weak. If he notices my reaction, he doesn't show it. "Can I come in?" he requests, his deep voice like dark chocolate melting on my tongue.

Gulping faintly, I step out of the way and open the door wider. Flynn's impressive frame crosses through the doorway, and he immediately looks to Bella, his movements slowing until he's standing a few feet away from her. "She won't bite you," I declare, closing the door. "Unless she thinks you are a threat, of course," I tack on as I move to stand next to him.

"A threat to you or to her?"

"Both," I clarify with a grin that is a bit more real than I mean it to be. Clearing my throat, I motion to where he still holds his hands behind his back. "I was told that there would be treats for me as part of your groveling."

He laughs at my boldness but moves to set two small white bags down on the table. His large hands then start unbuckling the leather straps at his side that hold the chest and back pieces of his armor. He is actually wearing it today.

"What are you doing?" I ask slowly, eyeing his motions like he's planning to strip everything off in front of me. *Would that be so awful?* The shift in my thoughts momentarily shocks me before I shake my head, as if to dissipate an imaginary fog.

He pauses, looking over at me with a wry smile. "Would it bother you if I took this armor off? It's just incredibly uncomfortable and limits my movements."

"Are you expecting to need your full range of motion while you are here, Flynn?" I ask in amusement. He stills as soon as his name is past my lips, his eyes fluttering shut for a split second before he's back to unbuckling his armor again. The moment was so quick that I briefly wonder if I imagined it. *Did I say something wrong?*

When he gets the three straps on his other side undone, he lifts the golden armor over his head and leans it up against the stone wall. Next, he unstraps his sword and lays it beside his armor. Even without the bulkiness of that little bit of armor, he still fills the room how I imagine a warrior would from the books I've read. The black tunic he wears does nothing to hide his muscular physique. I quickly draw my eyes away as he turns to walk to the couch and takes a seat like it's the most natural place in the world for him to be. Meanwhile, I stay standing where I am, a bit dumbfounded as I watch him pull the bags on the table closer. He starts unraveling the rolled paper material of one until it's open.

"I brought something for your fox? Is it okay for me to give it to her?"

"You brought something for Bella?" I stupidly repeat.

His eyes crinkle as his laugh weaves into the darkness between us. "I did. I hope that is okay?" At that Bella perks her ears up and lifts her head. Her snout starts making sniffing noises before she stands up fully and walks cautiously towards him. "Can she understand what we're saying?" he asks with a curious look.

I'm still standing like an idiot with my mouth open, hands on my hips, as I surmise that I've lost control of the situation. I'm not sure I ever had it to begin with. Without waiting for me to answer, Flynn takes out a small cookie from the bag and holds it out to Bella in his massive palm.

"It's a cookie made with ingredients safe for animals. The bakery mostly caters to domesticated dogs and cats, but there should be no reason that your fox—Bella—can't have one." I watch as Bella waits all of two seconds before she takes the treat from his hand with her mouth. Her tail wags joyfully as she chews. This isn't exactly what I had in mind when I told her to be nice to him. "I think she likes it," he grins, reaching out to scratch under her chin. I expect her to back away or move her head out of his grasp, but the fox instead leans into his touch.

"Are you freaking kidding me?" I grumble under my breath as he pulls out another cookie. When she's finished all of the ones in the bag, she contentedly lays on the ground near his side of the couch. My eyes narrow at her, and I mouth the word "traitor" as she watches me walk over to take a seat on the couch. She huffs a breath and then lays her head down, apparently not caring for my theatrics and ready for a nap now that her belly is full. "So this was your plan," I say as I take a seat a few feet away from him, "to feed my fox treats so she would like you? Then when you inevitably do something to upset me again, she won't attack you?"

Flynn barks out a laugh, pulling the other bag closer on the white table. "More or less," he responds, smiling proudly and then adding, "though I'm hoping not to make you upset in the first place."

I can see the truth of his words when his eyes meet mine, the glowing sincerity in them playing with an unfair advantage in what is supposed to be *my* game of pretend. He laughs again as I groan; he likely finds the exasperation in it funny, while I'm just trying to regain my equilibrium around him.

"Have you ever had a triple-chocolate brownie?" He pulls out a rectangular dessert from the bag and hands it to me. I try to ignore the way my skin tingles with awareness when our fingers brush.

"I haven't," I reply, holding the treat up close to my face as I eye it. Chocolate chunks in three different colors are layered throughout, the candlelight surrounding us making them all glisten.

"These aren't quite as good as the ones back home, but they are a pretty close second," he says before taking half his brownie with one bite. From the corner of my eye, I find myself briefly watching his tan jaw work as he chews before hastily turning my attention back to my own brownie. Taking a small bite, I nearly gasp as the brownie begins to melt in my mouth. Flynn laughs, leaning forward to rest his elbows on his knees. "That is the smallest bite I have ever seen someone take out of one of these," he says jovially, and his delight is nearly enough to bring a smile to my own face. "What do you think?" he inquires after a few moments.

I hum, closing my eyes as I continue chewing, slowly savoring each and every flavor that plays on my tongue. It's so decadent and rich that I'm not sure I'll taste anything as good ever again. When I'm finished with my bite, I have to restrain myself from taking another before I answer him. "It's unlike anything I've ever had before. It might be even better than lemon loaf, and I really thought nothing could top that."

He beams at me, somehow looking even more defined and handsome under the flickering gleam of the candles. A ridiculous part of me suddenly wishes I could spend my days just studying his face. I imagine I wouldn't ever find a single flaw. *But that is not what my future holds.* Cold realization brings me back to the present moment and my end goal. I need to befriend this guard only so that I can get any information he might have that could help me escape, nothing more. I set the brownie down, knowing I will get completely lost in its chocolatey goodness and abandon everything else if I continue indulging.

"You said these aren't as good as the ones back home. Where is home for you?" I query.

He turns and looks at me from where he is leaning forward, tossing the second half of the brownie into his mouth. He chews so incredibly slow that, for a moment, I wonder if I've upset him with my question. If asking this was a social faux pas somehow. When he finishes his bite, his tongue darts out slightly to lick away any chocolate at the seam of his lips. I track the movement, fighting the urge to mimic it with my own tongue. My eyes move slowly back up to his, and I nearly gasp at what I see reflected in his gaze. He's looking at me how the characters in my romance novels describe their lovers' gazes before passion consumes them. His irises are like liquid slate, threatening to devour me wholly from the intensity in them. Shadows from the candlelight writhe on the walls as a thick and heady tension between us keeps building.

Seconds or hours pass—I'm not entirely sure which—before he responds, the deep rasp in his voice igniting a new flame within me. "How about a question for a question?" he counters.

My lips purse together, wondering if it's smart to agree to answer anything he might ask. In the end though, my curiosity can't deny him. "Deal. Answer me first," I command, giving him what is supposed to be a hard look.

He smiles, like I've just given him an amazing compliment instead of an order. That's one thing I've noticed about Flynn—he is never bothered by me in any way. I'm sometimes short in my answers, sometimes awkward, but each time he just looks at me like it's normal. Like he's totally unaffected by the fact that he's talking with a girl who can literally count on one hand the men she's had any length of conversation with. The butterflies that never disappear when I'm around him respond in kind.

"Home for me is east, out near the edges of the forest." He looks towards the library as he answers.

I hear longing in his voice, and I wonder if he must be from one of those outpost border towns I had read about. "Do you get to go home often?" I ask.

He leans back against the couch, crossing an ankle over his knee with the kind of confidence that definitely makes that flame inside me grow larger. "That is two questions, Sunshine. Time to answer one of mine." The nickname rolls off of his tongue way too easily, and I don't know if I absolutely love or loathe it.

"Sunshine?" I repeat, an eyebrow raised as I subtly angle my body closer to his without a second thought.

"Yes. Now answer my question." He fights back a smile when I scoff at him. He stretches an arm out along the back of the couch and taps his long fingers there. "You said before that you hadn't stepped past the doorway. Did you mean that it has been awhile? Or did you mean *ever*?"

Of all the things I was expecting him to ask, that was definitely not one of them. The air feels thinner, like I can't quite grasp it enough to take a breath. He watches my reaction, probably wondering why I'm stalling. In truth, I'm calculating the risk of telling him. After a moment, I determine there really isn't anything he can gain from knowing that I haven't left this prison at all. "I have never left this tower," I reveal quietly, shrugging and dropping my gaze to my hands in my lap.

"Ever?" he asks incredulously.

I nod, taking a breath before continuing, "Alexi told me that after my parents were murdered, my uncle placed me in this tower under the guise of protection. That the people who murdered them—mages, he claims—had come for me as well." Flynn lets out an irritated noise, drawing my attention. He clears his throat, looking somewhat surprised at himself, before he gestures for me to continue. "Of course, you already know what he's told the kingdom as I've gotten older. But I have never left. When he visits—" I cut myself off there, realizing the guard—Flynn—doesn't need to know *those* details. "When I was a child, I had maids taking care of me here, but eventually the king ordered them to stop coming. Alexi stepped in when he saw that the king wasn't giving me an education or really any of the basic necessities beyond keeping me alive. Once I became an adult, he kept coming because I was so lonely." This feels much harder to talk about than I ever thought it would, though I suppose this is the first time I've ever talked about it *at all* with someone else.

"Did King Dolian ever wonder how you learned to do all of the things Alexi taught you?" Flynn asks gently.

"No, he hasn't exactly spent time getting to know me. He mostly— It's not important," I choke out quickly. I dare another look at Flynn to see if I can gauge what he's feeling.

Disbelief. Pure disbelief contorts the features of his face. His muscles are wound tight as he holds himself still, like he wants to jump off of this couch and hold someone responsible for what I've just said. "That's why he was leaving his post," he murmurs under his breath, avoiding my eyes. I study his profile, seeing something flash too quickly in his expression for me to comprehend.

"That was three questions from you by the way. You are now in my debt," I tease, smirking as I look him over.

Flynn smiles and runs a hand through his hair, pushing the locks back and holding them there for a moment before dropping his hand and letting the waves tumble back forward. "Eager to know more about me, Sunshine?" he provokes with a cocky grin.

"Perhaps I'm just trying to gauge whether or not I should still have Bella attack you?" His laugh is sultry, not at all threatened by my words. It could have something to do with the fact that Bella is happily sleeping at his feet. "And that is *another* question that you've added to your debt."

"Ruthless," he chides, though he looks transfixed as he watches me chew on my lower lip. I run through a list of things I *should* ask him, yet there is only one thing I really want to know at this moment, and imprudently, it has nothing to do with my escape.

"Did you ever talk with Alexi?" I ask quietly, a sharp hurt digging into my stomach. When Flynn doesn't respond, I wonder if that was a stupid question. It definitely was a heavier one than I think he was expecting.

"I didn't talk with him." His answer is solemn when he turns to face me fully on the couch. "Before he—before *I* came into this new position," he starts carefully, "I was stationed on guard duty near the front of the castle. My job was to walk the grounds out front during the day. Alexi was stationed here, so our paths just never crossed." I nod my head, settling back down in my seat and angling my body to face him. "But there was one time that I saw him get into a fight with someone."

My eyes widen in surprise. "What? Really?"

"Yeah," he answers, huffing out a laugh before continuing. "I was eating breakfast in the mess hall. It was my first year in the guard. I didn't hear the words said, but something set Alexi off."

I shake my head in awe. Alexi was always level-headed and calm with me. Nothing ever seemed to get a rise out of him. I know I had thrown many tantrums that ended in me giving up because he would just stare at me, unmoving in his resolve. "What happened?" I ask, my fingers absent-mindedly finding the ends of my hair and twirling them.

Flynn smiles faintly, looking down at his legs for a moment as he relives the memory. "He just started swinging, connecting every shot he aimed for this guy. Over and over until, finally, a few of the younger guys pulled him off. After he assured the guys holding him back that he was calm, Alexi walked over to the guard he was fighting and squatted down to him." I tilt towards Flynn, anxious to glean something new about Alexi—wanting to know what he was like outside of this tower. "He leaned in close to the other guard, but didn't lower his voice. It was like he was broadcasting it for everyone to hear. Alexi told him that if he ever heard anything as vile about 'her' again, he would make sure the man was no longer fit to work as a guard. I wonder if he was talking about you." His eyes hold mine, something new and fragile feels built between us—a bridge, perhaps, of understanding.

Tucking my hair behind my ear, I say, "He could have been talking about Alanna, his wife. She passed away in an accident many years ago."

Flynn nods, rubbing a hand over his jaw. To learn something unexpected about Alexi—even something so trivial, it loosens something in me. It's like letting a different sort of comfort slip through the tiny cracks in my armor, smoothing along their jagged edges.

"Alexi is the one who brought Bella to me," I confide as I lean my shoulder back against the couch and fully face Flynn. His arms fold over his chest as he adjusts so that he faces me as well. We mirror each other—our knees just delicately brushing. "I was seventeen, and he just walked in with her one night," I say, smiling vaguely at the memory. "He said he found her hiding in the flowers near the tower and that he just had a feeling that she was different. She's always been very keen—very aware. You would assume a wild animal would suffocate in this tower, but she doesn't mind it much now." I look at her sleeping form next to Flynn's boots, memories of that first night together a welcome reprieve.

"Now? Was it hard for her at first?" he asks.

"She would lay around most of the day like she was sick almost. I felt guilty." I pause as the happy memories melt away and are replaced with one of the night that I had made her leave the tower. "I still do. She deserves better than being trapped here with me," I whisper before wincing, not meaning to speak those words out loud. They feel too personal, too close to letting this stranger in. I can feel my small smile turn into a frown, the rare moment of genuine happiness fading. Flynn bumps his knee into mine playfully, drawing my gaze back up to his and stopping my emotional spiral into the darkness in its tracks.

"Do you want to talk more about him?" he inquires softly. But this already feels more personal than I ever intended this night to go.

"Maybe another time," I respond quietly. He nods as a different sort of tension thickens the air. It's not fully uncomfortable but instead a mutual understanding that sometimes things are too complicated to talk about. Even if, deep down, we have the desire to do so.

"I know I'm in your debt question-wise then, but I do have one that I need to know the answer to desperately."

"Okay," I respond slowly, watching him. He pinches his lips together like he is fighting off a smile, and a small part of me dislikes that because his smile is like a beacon. I can't help but be drawn to it, to indulge in it.

"Where does Bella go to the bathroom?"

"What?" I screech, rearing my head back.

He laughs as a true smile breaks across his face. And despite still feeling buried under the rubble of everything that has happened, starting with Alexi's death, I smile a little too. His eyes immediately dart to my mouth, his own grin faltering for a moment before he looks back up to me. Magnets—it truly is like magnets how often I find myself wanting to get lost in the dark depths of his gaze. I am not sure what that says about me, or if this is a normal reaction, because I have never felt this way before. While Alexi's presence was paternal and kind, Flynn's is so much *more*. And as each layer of protection that I have placed around my heart starts to crack and shift at his nearness, I realize that he makes me feel a multitude of things. He gently bumps my knee again with his, and I remember I still haven't answered him.

"She's trained to use the toilet," I say, nonchalantly lifting a shoulder. Flynn's eyes grow wide before he looks at Bella.

"Truly? That's incredible!" he exclaims, an almost childlike wonder crossing his handsome features.

I study his profile and the way the candlelight dances on each plane of his face. In the depths of my mind, I wonder what it would be like to drag my fingers over the smooth skin there. And then I shake my head at that thought because it's so far-fetched. Not to mention forbidden. Completely and utterly forbidden.

He studies Bella for a minute longer before he sighs. "I should go," he states, standing up and walking over to where his armor is.

I watch as he buckles the cuirass in place and secures his sheathed golden sword back around his waist. The metal gleams in the dancing firelight as I join him, the two of us walking beside each other to the door. He opens it and steps across the threshold, turning to face me.

"So, was my groveling enough?" he asks in a low voice, a teasing expression pulling on his brows and mouth. My heart skips a beat at his words and my perceived intention behind them. I must be misinterpreting something, but that look in his eye— Clearing my throat, I paste on a look of indifference that I definitely don't feel.

"I suppose if Bella is happy with your apology, then I am as well," I answer, gesturing towards her. We both look into the living area to find Bella sleeping peacefully on the floor.

"Then I will consider this a successful night. Goodnight, Sunshine."

"I don't know if I like that nickname," I retort, watching as he walks to the stairs. He laughs, the sound tickling my ears until a grin of my own breaks free.

When I can't hear his steps anymore, I close the door and take a moment to just stand there. I inhale a true deep breath for the first time in *weeks*. My mind whirls with indecision now on my plan to use Flynn for information, especially after how easily that excuse crumbled when he was near. The only thing I know for certain at this moment is that he will either be my downfall or my salvation.

Chapter Twenty-Two

RHEA

"LITTLE ONE, YOU MUST focus," he said as he placed the piece of paper back in front of me. He had written out math equations, and they might as well have been an ancient language. I couldn't focus enough to begin to solve them. Plus, even with the candles lit around the table, it was still so dark, and my attention kept drifting to the wiggling flames and the shadows they made.

"Why do I have to do this?" I pouted, throwing down the quill and slumping back against the couch. My head hurt, and I didn't want to try anymore. I just wanted to go sit by the window and wait for the lanterns to float in the sky.

"Because it's important," he responded, taking a seat next to me and pointing to the paper. "Knowing basic math is helpful for understanding the world around you."

I scoffed, looking at him from the corner of my eye. "Yes, very helpful from my tower to know how to do multiplication. For counting spider webs and dust bunnies," I snarked and turned away.

I begged Alexi to take me down to the grass and the water just for a moment—just so I could feel them. But he said his blood oath to my uncle prevented him from doing so. He said that the cost would be his life, and the scar on his palm told me he wasn't lying. Not that I ever thought he was. Alexi had been in my life for years now, and I never once believed him to be a liar. I only wished that there was a way to work around the oath so that I could leave for merely five minutes. I just wanted to step in the grass and drag my fingers across the wildflowers in the meadows surrounding the tower. Maybe dip my toes in the water.

I had asked my uncle why I couldn't leave, and he just told me it was dangerous because the people that had killed my parents—and had tried to kill me—were still out there. He didn't like it when I questioned him about my parents though. Often it resulted in him getting angry with me. He was scary when he got that mad.

"Rhea." Alexi's voice snapped me back to the present. The sun had just set, and the Summer Solstice celebration was about to begin. I wanted to go desperately, but as usual, I would be stuck watching from the tower. Well, that is if Alexi would let me skip doing this math stuff. "It's important," he said again, picking up the quill.

I groaned and threw my hands up in the air as I yelled, "Is it though? I don't need to know this. I can't even leave. You say it's to help me understand the world around me, but I understand it well enough. It's confined to the stones of this tower!" I waited for him to yell back, to get frustrated, as the king did. But his face just softened.

He dropped the quill on the tea table and stood. "Okay, that's enough for tonight. Let's go wait for the lanterns."

Squealing, I followed him to the library, bouncing on the balls of my feet in excitement. He sat down on the bench, opening the window enough to let the fragrant summer air in. The full moon shone, and twinkling stars surrounded and waved their hello to me. Finally, the first tiny lantern dotted the sky over Vitour. Then another, and another, until the sky was full of them. They glowed like golden dots speckled against the pitch black. The silver light cast by the true stars above the lanterns completely transformed the sky, like another world had temporarily let us borrow their night. Lanterns were also released from the gardens near the front of the castle. From this angle, I could only see a few of them as they floated up higher and higher.

"I have a birthday gift for you." Alexi's words drew my attention from the window.

"Is it lemon loaf?" I asked, clapping my hands in anticipation.

Alexi shook his head and pulled a small black bag out of his pocket. He extended his palm out to me, a minuscule smile on his face. "Go ahead and open it."

I gently picked it up and untied the strings, the fabric velvety beneath my fingertips. I felt the cool bite of metal as I reached my finger and thumb in and pulled out what looked like a bracelet. It was gold and dainty with intricate flower designs on the band.

"What is this?" I breathed, holding it up into the moonlight so I could see it better. I had only ever seen the king's rings or the necklaces and bracelets drawn in books, but this was better than them all. It was the most beautiful piece of jewelry I had ever held.

"A special gift for a special girl," he responded as he removed the bracelet from my hand and clasped it reverently around my wrist. I held my arm out in front of me, marveling at the delicate chain and how it looked against my skin. "Happy thirteenth birthday, Rhea."

I looked up at him and smiled widely before looking back down at the bracelet, tracing over it repeatedly with my fingers.

The memory fades away as I hold the bracelet up in front of me. I am too nervous to wear it in case the king stops by and demands to know where I got it. So I keep it in its little pouch, hidden in the drawer of my white vanity. I slept heavily last night, unbothered by nightmares or strange dreams. And though the memory of Alexi gifting me what—I would later find out—was Alanna's bracelet makes me yearn to see him again, I don't have that same gut-wrenching anguish that I had before. I am still sad, still miss him terribly, but I am also... happy to reminisce. I set the bracelet back in its pouch and tuck it into the drawer. I finish brushing my hair before tying it back with a ribbon and standing from the vanity.

After a morning spent cleaning, I have the urge to move my body and exercise. My magic wiggles inside of me, the warmth of it actually more dominant than that bone-deep cold today. Pushing the tea table out of the center of the room, I sit on the floor, closing my eyes and imagining a golden ray of light pouring from the heavens and landing on the crown of my head. I pretend the light spills down my body from my head, dripping onto my shoulders and hips and toes. I relax each muscle as the light hits it, warmth curling inside me as my mind begins to quiet. It is a different sort of silence than what I have been forcing it to be. This feels like pure stillness, like calm. It feels like an undisturbed lake underneath a sunny sky. It is warm and caressing and *light*. And without guilt, for the first time in a long time, I let myself relax in its softness. In the way my mind doesn't feel like a battlefield and how my heart has nearly gotten rid of all the shields I have been placing around it. Those things are still there—still tucked into the depths of me—but now there is space around them, enough for light to shine through. Like sunlight piercing a small hole in a dark cave.

As a teen, I thought these mind cleansing exercises were boring and often grumbled about it to Alexi, but now I understand their importance. They are meditative, like the kinds of practices I have read of mages doing in the Mage Kingdom. I take another breath, filling my lungs deeply, before I slowly release it and open my eyes. Coming up to stand, I work my body until sweat drips and fatigue sets in. I miss Alexi terribly, and a part of me still wonders if I should have defied his wishes and just saved him anyway. If I should have tried harder.

The boxes I have shoved all of those dark feelings and emotions into begin to rattle, as if to shout, *we're still here, and you can't ignore us forever.* I know that—of course I do—but for now, I enjoy the peaceful space between them.

The next ten days pass by with only letters from Flynn. He claims to have some sort of training or guard duties, and that is why he can't stop by. But every morning, I wake up to a letter, which usually consists of him explaining what boring thing he isn't excited to do that day followed by a question or two for me. And every evening, I leave one for him, laying outside on the landing in front of my door.

SUNSHINE,

TODAY, WE HAVE TO DO A MANDATORY TRAINING ON HOW TO FIGHT WITH OUR SWORDS, AS IF WE DON'T ALREADY PRACTICE THAT DAILY—OR AT LEAST I DO. IT'S BORING AS HELL. WHAT IS YOUR FAVORITE FLOWER? DO YOU LIKE TO DANCE?

SINCERELY,

AN ALREADY STRAPPINGLY STRONG GUARD WHO KNOWS HOW TO USE HIS SWORD

Flynn,

Why am I not surprised that you are well-versed in swordplay? Something about that just makes sense. At least you get to be bored outside, surrounded by other people. My favorite flowers are drangyeas; they were the first ones I was ever given. I don't know if I like to dance. I've never tried. I think with the right partner, I might. What is your favorite food? Favorite color?

Sincerely,

Rhea

SUNSHINE,

TODAY, A GROUP OF GUARDS IS BEING SENT OUT BY THE KING TO A SMALL CITY NEAR THE MAGE BORDER. THE CRUEL DEATH HAS HIT QUITE HARD THERE, AND THEY ARE TO SEE IF THEY CAN FIGURE OUT A REASON WHY. I'LL HAVE TO HELP COVER GUARD DUTIES WHILE THEY ARE GONE ONCE I LEAVE MY SHIFT AT THE TOWER. APPARENTLY, I WAS RECOMMENDED TO DO SO BY MY COMMANDER. LUCKY ME.

I MAY HAVE BEEN SURROUNDED BY PEOPLE, BUT DOES IT HELP TO KNOW THAT THEY ALL SMELLED TERRIBLE? FROM THE AFOREMENTIONED SWORD PRACTICE.

ANYWAY, MY FAVORITE FOOD IS PROBABLY ROASTED CHICKEN. IS THAT BORING? IT SEEMS BORING, BUT IT'S TRUE. MY FAVORITE COLOR IS A SPECIFIC SHADE OF GREEN. WHAT IS YOUR FAVORITE COLOR? HOW IS BELLA?

SINCERELY,

FLYNN

P.S. DON'T THINK I'M LETTING YOUR SWORD JOKE GO UNNOTICED. I'M STILL TRYING TO CATCH MY BREATH FROM IT.

Dearest Boring Flynn,

Yes, chicken is quite boring. Though I've never had it roasted before, so maybe it is good enough to be your favorite food? Mine is undoubtedly a sweet—lemon loaf. Alexi used to sneak me in pieces whenever the castle baker made it. I would have thought your favorite color is black, given it's all that you like to wear. My favorite color is purple. Bella is perfect; in fact, she is sleeping next to me while I write this.

I wonder what the king is hoping to truly accomplish by sending those guards there, as the Cruel Death doesn't answer to him. I hope they stay safe on their journey. The Cruel Death doesn't discriminate, does it? I'm sorry you have to cover in their absence, you must be exhausted. I'll be here, reading another book and trying not to go insane. What is your favorite season?

Sincerely,

Rhea—not Sunshine

P.S. I was merely stating the truth, at least from my point of view.

SUNSHINE,

THE GUARDS HAVE COME BACK AND ARE REPORTING THAT—AS YOU MENTIONED IN YOUR LAST LETTER—THE CRUEL DEATH DOESN'T DISCRIMINATE, AND UNFORTU-NATELY, THIS WAS EVIDENT IN THE VILLAGE. TODAY, I AM LEADING SOME OF THE APPRENTICE GUARDS THROUGH SOME RUNNING DRILLS. IT IS—AND I CANNOT EM-PHASIZE THIS ENOUGH—ABSOLUTELY AWFUL. I WILL SWING A SWORD ALL DAY, BUT I *DESPISE* RUNNING.

IT'S A TRUE TRAVESTY THAT YOU'VE NEVER HAD ROASTED CHICKEN. I'M AFRAID MY WARDROBE IS PROBABLY AS BORING AS MY FAVORITE FOOD CHOICE. LEMON LOAF IS VERY FITTING FOR YOU THOUGH. SOMETHING BRIGHT AND SWEET, AND PERHAPS A LITTLE TART AS WELL (IT'S A JOKE BUT ALSO, IS IT?).

MY FAVORITE SEASON... I DON'T THINK I'VE EVER BEEN ASKED THAT BEFORE, BUT I'M GOING TO SAY SUMMER. MY TAN GETS DARKER IN THE SUMMER, AND IT REALLY ACCENTUATES MY HANDSOME FEATURES.

WHAT IS YOURS? IF YOU COULD CHOOSE TO LIVE IN A DIFFERENT KINGDOM, WHICH ONE WOULD YOU CHOOSE?

SINCERELY,

A PROBABLY-THROWING-UP FLYNN FROM BEING FORCED TO RUN ALL DAY TODAY

Dear Sick Flynn,

Another sword reference? You're getting predictable. You're also so very humble; it's almost as if you are acutely aware of how you look. My favorite season is autumn. I love watching the trees turn colors, and there is this fragrance in the air that time of year—it's totally unique. I would, without a doubt, choose the Fae Kingdom. They have dragons, and I have always dreamed of riding one someday. What about you?

Sincerely,

Sunsh— Nope, I can't do it.

Rhea

P.S. These letters have been the highlight of my week, so thank you for indulging me.

Sighing, I set my note outside the door. Then, I light a taper candle and place it in the bronze holder, protecting the flame with my hand as I walk into the library. Sitting on the velvet-cushioned bench by the window, I grab the current book I'm reading, the one given to me by Tienne and Erica, and settle in, letting my eyes grow heavy as I imagine myself between the pages of the book.

"Little One, wake up." His hand shakes my shoulder as I startle awake.

"Alexi?" I ask, pushing the covers aside and looking up at him from where he stands next to bed. He looks exactly as he always did—his salt and pepper hair neatly trimmed, closer on the sides and a little longer on top. His golden armor is clean and shiny over his dark black tunic, trousers, and boots.

"We have to go, now," he says, reaching out a hand to help me up. Confused, I place my hand in his—it's ice cold. Panic blooms as he starts to pull me down the stairs and I nearly stumble from how quickly he is moving.

"Alexi, wait! What is happening?" I ask, tugging on his hand to stop him once we reach the bottom. I look around the living area of my tower, trying to figure out what feels off about it.

"Do you not want to leave this place?" he challenges, gripping my hand more firmly.

"Of course I do, but I don't understand what is happening. You can't help me because of the blood oath." My mouth parts slightly as I look around us again. "Where is Bella?" Alexi turns to me, his eyes filled with sorrow.

"Do you not remember what happened?" he questions, gesturing towards me as if I'm the culprit in her disappearance.

"What are you talking about?"

"You killed her," he intones in a hollow voice, his hand squeezing even harder. Shaking my head, I step back from him—something is not right. "You killed her, and then you killed me. And soon, you will kill him."

I tremble, trying to work my hand free from his—pulling and yanking—but it is to no avail. He grips tighter, the feeling of my bones nearly crumbling propelling my panic even further.

"Don't you see it? Don't you feel it growing within you?" He tugs me closer to him, my chest crashing into his as he nearly lifts me off my feet.

"Alexi, let me go!" I scream and flail, terror making my movements wild and uncoordinated. He finally lets me fall to the ground, dust kicking up from underneath me as I realize we aren't in the tower but somewhere else.

"I will never let you go," he says, voice morphing into something vile. The pupils of his eyes widen as they eventually take over the irises and then the whites as well. The darkness drips onto his cheeks, like how I've read sap seeps from tree bark. It slowly morphs Alexi's face until it turns into his.

"You are mine, Rhea," he growls, prowling to me as I try to scramble away. "You are mine," he repeats, his voice surrounding me from every side. "You are mine. Forever." His words pierce me as I sob and scream and claw the ground, trying to get away from him. I feel a hand on my ankle as he pulls me deeper into the darkness. The words chant around me and through me, and all I can do is scream and scream and—

My eyes snap open, a scream still echoing in the tower. I bring my hands to my face and feel the wetness there as I gasp for air. Bella whines next to me, her golden eyes glowing in the light of the moon.

Nightmare. It was just a nightmare. He isn't here. My heart beats so hard and fast in my chest that it's nearly painful. My hand rests on my sternum as my breath rushes in and out. Laying back down on my pillow, I stare at the ceiling above me, too afraid to fall back asleep as I wait for the sun to rise.

When the first golden rays peek past the horizon, I get out of bed and run a bath. I take my time scrubbing my hair and body, then drain the tub and dry off. Every time I close my eyes, the nightmare still plays in my mind—Alexi's eyes dripping black and then him morphing into the king, something I can't believe my brain would ever conjure up.

I stretch my arms overhead as I walk down the stairs, my long hair dripping water behind me as I go. I beam when I see the paper on the floor in front of my door. Practically running over, I unfold it quickly and read it.

SUNSHINE,

I HAVE A PROPOSITION FOR YOU. TOMORROW IS SUPPOSED TO BE A DAY OFF FOR ME, BUT I WAS THINKING WE COULD SPEND IT TOGETHER? I'M VERY CURIOUS TO SEE WHAT BOOKS ARE TUCKED INTO THAT LIBRARY AND WHICH ARE YOUR FAVORITES TO READ.

WHAT DO YOU SAY? LEAVE A NOTE JUST AFTER SUNSET IF THAT WOULD BE ALRIGHT. I'M NOT ABOVE BRIBING YOU WITH CHOCOLATE AS WELL.

SINCERELY,

FLYNN

P.S. YOUR LETTERS WERE THE HIGHLIGHT OF MY WEEK, AS WELL.

The butterflies in my stomach go wild as I read and reread the letter. He wants to spend a whole day with me? Here? My eyes lift to look at the tower around me, and the cold gray stones that line every wall make me want to scream. The old, worn-in wood floors tell the tale of not just my confinement here, but also the story of when this space was a watch tower and a guard's quarters.

There's something that feels so different about him seeing this place during the day versus in the shadows of the night, as if there is nowhere I can hide—even though I'm not sure I want to conceal anything. Flynn knows me better than anyone else alive, and that's after barely a few weeks of interacting with each other. While that thought is somewhat depressing, maybe it isn't the worst thing in the world to let him in. It's not like we can be anything more than passing acquaintances anyway—he is a guard with a blood oath to a monstrous king, and I am a princess secretly planning to escape my captivity in this tower. Somehow. But I suppose that doesn't mean that I can't at least enjoy his company until it's inevitably time for me to go.

I grab everything that I need to write my response to his letter and sit on the floor by the tea table. I keep it simple and agree to his bribery of chocolate for a day spent together. When the sun sets, I place the note outside the door, smiling as I do so.

Chapter Twenty-Three

BAHIRA

"I CAN'T BELIEVE WE are even having this conversation, Bahira Rose Daxel." I wince a little at the use of my full name by my father as he stares at me with frustration. He's dressed more casually today, a loose black tunic barely half tucked into dark blue breeches with black boots. The colors are reminiscent of what one would wear to a funeral. Shit, maybe it's *my* funeral.

"Father, I was defending my honor. He was spreading lies about me," I argue defensively.

Though it has been a week since my *encounter* with Gosston, word traveled pretty quickly and eventually made its way to my father. He has been so busy with the council lately that I was hoping he wouldn't have heard. I was wrong. Apparently, Gosston's father is furious that a member of the royal family "attacked" his son. He's been hounding the council and my father nearly every day since. My father sighs, tilting his head up to the sky like he's dealing with a petulant child.

"Why are you upset with me? I thought you would be proud that I stood up for myself." Sitting on the edge of my bed, I can't help but feel small under the scrutiny of my father's stare.

"Bahi, you know that I am. But things are chaotic within the kingdom right now. You were at the council meeting," he says, taking a seat next to me on the bed. "You saw how scared these men are. They feel a shift—we all do. Something unknown is lurking in the next realm over, and we are all on edge just waiting to see what it is."

"Have you heard from Nox?" I ask, turning to look at him. He simply shakes his head, his thumb tapping away on his knee. "And what about you, are you scared?" My father is the type of man that is secure enough to recognize his feelings and emotions and speak about them openly. He knows I ask the question out of pure curiosity, not of judgment.

Looking out into my room, he takes his time answering as he gathers his thoughts. "Yes and no. I worry about what your brother will find and how he will manage to get it back to this kingdom, if it truly is something that could be used to attack. I worry about our people and whatever is causing our magic to weaken. While we have trained warriors, the heart of our defense comes from that magic and the density of the forest around us." He turns his gaze to me, the truth of his fear reflecting in his eyes. "And if Nox is correct on the size of their army, then I worry even more about how we will protect ourselves." I exhale deeply, laying my head on his shoulder as his arm wraps around me. "And I worry for you," he confides while kissing the top of my head.

"I can take care of myself," I joke, biting back a smile. "Clearly."

"Do I even want to know what was said to make you attack him with your spear?"

"Oh, the same thing the men on the council give me shit about," I grumble. While that's obviously not *everything* he said, my father doesn't need to know the rest.

"Hmm," he replies, tightening his arm around me briefly before continuing, "and you let him goad you into fighting him over it?"

I jerk out of his embrace as I sit up quickly, ready to explain all the reasons that Gosston needed to be shut up—even if they will embarrass me—but my father holds up his hand.

Smiling at the scowl on my face, he says, "Let me continue. There is not a soul in the capital who doesn't know that you are working towards a solution to our fading magic," he states, wrapping his arm around my shoulders again. "I know that if anyone is capable of figuring it out, it is you." His words pour into me, filling me with an acknowledgement of the work I'm doing that I didn't know I needed. "I'm just worried that you're tying up too much of yourself in your pursuit," he adds.

"What do you mean?"

"Your worth and value are not a byproduct of how much magic you may or may not have. And I worry that, along the way, others have made you feel like it is. Maybe even myself or your mother—"

"No," I interject. My feelings around this entire conversation are exasperated at best, but I won't let my father place blame on himself for the lengths I've gone to in trying to fix our magic. "You and mother have always supported and encouraged me. It's just..." I trail off, my father staying silent as I find the words I can only voice around him. Around everyone else, I have to be strong, determined, unbothered, *unbreaking.* With my parents—especially my father—I can let that facade drop without judgment. "I just feel like I was meant for more. I don't know why or how to even quantify what that is, only that it's my job—my destiny—to figure this out. That once I do, I'll be rewarded with the part of my soul that feels like it's missing." My voice wobbles, an embarrassing wetness beginning to well in my eyes before I push it away.

The pressure placed on me from both myself and the opinions of others feels unbearable at times. Using it as motivation is the only thing I can do to avoid being crushed beneath it. I feel like I am carrying double my own weight—it's doable, but it doesn't mean it's easy.

"And what will you do if you fix the magic for everyone else and you still don't have any?" he wonders.

I shrug, not wanting to entertain that possibility. "Then I guess I'll make Mother happy and marry Daje after all."

My father chuckles, squeezing me once more before letting go and standing up. "Want to go to my council meeting for me?" he teases, winking in my direction as he not so subtly changes the subject.

"Father, we both know that for the safety of the kingdom, it's better if I don't." I follow him out the door, his laughter booming as his shoulders shake. "What will you be discussing today, anyway?"

"The Summer Solstice celebration," he sighs, clearly not at all interested in party planning. My father kisses the top of my head before leading us out into the hallway. "I will see you tonight. Do try to keep your fists to yourself today, if only for my sake," he implores.

I give him a noncommittal shrug—much to his delight—as we split directions. He heads towards the council room for his meeting, and I make my way to the library. I'm going to try my best to avoid worrying about an impending conflict within the realms—much like how I've been avoiding pretty much everyone since I fought with Gosston a few days ago.

Though I don't necessarily regret my choice to defend myself through *physical* means, I can recognize that it probably wasn't a healthy way to do so. The anger, and sometimes bitterness, I feel at the way that I am—at what I was born lacking—feels like it grips and shreds my rationality. Then there is the whole interaction with Daje. I've definitely been avoiding him specifically. In truth, I don't know what to say. *Thank you for using your magic even though I specifically told you not to,* don't exactly seem like the right words. We haven't ever fought like that. There's been a wall of awkward tension between us, growing larger every time Daje hints at his feelings for me and every time I ignore it in return. Guilt settles inside me, a boulder pushing on my insides, nearly making me go out to search for him, but I stifle the urge and continue my walk to the library.

My sandals scuff against the stone beneath me until I reach the many rugs that line the floors inside the building. I wave to Elisha in greeting, who dips her chin respectfully before she turns back to whatever old tome she is reading. Heading to the back, I climb the stairs to the second level where some of the oldest tomes and journals of our kingdom are kept, tucked away against the furthest wall. With so many failed experiments under my belt, I'm wondering if I need to start at the beginning again. There has to be something I missed. Something I'm not seeing and just keep overlooking.

At the top of the stairs, I turn left and walk in the middle of two tall bookcases. The bookshelves up here look ancient, like they might cave in at any second. I'm not sure if it's magic that keeps the shelves together or if the wood of the banya tree is just that durable, but I make sure to be careful and edge my way around them. Every time I graze against a shelf, I gather more dust on my black leggings.

The only light up here is that of the spelled flames lining the walls and hanging from above. At the back of the hallway, a long wall runs the entire width of the library, and built into that wall are wooden shelves that stretch from floor to ceiling.

These shelves house the journals of the king's council spanning back to the ancient mages. It is tradition for the council members to keep a chronicle of the kingdom in their time. Some write daily, including musings from the latest council meeting or updates from the last public forum day. Others only write when something of significance occurs, like when the princess of a kingdom shows not even a spark at her Flame Ceremony. While I've briefly glanced at them before—several so entirely boring I fell asleep with my face in them—if I go back far enough, will I find something of relevance? There *must* be an event in one of these journals that I can draw some sort of conclusion from.

Since there is no way to accurately predict how far back the magic issues go, I start with the most recent journals and work backwards from there. Grabbing a stack at the very end of the long bookcase, I make my way back downstairs to my usual table. Setting the journals down, I walk over to the front desk where Elisha is still reading.

She smiles and sets her book aside when I come into her line of sight. "Your Highness, what can I do for you today?"

"I was wondering if you had some blank papers and a spelled pen? I want to take some notes on what I'm reading but forgot to bring anything with me."

Her lips quirk to the side for a brief moment before she is moving quickly, her petite hands digging into a drawer next to her. She pulls out a beautifully bound black leather journal and a pointed pen. "Here you are, Princess. Is there anything else you need?"

My thumb grazes the outside of the journal. It's larger than most, ideal for making sure I can write all the things I might need to. "No, this is perfect. Thank you, Elisha."

She smiles broadly before picking her book up and returning to her reading. I walk back to my table, setting the new journal and pen down before pulling my curly hair up onto the top of my head and securing it with a hair tie. The chair creaks as I take a seat and pull the journal from the top of the stack.

I will have to start with the last entry in the journals and read backwards, working towards the first, to have an accurate timeline of events. Councilman Hadrik's is the most recent, and when I turn the pages, I find that the final entry is the council meeting that I attended last week. While some details are left out that are too private for just anyone to read—like Nox's letter—it does go over how the other councilmen have expressed concern about the "magicless princess and her ability to rule should something happen to the crown prince." I smirk at the following line, "King Daxel promptly put any unfounded concerns to rest when he reminded the council that rulers are chosen by merit and worthiness—as they also were hundreds of years ago—and not by the magic they may possess."

The journal then goes back, covering flame ceremonies from the previous week including Starla's. Hadrik is factual about his entries, merely noting the date and what happens. It makes my own note taking that much easier. Hours pass, the sun outside moving into dusk, the soft light trickling in through the canopy of the dense trees. I think I lost the feeling in my ass an hour ago, but I can't stop reading.

I move on from Hadrik's journal to Councilman Arav's next. His writing is less legible, his letters sloppy and loopy. My eyes eventually adjust to his penmanship, and I write out several things that he notes. He mentions a few flame ceremonies in the capital, but about halfway through his journal, an entry about the magic in his small town on the outskirts catches my eye. He talks about how the oldest of the mages there are nearly magicless now. How it takes more and more effort as people grow older to wield the magic they are born with. I set his journal down and write his observations in my own. Is it truly as drastic as he has written for the people of this border town, located less than five miles from the Fae Kingdom? I don't know if the proximity to the border means anything, but I write it down just in case. I read on for another hour or so before my body protests that I must get up and eat something. I take Arav's and two other unread journals with me before putting the rest back.

The walk back to the palace is quiet, perfect for my thoughts to run in my head as I try to pluck important data from the information that I am reading. I wonder briefly if a trip to the border is warranted. It would take days and probably be a bit of a logistical nightmare for my father, but it might be worth it to see firsthand how the older mages are losing their magic. Maybe even see if there is something *different* about the land there. Though I assume if there was something visible and tangible, it would have already been reported.

I walk right to the kitchen when I get home, ordering dinner and a glass of wine to be brought out to the veranda off the first floor. Spelled flames inside a glass vase in the center of the table provide plenty of light as I pull out Arav's journal.

Just as I am about to dig back in, footsteps alert me to an incoming visitor. My muscles tense as I pray to any god that might be listening that it isn't Daje. My prayers are answered when Haylee struts in, her flowing pink skirt rustling and bangles dangling on her wrists as she walks. Audibly sighing, I let my shoulders sink in relief, and Haylee chuckles in response as she takes a seat opposite of me.

"What are you doing here?" I ask as a formality though I'm sure I know the reason why.

"Can't I just visit my friend who has been hiding in a book cave since beating Gosston's ass?" She lifts a knowing brow, but I just shrug back.

"I'm not hiding," I retort, crossing my arms over my chest as I kick my heels up on the chair to my side. When Haylee just stares flatly at me, I groan. "Fine, I *am* hiding, but only until I figure out what I am going to do about Daje."

"Why don't you just put him out of his misery and agree to love him forever and ever until you're both old and gray?" she sings, fluttering her hands about like this is just the greatest of suggestions.

"Haylee—"

"Bahira, come on, there are worse things than having a guy pine over you."

I sigh, laying my hands flat on the table. "You know the reasons I can't say yes to him. I *can't*. I just don't—"

"You love him, don't you?" she asks almost incredulously.

"I do, but as a friend. Nothing more."

"That could blossom into something more, Bahira! Plenty of people go from friends to lovers. You haven't even *tried* to see him in that way."

I drop my gaze from hers, because that *isn't* true. I *have* tried. I have watched him sparring half naked and sweating, his muscles flexing as he lifts his sword in rhythmic movements. I have tried in quiet moments between just the two of us, where his mellow laugh fills the air. And I have tried in tense moments—like in the council rooms when news of Nox is sparse and my heart beats out of fear in my chest. None of those moments have ever made me feel anything for him except a deep appreciation of his friendship. But Haylee won't understand that. So instead, I settle on something else. It isn't a lie, but it isn't the whole truth.

"Not until I find the answers I'm looking for. Not until I fix our kingdom. Until I fix—" I hesitate, voice cracking with emotion I'd rather not express.

Haylee's eyes relax as she takes me in, her hands reaching out to cradle one of mine. Her eyes are imploring as she says gingerly, "I know. You deserve to be happy, Bahira, and despite what you may think right now, Daje could make you happy. Just— Don't count him out yet, okay?"

I stare at my best friend and the sympathetic look on her face. Slowly, I breathe out, nodding my head in agreement and squeezing her hand a little tighter for reassurance. Another set of footsteps sounds before the door to the veranda opens suddenly and a younger mage pops his head through, his chest rising and falling quickly.

"Your Highness?" he asks, looking around until he meets my gaze. "Your father sent me to find you. He's just received word from Nox."

Chapter Twenty-Four

RHEA

THE SUN REACHES ITS highest point in the sky when Flynn knocks. I take one last look down at my light purple dress, the built-in corset traveling around my subtle curves and flowing out into a long skirt that nearly touches the tops of my feet. The sleeves are billowy and land just above my elbow. The dress is delicate and pretty and so out of place for me to wear in a stone prison. Tucking my unbound hair behind my ears, I take a deep breath and walk to the door.

There is a slight creak as it opens and reveals Flynn standing on the landing. My next inhale gets stuck in my throat, my heart pounding like a drum as I take him in. He isn't wearing his guard uniform today—though he did opt for black trousers tucked into brown boots that go to his calf. A form-fitting dark green tunic draws my gaze, the golden tan pigment of his skin glowing against the rich color. The laces of the tunic at his neck are loosened enough that the skin of his chest peeks through. My mouth dries and swallowing becomes momentarily difficult as I tilt my head the rest of the way up to look at him. I watch as his gaze traces a searing line down my body. The survey is quick, his eyes back to mine in a flash, but the heat left in the wake of his perusal burns me from the inside out.

"You look beautiful, Rhea," he says, his deep voice rasping.

Heat rises to my cheeks as I dip my chin in thanks. I nearly respond with *so do you* but luckily stop myself in time. He extends a hand out to me that I hadn't realized was behind his back, a single flower in his grasp. The beautiful rose is perfectly bloomed, its petals a perfect pink and stem the most vibrant green.

"Thank you," I say shyly, taken aback by his kindness and... well, just *him*. Our fingers brush in a whisper of contact when he passes me the flower. Those incredibly soft-looking lips of his beam back at me, his handsome face lighting up with the movement. I nearly feel disoriented as I step back and let him in.

"Did you miss me?" As usual, his steps are graceful, his body laden with power as he walks through the threshold and into the tower. For someone as broad and tall as he is, he moves like a man half the size. It reminds me of the warriors I've read about and how they've honed their bodies to be perfect weapons.

I bite back a smile, rolling my eyes as he watches. "Did I miss you prattling on about how handsome you are? Hmm, I'm not sure." I tap my chin, feigning indecision.

"Notice you said how handsome I *am,* are you confirming what we both know?" His raven hair touches the tops of his brows, and I wonder for a moment if those few rebellious strands represent a side to Flynn that I have yet to see fully. It's physically torturous to stop my hand from ruffling through his locks as I walk to grab a small glass jar by the sink for my rose.

"You may pull from that whatever you need to hear," I remark with my back to him as I set my gifted flower on the tea table. His chuckle is luxurious, a heady sound that promises fantasies I have no business entertaining. *He is forbidden in every way,* I remind myself.

"So, what have you planned for us?" he asks, thankfully changing the subject. Bella walks over to him and leans her head in on his lower stomach, searching for pets while I stare at Flynn.

"What?" I squeak out, my heart picking up speed as panic sets in. I was supposed to *plan* something? Did I misunderstand what he had meant in the letter? Stars above, am I expected to have this whole day planned out? What can we even *do* here?

Flynn's laugh draws me from my thoughts as he steps forward. "Your cheeks are so red right now," he teases with a smirk. He rubs Bella's head before his affectionate eyes find mine. "I was just hoping we could read together."

Was that vulnerability in his voice? It is impossible for me to believe that this usually confident and magnetic man would feel self-conscious about *anything.* Let alone wondering if a woman stuck in a tower wants to read with him. *Not just a regular girl.* His words repeat in my mind. Huffing out a sigh of relief, I playfully roll my eyes to hide my embarrassment. Still, my nerves are simmering beneath the surface. Above all else, I really want Flynn to like me, and that leaves me feeling even more anxious than before.

"Do you want the official tour?" I question, waving my hand towards the room. His lips widen into a full smile, one that I find completely unfair. It's unfair to be that handsome and kind and funny and— *Get it together, Rhea.*

"Lead the way, Sunshine."

"We really need to talk about that nickname."

"Do you not like it?" he questions, studying me as we walk, his gaze burning into the side of my face.

"I just don't understand it. Why 'Sunshine'?" We enter the library through the arched doorway, and any response that may have been on the tip of his tongue vanishes as he gawks at the space. A strange feeling of pride bubbles inside of me while I watch him walk along the edges of the crescent-shaped room, eyeing the different titles that line the shelves. Bella curls up in a sunny spot on the floor in front of the bench and rests her head on her crossed paws.

"Can you even *reach* the ones up here?" He stretches an arm overhead and grabs a book from the very top shelf. That constricting feeling in my throat returns as I watch him. I'm feeling both flushed and somewhat jealous.

"No, but I always viewed it as a sort of prize to be won. Like once I finish all the books I can reach, the top rows are my consolation," I say as I take a seat on the bench by the window. The light and heat of the sun bathes the room in a beautiful brilliance, no nook or cranny left untouched by its rays.

"You can't be anywhere close to reading all the books here, can you?" he asks, looking around.

I shrug, leaning back and placing my hands behind me. "I used to think I'd never read all the books in here before I died. But reading is often the only thing that distracts me for a long time, and it's all I really have to do besides cleaning and exercising." I don't mean to babble, but my nervousness at having him here in this space outweighs my logic. "Anyway, do you like to read?"

He nods, hands clasped behind him as he browses the different titles. "I do. The library back home is massive and one of my favorite places to be when I'm able to get back there to visit."

"When was the last time you went home?"

He picks a book off the shelf, a small smile curving his lips as he flips through the pages. "About a year ago."

My eyes widen at the admission. That is such a long time to go without seeing family. "What made you decide to join the King's Guard?"

"This should count as part of our question game since I already owe you three," he says, still holding onto the book and coming to take a seat next to me. I bump his shoulder with mine, a movement he chuckles at before leaning back to mirror my position. "I love my family and would do anything for them. Joining the King's Guard was something I did for them, to help." His head leans back to look at the ceiling as he takes a deep breath, the longer top strands of his dark hair shifting with the movement.

I can't help but trace his face with my eyes, moving down to the strong column of his throat and then to his chest. My fingers grip the fabric of the bench as my heart pounds a little faster. He peers at me from the corner of his eye, making me stop my visual assault and instead reach for the book he chose. I flip it over and groan when I read the title.

"Are you kidding me?" I deadpan, letting it dangle from my hand like I find it offensive.

"What?" he questions, sitting up and running a hand through his hair to move the strands back in place.

What is it about his hair that I can't ignore? What a weird thing to constantly notice. "This book. It's one Bella picked out for me to read once. Then she promptly fell asleep from how boring it was." I turn to the first page of *The History Of The Five Realms* and snort again, the memory of Bella snoring away while I read playing in my mind.

"One, how did Bella pick a book out? Two, are you not a fan of history tomes?" His decadent laugh coaxes warm feelings from inside me as he takes the book back and lays it on his lap.

"She sort of tapped it with her nose," I reply, smiling at the memory. "And I'm more of a romance reader." Reaching back farther on the bench, I grab my current romance read before handing it to him.

"*Three Roses In the Wind,*" he reads out slowly, before giving me a skeptical look.

"What? I get lonely up here and these books make me feel less so. I enjoy reading about how lovers meet and what they do together and—" Flynn starts coughing, a fist coming to his mouth as he turns away from me. "Are you okay?" I ask, leaning forward slightly to see him. When he regains his composure, he looks at me with that heated sort of gaze he had from the other night. The type of gaze I have definitely read about in a romance book. It makes my toes curl.

"Yep. Yes, I'm fine. Tell me more about these books."

My eyes narrow as I watch him smile a little too innocently at me. I yank the book from his hand—his laughter filling the library—and grab the book Tienne and Erica gave me instead. "I've also been reading this one, and while it does have a little romance in it, it's mostly quests and battles." He hesitates for a moment before taking the book from me and tracing the lettering on the cover. I recognize it as an intimate touch I've always done with certain books that are my favorite.

"Do you like this one?" he asks quietly, looking over at me. His tone stirs something within me, like it's telling me this book might be important to him—meaningful in a way I don't quite understand.

"I do," I answer, leaning in a little closer. "Have you read it?"

He nods before opening up to the page I have bookmarked, smiling when he sees where I'm at in the story. "Would you want to read the rest together?" he offers.

The look he's giving me and the tension surrounding us combines inside me, creating feelings I don't know how to name or even what to do with. I don't know why that question catches me so off guard either. I've never shared a book with anyone before, and it feels far more personal than I think it should. But reading is everything to me—it's entertainment and escape and freedom through others' stories. And sharing that with Flynn makes those butterflies reappear in my stomach. My magic warms and hums inside me, the feeling of it tingling down into my fingers and toes. I nod my head and scoot back on the bench until my back is leaning against the stone wall lining it. Flynn kicks off his boots and does the same on the other side.

Our eyes meet, time standing still for a moment as we study each other. I wish I could ask him why he looks at me as if I'm the reason the flowers bloom. My knees draw into my chest and my cheek rests on top as I listen to him start to read, the energy between us comfortable—sweet even. His voice is soothing, and I swear I feel it soften some of the jagged pieces that lay shattered within me. Another layer of that heavy, oppressive ice melts away inside me.

⁂

Flynn leaves a few hours later. We finished the book quickly, taking turns reading chapters and talking over our favorite moments and characters. It might have been the most fun I've ever had, and I find it unbelievable that it happened within the confines of the tower.

When I asked Flynn how he is able to come in and out of the tower without anyone noticing, he told me that, apparently, there is a door at the very bottom that opens out to the meadows below. He said that he can walk under the bridge undetected and right to that door. He also said there is a pathway that leads from the bridge to the front of the castle and from there to a road that leads to the city of Vitour. It's a valuable piece of information, and I tuck it away in my mind, even if guilt flickers there for doing so.

The last thing Flynn said before leaving was that he had a surprise for me tomorrow night.

⁂

Candles line the tower floor, the flickering shadows of the flames on the stone walls sensuous in their motions. I'm standing in the middle of the living area when movement on the balcony catches my eye. I head towards the open doors, the night sky above filled with sparkling stars. The moon is completely full, its glow bathing the tall figure and causing his dark hair to shimmer in its silver light.

Flynn.

He turns around when I step out onto the balcony and leans back, his elbows resting on the railing as his eyes drag slowly down my body. I'm still for only a moment, letting his gaze paint over me in provocative strokes. My body then moves before I consciously command it to, my bare feet near silent as I step closer and closer. Flynn's eyes burn like smoldering coals as our breaths fall in sync. He watches me with a hunger that tightens his body and makes my own become more loose. I want him. I want him so badly my mouth practically waters.

He stands up to his full height but keeps his hands gripped on the balcony railing. His black clothing and tan skin stand out against the white stone at his back; his fingers holding it so tightly I wonder if he's trying to restrain himself. My hands come to his shoulders before I slide them down slowly over his chest, my fingers gripping his tunic there as I tilt my head up to look at him. He moves his chin down, his eyes only leaving mine to linger on my mouth. I lean fully into him, molding into each divot and plane perfectly. It is a fitting of two bodies in a way that feels like fate—like it was always meant to be. Rising onto my tiptoes, I hold him for balance and bring my face as close to his as possible.

Our breath becomes mingled, our noses barely touching, but he keeps his grip onto the railing. I'm done waiting, though, so I drag a hand up to his neck, fingertips gently pushing into his muscles, until I wrap them around the back of it. Feeling the tickle of his hair there, I curl my fingers, nails digging into his skin lightly. And I'm not sure who moves first, but our lips crash together in a sea of lushness and desire. He groans, the sound deep and intoxicating, as it unravels me from within. Our tongues meet, the feel of them sliding against each other heightening my arousal as I grow more slick between my legs, my body aflame with a yearning I've never felt before.

Finally, his hands leave the railing to come to my sides, yanking me even closer to him. They slide down my body slowly as we kiss, his taste and scent sending me into a frenzy as I grip onto him harder. When his own fingers graze the curve of my backside, I whimper, but Flynn doesn't stop. He grips the flesh there as his mouth leaves mine to place desperate kisses down my jaw and neck. It feels like he is everywhere and still, I need more. I let go of his tunic and slide my hand down his chest, down his firm abdomen, past the waistband of his trousers, stopping when I reach the outline of his—

My eyes open suddenly, the dream fading away until all I see is the ceiling of my tower. I inhale deeply through my mouth, still feeling that intense yearning despite being completely awake. *That was my first ever dream like that.*

"Holy gods," I whisper into the night as I squeeze my thighs together, surprise growing at the slickness between them. A burning desire to use my hand on myself to relieve the aching I still feel ignites within me, but then Bella's soft snores by my side quickly douse that flame. Still, when I close my eyes, all I see is the heat in Flynn's gaze. All I hear is the sound of his hungry groan. And all I feel are his hands gripping me in places no one ever has before. It takes a while for sleep to find me again.

✦✦✦✦ ✦✦✦✦

Bella and I spent the morning watching the sun rise on the balcony. The sky paints the land in gold and light blue while the warm breeze brings the scent of the flowers at the base of the tower with it. When the sun fully crests the horizon I come inside to draw a bath, leaving Bella outside. I managed to get some sleep last night, but while I didn't have another *sensual* dream, the desire still lingers on the edges of my mind, like an oath unfulfilled.

My fingers drag lazily across my abdomen, goosebumps rising in their wake under the water. Looking over the edge of the tub, I confirm that Bella hasn't come upstairs before sliding further into the water, my hand moving closer to that aching spot at my core. When the tip of my finger reaches the bundle of nerves there, I gasp at how sensitive it already is. My thighs squeeze together as I begin to circle, a languid feeling unraveling and moving up from my toes. As my mind starts replaying moments of the dream, I am reminded of the way it felt to have Flynn's body so close to mine. The way his mouth collided with my own as our tongues met in the middle. I bite down on my lower lip to stifle a moan, my hand moving quicker as I reach the brink of an orgasm faster than I ever have before. The memory of the dream morphs into my last visit with Flynn. It's not overtly sexual—just him sitting across from me, looking with rapt interest as he usually does—but it's enough. I gasp for breath as that tension builds and builds until it bursts open, my release barreling through me so intensely

230

that I have to cover my mouth with my other hand. I keep my finger moving in those tight circles through the wave, my hips jerking in tandem.

I wait for that moment after an orgasm where my body feels sated and relaxed, but it doesn't come. Instead, my finger keeps moving, and I slide my hand down from my mouth to gently circle over my nipple, causing it to peak under my touch. New fantasies flood my mind filled with images of him kneeling at the edge of the tub, replacing my delicate hands with his larger, calloused ones. A breathy moan, as quiet as I can keep it, leaves me as I bring myself back to that teetering edge again. All because of him—his hands and his mouth and that smirk and his hair. But it's also his kindness and humor and the way he looks at me like I'm someone of value. *Not just a regular girl.* I shudder, the coiling tension finally releasing, leaving me feeling boneless.

I relax again into the tub, letting the feel of the warm water calm my quickened heart. My magic pushes on my stomach and at the base of my spine as its warmth travels through my arms and legs. I haven't called on it since that fateful night, but the urge to do so now is nearly overwhelming. Lifting a hand out of the water, my palm facing up, I close my eyes and concentrate on directing the magic. Even with my lids closed, I can see the glowing white light there within seconds. I open my eyes and move my hand closer to me as I feel the staticky warmth tickling my fingers and palm. It lights up the gray stone around me, turning it into something completely different, something warm and bright.

I wonder if using my magic, even in this capacity, is something I should try to do more often. There is a sense of relief after using it, but I'm unsure if it's my own feeling or the magic's. Can magic even *have* feelings? It's one of the many questions I have about this *ability*, if I can call it that. Where did it come from? What else can it do? Is it alive? Knowing? Sentient? Can it be honed into something *more*? Which makes me wonder why I sometimes feel that ancient, dark coldness mixed in with the light. Is that magic as well? I think a part of me hopes that it is, if only to explain away why I sometimes feel so *other* when it curls and coils within me. And if it isn't magic, is it the consequence of boxing up my feelings and shoving them down within me? Did I accidentally create something in the dark abyss of my grief and sadness that mirrored the way I felt? And if I did, *how do I make it go away?*

Chapter Twenty-Five

RHEA

"WHAT IS ALL THIS?" I ask Flynn as he walks in, carrying a black basket and what looks like a knowing smile. I had spent most of the day balancing between trying to forget the dream I had of him and trying to forget the orgasms I gave myself because of it. Now that he's here, it's taking everything I can muster not to drag my gaze down his body. But I can't keep my eyes off of the way his hands grip the basket or my ears from hearing the strong cadence of his steps as he moves past me and into the living area. And then of course there is the way he smells and that secretive little smile and... *Damn it.*

I force myself to take some deep breaths as I step up next to him, my gaze anywhere other than his chest, which is at my eye level. When I finally get myself under control, I move to the couch expecting that's where we are going to sit, but his fingers gently grab my own, halting my movements.

"I was thinking we could go outside, on the balcony."

"The balcony?" I screech, nearly horrified. There's no way he could know what happened on that very balcony in my dream, but I can't help the blush that creeps up from my neck and onto my cheeks.

"Yes, is that okay?" he asks, a single brow slowly raising. His stupid handsome face glows in the candlelight, and I have to look away before I accidentally reveal how I'm feeling to him.

Gods above and below, *help me.* "Of course. Why wouldn't it be?" I stumble as I rush past him and out into the night air.

"Alright then." He laughs behind me, his steps following mine. He sets the basket down in the center of the balcony before coming to stand next to me, his hands laying flat on the wide stone railing. "Wow, it's a beautiful view from up here."

I gulp as I nod. My head is too filled with thoughts and memories of things that haven't actually happened—but felt real enough—to respond. After a few moments, Flynn turns and starts taking items out of the basket. I stand back and watch as he lays down a dark blue blanket and a variety of different foods in glass containers. Next, he pulls out two plates and two forks—an item I know how to use in theory, but in actuality never have. When he finishes setting everything up, he spreads his arms out to the sides.

"It's a picnic," he declares as he smiles at me. "Normally, you have them in a meadow or underneath a tree, and it's usually daytime, but we can make this work." He takes a seat on the edge of the blanket and gestures for me to do the same. The food in the middle smells incredible, the air now laced with things I have no name for.

"How did you get all of this?" I ask, my fingers trailing along the edge of my plate.

Flynn watches the movement, lost in a daze for a moment before he looks back up at me. "I had Tienne and Erica help," he explains, gesturing to the meat at the center of everything before continuing, "This is roasted chicken. Then we have a mixed green salad, roasted potatoes, and a special dessert that I'm keeping a secret." All foods that I have read about but have never experienced eating.

His eyes sparkle under the moonlight, doing nothing to ease the adrenaline coursing through my veins, making my body come alive just from being near him. He holds out his hand for my plate, and I tell him I want to try a little bit of everything.

"Let's see if roasted chicken is actually worth being your favorite food," I tease, poking a piece with my fork and bringing it to my mouth. The texture of it is silkier than I thought it would be, since nearly all the meat I've ever eaten has been dried for easy storage. Once, Alexi brought me freshly cooked pork, but that was much greasier than this. The flavors are savory and earthy and something else I don't have a name for. It's salty too, and when I clear my throat and move to stand up and get some water, Flynn quickly flips open the lid of the basket and pulls out a small glass bottle, the color too dark to see what the liquid inside is.

"This is just fruit juice," he says, noting the way I look warily at it. "I was going to bring wine, but I wasn't sure if you had ever had alcohol before, and I didn't want your first experience with it to be here." He uncorks the bottle and hands it to me. Tentatively lifting it to my nose, I sniff, the fruity scent pleasant enough that I take a drink. It's overly sweet and a little tangy, the flavors coating my tongue and throat delightfully.

I hand the bottle back to him as I respond, "It's really good. So is the chicken. I suppose it isn't the *worst* food to have as your favorite." I chuckle at his triumphant smile.

Flynn snorts, turning his attention back to his food as we eat in contented silence. Eventually Bella comes out, leaning over to try everything leftover on my plate. I've been full from eating before, but never quite like this. My body feels different in the wake of eating food freshly prepared. I offer to clean up the dishes once we are both done, but Flynn shakes

235

his head and carefully stacks everything up to place back into the basket, pulling a small bundle wrapped in parchment paper out before he does so.

"When I saw that the baker had made this for today, I had Tienne and Erica grab extra for us," he says as his hands begin to unwrap the item until a familiar scent permeates the air.

"You didn't," I whisper, a half-choked laugh coming from me. Laying in the center of the brown paper are two slices of lemon loaf.

"It's your favorite, right?" he asks. I can feel him looking me over, feel his excitement start to falter because of the way I freeze as I stare at the dessert. Emotions flash through me as a knot grows in my throat. Its jagged edges make it hard to breathe, hard to think past. "Sunshine..." His voice trails off as I meet his gaze, unable to stop the tears flowing out of the corners of my eyes. "What's wrong?"

"I'm sorry," I whisper, quickly wiping at the wetness now streaking down my cheeks.

"Talk to me, what can I do?"

I shake my head, clearing my throat as I look out into the night sky. "Alexi was the last person to bring me lemon loaf before he died. He was the *only* person to ever bring me any treat like this before you, and I just—" I inhale and hold it, my chest expanding painfully before I allow the breath to slowly seep out of me. "I'm sorry, I don't know why this keeps happening."

"What keeps happening?" He moves closer to me as he asks the question.

I keep my gaze on those winking stars, still imagining they are waving hello. Like how I'm drawn to the sun, the silver-flecked sky of night is one that brings a different kind of comfort. It's so similar to the comfort I have when I dream of the Middle. A dream that is not quite a dream.

"I keep trying to force myself not to feel," I start, my voice no louder than the rustling of the leaves on the trees in the distance. "And most of the time it works. I've tucked away emotions that will only remind me of how much I've lost—placing them into these dark pockets in my mind and locking them up tight." My gaze drops as my fingers play with the fabric of my dress. "But sometimes I feel like I've been dropped in the middle of an unknown forest with no direction. And I wander around, trying to find landmarks that signal a way out, but instead I just go in circles. Whenever I feel I'm close to freedom, I'm quickly reminded that I'm back where I started."

The double meaning of my words weighs heavily on me. I don't expect Flynn to understand, given what *little* he actually knows about me, but when I lift my eyes to his, he peers at me with a recognition that he shouldn't have. With a compassion that I'm surprised to see.

"Have you ever felt so desperately lost like that?" I whisper as my lip wobbles a little with the question.

Flynn slides his hand tentatively under my own, pausing to give me time to back away from his touch. Instead, I interlace our fingers, studying the way my fair skin gleams against the tan of his. Our palms connecting are like a tree taking root or a flower blooming in the sun. His warmth soaks into me, prodding at those dark corners inside me with something lighter.

"I have," he says softly, his thumb rubbing the back of my hand. "Recently, in fact." When I gesture for him to continue, he responds by shaking his head playfully and looking up to the stars. "For a long, long time, I felt the weight of what has been expected of me resting on my shoulders like an immovable boulder." His brows draw together, his concentration moving to where our hands meet. "And then one day, it morphed into something else. Suddenly, the pressure of those expectations shifted. And for the first time in my life, I felt what it was like to not know what to do—to be given answers and, in response, only have more questions." His dark smoky eyes hold mine then, conveying words that I don't know how to translate.

Well that was about as vague of an answer as mortally possible. "Do you still feel it?" I pry. "Not knowing what to do?"

His lips quirk into a smile that doesn't reach his eyes. "Yes, but also, no."

A breathy laugh escapes me. "Was that supposed to make me feel better? Because if so, you sort of did a shit job."

Flynn barks out a laugh, his eyes wide with surprise. "The princess curses. That is unexpected." His heated gaze cuts through that cold sadness that had settled into my bones.

"I never claimed to act like royalty, a fact you should be more than aware of by now."

Flynn chuckles, the sound pushing away that thick feeling of turmoil from earlier as he squeezes my hand before letting it go and saying, "That is true, though you are more regal than anyone in this kingdom."

I snort at that, tucking my hair behind my ear. Flynn cleans up the rest of the dishes and leftover food, leaving the lemon loaf on top of the basket before moving it off the blanket. Then he lowers onto his back, one arm curling under his head as he pats the spot next to him.

"Can you tell me about Alexi?" he inquires softly, staring up at the night sky. I study his side profile, noting the way that, even in the dimness of night, he glows like a star himself.

"Why?"

"For two reasons. One, I like hearing you talk," he says seriously as he pats the ground next to him again. "And two, because you shouldn't have to hold in what you're feeling anymore. He was important to you, Rhea, and the more you fight that urge to speak of him, the more it will fester inside of you like an unhealed wound."

I suppose his words make sense, enough to at least move my body so that we are lying together, shoulders just barely touching.

"You also aren't alone anymore," he adds, interlacing our hands again between our bodies. We both turn to look at each other, the sensation of our closeness making my magic hum in what feels like approval and lighting me up from within. I'm sure it must be noticeable, but Flynn's eyes never stray from my own. "Tell me," he says again.

So I do. I start with the first time I saw Alexi when I was a small child and how his imposing presence frightened me. I recall how he acted as my teacher and all the many things he took the time to make sure I knew. I tell Flynn about how Alexi brought me Bella, though I leave out the part of me healing her. As I continue sharing memories and moments I've never told anyone else, I can feel it—that impossible, invisible weight easing partially off of me. Like someone starting to saw through the chains that attached me to it. No, not someone, *Flynn.* We laugh together when I talk about how Alexi avoided my questions on sex—though my mind does briefly return to the previous night's dream. He asks me questions all throughout, eagerly engaging me to share more and more.

Then it's time to talk about Alexi's death, and my voice stalls. Flynn squeezes my hand again, a steady reminder of what he said earlier. *You aren't alone anymore.* So for the first time since I watched it happen, I recall every detail of that night. My body trembles as I talk, my heart beating soundly against my bones like it's rattling to break free. Flynn is so still as he listens that I have to look at him a few times to make sure he didn't fall asleep. When I finish, a tear trailing down my cheek as I explain my raging guilt at being the cause of his death, Flynn pulls us up to sit. He gently wipes my tear away before he drags his finger across my jaw to hook under my chin, tilting my head up to look at him. Like this, there is nowhere for either of us to hide except in the depths of the other's gaze. With the moon shining above and a gentle floral-laced breeze blowing through, a shift happens between us. It is soft and sweet and completely unexpected in a way that feels frightening—and also thrilling.

"I'm *so* fucking sorry, Rhea," he says, his thumb gingerly sliding across my skin from where he stays holding my chin. "None of it, absolutely *none* of it, is your fault. I need you to understand that."

"But how can it not be? *I'm* the reason the king was angry. *I'm* the reason Alexi was being watched."

"Because *you* aren't responsible for the actions of King Dolian," he declares, his voice low and menacing as he says my uncle's name. "And the fact that he's made you feel this way, made you feel like *you* were the one who drove that sword in, it makes me—" He cuts himself off abruptly, letting go of my chin to run a hand through his hair. "It *infuriates* me. You don't deserve it. *Any* of it."

My eyes move back and forth between his as I read the emotions on his face. Anger, yes, but something else lies there too. His hand drops to his lap, the other still firmly laced with mine as his thumb runs back and forth in comforting strokes. A coiled quiet lingers, and I don't know if it is filled with tension because of the topic or because of words left unsaid. Either way, I decide to break it with some humor.

239

"Any fascinating stories with your legendary swordplay?" I ask, bumping his knee with my own. Flynn nearly chokes on his laugh, dragging us back down until we are looking up at the sky again.

Our hands stay holding onto each other for the rest of the night. The moon is already in the west when Flynn decides he should leave. Standing on opposite sides of the doorway, he leans over and kisses the back of my hand with a wink, which makes me roll my eyes. And when I climb the stairs to my loft, exhausted but inexplicably at ease in a way that is so foreign to me, I can't help the smile that breaks through.

When I awake, after a few hours of restful sleep, I find a note on the floor in front of the door.

SUNSHINE,

I AM GOING TO VISIT YOU THIS AFTERNOON. LET'S READ TOGETHER AGAIN. ALSO, I BELIEVE YOU OWE ME A QUESTION IN OUR GAME, SO CAN YOU TELL ME WHEN YOUR BIRTHDAY IS? THINK OF SOMETHING GOOD TO ASK ME IN RETURN.

SINCERELY,

FLYNN

"This afternoon?" I squeeze the letter to my chest. The mental list of questions that has only grown the longer I've known Flynn runs through my mind.

Bella comes down, stretching her legs and yawning as I get our breakfast ready. Taking my meal out on the balcony, I sigh as soon as the rays hit my skin. The magic inside of me curls and hums, warming me up from the inside as well.

My eyes look out over the glistening water at the same few ships I see floating there every morning. It's easy to be reminded of the monotony of my day, of the way my life replays itself like I'm stuck in a loop. Except that's not exactly true anymore. The loop was disrupted the day a guard named Flynn showed up and saw me. Truly saw me. I chew on my lip as I think about the fact that I will have to leave him when I escape. I wish I could ask him to come with me. My heart flutters a little at that thought.

He probably has an established life here, however, and friends that rely on him. My thoughts keep tumbling over themselves as I reach for a piece of bread off of my plate when my hand freezes halfway to my mouth. What if he is *with* someone. I assume he isn't married because there would be a ring on his finger. *Wouldn't there?* But he could definitely be seeing someone and I wouldn't have a clue. I don't want to believe he would do something like that, but how would I know? With my limited experience, am I really the best judge of character? I know what my question for Flynn will be.

Groaning, I set the food back down and tilt my head up towards the mostly blue sky, just a few fluffy white clouds floating overhead. Bella comes to sit at my feet, my hand immediately dropping to the top of her head.

"Bella, tell me everything you know about men." I look down at her, her golden irises gleaming in the sunlight as she turns her head to look at me. She huffs out a breath and turns back to look at the lake through the railing. Leaning down, I kiss the top of her head and chuckle. "Yeah, that's about as much as I know too. Though maybe I know a bit more since I can read books." Bella shifts to look at me again, and I burst out in laughter. She almost looks like she is scowling.

I finish my food and head up to my loft to bathe and get dressed. My fingers drag across my collection of newer dresses that I've laid on my bed after my bath as I try to decide which one to wear. There is a cream-colored one that is more flowy than the others, the fabric silken. Slipping it on, I delight in the feel of it against my skin. I sit at the vanity and brush out my hair before tying the long strands back into a low ponytail.

When knocking sounds downstairs, my heart flips in my chest. I quickly make my way to the door and pull it open, but my smile falls a little when I take in Flynn's appearance. He has dark circles marring the tan skin under his lovely eyes.

"Are you okay?" I breathe out, worry twirling in my stomach.

Flynn just smiles—a world-endingly beautiful thing—before he nods his head. "Yes, perfectly fine." I step to the side to let him in, shutting the door. "You look beautiful," he says smoothly, and heat rises to my cheeks as I dip my chin.

"Thank you." I reply, nervously tucking a strand of hair behind my ear.

"Have you picked out a book for us to read?" My eyes follow him as he takes a step towards the library, unable to help the way they drag up and down his impressive figure. The muscles of his thighs strain against his black trousers, while the size of his shoulders speak to the strength he must possess. Swallowing, my inspection of him continues until my gaze finds his again.

"Sunshine," he murmurs as he runs a hand through his hair. *Is it odd to be jealous of that hand?* "I would love to know what you are thinking about right now."

My lips pinch together as I gesture ahead of us and completely ignore his request. "Shall we?" He blows out a breath through his grin, shaking his head as he follows me into the library. "Is today a day off for you?" I ask as he browses the books.

"It is," he says, glancing down at me with a smile.

We jokingly argue over which book to read, Flynn picking out another history book as dull as *The History Of The Five Realms,* while I gravitate to one of my romance stories with the hope that it will mean Flynn has to read a more *sexual* scene. I laugh internally at the thought and employ everything in my arsenal that might work to get him to agree—which just consists of me pushing my lower lip out in a pout and fluttering my eyelashes at the same time. It works though because Flynn gives up and agrees to read from *I Have A Dream,* a romance about two ill-fated mortals falling in love.

Facing each other on opposite sides of the bench, we take turns reading, alternating chapters and often doing ridiculously exaggerated voices for the characters. It's when we are about two-thirds of the way through that I realize my plan has backfired. The chapter begins with the two characters kissing for the first time, and my face heats as I read about the way their hands travel over each other's bodies. I keep my eyes on the book, holding it in front of me like a shield, not daring to look at Flynn who hasn't moved once since I started reading. When the characters start undressing, I pause, my mouth opening and closing in silent protest.

"Why did you stop, Rhea? It was just starting to get interesting." I lower the book just enough to see the roguish grin on Flynn's face. He has one leg extended, one knee bent, and his arms folded over his chest.

My eyes narrow as I clear my throat and look back at the words on the page. "His hand brushed against the underside of my breast, sending goosebumps across my flesh. My breath hitched as he moved his hand higher, his other traveling further south to where an aching need had taken root." Gods, I was burning up on the inside, and I wasn't sure if it was because of embarrassment or desire. Or both. "I begged him to move quicker, to bring his large fingers to where I needed them. The first brush of them against the sensitive nub at the apex of my thighs was a fire roaring to life. It raged and burned the longer his fingers toyed, until he plunged one of them inside me." My toes curl, a motion I am sure Flynn can see where he sits across from me. My voice is a mortifying breathy rasp as I continue. "The fingers of his other hand toyed with my nipple as he pressed himself closer to me. The outline of his large cock—"

"Fucking gods, stop." It is a gentle command, but when I lower the book again to look at Flynn—my heart in my throat—he appears to be anything but calm.

His face tilts up to the ceiling, a faint flush on his cheeks, while his fingers grip the pillows on either side of him so tightly I am nervous that he will somehow tear them to shreds. The column of his throat begs me to caress it with my stare. Something ravenous blooms in my chest when he looks at me—hunger swirling in those dark eyes. I need to break this tension; not because I want to, but because it appears like he does. Like he is holding himself back. Though, that is the smart thing to do. He is a guard, and I am a princess locked in a tower by a ruthless, vile king. We are forbidden in every way, and the last thing we need to add to that complicated mix are actions that can't be undone.

"Summer Solstice," I blurt out with a grimace.

"What?" My words clear the glaze from his eyes as he blinks rapidly and loosens his grip on the pillows. Inhaling deeply through his nose, he blows it out through his mouth slowly as he levels his gaze at me.

"My birthday," I clarify. "It's on the Summer Solstice."

"That is soon," he states, his shoulders rolling back as he relaxes a little bit more.

Nodding, I lay my book down at my side and chew on my lip as I contemplate. "Can I ask you a question?"

He stares at me for a moment before nodding. "Anything."

It's quiet while I think, the sunlight coming in from the window bathing us in its glow. "Are you with anyone?" It comes out hardly more than a whisper, barely more than a feathering of words past my lips.

"What do you mean?" He is looking so intently at me that I have to remind myself to take a breath.

"You know, a partner. A companion." I gesture in the air with my hands as I continue, "A lover."

"Ah," he says, sitting up and scooting closer until one leg hangs off the bench and the knee of his other brushes against my own. "It would be odd that I was coming here to see you if I was, don't you agree?"

"I do, but then again I don't exactly know how things work in the outside world. Maybe that would be a normal occurrence for a man," I shrug, letting a little of my insecurity out into the open between us. He leans in, his perfect scent surrounding me as I breathe in deeply. It unfairly clouds my mind so that all my thoughts are about him. Though in truth, that's always the case whenever he is near.

"It might be a normal occurrence for a different man, but not for me. There is no one else—here or back home." His eyes are dark pools of glittering sincerity before he adds, so very quietly, "There is only you."

Chapter Twenty-Six

BAHIRA

IT HAS BEEN OVER a week since Nox's last letter. After the young mage informed me we had new correspondence, I hurried to the council room and was met with my father's worried gaze. His face was lined with tension as he held the letter out to me from where he stood at the head of the long table. Reading it over, my heart had palpitated in my chest, my eyes taking longer to focus on each word. Nox thought he found the source of the magic, and apparently, he was close to figuring out exactly *what* that burst we felt was. He—most inconveniently—didn't say what his suspicions were, but either way, the members of the council have been even more on edge ever since.

Summer has descended upon the Mage Kingdom, the heat from the sun beats down on the tops of the trees and mixes with the humidity from the thick foliage of our realm, making my workshop feel stuffy. My brow is dotted with sweat, a bead rolling down my temple, as I lean over to peer through the eyepiece of the magnifier on the table. Clicking another glass lens in place, it zooms in on the glass slide underneath. Looking down the scope, I watch the organisms move around in the small drop of magic-infused water I had placed there. I don't see anything unusual, so I click another glass lens into place to zoom in even further. I study it through the scope, trying to find something—*anything*—out of the ordinary. But there is nothing unique about the water. I zoom in again, only two glass lenses remaining to click into place. Holding my breath, my hands braced on the table on either side of the magnifier, I stare. And stare. And *fucking stare*, but there is nothing. Nothing to even signify the water has been infused with magic.

"Fuck it," I grumble as I push the remaining two glass circles into place, zooming in as far as the tool will allow. I close my right eye as my left looks down the scope, and it takes a second to focus the image, but with it this magnified, I can see the cells of the spring water. My vision blurs, probably a combination of not getting enough sleep and looking through this damn scope for too long. Mentally, I start counting to ten, making it to four before I swear I see a flash of light. It was quick, too fast to be certain if it was a trick of the scant sunlight shining in or actually coming from the water cells. I restart my count and make it to ten without seeing the flash again. Blowing out my breath, I stand up and stretch my back out before leaning against the black stone counter behind me.

I haven't been back to my workshop in weeks, partly because I couldn't figure out what the hell to experiment on and partly because I've been too nervous that I might run into Daje here. I still haven't spoken with him since the day I challenged Gosston, and it doesn't evade me that this is the longest we've gone without speaking.

Children run past my workshop, laughing and screaming as they chase each other, which brings me back to the present. My little lab built into an albero tree is off one of the main roads and usually pretty quiet, but with the warmer temperatures of the summer season, everyone has been more restless—including the children. Or maybe it is just *me* who has felt that way. Between the loss of the magic, Nox's mission, possible impending war, and my lack of progress, it feels like we're standing at the gates of something huge, unable to see what's on the other side.

"Shut up, Barren!" a small girl's voice says, drawing my attention to the door.

"You can't tell me what to do; you barely have any magic!" My brows draw together as I take an unconscious step closer to where I hear their voices.

"I said, shut up!"

"You can't play with us. You need stronger magic in order to be in the game." Someone—Barren, I assume—says in a high-pitched voice, the cadence of it grating on my nerves.

I step across the threshold of the doorway and out onto the gray stone-paved road. My eyes dart around until I see them, a half circle of children all facing one lone girl—Starla, her curly brown hair recognizable from her Flame Ceremony. She furiously wipes away the tears tracking down her cheeks as she holds her ground against them. But I can see how she reacts to their words, the small deflation of her shoulders and the way she can't stop the slight wobble of her lip. The whole scene feels so familiar to me.

"Go play with the plants! They'll be your friends," Barren snarls, swiping his stringy blonde hair out of his face as the others around him laugh loudly. The children appear to range in age from eight to pre-teen, leaving Starla the youngest among them—impressing me even more to watch her stand toe-to-toe with them. "Poor Starla, hated by the gods so much that not even your parents wanted you."

My eyes narrow, anger rising within me, but I force myself to stay put. I know firsthand what it is to have someone step in when you don't want them to, and something in her stance tells me that this little girl would rather defend herself than have someone do it for her.

Starla folds her arms over her chest and gives Barron a scathing look; a move that is so reminiscent of something I might have done at her age that I can't help but smile. "I may be an orphan, but at least I'm not an idiotic prick with zero brains!"

I bark out a laugh, the sound crossing the distance to the children who all look my way. Their eyes widen when they see me, Barren's growing the biggest of all. The group disbands quickly, running away without a second glance and leaving Starla all alone. I walk towards her, smirking when Starla turns and gives me her back.

"I don't need help," she growls, her shoulders tensing slightly before she adds, "Your Highness."

"I know," I answer as I walk around Starla until I'm in front of her.

She stares off at the trees behind me before taking a deep breath. "I'm sorry I called him a prick." Her lip wobbles again before she rolls them together.

"No, you aren't," I say, squatting down until we're at eye level. "But between you and I, he is a prick." Her shoulders slowly relax, a ghost of a smile replacing her earlier glower. "If you ever want a reprieve from said pricks, I wouldn't mind an occasional lab assistant."

I don't know why I offer; I prefer to work alone when I'm doing my experiments. Still, Starla reminds me of a younger version of myself. The memories I have of trying to navigate a world where everyone else had something I didn't tugs on my heart uncomfortably. At least I had Haylee and Daje— My throat goes tight at the thought of him. I blink away the emotions and stand back up, suffusing my voice with indifference once again.

"You will have to learn not to let the things they say bother you. If they see that they are getting to you, it will only make it worse." She lifts her chin higher but avoids my gaze. Snorting, I step around her and begin walking back to my workshop. "Think about what I said," I shout over my shoulder.

My head leans back against my chair on the veranda outside of my room, another mage journal in my lap. A warm breeze rustles the leaves on the trees surrounding me as I listen to the humming of bugs and the chirping of seasonal birds, back from their migration to the Nalka Mountains in the east. Summer Solstice is in a few days, and my father has been trying to distract the council with celebration preparations until we receive our next letter from Nox.

My mind wanders to the last time he came home for a visit. His hair had grown longer than he usually kept it, and I swear he even appeared more tan. My brother always had an affinity for being serious, particularly when it came to talk of his mission, but it grew with time away from his kingdom. He had changed so much in the four years he had been gone that each time I saw him, it almost felt like meeting a new person. Even his best friend, Cassius, couldn't draw the same level of mirth from him as usual. But when it was just us, he would let the undercover crown prince façade fade a little and become my caring older brother again. He relaxed and laughed more, always asking about whose ass I was kicking and how my experiments were going. I often wanted as many details as he could give me about where he was, but all he wanted to talk about was what I was doing while he was gone. I know he hated lying to our people about where he truly was and what he was doing, but he did it for their safety. My parents cried when he left, supporting his decision to put his people in front of his own desires but feeling the weight of his absence in their bones. We had no idea his sacrifice would bleed into years, and all I can hope for now is that it's nearing an end and he will be home for good soon.

Letting out a sigh, I flip the page of the journal and continue reading. This one is from a year ago, and for a few pages now, the councilman has droned on and on about how he isn't happy with the newest group of young mages because they "all appear weak." My eyes roll, and I keep turning the pages until I finally see a new entry. Reading through the journals has been eye opening in a way that unfortunately isn't yet helpful in my pursuit to fix the magic, but instead shows me what some of these men in particular are truly like. I wonder briefly if any of the council members had documented that I fought with Gosston in their current journals, and a cackling laugh bursts out of me at the thought.

"What's so funny?" my father asks from behind me.

My scream of surprise is so loud, dozens of birds take flight from the canopies above. "Father, what the hell!" I shout, hand clutching my chest as I try to take a breath while my father laughs as he comes to stand beside me.

"You make it too easy, Bahi." Ruffling the hair at the crown of my head, he continues, "For such a fierce warrior, you sure do scare easily."

"I do not expect to be ambushed in my own room, *Your Majesty*. It has been a while since we sparred. Perhaps you would like a reminder of just how old you are getting?" I try to remain serious, working to keep a smile off of my face, but I fail miserably. My father holds his hands up in mock surrender as he takes the chair next to mine. We sit in comfortable silence for a moment, just taking in the trees and flowers and wildlife that surround the palace.

"Whose journal are you reading today?" he asks, crossing an ankle on top of his knee. I hold up the red book, Councilman Dune's name engraved on the front. My father knowingly chuckles while shaking his head, and no other words need to be said for him to understand that the content I'm reading is less than useful.

"While Dune's has been unhelpful so far, I have been able to pull enough information from the other journals to start charting patterns and data on how the people's magic is being affected," I say, reaching over to the side table where my own journal and pen are.

Turning to the page that houses the first part of my graph, I show my father the dots that represent the Flame Ceremonies and the measure of magic at each one. Then I have small x's marked anytime there is mention of a disturbance in magic. A key drawn to the side shares where those disruptions take place within the kingdom, as well as the severity of them and an additional timeline if this was not the first occurrence. Like with

Councilman Arav's mention of the older mages of his small town losing their ability to wield their once-strong magic. The graph is ordered by time, with the left end signifying the most recent date and then going back farther and farther as you read right. My father takes everything in, systematically reading it all before looking up to me with a broad smile.

"This is fantastic, Bahira. This sort of timeline and data analysis has never been attempted nor studied before. This very journal will be added to our archives; I have no doubt of it."

I snort at that, but a small part of me hopes that he's right. While I may not give a second thought about a compliment given to me for my looks, I absolutely crave being recognized for my mind. The discovery—and prompt fixing—of what's plaguing our magic will be something written in history. Especially when that discovery will return my magic to me. It has to.

"My loves." My mother's voice calls out to us from my room, and my father turns to look at her, pure love and adoration in his eyes, when his smile drops and his brows furrow in concern. I whip my head around to look at my mother. Her face is pale, and her hand is shaky as she walks up and holds a sealed letter out to my father. "It's from Nox," she says, clasping her hands in front of her. It doesn't stop their trembling. "It's addressed only to you."

It's my turn to look confused as my father reaches out a hand for my mother and guides her to sit on his thighs. Once he is sure she is comfortable, his arm wrapped around her waist, he opens the letter and begins to read.

I watch both of their faces for signs of what the letter could say, but besides their eyes going round, there are no other hints. When they both have read it, he hands the letter to me.

Father,

If you deem it safe, I would like this letter to remain between us. I sent my last letter to appease the council so that they do not grow anxious when they don't hear from me, but I have found the source of the magic. It is not what we were thinking it might be, but it is no less important and valuable to the safety of our kingdom.

My plans have changed, and I will be leaving soon. I will be bringing the source of the magic with me. I ask that when I arrive, it is just our family that greets me. We will need to decide together how to proceed and how to keep the source of the magic safe.

If I am able, I will send word while on the road. Otherwise, I will see you soon.

I love you all.

Nox

I reread the vague letter again, vowing to punch Nox in the face when I see him for being so cryptic *again*. My father pinches his lips together while laying his head against my mother's arm.

"What do you think it could be?" I question, looking at them both.

"It could be anything. I—"

"Your Majesty!" a young mage's voice calls out.

"Gods, how many people are going to traipse into my room today?" I mutter, catching my mothers wry smile as I turn and look back at the out-of-breath mage.

"Your Majesty, King Kai Vaea of the shifter isle has summoned you through the Mirror. He is waiting for you now."

Chapter Twenty-Seven

RHEA

B ELLA AND I SPEND the next day reading and relaxing, which I suppose is like every other day. Despite the repetition, I can't stop looking outside to see how close the sun is to setting, knowing Flynn's shift will end and he will be here soon.

I choose an incredibly soft dark blue dress that is sleeveless and comes down to my ankles. Small suns with wavy flares embroidered in golden thread cover the bodice. The billowy skirt flows from the waist where additional golden thread cinches it, showing off more of my figure than I'm used to. The dress has more buttons than any of the other ones I own, and there is a small gap where I couldn't reach them all. Twirling back and forth in front of my vanity, I stare at my reflection, noticing that my eyes look a brighter green today.

My heart skips a beat at the thought of wearing a dress like this in front of Flynn. My emotions have felt so complicated since he came into my life. Despite the fact that I've done everything I can to keep things locked in boxes and pushed into the darkest parts of me, some of my emotions keep rising to the surface, like oil in water. One moment I'm washed away by the tidal wave of heartbreak, and the next I'm set back up and standing at the shore again. Like now, as I wait for Flynn with happy anticipation. Maybe that's why I feel so jumbled up inside—a war is going on with two halves of my soul. I experienced happiness with Alexi, but it was only in pockets of time where he would sneak in to visit me. There was always an underlying sense of urgency to it. With Flynn, it just feels different—new and utterly complicated.

To get my mind off of everything I'm trying not to think or feel too deeply about, I write a letter to Tienne and Erica. Besides wanting to thank them for all the gifts they've given me, I also know I need their help to get supplies for my attempted escape. Grabbing the ink and quill, I practice a few lines on a separate piece of paper before starting my letter.

Dear Tienne and Erica,

I wanted to thank you for the dresses! They are so lovely and much nicer than anything I've ever owned (as you are probably aware). I hope to be able to repay you for them someday. I also wanted to thank you for all the other gifts you've given me. I was hoping I could ask you both for one more favor. Is there any way a satchel and a pair of shoes could be brought to me?

I pause, lifting the quill up from the paper as I contemplate about how much I should tell them. The letter is rather vague if I just leave it at that, but I can't word it in a way that won't clue them in to my plan of escape. What if they were also forced to take a similar blood oath as the guards?

It's safer for both myself and them to not say too much. While I want to trust them, what if their kindness is an act? *Just as Flynn's could be.*

I force that thought away and finish the letter by simply signing my name. If it is considered rude, well, I've been locked up in a tower for nearly twenty-two years, so surely they will show me some understanding. Keeping the letter on the tea table for Flynn to deliver, I sit on the couch with Bella—a book in my hands to distract me. The sunset eventually gives way to night, and when it's too dark to see the words on the page, I light candles all around the room. I'll have to ask Flynn to bring me more, as I have never used this many at once.

When his knocks finally sound, my pulse increases as I run my fingers through my hair to smooth it out and straighten my dress. My nerves leave me feeling frazzled, even my magic coils inside me in anticipation. But that excitement is momentarily clouded with guilt, like fog rolling in from all angles and covering those caged emotions as they rattle again to remind me that they are still there. My promise to Alexi replays in my mind.

Still, when I open the door to him standing on the landing, there is no stopping the way my stomach dips and my breath hitches. His eyes catch mine as they always do, and like those galaxies I see in my dreams, I'm powerless against their pull. He smiles, and the fullness of it causes my already pounding heart to skip a beat in its flutter. He's dressed in all black again today, though I swear his tunic is tighter along his chest and biceps. *Breathe, Rhea.* As if waiting for the command, my lungs suck in a shaky gasp of air.

"Hello, Sunshine," he says, walking through the doorway as I step back to give him room.

"Hello, Fly—" My words are halted when he pulls something out of a black satchel he has with him. He holds a small glass bowl that's illuminated with a bright golden light. It subtly lights a small portion of the room instantly in a liquid golden color, like Flynn has pulled a tiny chunk of the sun down into this very space.

"It's a flame gem," he says, walking over to the tea table and setting it down. The gem is no bigger than a small pebble, but it casts enough light that everything within a three foot radius is lit. "I figured you would enjoy having a light that you can move around with you more easily but that won't be seen from the castle. You'll have to charge it in the sunlight during the day and then use this cloth to cover it at night when you're ready for bed." He lays down a small square of black fabric next to it on the table, his eyes moving to mine.

My hands are layered over my chest, feeling the thump of my heart as I look at the gem. Pure joy tugs the corners of my lips as I laugh, thinking about how much easier it will be to read at night. How I won't have to huddle up to a small candle flame to try and make out the words on the page. My heart flips at the idea that he thought of me while finding this gem—one I didn't believe was *real*. He had said they were difficult to get, so I wonder how he came across this one. When I look at him to thank him, the words get caught in my throat. He looks at me with wide eyes, an astonished gleam to them.

I lift a brow and gesture towards the table. "Why do you look so surprised?" I ask. Confused, I turn my head to look around the tower, trying to see what he sees. I'm not sure I could ever see this place as more than just a cold, suffocating prison, but I suppose the golden light pouring out of the gem does cast a pretty glow against the stones. "You said these gems were all over the castle, yes?" I ask lightly.

"I have never seen you smile like that before," he says, voice gravelly and much closer behind me.

I gaze over my shoulder, having to tilt my head back to look at him. His dark irises sparkle—flecks of silver mixed into the slate color reflecting the gem's light.

"You missed a few buttons on your dress," he whispers.

Excitement tingles my fingers and knots my stomach as I nod my head at my purposeful mistake. I don't know what possessed me to wear a dress I could barely reach all the buttons for, but as I slipped it on earlier, I had the idea that maybe if I left a few undone, Flynn would notice. Like he did the first time we met when I was too nervous and heartbroken to let him near. But now, every time I picture him, a need once foreign to me claws up my throat. I should ignore it; a relationship of any kind is forbidden.

Forbidden by the king, forbidden by the fact that he is supposed to be my guard, forbidden by *common sense*. And yet...

"I did," I counter with equal quiet.

Two words, yet it feels like the world pauses at them. He takes a step closer until there's only a small space separating us, the heat from his body caressing the skin on my back. He doesn't say anything or reach out to touch me, waiting for me to give him permission. Flynn's always been so attentive to my reactions around physical touch, but right now, all I can focus on is how near he is to me and how I'm silently begging him to move even closer.

"I need you, Flynn," I breathe out the words, my heart racing and blood pounding in my ears, "to help."

His eyes grow impossibly darker as he inhales a sharp breath. The air feels thick around us, my body buzzing from his proximity. I'm acutely aware of the naked skin on my upper back, though I feel like so much more is exposed. Tension builds like that of a thunderstorm—taut, electrifying, and wild. I look away from him as he slowly and gently gathers up my long hair. His fingertips graze the base of my neck when he bundles the strands to one side and drapes them over my shoulder. Heat follows where his skin meets mine, yet shivers break out over my body. Deliberately, leisurely, his deft hands work to put all the remaining buttons through their matching loops, pausing longer than necessary on the last one. Breathing deeply, I'm surrounded by that incredible scent of his—it's crisp and clean and wholly like a breeze that's been scraped along the nearby trees.

"You look so beautiful." His voice is a low, decadent ribbon that slowly and seductively wraps around me. "Do you want to dance?"

I still as panic flares within me. "I don't know how to dance," I rasp, nerves causing my hands to tremble.

"I will show you." His fingers grip mine slowly before he walks around to face me. My smooth skin brushes against the calluses of his palms, and a curious ache to ask him how he got them blooms in my stomach. Is it strange to want to know everything about him? To have the desire to spend hours talking about his past or what he likes to do for fun or his favorite food? My face feels flushed at the thought as I tilt my head up to look at him. Taking in my expression, his hand tightens on mine. "We don't have to if you don't want to," he says, his chin dipping and causing the strands of dark hair hanging over his forehead to rustle.

"I do," I exclaim quickly, "it's just... what if I'm terrible at it?"

"Then I'll help you get better," he answers, his smile bright even in the subtle light. And isn't that the truth of it—of how he treats me? I have been shaped and molded by the confines of this prison all my life. Beaten and broken by a man with no compassion or love for me. But I never get the sense that Flynn wants to form me into anything other than who I already am. As if this splintered and heartbroken version of me is exactly what he wants. He doesn't want to change me; he only wants to help. "Besides, I'm good enough to counteract how bad you will be."

I scoff, slapping his arm playfully as he places his hand on my lower back. The touch is light, barely any pressure, and yet it's all I can focus on. My chest rises and falls in harsh movements as I lean into him a little more.

"Put the hand I'm not holding on my shoulder," he instructs. I do as he says, my fingers pushing onto the fabric of his tunic and into the hard muscle underneath. "This is called a box step waltz," he says before launching into the details of the dance and how I am to move my feet. I fail on the first few attempts, constantly tripping over myself and him. Flynn enjoys it when I mess up though, and part of me wonders if it's because he gets to catch and balance me when I'm about to fall over. Or maybe it's because of the way I laugh at myself in embarrassment as I trip, his eyes lingering on my mouth when I do. As moments pass, we move closer and closer. His large hand engulfs mine as he holds it tenderly to his chest.

"Where did you learn to dance like this?" I ask, trying not to focus too hard on how I need to move my feet.

"My parents made me take dancing lessons when I was younger," he says, laughing at the surprised look on my face. He continues to guide my steps, our pace beginning to quicken.

"What are they like?" I feel I've barely scratched the surface of knowing who Flynn is, despite our letter passing and time together. It's like every part of me is begging to find all the details that shine a light on who he is. I want to know everything.

His head tilts to the side in contemplation, his eyes gleaming and looking just past me, as if he can see his parents here now. "My mother is very kind and empathetic. She's soft-hearted but fiercely protective. My father is patient, loving, incredibly smart, and devoted. They were wed relatively young but fell in love at first sight," he chuckles, giving my hand a little squeeze. "Or so they say."

I hum in response, dropping my gaze to his chest. "I wish I had gotten to know my parents," I whisper, my feet now moving to the steps of the dance without conscious thought. I dance on the tips of my toes, and because of Flynn's height, my eyes are in perfect alignment with his lips.

"I'm sorry," he says gently, offering support in his words without trying to fix what can't be undone. My dress flutters around my legs as I move through the waltz. A content silence blankets us, the flame gem and candles illuminating the space with golden light. It is all too fantastical—to be here in this moment with him.

"I think I like dancing after all," I beam, shifting the conversation. His lips part and his eyes search mine as our bodies continue moving. The attention from him makes me feel warm and cared for, like a rose tended to in a garden.

"I guess that means I'm not so bad of a teacher, then," he grins, those dark eyes ensnaring mine.

As we dance to a made-up melody only we can hear, the tower begins to fade away so that I only see him. Awareness of the way his body is pressed up against mine as we move sets me ablaze. Every point of contact is a spark, my body seeking the heat of it until I can't push myself further into him. The thought causes a flush to rise to my cheeks, one I'm hoping can be explained away by the exertion of dancing. Flynn's movements falter for the first time as his eyes bounce between mine. Whatever he sees in them is enough to distract him. It takes me a moment to realize we've stopped moving, the surroundings of the tower slowly coming back into place—though the details are hazy. Only Flynn remains crystal clear.

"You are absolutely stunning, do you know that?" he questions, his eyes never leaving mine. "I believe you are the most alluring person in all the realms." The light of the flame gem gives the skin of his face, neck, and forearms a golden hue. His features are so striking—so perfect—that he almost looks otherworldly.

"No one has ever said that to me," I breathe. This moment feels impossible, like trying to walk on a cloud but hesitating with each step and expecting to fall through to the ground below. To find reality again. "And you haven't been to the other kingdoms."

"I don't need to leave this one to know that those words are true," he counters, lowering his head slightly.

The softness of my body fills in the gaps left by the firmness of his, and it creates a sensation that feels like I'm transcending the limits of what it means to *exist* in this moment. That's the thing with Flynn; being with him feels like I'm running forward through time. Sunrises, sunsets, the moon and stars... they all are meaningless when he's here with me. Especially when he looks at me like I might be someone he cares about—like I matter to him.

His eyes dip down to my lips for a moment, the movement making me lift just a fraction higher on my toes to try and close that last remaining distance. *Kiss me.* The thought of his mouth on mine has heat flooding through me with each breath that I take. That craving sweeps away every rational thought in my mind, every reason why we shouldn't do this. The sensations of my dress rustling against my skin, his warm hand holding mine, our bodies pressing so closely—it's a heightened realization of just how much I am yearning for him. He lowers his head slowly towards me, his breath tickling my lips as his gaze holds mine and—

A high-pitched whining sounds from behind us, startling us both into taking a step apart. The intoxication of the moment dissipates as we both turn to look at Bella, who is stretched out on the couch. She lets out another high pitched whine, the sound like a frustrated wail. Flynn chuckles, letting my hand go to walk over to Bella. He squats down and scratches the top of her head and bottom of her chin.

My cheeks puff up with air before I blow it out and tuck my hair behind my ears. My magic is lit up inside me, pure warmth buzzing and coiling until I sense it all over. If it is a sentient thing, it definitely likes Flynn as much as I do. Gods, I feel absolutely insane right now. Needing the fresh air, I head out onto the balcony, closing my eyes as I lean against the railing. I breathe in deeply, letting the earthy scents clear out my murky thoughts. *Dangerous. This is so dangerous.* For a multitude of reasons. Even with my eyes closed, I feel him come out and stand next to me quietly, his presence wholly consuming me.

"I should probably get going," he says almost regretfully. I plaster a smile on my face and nod, but I can't help how disappointed I am at the too-short-lived moment.

I follow him to the door, waiting for him to say something—*anything*. Instead, he faces me on the other side of the threshold and extends his hand out. Without hesitation, I place mine in his, holding my breath. He brings the back of my hand to his lips, planting a sweet kiss there before giving it a squeeze and letting go.

"I'll see you tomorrow, Sunshine." He moves to step away, and I remember that I have a letter for him to give to Tienne and Erica.

"Wait!" I yelp, running over to the table and grabbing up the folded letter. "Can you give this to Tienne and Erica?" He takes the letter from my outstretched hand and holds it up to look at it. "You can't read it though. It has... womanly stuff in it. It's only for ladies to read."

Flynn laughs—a hearty, true sound of amusement—before tucking the letter into his pocket. "I swear that my extremely handsome—but decidedly not female—eyes will not read your letter." He winks at me before taking a step back again. "Goodnight, Rhea."

"Goodnight, Flynn," I say back.

His face lights up, brighter somehow even with only the light of the torch in the stairwell. Then he turns on his heel and leaves, his steps echoing down the stairs. The only thought I can muster as I stand there, staring at the stone walls, is that I am so completely in over my head.

Chapter Twenty-Eight

RHEA

"Have you played cards before?" he asks from where he sits across the tea table from me the following night.

"Alexi and I used to play on occasion," I answer. I study the cards in my hand, sadness taunting the edges of my mind and reminding me it is never very far away.

"So I shouldn't take it easy on you?" His grin is cocky as he looks at me.

"I doubt you'd take it easy on me even if I hadn't played before," I reply sarcastically, eyeing him suspiciously over the top of my hand. He returns his own mock-menacing glare before he motions for me to go first. Back and forth we go, placing cards down and picking new ones up, making small conversation and telling jokes as we play.

"If you could be any animal, what would you be?" I ask him as I tap the cards in my hand to my chin.

"Something very formidable and fierce, like a jaguar or forest tiger," he declares, flexing his right arm. I snort but definitely notice his muscles through the thin black tunic as he moves them. I pretend to be unaffected. "What about you?"

"I've read about these bears that live in the Nalka mountains of the Fae Kingdom. They are smaller, have black and white striped fur, and live in packs," I reply, laying my card on top and looking at Flynn. "I would like to be one of them."

"Why?" He eyes me curiously, and I wonder if it was a silly thing to say.

"Because they stay together as a family. Even when they get old and can't move around as much, they don't leave anyone behind," I answer, watching as Flynn lays a card down and picks one up from the deck. "No one is ever alone." I stare at my cards, planning my next move when I realize that Flynn hasn't responded. I peek up at him, noticing the slight frown of his lips.

"Are you okay?" I quickly replay our conversation in my mind in case I've said something offensive.

Flynn clears his throat but doesn't speak for what feels like an eternity before giving me an appeasing smile and murmuring quietly, "That's a great choice." We resume our game in easy silence until we reach the end of the deck, each of us holding one final card. "How about a little wager?"

I look him over where he sits: feet flat on the ground and knees spread, elbows resting on top and hand dangling in between holding his card. He looks more well-rested and relaxed today, with a kind of ease that comes so naturally to him.

"What are you thinking?"

"The winner gets to ask any question, and the loser has to answer it," he smiles, wiggling his eyebrows in a way that's probably meant to be silly but on him looks suggestive.

Control yourself, Rhea. I pretend to hem and haw, finger tapping playfully on my chin. Flynn laughs, the sound of it wrapping around me like a star-kissed breeze. Looking down at my last card, I know there is only one in the entire deck that is higher in value, though I can't remember if it has already been played. However, the potential to ask him anything and know he *has* to answer is too enticing.

"Deal. Beat this," I taunt smugly, laying my card down on top of the pile. I watch his face for the moment he realizes he's lost, a question for him already on the tip of my tongue. But he doesn't look defeated or even surprised. My fear is confirmed when he lays down the one card that could beat mine. I scoff, acknowledging my defeat with a childish pout. He laughs again as he sits up, placing his forearms on the table. In the light of the gem between us, his eyes take on a dark silver hue. "Fine," I concede, leaning back against the couch, "what do you want to know?" The teasing smile melts slowly from his face and is replaced with a thoughtful look instead. His jaw catches the light in a way that it shows the cut of it more sharply, accentuating it along with his cheekbones.

"There are many things that I would love to know about you, Sunshine." Gods, that nickname. I open my mouth to ask him, again, why he insists on calling me that, but he continues speaking before I can voice it. "But there is one thing that I can't stop wondering about," he says, pausing before adding softly, "do you wish to live outside of this tower?"

I freeze, my eyes trapped by his. I don't know how to answer that. I mean, I know *what* my answer is, but panic is preventing me from voicing it. Why does he want to know? The blood oath makes it so that he can't help me leave—at least that is how Alexi explained it—but could it be that he would also have to act if he thought I was even *thinking* about it? Would he have to report to the king that I'm planning an escape? His words are careful—specific—not asking me if I want to escape but if I want to live elsewhere.

"Rhea, don't panic." He gets up from the floor and makes his way to sit next me, our knees touching where he's angled his body to face mine. "I'm just wondering because I want to help."

My lips part as my emotions tumble inside me. I wanted this. I wanted his help. And yet now that he's offered? I'm overwhelmed with anxiety about it.

"You can't help me," I say, confusion and indecision roiling inside me at how much I should tell him. At how truthful I should be when the magic of his blood oath might make him stop me. His brows draw down over his eyes while his mouth settles into a thin line. My heart aches at the look on his face, like he's betrayed by my rejection of his help. "Not because I don't want you to," I add with a shaky breath. "It's just the blood oath..." I trail off.

"You don't need to worry about that," he declares.

"Of course I do," I state, trepidation echoing with every beat of my heart. "Alexi told me that it prevents any of you from letting me leave. Are you telling me that's a lie?" The thought that Alexi could have helped me this whole time makes my stomach lurch and chest squeeze. I can't handle anything that devastating on top of everything else I'm keeping locked up inside. It is enough to destroy me.

"No, it's not a lie," he answers quickly. "The blood oath all of the guards take includes a line about not letting the princess—you—escape the tower in any capacity." His jaw clenches, a muscle moving in his cheek. "The king says it's because you aren't in your right mind."

I snort at that, rolling my eyes and shaking my head. I need to change the subject and get away from the severity of this topic. To move away from how close he is to discovering that I'm planning to leave on my own. So, of course, I settle on the first thing that pops into my head.

"What has the king said about the Cruel Death lately?" I ask, wincing at my lack of tact. Flynn's eyebrows shoot up momentarily, and the speed with which he's moved from dismay to shock is almost funny enough to make me laugh.

"You are terrible at being subtle," he mumbles, running a hand through his hair.

"I wasn't trying to be." I smile with forced sweetness. He huffs out a laugh, but I don't miss the way his eyes linger on my lips, like a smile is so rare from me that even a fake one is worth taking a double look at.

"We will be revisiting this topic," he says pointedly before sighing and leaning back against the couch. "And the Cruel Death is steadily getting worse. So many young men and women have fallen victim to it. The king keeps telling everyone that he is working on a solution, but no one other than him knows what that entails."

"Of course," I snark, not at all surprised by the lies my uncle tells. He's nothing if not a skilled manipulator.

"I get updates from the other guards about cities outside of Vitour, but the general consensus is that it mostly targets men of age to serve in the king's army and women in their child birthing years."

"Have you ever seen someone die from it?" He nods, but doesn't offer anything else, so I continue, "Do you know if the Cruel Death is in the other kingdoms?" I wonder if they have this affliction too.

"I'm not sure," he replies, tapping his knee with his finger. There's a silence in the air that holds a different kind of tension. It's the strain of unsaid words and secrets kept. I feel the weight of it all, heavy on my shoulders. "What are you thinking about?" Flynn asks, reaching over to gently tug on a strand of my hair.

I consider telling him everything. *Everything.* My promise to Alexi. The truth about what the king does to me. I think about sharing that I *am* finally ready to escape, that I believe I actually can. Briefly, I contemplate telling him that I'm composed of a myriad of broken and mismatched pieces, but talking with him makes me feel like maybe I'm not *just* those things. That being with him makes me feel softer—less jagged. But when I try to speak, the words won't come out. My mouth closes, and all I can do is stare at him and hope he understands. Hope he sees that I want to try opening up more to him, but there is an intrinsic part of my soul that has been keeping track of every time I've had something precious and every time it was ripped away. My parents. My freedom. My autonomy. Alexi. Nearly Bella. My *life.* More than likely my future. And Flynn, he's precious to me. Even if it pulls the frayed strings of my heart farther apart, I'll take being the cause of his sadness over the cause of his death.

I expect him to be angry with me. Pulling in a breath, I brace for the irritation to come over his face. For him to see me as I see myself: someone completely out of place. But his eyes only ease further as his lips tug into a small smile. He holds his hand out to me in the darkness, palm up. Like a rope thrown into the chasm, it's an offering of physical comfort. I reach over slowly and lay my hand onto his, interlacing our fingers, and my entire body relaxes.

"I don't know what it has been like for you here. Not wholly anyway," he states quietly, gesturing to the space around us with his free hand. "But I would like to know. One day, when you're ready, I would like to know everything about you."

"You claim that, but my life hasn't been one of joy and whimsy. There has been no fairytale happy ending," I whisper, willing the tears in my eyes to stop.

"Then it is not your ending yet," he says. "I haven't known you for very long, Sunshine, but you are stronger than you give yourself credit for." I start to disagree with him, but he squeezes my hand in a silent protest, never actually speaking over me. I pinch my lips together—a move he chuckles at—and let him continue. "I think you are too hard on yourself. You have lived—no, *survived*—in this place for your entire life. And you've done it mostly alone. There are men walking around this tower acting as guards that don't have half the courage, half the perseverance, that you do." I huff out a breath and turn my gaze down to my lap. The way he's looking at me, like I'm something to be admired, is too much. "Rhea," he rumbles, the sound laced with a richer, deeper kind of intent.

When my gaze meets his again, the pained sincerity in his eyes nearly undoes me. He truly believes everything he's just said. It's written on his face and in the way he holds himself steady, not shifting under my stare. I may not be able to tell when people are pretending around me, but Flynn wears his feelings out in the open for me so that I don't have to search for them.

"What are we doing?" I quietly ask.

"I don't know," he answers raggedly. "When it comes to you, I am cast out to sea without any sense of direction. I—" He pauses and swallows. "I have never felt this way about anyone before. I've never felt so lost and so sure about someone at the same time."

"Me either." Smirking, I add, "Obviously."

He laughs at that, reaching over to tuck a strand of hair behind my ear. "Just consider what I asked before. Please."

Please. That word from his mouth, the pleading I see reflecting in his eyes... it weakens all of my defenses. It's impossible to deny him, so I nod my head. Flynn sees my hesitancy but recovers quickly—giving my hand a small squeeze before letting it go and returning to the other side of the tea table. We play another round of cards before he leaves for the night.

Laying in bed later, I stare out at the night sky and wonder who will hurt more when I leave: me or him?

A warm breeze—the sign of summer evident in the air—rustles my hair the next day as I stand on the balcony, my head heavy. It's calm—deceptively so. Like the world has paused momentarily, not to let me bask in it, but to give me a warning. I don't have to wait long to know what is coming—*who* is coming. My door is thrown open, the silence only interrupted when it bangs against the wall. As I whip my head around towards the invasion, terror heedlessly grips my throat like a noose.

And he walks in. "Rhea," the king purrs as he enters the tower, dressed in his usual finery.

I watch as his guards carry in a wooden table and chairs. Two more guards follow behind with what appears to be a porcelain tea set. The entire scene is disorienting as I watch them set everything up, first laying a pure white tablecloth down and then a steaming teapot. Small mugs and plates are placed out next, and another guard sets down little jars in the middle.

"Have a seat, my darling," King Dolian says as he pulls a chair out and gestures for me to come. Stillness holds my body in place as my wide eyes take in the entire setup.

What is happening?

His voice drops an octave lower as he continues, "It is rude to make your king wait, Rhea. I may have told you not to bow before me anymore, but I do expect obedience." That makes me move faster, my bare feet padding on the wood floor as I step up to the chair. "This dress is a beautiful color on you. It reminds me of dresses one might see on the ladies in court," he drawls, a finger dragging lazily on my shoulder.

I had chosen one of the pink dresses Tienne and Erica brought me because I liked how I felt in it. Its unique color brings to mind the rose Flynn brought me. The gold of my hair and green of my eyes seem to brighten when I wear it. The cut, like most of the dresses I was given by the maids, has a built-in bodice and a flowing skirt. It's a beautiful dress that makes me feel like I am absorbing some of its beauty into myself, and a naïve part of me thought maybe Flynn would like me in it as well. Now, I want to rip it off and place a formless, ugly brown blanket of a dress on myself to hide from the king's hungry stare. It makes my stomach churn and my magic writhe inside of me, like it's trying to bury itself under my skin to hide from him. Or maybe break its way out to protect me.

"Thank you, Your Majesty." I force out the words, thick like mortar as they push through my teeth and lips.

My uncle smiles, and instead of the usual brutal twisting of his lips, it's a subtler one that I've never seen from him in the past. He pours what I assume to be steaming hot tea into the small cups in front of us, not asking for my input as he adds things in and stirs with a small spoon before tapping it on the side. When he's finished, he carefully slides the cup—nestled on a small plate—in front of me.

"This is how she liked it," he says with a voice that is uncharacteristically soft and gentle. It should put me at ease, as he's clearly in a good mood today, but all it does is leave me feeling like I'm teetering on an invisible edge. My fingers desperately grip the fabric of the dress in my lap.

"My mother?" I dare to ask. He nods, sipping from his tea without making a single noise. Something I doubt I can also achieve, so I don't drink any at all. "Did you—" I pinch my lips together, not knowing if I should speak or what exactly he is expecting of me in this conversation. There's a terrifying feeling in the air, like wading through fluffy clouds only to realize it is actually smoke and you're surrounded by fire. It's so jarring, I don't know how to move or what to think or say.

"Do not be afraid to speak in front of me." He phrases his words politely, gesturing elegantly for me to continue. I nearly scoff in shock, but manage to reel it in at the last second. "Do you want to know about your mother?" he coaxes, crossing one leg over the other and resting his hands on top of his knee. It's the type of royal indifference that he's mastered so well.

"Yes," I say in earnest because, despite it all—the abuse and the manipulation and the lies—I can't help but crave knowing more about my parents. When the king speaks next, the compassionate lilt of his voice catches me completely off guard.

"She arrived at the castle when she was just a few years younger than you are now. The head housekeeper—a burly woman named Imelda—took her in from the streets when she saw her wandering in the capital square, barefoot and disheveled." He chuckles at the memory. His laugh is so real, so *mortal,* and for a second, I let my own smile break through in response. His eyes zero in on my lips, a million different emotions flashing in them before he continues. "She worked her way up in the staff and had been employed in the castle for nearly a year before she was assigned to my wing. I'll never forget the first time I saw her," he confesses quietly, seeming ambivalent before he clears his throat. "She was walking down the hallway that led to my room, a bundle of fresh linens in her arms. The sun was shining in just the right way through the windows, making the crown of her head"—he gestures with his hands, placing it on the top of his head—"glow golden. She looked like a queen, even then in just a maid uniform." He lifts his tea cup to drink, the movement fluid and practiced. I still leave mine untouched.

"Did you become friends?" I ask carefully. I know from his previous words that, at the very least, he cared for my mother in *some* capacity—that he may have even loved her. He keeps his eyes down on his cup, a sort of reverence that is so completely out of place that I'm afraid to breathe and disrupt it.

"We did. Over the course of a few years, we talked nearly every day. Everyone in the palace loved her, even my father. He saw her beauty, grace, and kindness, and it actually subdued something in his otherwise-cold heart." His brows draw down as he speaks of my late grandfather. The hand he has resting on the table clenches into a fist, his knuckles turning white. "I was going to marry her," he nearly whispers, bringing his eyes up to meet mine. For the first time in all the years that I have known my uncle, I see true and utter sadness looking back at me.

"But she married your brother," I state. Like flipping the pages of a book, I watch as the sadness quickly changes into fury.

Burning, unrelenting anger lights his hazel eyes and warps the features of his face. "She chose wrong, and as she died, she realized that truth."

I'm rendered speechless by his words, by the meaning behind them and the rage pouring off of him in waves. My body stills, like a deer caught in a hunter's gaze.

"That is why you are so important to me, Rhea," he says, dropping his chin slightly as he glares at me. I bite the inside of my cheek, forcing each breath I take in even though my chest feels too tight to take it at all. "Everything I have done has been to protect you. To help you not make the same mistakes as the woman who bore you."

"Protect me?" I whisper, unable to stop myself. The warm feeling of my magic stirs inside of me, but that other feeling—frozen and dark—mixes with it as anger and confusion thrash in my blood. In my soul.

"Do you not see the benefits to living this life? I have given you everything you could need, kept you safe, and all I've requested in return was that you stay here until it was time," he quips, and for a moment I wonder if he's trying to convince me or himself.

Like I had a choice in being a prisoner. Like he hasn't ruined my being so completely that I will never know what it is to feel *normal*. He takes in my slack jaw, the widening of my eyes, and his own eyes narrow in return. *It enrages him.* It enrages him to know that I don't view the last twenty-one years of my life as a blessing bestowed by his hand. It's quite the opposite.

"I see I still have work to do then," he sighs, standing up abruptly and moving to my side of the table.

My throat constricts as his hand slides into my hair and grips it so tightly that a pained noise is forced from me. His other hand races forward with a slap so loud that it causes my ears to ring, the stinging on the side of my face so strong that I feel it from my temple to my chin. He yanks my head back as he leans over me, a towering darkness snuffing out any remaining light within.

"In time, my darling Rhea, you will see just how much you mean to me." His lips trail over my forehead as a tear slips free and runs down my cheek. With a deep breath, he lets go and walks to the door. His guards filter in, cleaning up the furniture and tea like it was never there. If it weren't for the sensitive skin on my face, I might have thought I was hallucinating.

When the guard that held Alexi's hair comes over to get the chair I'm sitting in, his dark eyes meet mine in a piercing stare as he gestures with his chin to get me to move. My steps off the chair are wobbly, and I nearly fall before he shoots out his hand to grip my arm. His long black hair slides over his shoulder with the movement. Quickly jerking his hand away, he lifts the chair and walks towards the door, closing it behind him.

Bella walks out of the library, her steps sure and quiet as she comes to stand right next to me—nuzzling her head into my stomach. The hand not cradling the throbbing side of my face absentmindedly scratches behind her ears. We stand there, frozen in time for a moment. All of the king's words replay and swirl in my mind like a tornado, none of them stilling long enough for me to grasp onto and understand what they mean.

Chapter Twenty-Nine

BAHIRA

"WHY DO YOU THINK he's summoned you?" I ask my father, peering at where he sits across from me, my mother still on his lap. The mage who had come to inform us of the shifter king's message waits in my room with his hands clasped behind his back. My father cants his head, watching as my mother stands, before standing himself and reaching his hand out to me to help me up.

"I do not know. We haven't had communication with the Shifter Kingdom since before the Spell was put into place. Though they recently crowned a new king, young by their standards. Perhaps he will be willing to form an unlikely alliance with us," he ponders, holding Nox's latest letter up. "Come, let's go meet the new king of the shifter isle."

I follow my parents down the stairs to the first floor, the unsteady beating of my heart matching our quick steps. I turn to go into the throne room where I expect the meeting to take place, but my mother grabs my hand and tugs me back into the main hall.

"We should have this meeting in the council chambers," she says, looking over to my father who nods his head in agreement.

"Tomas, has the council been told of this?" When Tomas shakes his head, my father sends him off with instructions to find all the council members and tell them to meet us in the council room as soon as possible.

My eyes flare wider as we enter, the new addition conspicuous from its place near the head of the table. The oval mirror stands tall at eight feet and is framed by dark brown banya wood. Tree bark twists around the edges almost as if it had grown that way and was cradling it. The current sigil of the Mage Kingdom, an ancient albero tree under a sky full of stars, is carved on the bottom curve of the Mirror while the old celestial sigil of the last Void mages—who ruled before us—adorns the top. Possessed by the ruler in each kingdom, the Mirrors are spelled objects given their power by the magic of the continent, allowing every ruler in Olymazi to communicate with each other. Normally, our Mirror is kept in a small, closed-off area attached to the throne room. A guard stands outside to both sway anyone from attempting to mess with it and to listen in case a voice comes *out* of it. Looking over the rippling silver of its center, I notice that the glass looks liquid and pliable. I move to step towards it, but my father halts me with a hand on my shoulder.

"The image will start to clear as soon as I, or someone of my bloodline, step near. We should wait until everyone from the council is here." I nod my head and step back in line with my parents.

Within a few minutes, every man and woman sitting on our council is here, none of them actually taking a seat. They all spread out in the room, but stay close enough to make sure they can see the Mirror. There's a nervous energy as I look around and see lots of shifting eyes and feet and hands tucked into pockets. And then at the last moment, another mage comes in and shuts the door behind him quietly. He lifts his head, his gaze meeting mine briefly. *Daje.* I frown slightly as I stare at him, trying to read if the tension lining his body is because of the situation or because of me. The trickle of sunlight flowing in from the windows at the front of the room makes the space between us glow brightly, while we are cast out in the dark edges. It feels symbolic. My father clears his throat, and I turn forward again, though I can feel the skin in the middle of my back prickle from Daje's stare.

"Ready?" My father asks the question quietly. I nod, looking at my mother who does the same, and together we step up to the Mirror. It is unusual for him to ask me to be a part of this, only in the sense that I generally avoid any matters that are political in nature. Yet something deep within me recognizes that this is an important historical moment and that I need to be here even if only to witness it.

The cloudiness of the Mirror begins to dissipate as we move closer, two blurry figures taking shape.

"King Kai Vaea, it is a pleasure to meet you," my father speaks, his voice dignified and his posture that of regality.

On the silvery surface, one of the men takes up nearly the entire image. I can't tell if he's just that large or if the Mirror is making him appear bigger than he really is. His dark brown eyes stare intensely at all of us, wild and predacious, but he doesn't respond to my father's words. Black tattoos cover nearly all of one arm, the ink stark against the light golden tan of his skin. I can't decipher their designs.

"This is my wife, Queen Alexandria, and my daughter, Princess Bahira," my father continues. My mother executes the most perfect curtsy, while I simply dip my chin slightly in respect.

The shifter king smirks at my display before gesturing to the man standing next to him. "This is Tua, my advisor. Thank you for answering my summons," he says, his deep voice lilting with a light accent so different from our own. This is the first time I've ever seen or heard someone from the shifter isle. His hands clasp behind him as the advisor, who is about six inches shorter and twenty years older, holds his own in the front. One is a stance of command and dominance, his broad chest flexing with his hands behind him, noticeable even in the slight distortion of the Mirror. The other stance is more diplomatic and peaceful. I also notice both the king and Tua have the same colored hair and eyes.

"Are you interested in my advisor, Princess?" the king asks sardonically. "I'm afraid he is already married. But if the Mage Kingdom is lacking, perhaps a visit to our isle is in store. There are a few males here who would be more than interested in playing with a princess." King Kai mocks me—his shoulders relaxing a fraction, while Tua suddenly loses all color.

"Tempting," I reply, shifting my weight onto one leg as I tilt my head to the side. I dramatically drag my eyes down the shifter king's body. It's more of a way to let him know that he doesn't intimidate me and less because I find him pleasing to look at. *Though he isn't terrible.*

"But I only *play* with males who have the intelligence to see me as more than a royal commodity. Is your kingdom so boring that you find accosting females entertaining, Your Majesty?" I add. The slight gasp from my mother and low grumbling from the mages behind me reminds me that I'm not acting very *royal* during a time when tensions are high.

King Kai chuckles, the sound powerful even from where we stand an ocean apart. "What makes you think I was talking about myself?" he practically purrs.

My eyes narrow, and I'm about to let my temper get the best of me when my father and the island king's advisor clear their throats at the same time. I hold the shifter king's gaze for a few seconds before my father starts talking and he is forced to look away. I childishly grin at him for breaking contact first. It's a move he notices and clenches his jaw at.

"We are curious as to why you have reached out," my father intervenes, clearly trying to diffuse the situation. "It has been many decades since our kingdoms last interacted."

The island king crosses his large arms across his chest, taking a deep breath before answering, as if calculating exactly how much information he wants to provide despite being the one who reached out. "We know your secret."

The voices behind me quiet immediately. My eyes dart to my father, who stops his nervous tapping on his thigh and states calmly, "I'm not sure I know what you mean, Your Majesty."

The king of the shifter isle glares, his stance preternaturally still, before growling, "Let's drop the pretenses, King Sadryn. I know that mages are not susceptible to the same consequences of crossing the Spell as the other peoples of Olymazi are." A ringing sounds in my ears as utter silence descends upon the council room. "I would like to propose a deal—a service in exchange for our silence on your *special* ability."

How the hell does he know?

I grit my teeth together, my anger flaring at the casual way he is holding our kingdom's safety in his hands. If any of the other kingdoms discover that we can cross through the Spell unharmed and unchanged, who is to say what sort of chaos would ensue? How could we even begin to predict the repercussions of that?

Daje's father clears his throat behind us, my father briefly glancing at him over his shoulder before turning back to face the shifter king and asking, "King Kai, what is your price?" I can feel my annoyance and frustration building with each second that passes in which he doesn't respond.

Finally, after a glance from his advisor, the island king speaks. "One of your mages."

I gawk, releasing a wholly undignified sound as my hands fist at my sides. My father holds his hand up towards me in a rare show of his dominance as king.

"Please explain," he demands, gesturing to the tall, arrogant ruler that I'm beginning to absolutely despise on the other side of the Mirror.

"At the risk of sounding vulnerable to another kingdom, consider this a show of our good faith," he starts, speaking slowly, as if this is a rehearsed speech. The slight nod from his advisor silently confirms that it probably is. "We believe there to be a blight on the magic in our kingdom. It is acting strangely and has been for some time."

I hate that his words pique my interest. And the interest of the council behind me, if the shuffling feet and bodies I can feel moving closer are any indication.

"In exchange for our silence, we would request that one of your strongest mages come and help us figure out how to fix the affliction."

"And how would one of our people be able to help?" my father queries, a line forming between his brows.

"Is mage magic not the rawest form of magic in our realms?" the shifter king asks, his advisor nodding subtly next to him. "And are mages not known for their ability to control and manipulate that magic?"

"It is," my father answers slowly. Though he of course leaves out the fact that the raw magic of our kingdom is dwindling.

"That is my price: keeping your secret safe in exchange for the time of one of your mages to help with our problem. It feels like you're getting the better end of the deal, does it not?" He lifts a mocking brow, and gods above, I want to knock that look right off his face. I don't realize how tightly I'm squeezing my hands together until pain lances my palms from where my nails are digging in.

Hadrik and Kallin step up to my father's sides, whispering in his ear as the shifters look on. After a few moments of discussion, the councilmen step back and my father leans in to whisper something into my mother's ear. Her gaze slants to him as she listens intently, thinking on something before imperceptibly nodding her head.

"We would like to suggest an additional condition to our deal," my father proposes. King Kai and his advisor glance at each other briefly before the king gestures for my father to continue. "I'll get straight to the point—we have a potential problem on our hands from one of the neighboring kingdoms."

"What sort of problem?" Tua questions. "And with which kingdom?"

I can practically hear the council members holding their breath in anticipation of my father's pause.

"I am waiting for my son to confirm what he has found there before I give names. I don't claim to be perfect, and there is a chance—though small—that we could be wrong," my father confesses, holding the king's eyes. "Because of that, I'd rather not say which kingdom until I have proof. And as far as the problem, about four years ago we felt what can only be described as a blast of magic. Since then, the heavy presence has been felt in waves." Tension lines King Kai's face, his lips forming a straight line while his dark brows draw in. My father goes on to explain a little about what the magic felt like and why he is concerned. Enough detail for them to know we're not lying, but not so much that it gives anything critical away. I watch the shifter king's reaction, but he's much better at keeping his face neutral than his advisor is. Tua's brows shoot up his forehead as my father continues. "My son volunteered to go investigate and see if this presence is something we should be preparing for—"

"By investigate, you mean he has infiltrated another kingdom, correct?" King Kai nearly growls. His advisor briefly cuts him a look from the corner of his eye.

"He has, and I have no doubt you would have done the same had you thought your kingdom was under threat," my father says, firm and calculating. The two men hold eye contact, a battle of two realm leaders, strong and defiant in different ways. "We might need to prepare for war if this item is capable of bringing down the Spell."

"And is it?" King Kai asks, subtly adjusting his stance. I see more clearly that his tattoo actually starts on the back of his hand, running up his arm and going underneath the sleeve of his tunic.

"We are not sure. My son believes he has found the source of it but is confirming as we speak."

"And what is it you believe we can do for you from the shifter isle?" he challenges, lifting his broad chin. Like he relishes the decision that our people's fate could very well lie in his hands. It's a move that makes me sneer involuntarily. Which in turn makes him smile, though it's more a baring of teeth, like a wild animal. *Asshole*.

"I ask that if this object is indeed strong enough to break through the Spell, enough to wage war on our kingdom, that you help bring our people to your island for safety." I work to keep my face impartial, but the surprise of my father's words leaves me feeling wobbly. Mages have never left in mass exodus from the kingdom. Not even for The War Of Five Kingdoms two-hundred years prior. To do so would be unprecedented.

"Is there a reason you feel you can't defend your own people from an imaginary attack, King Sadryn?" My father bristles at his accusation, just enough to cause me to grit my teeth. "And what would be the benefit to us for doing so?" The island king continues. The advisor at his side grimaces at his tactless words. Still, he doesn't correct his king or offer a more courteous response.

"You will not save innocent lives from the gore of war?" I ask incredulously. King Kai trains his gaze on me, but it betrays no emotion. His face is made up of hard edges and stone cold callousness. I would very much like to punch him.

"No. We have our own people to worry about. So I ask again," he replies, the muscles of his biceps bulging as his fisted hands push into them. "What would be the benefit for us?"

"If there is something that can take down the Spell, or allow armies to pass through, do you trust they will stop at just one kingdom?" my father questions, tilting his head to the side. "Your kingdom would be just as much at risk as ours would."

Tua leans in close, whispering something to the island king that has him tensing before giving a sharp nod. King Kai's voice is terse as he speaks. "Then the agreement is made. We will start preparations to sail to your southern shores tomorrow with the plan to arrive in seven days' time. Once in person, we will seal the deal in blood and the magic will choose the mage best fit to help us. Does this sound acceptable?"

My father looks to my mother for her opinion, a move that the shifter king is pleasantly surprised by if the slight tilt of his lips is any indication. When my mother nods, my father looks at me. My eyes move back and forth between him and the island king, but I know there really is no other option. If Nox believes this magical object is a threat to our kingdom's safety, then we must do whatever we can to protect our people. So I nod my head as well and take my father's other hand. Together as a family, with the fate of the kingdom on our shoulders, we agree to a deal with the king of the shifter isle.

Chapter Thirty

RHEA

"*R*HEA." *A VOICE LIKE the moon and stars and eons past envelopes me from every side, cradling all my broken pieces. Holding them together in a loving embrace that temporarily ceases the aching in my heart. "Wake, Rhea," she says.*

My eyes flutter open, and the illumination of infinite stars and galaxies meet them. Each flicker of starlight, each swirl of a new world draws my eye.

I am mesmerized as I watch the colors bleed and blend. It's as beautiful as it is overwhelming, and it calls to me.

"Hmm," *the lovely voice hums, a sound that reverberates through my bones.* "The magic inside you grows. As it does, coming here and interacting with everything around you will become easier." *Stardust surrounds me as she speaks, each tiny speck glinting and gleaming as it twirls around my body.*

I don't respond, as I'm not sure what to say. This place—the Middle—is peaceful and magical, and it feels like a part of me recognizes it, but I can't say why.

"Why can't I see you?" *I ask faintly. I* feel *the woman smile, and like a vision on the edge of my mind, I can see the delicate curve of her pink lips.*

"We don't have much time together," *she replies, the scent of jasmine winding through the universe I lay in to embrace me again.* "It is time for you to leave." *Her voice sounds much closer to me than it ever has before. I tilt my head to the side as much as I can in both directions, but I see no being.*

"He will never let me go," *I whisper, knowing in some way that she is telling me to leave my tower. The woman hisses—surrounding me with an eerie rumble—but I know she is not angry with me. Her fury visibly passes by me as I lay there, reds and blacks and grays of all shades on a mystical wind which holds so much contempt that it sends shivers through my body.*

"He is a broken man. Now so twisted and consumed by rage and revenge that he cannot see what he has become. He cannot see that he is something he onced feared," *she intones as a calming and comforting breeze grazes my skin.* "It is time to go east. To follow the stars above the ancient trees."

"I don't know how." *My voice sounds small and cracks with the truth of those words.*

"You have everything you need to leave," *she cryptically answers.*

I sigh because I don't. I'm not strong enough or brave enough or—

"You are," *she interjects, that floral breeze again caressing me.* "You are all those things and so much more. But you cannot linger. It is time to go now."

This is the closest the woman has ever come to sounding aggressive while speaking to me. My mind weighs her words and the inflection with which she speaks them. How can she believe that I'm strong when I am so broken? I turn my gaze up to the stars twinkling above me, my hand lifting to try and grasp at them, but failing. They surround me in all directions but are an eternity away at the same time.

"It is time," she repeats.

"Okay," I whisper as my hair begins to whip around me. A warm sensation wraps around my heart, weaving in with the icy shadows. Overwhelming them until all I feel is safe and cared for and— I sense myself become heavier, each layer of me starting to fall back into place piece by piece.

"He is good—" Her silvery voice is cut off as my soul is knit back into place within my body and I fall and fall and—

The tingling of my skin wakes me as I sit up quickly and look around the library that has grown dark as the night progressed. After the king's visit, I was too wound up, so I came here to read. The flame gem on the table in the corner of the room glows, lighting the rows and rows of books. I'm lucky King Dolian didn't come in here.

My chest tightens as I remember my visit to the Middle and my instructions to leave *now*. I wish I could understand the feeling of familiarity I have and why I just *know* that these visits and the woman I speak with aren't fragments of my subconscious. It isn't a dream despite the fact that I have only been able to end up there while I've been asleep.

A painful reality that I've been avoiding is now laid bare before me. I have been pretending, enjoying the distraction and the daydreams of "what if." But the chilling truth is that I have to leave this tower, and I have to do it tomorrow. *Alone.* Even though I want Flynn to help me—more than I have ever wanted anything, besides saving Alexi—the truth is that he can't. With the blood oath, he can't help me escape and, therefore, he can't know about my plans. I think about his offer, the way his eyes lingered on mine, our almost kiss... and a tear falls. Because, while Flynn may want me, I think a part of him knows that I could never be what he needs—what he deserves—in return. The pieces of my soul are scattered in the wind, ripped out of me too many times to ever fully be put back together again. I'm a shell of a person and he is like a full moon in a midnight sky—brilliant, comforting, and amazingly beautiful but also completely out of reach. Like trying to hold onto a smoky tendril, my hands will never be able to fully grasp him. And maybe that's why he's never acted on the invisible string that feels pulled taut between us.

I let the tears fall, mourning the life I might have had in a different time—a different world—and then I wipe them away and begin to plan.

⚘⚘⚘⚘ ⚘⚘⚘⚘

The entire next day moves much too quickly while I try to figure out how I can leave with next to nothing. My dresses are laid out on the bed in front of me as I wonder if I can somehow tie them together to make a sort of bag to carry supplies within. Suddenly, the door to the tower swings open and slams into the wall. I yelp in surprise as Bella ducks down on the bed. Walking over to the railing, I look over and see the gruff dark haired guard that is part of the king's trusted standing with a medium supply box in his hand.

"Your supplies are here," he grunts, like the mere act of giving me anything at all is too much of a burden for him.

I stare in pure confusion as I try to work out the days in my mind. I definitely received a delivery last week. Flynn brought it in and helped me unpack it. Which means Flynn doesn't know about this delivery. *Tienne and Erica—it must be from them.* My brain must be functioning too slowly for this guard because he dramatically grumbles and then drops the box on the ground unceremoniously.

"Empty the supplies out, and leave the crate outside the door." The guard then turns to leave before I answer.

Once the door is shut, I bolt down the stairs—Bella on my heels—and grab the box. For a second, I start to slide the lid off before I realize that I should open it in the loft in case my suspicions are correct. Running back up the stairs, my heart beating fiercely, I plop on the bed with the box. Peering inside of it, it would look like any normal supply drop off: various foods, some more soap and paste for my teeth... It's all that is visible from the top with the lid off. But as I take more and more of the items out, I see something hidden at the bottom. It's as wide as the box itself, and a strap lays across it diagonally. A rich black leather satchel, big enough to fit clothes and food in, is tucked at the base of the box. Lifting the satchel out, I marvel at it—dragging my fingers along the supple front of it—and the timing of receiving it just now. It's as if Tienne and Erica knew that I would need this before tonight. Reaching for the lid, I'm about to slide it back on when I see the box is not empty.

Gasping, I shakily reach in and grasp the pair of shoes that were hidden under the satchel. No, not shoes—boots. They are just as soft as the leather of the satchel—except, instead of black, they are a beautiful, rich brown. Instead of being tall and bulky like the King's Guard uniform boots, they are slender and only appear long enough to go past my ankles. Immediately, I sit on the edge of my bed and pull one of the boots on. It feels... odd to wear them. There is a slight pinching around my toes, but I suppose that makes sense considering I've never worn shoes before. Pulling the other one on, I stand up to walk and nearly trip myself.

"Bella, look at me!" I yell, trying to get her attention as I gingerly move around the loft until I start to feel a little more confident. Her pointy snout twitches in what I imagine is amusement while her eyes scream indignation. "We are leaving tonight, Bella! We have everything we need now, and with the extra food I—" I'm interrupted when the door to my tower opens and the guard walks in. I quickly hide behind a wall and start working to get the boots off. The first one comes off after a few tugs, falling to the floor. I cringe, freezing for a moment before I move on to the other foot.

"I asked you to put the box outside," he grumbles, steps sounding on the wood floor below. "Are you up there?" His voice trails off before I hear him start moving again and his boots sound on the metal staircase.

I curse under my breath as I try to get the other boot off. My heart beats furiously as I pull and pull until *finally* the other boot pops off. I toss it on the ground and run to grab the box. Three steps later, I'm standing at the top of the stairs blocking the guard from going up any farther as I hold the box out to him.

"Here you go," I say, the honeyed smile on my face making the guard's steps falter. He tries to look past me while grabbing the box, but I angle my body to block his view, leaning my shoulder against the wall. His dark eyes narrow, nearly level with mine from where he stands on the stairs. I've never stood this close to one of the King's Guardsmen before, and my nervousness grows as I take in his appearance further. The gold armor makes his lightly tanned skin gleam—so different from how Flynn's olive complexion seems to glow on its own—while long layers of raven hair frame his sharp jaw.

"Next time, follow directions," he snaps before turning to go back down the stairs. I watch him the entire way, keeping my fake smile on as he takes one more look in my direction. For some ridiculous reason, I throw my hand up in a little wave, wiggling my fingers until he scoffs and finally walks through the door.

Once it closes, I drop my smile and let my shoulders sag. Opening the trunk at the foot of my bed, I take out my single pair of trousers and Alexi's old undershirt and set them, along with a clean pair of undergarments, onto the bed. I then grab additional undergarments and one of the more simple dresses I own and place them in the bag, figuring ease of movement is more necessary than looking good in the forest. Moving to my vanity, I grab the hairbrush and a ribbon. I eye my toiletries. As much as I want to bring everything, I don't have room for it all when I consider the food that still has to be added. So I choose a bar of soap, a container of mint paste and the brush for my teeth.

The last thing I put in the satchel is the food I was given today. It makes the bag bulge, and I have to heave it over my shoulder, but everything I need to finally leave is there. Taking the bag off and setting it up against the wall downstairs with my boots, I decide getting Bella and I clean should be a priority, since I'm not sure what the bathing situation will look like while I'm traveling. So I take my time, soaking in the steaming waters and scrubbing myself twice over.

When I'm done, I drain the tub and put in fresh water, coaxing Bella in. Bathing her today takes much less convincing than it normally does. Maybe she really does understand that we are leaving tonight. The rest of the day is spent reading, both out of comfort and out of nerves. Holding *The Little Sun,* I sigh, chewing on my lip as my eyes glaze over the words. Though he hasn't left a note, I assume Flynn will stop by tonight after his guard duty ends. My heart feels stretched thin at the thought of him knocking on the door to an empty tower. Feeling too antsy, I lay the book down on the bench and walk out of the library.

For the final time, I open the balcony doors and step out. My gaze draws east as I take in the field of wildflowers that leads up to the forest. My eyes close as I picture what it will be like to finally drag my fingers along them, feeling all of their delicate petals for the first time. I get so lost in the daydream that by the time I open my eyes again, the sun is getting ready to set. Walking back inside, I slip my feet into my boots, clasping the three small buckles, and lift the stuffed bag over my head. The strap settles across my chest as the weight of the satchel digs into my shoulder.

"Are you ready to go, Bella?" I ask, words I never thought I'd get to say to her. She follows me back down the stairs, and together we walk to the front door. My hand pauses on the handle as I look back over my shoulder at the place that I've been trapped in for nearly twenty-two years.

With a gentle nudge from Bella's snout and another deep breath, I turn the handle and swing the door open, taking a step towards freedom for the very first time. It's strange to hear the door close from this side, a slight echo working its way down the staircase. My boots make quiet scuffing sounds against the eerie gray stone as I walk to the first step. A small window is cut out of the wall, and I stop in front of it, taking in a new view that faces the castle. I knew it was big, but seeing it straight on like this makes my lips part on a breath in wonder. It's so massive, much larger than anything I could have dreamed up.

Shaking my head, I turn back to face the stairs and take my first step down. Then another. And another. Until I've rounded the first of many spirals. Bella follows closely, moving with grace and agility while I keep a hand on the wall for support and balance. The center of the tower is hollow after that first spiral, providing a clear look to the ground below. Looking down makes my stomach clench, so I keep my gaze on the steps in front of me.

Minutes drip by as we continue down the tower, pausing anytime I think I hear a voice or a noise. As we descend, the fading golden light of the sun peeks in through small windows, illuminating just enough of the steps to make sure I don't trip. Finally, after what feels like a small eternity, a landing appears in front of me. I can either go through a door or continue farther down into darkness. *Is there a part of the tower that goes underground?*

"We have to be at the ground level by now, right? Do you hear anyone?" I ask, leaning my ear against the door. I watch Bella as her ears twitch back and forth, but her demeanor remains calm. I wait another few moments, hoping that we're at the bottom and out of sight of the guards. All I need is ten seconds to walk out of here and run towards the meadow. Ten more seconds and we're free. *We're free.*

Steeling myself, I slowly open the door, the hinges surprisingly quiet. The setting sun shines directly into my eyes, blinding me for a moment. A hand goes to my forehead to try and shield them from the waning light. When my vision clears, I suck in a breath, my eyes widening. Though the space is empty, I quickly realize that I'm not at the bottom of the tower. Panic curls in my stomach at my mistake. A large gray stone bridge is in front of me, the width so much grander than I ever could have imagined. *How could I forget about the bridge?* My eyes dart to the sides, confirming that no one is here at the moment—a *huge* stroke of luck. Despite knowing that I shouldn't and that I'm risking getting caught, I can't help but take one step out onto the gray stones.

Birds soar overhead as I tilt my head back and look up to the place that's been my prison, my cage, for my entire life. An odd pang of despondency flickers inside of me. The tower just looks so unassuming from the outside. Inside, it was my entire life. Everything about me was confined within those stone walls, but now that I'm out here gazing at it... it just blends in with everything else. Like it wouldn't matter what or *who* was in this tower at all. It feels like confirmation that my very life has been an insignificant speck in the grand scheme of existence.

Bella nudges my hand, bringing me back to reality.

"Okay, Bella, we should keep going down the stairs," I say in a low voice as my eyes catch on something farther down the bridge. I hadn't noticed it before, with the sun practically blinding me, but now I see two black and gold figures talking with each other. Slowly, I start inching back to the tower door, beckoning Bella to follow me.

"Hey, you!" a male voice shouts, followed by the sound of footsteps. Bella and I take off, darting back to the staircase inside the stone column. I chastise myself, knowing that, in my haste, I made a mistake. I can only hope it won't cost us our chance at escape.

My feet start to ache in my boots as I move in the near darkness, going down farther and farther with Bella right next to me. I hear the tower door to the bridge open, boots on steps sounding closer and closer behind us, yet we still haven't reached the bottom. Finally, as we round the stairs, I can see the golden light of the sunset outside filtering in around the edges of a door. Just a few more turns around the staircase and we'll be there. My heart beats in my ears as I command my body to move as fast as it can. My legs pound and arms pump as the echoes of footsteps surround me. I finally reach the landing just a few steps after Bella. My hand reaches out for the door handle, the tips of my fingers barely grasping it to turn. Bella uses her head to push it all the way open, darting outside. I follow closely behind, the tip of my boot making it through the door—the view of the meadow that leads to the forest right there in front of me.

A rough hand grips onto my arm and yanks me—my back slamming into something firm as a scream rips from my throat. Another arm bands around me, hot breath skating across my hair. "What are you doing?" he asks as I turn and see the face of the guard who had just dropped off the box of supplies.

I try to jerk and get out of his grasp, but his hold doesn't falter. The door in front of me closes as Bella—noticing I'm not with her—turns around. She darts back towards me, but it's too late. I scream at her, pleading for her to take her freedom, "Keep running, Bella!"

The door closes on her, sealing us into different fates.

Chapter Thirty-One

RHEA

"I HAVE TO ADMIT, Princess, I didn't think you had it in you to try to escape. And was that a fucking fox? Have you been hiding that beast up there with you this whole time?" He hauls me around to face him.

"Let me go!" I shout, trying again to rip out of his clutches. But his hand is firmly wrapped around my arm.

"Back up to your room," he growls before pushing me towards the stairs.

"No!" I yell, my boots scraping on the stone as I try to push myself away from him.

"We don't have time for this. Back. Upstairs," he grits out before he hoists me over his shoulder, my shriek reverberating off the walls.

My magic starts to writhe inside of me, pushing against the barrier of my skin like it will somehow be *useful*. But I'm not sure how having the ability to heal can help me get free, so I ignore the sensation in favor of trying to break free of this guard. He pins my arms to my sides as he climbs the stairs, ignoring my attempts to wriggle free from his tight hold.

A noise sounds above us, like that of an opening door, and then I hear a familiar voice. "Xander, are you down there?" Flynn shouts. I nearly answer in return before I stop myself at the last moment.

"Yeah, it's me," the guard holding me shouts back, the sound a bit breathless before we round the final curve of the staircase and come to the platform that opens out onto the bridge. "I caught the princess trying to escape." Flynn's boots step into my line of sight, and I trail my eyes up his body until I meet his rounded gaze. Shock contorts his features as he lowers his drawn sword.

"Sun—" He clears his throat, stopping himself from using his nickname for me. "Trying to escape?" he asks, his eyes leaving mine to meet the guard's.

Xander's black hair tickles my arm as he nods his head and answers, "She had a fox with her as well, but it was able to escape through the door. We'll have to alert the others to be on the lookout."

I grit my teeth together, my body jerking side to side as I try to free myself. He snorts, my strength nothing compared to his, as he squeezes me more tightly to halt my movements. I hiss through my teeth in frustration, my body deflating as I all but give up my struggle.

"She's more fiery than I would have given her credit for," Xander mutters, turning somewhat so that I can see Flynn again.

I watch as his eyes fixate on Xander's hold on me, the hand on his sword flexing tightly. "Are you taking her to the king?" Flynn questions, his voice laced with a dark challenge as he shifts subtly so that he's blocking the door.

Xander tenses faintly—a motion felt more than seen—as he shifts his body again so that he's facing Flynn, my own view of him now blocked. "No," he says slowly, "I'm taking her back upstairs." A strained silence clouds the landing, my own frustration at being held like this adding to the tension.

"I'll inform the others about the fox," Flynn states. Xander moves his head in what I assume is a nod and then turns, beginning to climb the stairs back up to my prison.

I try catching Flynn's gaze, but he is already stepping out of the door and onto the bridge, not even glancing back. With each step, a bitter awareness starts to prickle in my veins that not only did I fail, but I also lost Bella in the process. My chest squeezes in on itself, and my breathing becomes more labored. Panic floods my body like water crashing through a broken dam. I was so close, but I failed. *I failed.* I don't know whether to scream or cry or just reach for that dark chasm within my chest and beg it to consume me again. I have no doubt that when the king finds out about my attempt, my life here will become even worse. If anyone can figure out a way to torture me further, it's him.

When we reach the achingly familiar arched door, the guard opens it and simply sets me down. Not speaking another word, the door closes, and I'm once again alone here. Truly alone this time. Even that tiny bit of freedom I experienced, the few seconds where I just gazed upon everything from the bridge, makes being back inside so much worse. It looks so small in here, so cold and empty and *awful*.

Slowly, I lift the satchel off of me and set it down near the stairs. Pulling on the boots, the slight swelling in my feet makes it even harder for me to get them off. Nighttime smothers the sunset, leaving the tower in pure darkness. Not wanting to go to bed alone for the first time in years, I grab the flame gem from the library and bring it out into the living area.

Taking a seat on the couch, I hug my knees to my chest and close my eyes. I create a new box in my mind, one that will allow me to just *not feel*. I imagine my hands grasping and pushing and yanking each feeling into its new prison, quickly sliding a lid over top and locking it. My mind then goes cold—that dark iciness that had started to diminish within me over these past few months now back in full force. Perhaps caring about what happens to me is pointless. The king can do whatever he wants, and I won't fight it. Resisting my fate all these years has done nothing but leave me feeling more empty, more broken, more alone. So maybe I should resign myself to becoming whatever it is he wants to mold me into. As I start to shove the last of my determination to be someone outside of this jail into another mental box, I see a small flame flickering in my mind: the last remnant of hope that is left within me. I walk up to it, lifting an imaginary booted foot to officially snuff it out, when there is a quick knock on my door before it opens.

Flynn doesn't walk in, but he stares at me, his chest heaving like he's just run the entire way up the tower. I startle at the sight of him. The hair around his temples is curled with sweat, and red splatters the front of his golden armor as his hands brace either side of the doorframe.

"Can I come in?" he asks, but his voice— It doesn't sound right. He doesn't sound like the man I've gotten to know. Still, I nod, and he walks through the door. I'm about to speak—to say what, I'm not sure—but then a knot forms in my throat at the sight of the giant white bundle of fur following at his heels.

"Bella!" I yell out, voice breaking as I bolt off the couch and fall to my knees when she meets me halfway. "I thought I lost you," I whisper, kissing the top of her head. She nuzzles her head into my chest as I hug her tightly, unrelenting relief relaxing that strain on my heart. "The moon may have the stars, but at least I have you," I recite with a quiet voice.

Flynn stands near the door, his armor and sword already off and leaning against the wall. My eyes catch the red again—blood, I realize—splashed across the front. I study his body, looking for any signs of injury, but because he is wearing all black, it's not obvious if there is one.

The silence stretches between us, so tinged with anger and disappointment and fear that I swear I can taste its bitterness.

"You should give us some space," I whisper to Bella, placing one more kiss on her head before watching her make her way to Flynn. She rubs her head on his hand, begging for a pet—which he hesitantly gives—before she climbs the stairs to the loft. Flynn's hands brace on his hips as tension brackets his shoulders. His head hangs low for a moment more before he slowly lifts his eyes to meet my gaze.

"Why didn't you tell me you were going to escape? I told you I wanted to help you," he implores, his voice rising faintly. Words dry up in my mouth as we gawk at each other, both weighed down by everything left unsaid. "Were you just going to leave without saying anything else to me?" There's a slight break in his voice at the end, hardly there but noticeable to me all the same.

"And why would I tell you, Flynn?" I counter, hating myself for doing this—for pushing him away. "Why would I tell you when you are *sworn* to not help me? When your very blood has magic running in it that would make you stop me?"

"Rhea, I told you that you didn't have to worry about the blood oath—"

"Yes, but you've never given me a reason why!" When he doesn't respond, I huff out a breath and shake my head, turning to gaze outside to the balcony. Chewing on my lip, I let my eyes close. "Why did you start visiting me? Why risk getting caught by the king?" It's a question I never wanted to give voice to, a worry I never wanted to let him see.

"What?" The sound of his steps echoes throughout the tower as he comes closer. I swallow down the pain radiating in my throat, the guilt and regret and every other negative emotion that has been locked inside of me for some time.

"I've been told that a man would only visit me for one reason," I murmur, remembering King Dolian's words. "Is that what you were hoping for? The chance to bed the princess of the tower?"

My head swings to look at him as I finish the sentence, wanting to see his reaction. Waiting to see the truth of those words reflected before me. Hoping it will be easier to leave Flynn behind if he admits that I was nothing more than a conquest. But that isn't what happens.

His head jerks back like I've physically slapped him, disgust curling his lip as he snaps, "Are you seriously asking me that?" His body practically vibrates with frustration and anger. He's *angry* with me. Panic sits heavy on my chest, constricting my breath. "Rhea, do you really think I'd spend time getting to know you—"

"I don't know you, Flynn. Not really," I argue, taking a step towards him, my head tilting up to hold his gaze. "We've only spent small pockets of time together *here*, secluded in a tower, where *you* can pretend to be whatever you want and *I* won't be any wiser." My arms fold over my chest, hands squeezing tightly into fists. "What are your motives? What are you really here for? What makes you keep coming back—"

"Because I fucking care about you!" he shouts, throwing his arms out to the side. "Gods, is it so impossible for you to believe that?"

"Yes!" I yell back, my chest heaving as my insecurities burn through me.

"Why?" he asks, stepping forward again until we are barely an arm's length apart, his face tense with confusion.

"Because the only people who ever cared about me are dead." The words come out in a shockingly low pitch, a near growl that surprises even myself. Cold seeps through my body, tingling the tips of my fingers. I heave a shuddering breath and point out to the city beyond this tower. "There is an *entire kingdom* of people who know that I live here day in and day out, and they don't care enough to wonder if the king could be lying about why I'm here." Frustrated, I wipe roughly at the tears that trace down my cheeks, but they don't stop flowing. "Twenty-one years and not one person has ever thought to themselves that maybe it's a ridiculous notion to assume a person is grieving for that long. *They don't care!*"

I laugh callously, the sound laced with the pain I've held onto. Each inhale I take burns my lungs as I gasp for air, the room blurring around me. Gods, this pain is infinite. I've been falling down into an abyss of desolation for so long that I forgot I was even moving. Flynn made me hope that maybe I'd finally found the ground, hit rock bottom so that I could begin to climb back up. But the darkness has just continued to grow.

"And maybe that means *I* shouldn't care either," I cry, my chest caving with an ugly truth I've never voiced before. Flynn's eyes widen with realization as he stares at me, the shock of my words and their intent leaving him momentarily frozen. Unable to handle the weight of his gaze, I turn away as I try to suck in a breath. "So how can I believe that *you* do?" Seconds that feel like hours pass before I sense him coming up behind me. Near but not touching.

"Well, you are wrong," he states, his voice excruciatingly soft.

"Stop," I gasp as I squeeze my eyes shut. "It's too late now. It doesn't matter."

"Of course it matters." His breath tickles the top of my head as he speaks. "*You* matter." I drop my head as a sob tears me apart. His rich voice is a tender plea that only works to unravel me further as he continues, "Rhea, look at me."

I try not to turn around because I know. I know that if I look at him, it's going to be so much harder to shut him out. It's going to be so much harder to pretend that he hasn't been one of the bright spots in my life since Alexi died. That his notes and jokes and the time we've spent playing games and reading together have meant more to me than he'll ever realize.

His hand faintly brushes the very outside of my elbow, just a whisper of touch so that I don't startle. He begs again, "Please look at me."

I can't deny him. I've never been able to. The beating of my tattered heart quickens as I slowly turn, my gaze staying glued to the floor. His hands lightly cup both sides of my face, the warmth of his fingers across my cheeks seeping into my skin. Immediately, my magic perks up under his touch—as it always does—but it's the way I can feel some of my own tension and anger and *hurt* melting away that leaves me breathless. My head tilts up to look at him, his molten eyes boring into mine with the kind of intensity that leaves no room for deceit.

"I never want you to doubt anything when it comes to me, so let me tell you some truths." He smiles, taking a deep breath to fortify himself. All of my attention is focused on him as I wait for his words, the anticipation so heavy that it feels as though the universe itself is leaning in to listen. "The truth is, I find you so captivating that the risk of getting caught visiting you is inconsequential in comparison." His thumbs gently wipe away new tears as they fall down my cheeks. "I have thought of nothing else—no one else—but you since the moment our eyes met for the first time."

My lips part as the air around me is sucked out of the tower. My hands grab onto his chest, gripping the tunic there tightly.

"The truth is that when I look at you," he rasps, "it's like peering into a blazing sun. I'm drawn to you, and I would happily go blind if your face was the last thing I saw."

My gaze is latched onto his as my chin tips further up. He compared me to the sun, but I'm more like a flower drawn to *his* light.

"And I'm terrified, because the truth is," he whispers, leaning in even closer, "I feel that there is no limit to the things I would do for you to keep you safe. To make you happy. To see you smile and hear you laugh."

Something overwhelmingly tender floods my body, wrapping me safely in its warmth. It feels as though the world around us is shut out and only he and I remain.

"Do you understand what I am telling you, Sunshine?" he pleads, our chests rising and falling in tandem. "I don't expect anything from you. I'll only accept what you're willing to give me." He lowers his head until our foreheads touch.

I've experienced my heart being ripped apart before—more times than I ever want to remember—but I've never felt what it's like to have someone piece it back together again. I've never experienced what it's like to have someone consume me so thoroughly with their words that I feel wanted, as I am.

"A minute, an hour, a day," he says, continuing reverently and breathing in deeply, "or more, I don't care. I first came to this tower because it was part of my job. I kept coming back because of you, because I was selfish and wanted to learn more about you. I was weak and couldn't resist trying to make you smile. Because you enchanted me so much that I was willing—*am* willing—to risk nearly everything just for that minute, or hour, or day where you look at me like you see me—the real me."

My magic flutters inside of me, coiling and twirling around, as his words permeate through any of the darkness that might have remained. Staring at him now, I nearly forget how to breathe. He's always been so indescribably handsome, but now as he looks at me like I *am* the very sun his universe spins around, I realize that this version of him might be his most appealing. Vulnerability and desire blend in his expression, mirroring my own feelings.

"Flynn." His name comes out on a ragged breath. How could I even begin to voice what he means to me? How could it compare to everything he's just said? Perhaps more words aren't needed. Maybe an act or a gesture can mean more than anything spoken.

At this moment, there is only him and the way he is looking at me. And I can't deny either of us any longer. Closing the infinitesimal distance, my lips slide across his, the featherlight touch igniting me from within. A burst of panic flares through me briefly, fear that I may truly be awful at kissing or that he might not actually want this, causing me to pause. But Flynn gives me no time to dwell on it. One hand slides to the back of my head, tilting it delicately to the side while his other moves down to my lower back. His lips press more firmly against mine, guiding me with his own movements as the world around us does indeed fade away. The need to be closer to him—to have every part of me touching every part of him—is nothing like I've ever felt before.

I slide my fingers into the silky softness of his hair. *Finally* feeling it the way I've always wanted to as I gently grip it. In one swift move, Flynn lifts me off the ground, my legs instinctually wrap around his torso, bringing us even closer than before. A deep groan rumbles from him as I squeeze my legs tighter. My mouth opens on a gasp, the tantalizing slide of his tongue against mine causes a demanding ache to pulse at my core. The taste of him is indescribable. It reaches into the deepest parts of me, forging new pathways and unlocking parts of my body previously untouched. That unique scent of his envelopes me, creating a hazy cloud of desperation and lust. And I know instantly that a metaphorical line has been drawn in the sand.

There was my life before this kiss, and there is my life since. There was the Rhea of the past who existed alone, with so much fear and so much guilt that she never truly lived. Then, there is the Rhea of right now, kissing a man who makes her feel wanted and safe and precious and *alive*.

And nothing would ever be the same again.

Chapter Thirty-Two

RHEA

Flynn slides both of his hands down to grip the bottom of my thighs. My body shivers under his touch, and I can't help but tighten my hold on his hair. If this is what kissing him is like, I can't imagine—

He pulls his mouth away from mine, only to plant searing kisses down my jaw and neck. My back arches in response, small gasps seeming to echo off the walls. When his lips are on me, I feel transformed, remade. Like a different version of myself that has been locked away and hidden is now brought to light.

"You are perfect," he rumbles in between the pressing of his lips on my skin. I'm blazing, feeling more alive, more wanted, more undone—just *more*—than I ever have before, as my body moves against his. I have no idea if what I'm doing is right or if I'm affecting Flynn the same way, and that small hesitation in me causes him to pause and look up at me. His eyes are wide and filled with a hunger that I know is reflected in my own. His perfect wavy black hair is tousled from my hands, eliciting more of those thoughts of what it would be like to do this completely uninhibited. Heat crawls up my cheeks as I chew on my tingling bottom lip. Flynn frowns, leaning in to kiss me, forcing the lip free and asking against my mouth, "Do I want to know what is making you blush so fiercely?"

"Nothing," I respond too quickly, causing him to laugh. My body trembles from the sound, and I'm not sure if it's my magic reacting or just me. Or perhaps it's both—it likes Flynn as much as I do.

My hands slide down from his hair to hold the sides of his face, so similar to the way he held mine. I pull him in for another deep kiss, feeling like I could exist off of only this. Off of only *him*. Like two choruses fusing together, our lips create an exquisite melody—a song unique to us. When we separate again, both panting for air, he groans as he adjusts his hold on me. His large hands slide farther up my legs and closer to the center of my body.

"What's wrong?" I ask, worried that he was injured earlier or that maybe he's tired from holding me.

"Everything is perfect. It's just—" He laughs, his olive skin flushing at his cheeks as he leans in to kiss the tip of my nose. "I have been thinking about this moment for a long time. *You* have consumed my thoughts for a long time."

Warmth brushes the edges of my mind as my fingers fan across his cheeks and chiseled jaw, gently stroking the smooth skin there in response. "You have consumed mine as well," I say quietly, my heart fluttering at how his eyes glaze at my confession. "Was it— Was I—" I stammer, not able to find the bravery to question what I'm afraid to know the answer to. Flynn reads the unspoken words on my face, though, and just laughs in that all-consuming way he does. His forehead comes back to rest on mine, his eyes indulgent as he pins me in place.

"Do you believe everything I told you?" I nod my head slowly as his earlier declarations replay in my mind. I want to brand them onto my brain—an eternal reminder of what he feels for me. A dedication of the moment we became something *more*. "Then know that this is the truth too. All I can think about now is how you taste," he avows in a dark velvet voice. His tongue darts out to lick his lips like he's desperate to see if there's any part of me still lingering there, causing my legs to squeeze around him tighter in response. "And I am now burdened with not only the knowledge of that taste but my desire to consume you again."

Gods above.

Our bodies are so closely pressed together that I can feel the evidence of how much he wants this—of how much he wants me. I let out a pathetic whimper, while inside of me is an inferno fueled by the knowledge that his desire for me is so... prominent. My earlier thoughts of what it would be like if all the barriers between us were removed pushes to the forefront of my mind again. My magic agrees with the direction of those thoughts as it warms me from the base of my spine to the top of my head.

"I don't want to rush things with you," he breathes as his lips skim across mine. "But make no mistake, Rhea, you have complete and total power over me."

I have no idea how that can be true when just my name from his lips has my legs weak and my heart skipping beats. He's holding more of me than he knows, and the longer I stare into the depths of his eyes, the more I would give him anything he asks. Any broken part of me he might desire, it's already his.

"What if I don't want you to go slow?" I whisper, looking at him from under lowered lashes.

His fingers grip my thighs more tightly, enough to let me know that he's holding back, but not enough to hurt. Unburdened desire floods my veins as I watch his eyes widen and brows draw up. For the first time since meeting Flynn, I think he might be speechless.

"I just assumed that we should since you haven't—"

"I have," I interrupt. His surprise morphs into confusion for a few beats, but then another emotion bleeds in. His eyes narrow faintly, and the corners of his mouth tighten as a near grimace takes form.

"With who?" The words are clipped, the change in his demeanor catching me off guard.

My eyes hold his, trying to decipher what I said wrong as I ask, "What do you mean with who?" We're both staring at each other, an unpleasant tension pushing us apart as I lean back a little to see him better. The tightness of his lips relaxes a fraction, but he's still looking at me like he's learned something new he doesn't like. And that thought makes me nauseous with panic. "Flynn, what are you talking about?" I suddenly feel shy with the apex of my desire still flush against his body.

"What are *you* talking about?" he counters.

"You can't answer a question with a question," I mumble. When he doesn't say anything and instead tilts his head forward, encouraging me to respond, I sigh and slide my hands down from his face. "Aren't you getting tired of holding me?" I deflect, a different heat rising to my cheeks as I now realize that perhaps I *don't* want to vocalize my thoughts.

"Don't insult me," he scoffs lightly, easing some of my worry. "Tell me what you are talking about."

My cheeks puff with breath as I pinch my lips together, my fingertips digging into the hardness of his muscular shoulders. Awkward seconds pass that only grow more so as time goes on. Finally, I exhale and dip my chin, hoping it doesn't sound as bad as it does in my head when the words start tumbling out of me.

"I just meant that I know I've been locked in a tower and have barely had any mortal interaction, but I know what it means to be... intimate. Or I have read about it, at least." My whole body tenses as I cringe—it definitely sounds worse out loud.

Flynn is silent, though his shoulders underneath my hands relax and lower. Suddenly, we're moving until he gently pushes my back up against a stone wall. Bracing me there, a hand leaves my leg to cup the side of my face. His eyes hold mine for a moment before our lips meet again. The feel of our tongues sliding together draws an indecent moan from me, my legs once again squeezing to bring him in closer. His hips push into me in response, and my mind goes blank—utterly blank. Thank the gods he is holding me up because I'm completely undone under his touch. Flynn pulls back slightly, our lips separating but still close as we breathe each other in.

"We need to slow down," he whispers. I let out a frustrated groan in response—to which he just chuckles darkly. With one more searing kiss that ends far too quickly, he lowers me to the ground and guides me over to the couch. "We also need to talk," he says, tone going serious.

I nod my head because I know. I enjoyed a few minutes of distraction where it felt like, for once, my world was coming together rather than falling apart. Unable to stop the quiver of fear that alters my voice, I ask, "How long do we have before the king finds out what I've done?"

"He's not going to find out," Flynn growls. A muscle in his jaw pulsates as he grinds his teeth together.

"But... the guard?" My skin tightens at the memory of his hold on me. One look at Flynn and I know his thoughts are the same.

"Is no longer a problem." The words are solemn as he holds my stare, unyielding in the fierce way he looks at me.

"The blood," I whisper, eyes rounding as realization clears away the remainder of the lust that had been coursing through me. "You killed him?"

"I should have, for the way he touched you," Flynn snaps before seeing the look on my face and exhaling loudly. "No, we fought, but I was able to subdue him. He's tied up at the base of the tower." A crease forms in the middle of his brows, his gaze dropping from mine like he's ashamed that he didn't do more.

"Flynn, you made the right choice." I bring my hand up to cradle the side of his face and tilt his head up to look at me, my thumb caressing his skin. "I don't want you to kill for me," I plead. "I just want *you*."

He huffs out a laugh, his rueful smile piercing straight through my heart, and leans in, planting a sweet kiss on my lips. I feel his atonement, as well as his protective spirit, in the way he moves his mouth against mine.

"And I want you. Do you have any idea how terrifying that is?" He swallows, a hand coming to rest on my knee. And there, in the slight tilt of his head and furrow of his brows, he shows me the small hurt that's inside of him. The one he won't voice but that is there all the same.

"I'm sorry I didn't tell you anything about me leaving," I say with a breath, my hand coming to rest on top of his. "I wanted to ask you to come with me, but I didn't think you could. Wait, how *are* you able to help me?"

Flynn goes still in response, eyes searching mine. I take our intertwined hands and flip them so his palm is facing up. When I untangle mine from his, I look for that slash of a scar that signifies his blood oath, like Alexi had. But the skin there is smooth. Grabbing his other hand and flipping it over, I see the same thing. Confused, I look at him as a tiny seed of doubt winks into existence within me. "I don't understand. Why don't you have a scar from the blood oath?"

"Because the oath, it didn't take." He takes my hand in his once more, thumb lightly trailing along the back, as he speaks.

My eyes widen as they dart from his eyes to his hands and back again. "How is that possible?"

I don't know many details about how magic works in our kingdom or beyond, but I do know from the history books I have read that magic is in the very land of the Continent. And that, when mortals give a drop of their blood and speak certain words with intention, it creates a sort of contract bound within the confines of that magic.

"That's a story I promise to tell you when we are long gone from here. For now, we need to talk about how we are leaving tomorrow."

I want to ask more, to implore how he was able to skirt around *magic,* but my attention gets snagged on his words. "Tomorrow?" I breathe, watching as he nods his head in response.

"Yes. Tomorrow, you and I are leaving this place *permanently.*" He squeezes my hand one more time before standing and walking over to the satchel I had dropped when I first came back into the tower. After sifting through the contents, he places it back down.

"This is well packed. And you have boots," he points out, as if noticing them discarded at our feet for the first time.

"I thought it would be better to have them. Though I have to admit that they hurt my feet." I reply, shrugging my shoulders.

He nods before a slow-growing smile breaks out across his face. "Were the bag and boots the 'womanly' things in your letter?" he asks.

I snort but nod in response.

"This is perfect, Sunshine. Keep this bag packed how it is. We will leave at sunset after my shift. We need enough light to get us to the edge of the forest, but once we are in there, the cover of darkness will help keep us hidden." My fingers nervously fiddle with the fabric of Alexi's shirt as I let his plan of escape sink into me. Flynn extends a hand to me, helping me up to stand before pulling me in for a hug. "For today, rest," he says quietly, lips moving on the top of my head, "Bathe in the afternoon tomorrow since it will probably be your last warm one for a few days."

I don't know how I will be able to rest with everything that has happened. My emotions are even more tumultuous than before, rising and falling within me like the tide I often imagine. So many opposing thoughts and feelings are fighting for space that I feel I might burst at the seams from it. But I agree all the same because the truth is, I know I want to leave this tower, and I know I want to do it with Flynn. If those are the only two truths I have, then that is what I will focus on. Wrapping my arms around him, I close my eyes as I breathe him in. Being this close to him, letting him hold me and surround me with his very essence, is magic in itself. Somehow, it feels like *he* interacts with my magic.

My eyes shoot open as I realize I will have to tell him, eventually, about said magic. I squeeze him harder in response as fear takes root. *Will he be angry that I am hiding it from him? Will he care that I have it at all?*

After a few moments of protest, I finally let Flynn go and walk with him to the door. Looking out onto the landing, he sets his armor down on the ground again before his eyes find mine. Like he can't help himself either, his arms wrap around me again as he steps in closer and takes a deep breath. A hand slides down to my lower back, and desire immediately comes racing back into my veins. My body is like sand struck by lightning; I'm completely altered under even the simplest of touches from him. I finally understand what the characters in the romance novels mean about being electrified from just a small bit of contact.

I shiver when his towering, broad form leans over me and his lips come to the edge of my ear. "The ability to touch you like this—to watch you react to my touch—is better than anything I could have dreamed of," he murmurs.

My breath squeezes out of my chest at his words as my thighs clench together. And despite the fact that today has been a confusing mess of highs and lows, I would happily ignore everything if it meant I could be wrapped up in Flynn for even just a moment more. I arch my neck, giving him space to continue sliding his lips and nose down it. He breathes me in like I so often do with him, and the feel of it has me dizzy with a craving that can only be filled by him. Is this normal? To literally ache for him like this? To feel so complete when he holds me?

"When we are safe and away from this place, I want to explore every single inch of you." His sensual voice unravels down my spine. *Oh gods.* My lips pinch together, holding in a moan that nearly escapes.

"Is that what you want?" he asks, peppering light kisses down my neck.

"Yes." The word comes out breathy and laced with need.

"Good." I can feel the smile on his lips as he presses one last kiss to my scorched skin before standing back up to his full height. "I will see you tomorrow at sunset."

I close the door and slow my heavy breathing. There is a deafening silence that screams into my ears as it descends into the tower. It holds the guilt of nearly losing Bella again, the anticipation of *actually* leaving, and the nervousness at being caught for it all. Like a tree breaking loose from the ground, it feels like the moments before it hits the earth—quiet before destruction. I undress, not bothering to grab a nightdress and just crawling under the comforter instead. Despite my earlier worries, my eyes do grow heavy and my limbs sink into the mattress as Bella rests her head on my thigh over the blanket. I guess I am more tired than I thought. Flynn's face is all I see in my mind before I quickly fall asleep.

I awake the next morning, realization settling in that I slept through the rest of the night without interruption. My arms stretch overhead as the warmth of the sunlight streaming in through the window blankets me. It is my last morning in the tower. My last time waking up in this bed surrounded by these walls. For sure this time, because I'm not doing it alone. I should feel pure joy at that, and I do, but fear penetrates my thoughts as well. Maybe it's from my failed attempt, or maybe it's because I'm going to be leaving behind the only life I've ever known. All I've wanted is to be free from this place, and yet now that the time is almost here, a part of me wonders if I can even survive in the world outside.

You aren't alone. Flynn's words make me smile and my magic hums at the thought. I notice it feels so much stronger and brighter lately. The woman from my visits to the Middle said my magic is growing, but I didn't give myself time to register what she was even saying until now. Closing my eyes, I try calling the light up to my palms. It responds immediately, the humming sensation mixing with warmth as my eyes open again to see the white shimmering magic. It almost looks like starlight or if you mixed the sun's rays with the moon's glow. I stare at it a moment longer before letting it slowly fade back into my body. That small use of magic feels like a release within me, and I again wonder if not using it every so often comes with consequences. The warmth inside me dances at the thought. *Great, I'm talking with the magic now.* Feeling absolutely deranged, I slide out of bed and head to the bathroom.

After bathing, I put on one of the more simple dresses I own, a light purple one with small eyelet details throughout and a simple square-cut neck. To keep my mind distracted, I start cleaning the tower for the last time. I'm so lost in thought, my attention focused solely on using a broom to get a cobweb out of a high corner, that I don't hear the king coming until he's already opening the door. My eyes dart to the loft where Bella is laying on my bed before they fall back on the king. I steel myself for whatever this visit will entail, moving to lean the broom against a wall. He confidently walks into the tower, his trusted guards blocking the door behind him. I notice there are only four now instead of five, so the guard that captured me yesterday must still be tied up.

"Rhea, we have much to discuss today," he starts, clasping his hands behind him as he begins to walk around me. I keep my body still, trying to shrink in on myself to take up as little space as possible. "Do you know what is happening in a few days' time?" he asks as he drags a finger across my upper back. My mind whirls for a response, and when I don't answer, King Dolian smacks the back of my head. I jerk forward with the strike, keeping my eyes down at my feet. "Answer the question, Rhea."

"Do you mean the Summer Solstice?" I hate the way my voice comes out small and weak. I despise how my uncle has come in like a vicious storm and washed away any of the excitement I was feeling just moments ago.

He walks around me in determined steps until he comes to my front, his shiny black boots nearly standing on my toes from how close he is. The king's thumb pushes under my chin to lift my head up until I'm forced to look at him. The sunlight streaming in from the balcony hits his face just right, making his eyes brighten—the skin beneath them left in the shadows. It's frightening and ominous. His other hand trails down my arm, the hair on the back of my neck rising as I fight the urge to push him away from me. I can tell that my magic is paying attention to everything that is happening but, as of right now, is making no move to try and make itself known. Not that I would allow that anyway.

"Do you know," he begins again, cutting into the piercing silence, "that this Summer Solstice marks twenty-two years since your parents died at the hands of mages?" I grit my teeth together because *of course* I know. Otherwise, I don't move, afraid to do or say anything else. Afraid to see where this conversation is going. "Which means it's been twenty-two years since you were born."

The beat of my heart is furious, and ringing starts in my ears as dread begins to crush my chest and filter ice into my veins.

"Do you know what turning twenty-two means in our kingdom?" he challenges, leaning forward and invading my space more and more. I try to inch backwards imperceptibly, but he notices and curls his fingers around my arm to jerk me even closer to him. "I grow tired of asking you the same question twice," he hisses in my face.

"It is considered the time when women come of age. When women may—" I hesitate, swallowing the bile that is working its way up my throat. "When women may marry." A macabre smile twists his lips, causing my stomach to bottom out. There is no way he is suggesting—

"We are to be wed soon after the Summer Solstice, my darling. Or should I say, My Queen." He tugs me impossibly closer to him, until I can feel his warm breath skimming my face, the fabric of his finely made clothing brushing against my skin. This time, I struggle to get back from him as my mind tries to come to terms with what he is suggesting.

"But you are my *uncle!*" I squeak, a horrifyingly terrified noise. "You *cannot* marry me."

He chuckles, but there is no mirth on his face. "I am the king. I can do whatever I want—with *whomever* I want. Besides—" He pauses, ticking a corner of his lips up before speaking again, "it wasn't that long ago that ruling families wed within their own bloodlines to keep things pure."

Despite wanting to pinch my lips closed to keep them as far away from my uncle as possible, I can't help but let my jaw slacken in shock. I always assumed that I would be safe from this particular type of touch—despite his lingering glares and confusing words—but I'm just now realizing how utterly ridiculous that thought was. Of course I'm not safe from him. I never was. I never have been. I never *will* be. As long as I stay here, I will be damned to fit into a role I was never meant for. I may be the rightful heir to the throne, but I was never meant to rule with *him* by my side. Those times I saw a look flash in his eyes that I didn't know how to define—I know what it was now. Desire and yearning—all things that I have now seen in Flynn's gaze; except with him, I am undone. With Flynn, I return those feelings. With the king, I would rather *die* than let him touch me in that way. I would rather impale myself on one of these guards' swords over and over again before allowing the king's body to touch any part of mine.

Abruptly—like he knows where my thoughts have gone—he lets me go, the movement so quick that I stumble trying to regain my balance. There's no time to react before his hand comes down on my face. The pain lances through my head and neck as the sound of the slap reverberates off the stone walls. I turn back to face the abhorrent monster wearing king's

309

clothes that dares to call himself my future husband. His chestnut hair glints in the sunlight; his cheeks—visible above his trimmed beard—are red from anger while lust swirls in his hazel eyes. Everything in me recoils from him except for my magic, which is now fighting to get to the surface.

"You can try to fight it. You can even pretend to hate me with every fiber of your being, but it won't matter, Rhea. You are mine. You always have been. From the moment I saved you from death and brought you to this tower, I have been waiting for this day."

"No," I whisper as I shake my head. "I am not your consolation. She didn't choose you, and neither do I." I hold his gaze, my fear not yet enough for me to submit to the fury I can see burning in those depths. He grips a bundle of hair right near my scalp and yanks me forward. A yelp of pain that I can't stop wrenches from me as his lips graze the spot where Flynn's had just the day before.

"You're right," he says against my neck. "I gave her a choice, and she chose my so-called *perfect* brother. Which is why I am making the choice for you, darling." His hand slides down my arm, squeezing tightly as he holds me in place. "You will earn your title, and I will continue to do what needs to be done until you are worthy of it. Enjoy your last few days in the tower," he growls before suddenly shoving me back.

The force of it sends me flying into the tea table, cracking it right down the middle from the impact. My eyes go blurry, my head swimming in pain as I watch him stalk towards me and lean over. His gaze crackles with a vile intensity that makes me flinch before blackness starts to creep in at the borders of my mind.

"The night after the Summer Solstice will be spent in my bed."

Chapter Thirty-Three

BAHIRA

MORE ANXIETY THAN USUAL has been simmering within me since our deal with the shifter king was made, so I engage in some target practice to hopefully help ease it. At this moment, he sails to our shores with the hope that one of our mages can help with whatever magic problem his kingdom has. A part of me wants to laugh at the irony, but really, I just hope he keeps his end of the bargain and helps our people escape, if it ever comes to that. Although I suppose with the blood deal, he won't have a choice *but* to do it. His smug, arrogant face drifts into my mind right as I release the arrow pulled taught on my bow. It penetrates the wooden target one hundred and fifty feet away but just barely underneath the center circle I was aiming for.

"Shit," I hiss, grabbing another arrow from the quiver on my back. I roll my shoulders back, exhaling sharply before nocking the new arrow. My muscles flex in preparation as I drag in a deep breath and draw the bowstring. I clear my mind of anything related to the infuriating island king and, instead, narrow my gaze on the target. There are a few seconds before I release the arrow where the world seems to still, the only sound and feeling that of my thumping heart. My mind is blissfully quiet, my anxiety non-existent. I pretend, as I let the arrow fly, that it carries the weight of my worries, of my self-imposed pressure. This time, when the arrow plunges into the exact center of the target, the corner of my mouth lifts in triumph. The wind blows tendrils of my curly hair across my face from the ponytail high atop my head as I let the last five arrows fly into the target. All of them hitting the center circle.

My mind wanders to my afternoon plans as I walk back to the palace after training. I had last worked with the magic-infused water from Councilman Hadrik, comparing it to a young mage named Alba. Alba's magic brought some life to the dead pirang leaves, but once the magic was used up, the leaves returned to their decayed state. With Hadrik's magic, they not only came back to life, but they also sprouted new life and continued to grow. I want to test and see how much stronger the reaction will be when the magic comes directly from the source and not from a dilution of magic in water. I want to chart how long the young mages' magic will work to keep the leaves looking alive before it begins to wear off. Generally speaking, mage magic should ramp up with age, hitting a peak at twenty-two and then staying there until death. What was happening that the magic is now losing its potency over generations? Are there other connections between magic and time passing that I am missing?

My sandaled feet are quiet against the pitch black stone as I walk to my father's office, a heavy sigh escaping my lips. Along the way, I reach one of my favorite tapestries in the palace. It hangs on the wall to my right, the large piece of art depicting the last of the Void Magic users, Queen Lucia Vasiris, in a council meeting. She sits at the head of the table—where my father now does—while the mages around her look on admiringly. The artist depicts her as literally glowing with her magic. She's beautiful, and her smile is serene as she looks out onto her council. I ponder the sacrifice she made when the war grew too close. She was the most powerful magic user on the Continent, yet she sacrificed her life to separate the beings fighting when she could have just ended them herself. Or at least, that is what our history books conclude. Only the fae and sirens have long enough life-spans that some could still be alive today from when the Spell was cast.

"I thought we were meeting in my office," my father says as he strolls forward from one of the long hallways in front of me. I hadn't realized I had stopped walking to study the tapestry.

"Do you ever wonder what Queen Lucia was thinking about in her last moments? Before she cast the Spell?" My eyes flick to my father next to me.

He folds his arms over his chest as he ponders my question. "I remember as a boy reading about her in some old book," he gestures towards the small palace library behind us as I snort. "They claim that she was not just a kind, gentle woman but also smart and incredibly empathetic. She understood the weight of the magic she carried, and I suppose that makes sense, considering Void Magic was inherited based on worthiness." He looks back to me, his face soft as he takes me in. "I think she thought about the people and the kingdom she loved dearly. I bet she probably felt the impact of such a hard choice but saw no other way to right the wrongs that were happening."

I nod my head, turning back to the tapestry and the petite woman who held so much magical ability. What factors went into figuring out if someone was worthy of that gift? And if there was some all-knowing being who could decide who *was* worthy, did that mean they could also choose who wasn't? Is that why I didn't have any magic? Not because it was being blocked, but because something, somewhere, established I wasn't good enough?

A tightness clenches my chest and twists my stomach at the thought. Trying to change the trajectory of my thoughts, I ask, "Do you think our ancestors expected to be in power for this long? That it would be two-hundred years and still no blue flame to indicate the next true ruler of the Mage Kingdom?"

"No, I bet they assumed that the remaining mages from her line at the time would eventually produce an heir that would inherit the magic. In fact, your great-grandfather dedicated a room here," he says, motioning down a hallway to our left, "for the moment he attended a ceremony that produced a blue flame." I hadn't realized we had such a space here. "Are you ready to go? I'm afraid I'm needed for more party planning for tomorrow's celebration, so time is short."

I steal one more glance at the tapestry before turning and walking with my father to my workshop.

꒜꒜꒜ ꒜꒜꒜

Haylee and a young mage named Erick are already at my workshop when my father and I arrive. Joining them inside, I walk over to three glass bottles containing the dead pirang leaves and spread them out on the table.

"I need you to just feed your magic into the leaves for a minute straight." I point to the glass bottles I want each one to stand in front of.

Going to the desk Haylee and I share, I open one of the drawers that holds the folders I use to organize my data. Inside the top folder, I grab a paper that lists the data from my last round of experiments. Grabbing a spelled pen, I walk around the table to stand on the opposite end. My body nearly trembles with anticipation as I tap the pen steadily against my chin.

"Go!" I shout, flipping over my tray of hourglasses to begin the count-down. They each point a finger to their respective bottle and begin infusing their magic directly into the plants. The bottle in front of my father glows a light purple, and instantly, the dead leaves begin to transform, health and life coming back to them. Haylee's magic flares a bright yellow—similar to her hair—as the leaves in her bottle take a few seconds longer but also begin to turn green. Erick's magic is red, and his slight hand shakes with the effort it takes to concentrate on sending it into the bottle. His leaves are the slowest to transform, cycling through many color gradients of brown before finally hinting at green.

"A few more seconds," I say loudly, nervously pacing back and forth in front of the table as I watch the one minute hourglass timer near its end. When the last granule of sand falls, I hold my hand up to halt them. Their magic fades away from their fingertips, momentarily making the leaves glow. In my previous experiment, Alba's magic had lasted for approximately five minutes before the leaves started to wilt again. Hadrik's had given actual life to the leaves, and I expect my father's to do even more as he is an even stronger mage. Haylee is like a control element—her generation between my father's and Erick's, so I expect her magic to react in the middle as well.

My attention is drawn to the two minute hourglass, my father giving my forehead a quick kiss before he ushers Erick out of the room to let me work. From the corner of my eye, I see Haylee move to the desk and sit down on the edge of her seat. My eyes move between the three glowing glass jars—watching as the row of hourglasses reaches the two minute mark. The leaves in my father's bottle have sprouted roots, new buds forming and blossoming as it uses up the magic to sustain itself. Over and over, I watch as each dead leaf does the same thing. The bottle of Haylee's magic moves slower, no new life sprouting—which is surprising to me—though the leaves turn a vibrant green one by one. But when my eyes fall back on Erick's bottle, the light green leaves have already begun to revert back to their decayed state.

"What?" I whisper, walking over to his bottle to squat down in front of it.

I watch as each leaf that was green fades to dark brown in a matter of seconds. I look over to Haylee's bottle, and without glancing at the hourglasses, I know that it can't have reached the five minute mark yet. The plump bright green leaves start shriveling—more slowly than Erick's leaves but decaying all the same.

"What the hell is happening?" I question under my breath, abject panic quickly replacing any excitement I had.

Haylee's chair screeches as she pushes it back and stands. Her footsteps and my racing heart fill the otherwise-quiet room as she comes to stand next to me. She watches the final leaves in her bottle shrink back to brittle and lifeless pieces. Tension builds in the air as we both look at the remaining bottle with my father's magic. It has already stopped sprouting new roots and buds. This was strong magic, *the mage king's* magic. Only one other person in the kingdom has stronger magic than him, and that is Nox. And yet in this experiment, his magic has stopped working more quickly than Hadrik's had. My hypothesis was that having the magic come directly from the source might result in it *feeding* the plants longer. But in all three instances, the magic fails more quickly than in my last experiment. It doesn't make sense that magic diluted in water is stronger than magic directly from a mage's hand. It doesn't make sense that the leaves would absorb and use the magic up so quickly that they then began to decay at an even faster rate. *None of this makes any fucking sense.*

My heart beats furiously as my breath starts to rush in and out of me. I pace around the table, trying to figure out what I am missing. *I have to be missing something.* All the insecurities and fears I've spent nearly a lifetime trying to squash burst out of me at this newest failure. I have spent *years* on this. Years consumed by combing through texts and laying out experiments that would help me quantify and translate why we were losing magic and how we could get it back.

I think Haylee says my name, but I can't be sure with the ringing in my ears. I squeeze my eyes shut, my stomach beginning to twist into knots as I gasp for breath. I've been desperately obsessed with trying to fix our magic, but I've made zero progress. Nothing to show for all of my *tinkering,* as Gosston had put it. Maybe he was right. Maybe he and all the others of this kingdom that see me as weaker and less-than would finally get what they expected from me. Maybe I should just stop fighting what nature or the gods or the fucking universe intended for me to be. All this time, I thought I was made for more. That I could actually be the one that could give some sort of answer to our people for *why* this is happening, but I've fallen short.

For the first time since my blood dropped into the Cauldron of Vires, I am utterly hopeless. I feel insignificant and unintelligent and just... pathetically undeserving. *Of my title.* My hands form fists as I pace back and forth. *Of my place in this kingdom.* Tears form in the back of my eyes, my frustration a thickening thunder cloud waiting to unleash. *Of everything.*

"Bahira," Haylee says, and I snap.

"What?" I scream out, swinging around, my hands accidentally slamming into an empty glass bottle. It hits the floor and shatters, shards of glass flying everywhere. "Shit," I grumble as I bend down to start picking them up. Haylee comes over to help, an awkward silence in the room as we work to clean up my mess. Carefully laying another piece of glass in my palm, I tell her, "I'm sorry, Haylee."

"It's okay. I understand—" Her words halt when she hisses out a breath, cradling her hand close to her. Blood begins dripping off her hand and onto the floor as she stands up. I quickly run to a drawer by the sink—throwing it open as I grab two clean white cloths and rush back to her.

"Give me your hand." I reach across the table with my failed experiments. Her blood drips rapidly, small drops plop and splatter while I clean the wound out before she uses her magic to heal it. Unable to stop the guilt creeping up the column of my throat, I ask, "Are you okay?"

She nods her head, a pitying look crossing over her features—causing my teeth to grind together in response. "Bahira, why don't we—"

"I just need to be alone," I interrupt sharply, forcing a curve to my lips as I look at her. The smile doesn't convince either of us in any way, but Haylee doesn't call me out on it. Instead, she nods her head, sending me one more look before walking out of the workshop.

I continue picking up the pieces of glass, kneeling on the ground as my hands start to tremble. The first tear falls, then the second, and before I know it, my vision is completely blurred. A harsh cry breaks free as I throw the glass across the room before slamming my palms down on the ground, pain prickling my hands. My body folds over my knees as I let my failure manifest in the tears falling from my eyes.

I cry for the woman who walked into this workshop today with hope that she would discover a breakthrough. I cry for the princess of the Mage Kingdom who just wants to find her value and to contribute in a meaningful way. I cry for the teenager who had to deal with snide comments and dirty looks because of what she was born lacking. And I cry for the little girl who made her father prick her finger five times before she let him embrace her in a hug. Who feared that her parents might not want a magicless daughter.

Chapter Thirty-Four

RHEA

BOOTS TAP AGAINST THE wood floors, the sound getting closer and closer. I try to move my body—my legs or arms or *anything*—but pain singes my nerves, causing me to groan. Panic then pierces my gut. What if I slept through our escape plan? What if I slept for days and now the king is here to get me? To force me to marry him in some sick, desperate attempt to recreate what he never had with my mother? To force me to bed him? When hands grip my shoulders, I scream out—my vision blurring and head aching.

"It's okay, Sunshine. It's just me." I know his voice, but what if it's an illusion? Or a terrible mixture of dream and consciousness? I have to fight and get away. I need to leave now before it's too late. A sob leaves me, broken and full of despair. It isn't until his arms wrap around me, pulling me carefully to my knees, that I let myself calm. He cradles me, my head laying against his chest as I breathe in the crisp scent of autumn and relax in the safety of his touch.

"Flynn?"

"It's me. I'm here," he repeats, cradling my body to his. "Did he do this to you?"

I don't answer, words beyond me as a slight tingling sensation prickles my back, but he knows. He knows only one person could be responsible for this. His arms band tighter around me like he can absorb the pain radiating through my body into his own.

"Never again," he whispers into my ear as his hand strokes soothing lines down my back. "I swear to you that he will never touch you again. I will fucking *kill* him before that happens. I don't care if this kingdom falls because of it." Leaning back, he wipes the tears from my cheeks and kisses my forehead, lingering there as he holds me. Invisible tethers draw me closer to him, forcing me to take the support he so selflessly offers. His deep voice is a melody of vengeance and retribution as he makes a vow to me that feels inked in blood. "His head will roll for what he's done to you." I stiffen, feeling the truth of those words settle into my bones. The warmth of my magic focuses on my chest, healing what must have been a bruised or broken rib. I realize I have never really felt myself healing like this before.

"What time is it?" I grunt out, my hands going to his shoulders for support.

"Nearly sunset. I would say we should wait another day for you to—" He pauses, closing his eyes before continuing, "heal, but I don't want to spend another second in this kingdom." I take in the lines of his face, the tension and anger held in his eyebrows and jaw. "I'm sorry I wasn't here," he rasps, laying his self-imposed guilt out before me. And it hurts more than any time the king has placed a hand on me.

I wrap my arms around his neck, my fingers diving into his hair. "You're here now," I whisper, scraping my nails lightly on his scalp and melting at the way he embraces me tighter in response. Kneeling, we hold each other, the last of the sun's golden rays blanketing us in its light. "And I'm okay. With you, I am better than okay." My lips graze his jaw as I place a delicate kiss there.

It's strange but exhilarating to be able to touch him in this way. It's the most natural feeling in the world, and yet I can't believe I get to do it. Everything around us feels momentarily still, a pocket of quiet where we simply hold each other. Months of near-touches and glances and fluttering heartbeats all led to here and now.

"Then lets get the fuck out of here," Flynn states after a few moments, breaking the silence.

I inhale deeply, my nose grazing the base of his neck before he slowly untangles us and helps me up to a stand. I stretch and wince from the tightness in my body, but all the pain is now gone. "I'm alright," I insist, noting the creasing of his forehead. "I just need to change."

I take the steps up to the loft, grabbing my change of clothes. Once dressed again in trousers and Alexi's undershirt, I pull my hair into a ponytail and secure it with a ribbon. Walking over to my vanity, I open the drawer and pull out the little black pouch holding Alanna's bracelet. I clasp it on, smiling faintly at the small comfort it brings before placing the now-empty pouch back in the drawer.

"I've never heard you curse so much," I muse as I join him back downstairs, hoping to ease some of the tightness that still lines his face.

"I'm sorry, Sunshine," he says lightly. My heart beats in my throat when he kneels before me. I notice that he has his sword in a sheath now placed across his back but his golden armor is gone. Instead he wears the usual all-black tunic, trousers, and boots.

"First, don't be sorry. I like it," I respond, without a second thought. His head snaps up to look at me in surprise. "Second, what are you doing?" I gesture to where he is before me.

"I'm helping you put on your boots. Put your hands on my shoulders," he instructs. I do so, watching as he places one boot before me to step into, followed by the other. I notice immediately that they feel much more comfortable than the first time I wore them. When I express that to Flynn, he pinches his lips together, his shoulders shaking with laughter. "You probably had them on the wrong feet."

I scowl at him and narrow my eyes. It just makes him laugh harder, and though it's at my own expense, I'm grateful for the sound and the way the agitation eases out of him. We walk over to where I set the satchel in the library—a move I am grateful for since it concealed the bag from the king.

Flynn sighs as he walks in, looking at all the books that line the walls and saying wistfully, "It's a shame that we didn't get to spend more time here."

I hum my agreement, stepping farther into the room and looking around. For years—decades—this room was my only escape. I was physically barred in and forced to remain here, but mentally, I was able to leave through the stories that these books provided. Over and over, I traveled to different realms and became different heroes and heroines, and had it not been for the words written on those pages, I might not be here at all. The tightness of my emotions grips around my throat as I try to swallow the feelings down. I reach my hand out for his, interlacing our fingers before taking one last glance at the shelves and walking to the door. Flynn slides the satchel over his shoulder, not at all affected by the weight of it like I was. It's then that I notice he has another bag slung over the opposite shoulder.

"I never asked you, how did you acquire all those books anyway?" he questions.

I shrug, leaning into him. "I don't know. According to Alexi, this tower was already built like this—books and all—when I was put here as a baby."

He turns towards me, tucking a piece of hair behind my ear. "I'm sorry."

"You have nothing to be sorry for," I say, tilting my head up to catch his dark gaze.

"But I was one of those people," he mutters, guilt thick with every word. "I was one of the people who knew you were here and just assumed that the king wasn't lying about why." It's quiet for a breath before he adds, "I meant what I said, you know."

My brows draw together in confusion as I survey him, my body drawing closer to his and my magic humming its pleasure at our proximity. His kind eyes and luscious mouth and the way he feels under my hands— I clear my throat to stop that train of thought. "What part?"

"All of it," he states, leaning down to kiss me. Even the gentlest of touches from him causes a wave of desire to completely consume me. I'm sure he is referencing how he promised to keep me safe and kill the king if need be, but all I can focus on is how he said that he wanted to explore every part of me. Gods, do I want to do the same with him. A wicked smirk tilts his lips as he leans in closer, my eyes closing on instinct. "I can tell what you are thinking, Sunshine," he whispers. "And it's going to distract me too much." I smile, a shiver rolling though me as he kisses the shell of my ear before taking a step back and shouts, "Come on, Bella!"

Flynn opens the door and pulls me through, my world still unbelievably off its axis from his touch, his words, his *mouth. Focus, Rhea.* Despite moving down the stone steps quickly, it still feels like an eternity until we reach the small platform that leads out to the bridge. We stop, mostly because I need to catch my breath.

"I probably should have asked this earlier, but what is the plan?" I huff out, looking down at the few spirals of the stairs remaining until the bottom of the tower.

"We will head all the way down to the lowest level that opens out into the meadow," Flynn answers, taking a deep breath of his own. "Then, all we have to do is cross the wildflowers and get to the forest."

"And then we head east, to your home?"

"Is that where you want to go?" There's apprehension in his voice as he studies me, his black waves tumbling over his forehead.

"Yes." I exhale, examining him as I lay one of my own truths at his feet. "I want to be wherever you are."

His answering smile is breathtaking—as always. He's the manifestation of a dream I never knew I had. Perfection brought to life in the form of sweet smiles and gentle touches and kind words. *There is only you.* That's what he said to me as we sat together in the sunlight surrounded by books. I thought men like him might only exist in the worlds I read about, but he's real and he's here... and I think he might be mine. And a growing part of me hopes that he realizes that all the shattered pieces of me are his. Only his.

"I swear to the gods, Rhea. You cannot look at me like that, or this trip is going to take twice as long," he groans, his voice echoing in the stairwell of the tower.

"Why would the way I look at you make our trip longer?" He quirks a brow, that provocative grin growing. It takes an embarrassingly long time for me to understand what he's referencing. "Oh. Oh, I—" I stammer, knowing that my cheeks are pinker than the sky at sunset.

Flynn laughs, leaning in to kiss the top of my head as Bella whines and works her way in between us. "Okay, okay. Bella's right. We need to go." Flynn holds my hand and guides me down the darkened steps until we finally reach the true bottom of the tower. "Remember, we run through the wildflowers and straight to the forest. Do not stop until we reach the trees."

"Alright," I say, fear and determination intermingling inside me. My magic begins humming more intensely, as if also showing its agreement with Flynn's plan. Suddenly a deep moan startles me, my hand reaching out to grip Flynn's forearm. "What was that?"

"Shit," Flynn says with a sigh. The bottom of the tower is nearly pitch black, just a small amount of light shining in from a cutout above. He lets go of my hand and walks over to a darker corner of the space. I hear the sound of something dragging across the stones, and then a bloodied face comes into view.

"You left him down here?" I rasp, bringing my hands to my chest.

"I couldn't exactly let him go." He drops his hold on the guard—Xander—as he points out what should be obvious to me. His wrists and ankles are bound, and a piece of fabric that must be covering some sort of gag is tied across his mouth. "They'll find him here, Rhea. I promise. But we have to go."

I keep my eyes on Xander until Flynn steps into my line of sight. My head tilts up to meet his gaze, a slice of golden light illuminating just one eye and a part of his forehead.

"I know you don't like leaving him here, but I need you to understand," he says softly, a hand gently cupping the side of my face. His calloused palm lightly scrapes against the smoothness of my cheek, his thumb tracing my bottom lip. "When it comes to your safety, I don't fucking care who is standing in my way. We are leaving this place behind, and no one—absolutely no one—will lock you up or force you to do anything you don't want to do ever again. And he"—his voice rises as he points to the guard laying on the ground—"would turn us over to the king the moment he was free."

My breath hitches, my hands somehow finding their way to Flynn's tunic and gripping the front of it. His words press into me. They force their way into the space of my mind not already occupied by boxed-up emotions.

"Tell me you understand," he demands.

All I can do is nod. Because while I do understand, I can't help but feel like everyone who comes into contact with me—one way or another—gets hurt. And even though I don't have fond feelings for this guard and I remember in excruciating detail how he held Alexi as he was killed, I don't want to be the one responsible for causing his discomfort. But Flynn is right, we need to leave and this guard would stop that. "I understand," I finally whisper.

Flynn drops his forehead to mine for just a moment before placing a kiss there and turning towards the door, Bella waiting behind us. With another deep breath, he pushes the door open and we move. Flynn is the first one through, my hand still firmly gripped in his. I see the flowers just ahead, beckoning us with each step we take to freedom, when Flynn suddenly tenses—his grip on my hand tightening. I don't have any time to react as I see a flash of gold swing through the air.

In horror, I watch as a King's Guardsman steps in front of me and drives his sword into Flynn's torso, the force of it so strong that it spins Flynn around to face me. A blood-curdling scream cleaves through the air as the guard yanks the sword back out, crimson dripping from the blade. Time slows down as I witness Flynn drop to his knees, his hands immediately going to his stomach and putting pressure on the wound. He looks up at me—eyes widening as his face contorts in pain. Silence rings in my ears as we stare at each other and my world implodes around me, crushing me in its destruction. The warmth of my magic begins to rise inside of me, but so does that primitive, lingering darkness. They twist and coil together, and I start to call on it so that I can heal him when I notice peripheral gold glints on both sides, temporarily distracting me. Flynn throws a bloody hand out to me right as a strong arm wraps around my waist and yanks me back into something hard.

"Going somewhere, my darling?" His rough voice scratches down my spine, but I keep my eyes pinned on Flynn.

He's bent over his knees, holding his wound, and his jaw is clenched in pain. Another scream leaves me as I struggle to get away from King Dolian, but his arms just band tighter around my waist. Two guards flank Flynn on either side, their swords drawn—but only one dripping blood. We were so close to the meadow; just a few more steps and we would have been encased in flowers of all colors. *Just a few more steps.*

"Well, isn't this *interesting*," King Dolian declares, holding me tightly to him as I watch Flynn lift his head.

Flynn's slate eyes, usually bright and full of personality, look a little duller as he clutches his hands to his stomach. Blood begins to pool around him, staining the bright green of the wet marsh grass that ominous deep red. His gaze holds mine, but there is no fear there. No, the emotion in Flynn's eyes reminds me of the calm look Alexi had on his face right before the king drove a sword through his body. And that is so much worse because I don't want Flynn to accept this fate.

"Did you really think that you could leave me?" the king whispers in my ear.

I try to cringe away from the feeling of him pressed so intimately behind me, but no matter how I move, he doesn't ease up his hold on me.

"Do you want to know how I thought I might find you two here?" he taunts, speaking loud enough for Flynn to hear. "I learned my lesson with

Alexi and made sure there was *always* a second pair of eyes on your guard." He gestures to Flynn with his chin and I watch as Flynn stills and flicks his eyes to the king's. "And imagine my surprise when I caught him leaving his post earlier today after my little visit with you." He drags his fingers down the side of my cheek until they reach my neck. They halt there, right over my racing pulse.

The sun's light is nearly gone, the moon not quite risen, but even with the impending darkness, my eyes are still drawn to Flynn's. I've always been drawn to him. From the first time I met him—scared and reeling after losing Alexi—he has never made me feel afraid or unwanted. He has always soothed me in ways that I never understood but intimately craved. And I know without a shadow of a doubt that if I watch him die, I won't survive it either. He brought me out of my loneliness and anguish and showed me what it was like to feel cared for, cherished. Though parts of me are still jagged and broken and I know I can never again feel true peace, I could have gotten close being with Flynn. I thought we would have that time together to try—to try finding our own version of happiness.

"Rhea, it's okay," he whispers, looking up at me with those gorgeous dark eyes. Trying to soothe me even now. But it's not okay. *I'm not okay.*

"Guards, seize him," the king says in a harsh voice. He's more than willing to kill Flynn in front of me to prove a point. I watch as two of the guards remove both of the satchels and his sword from him, tossing them to the ground. They stand on either side of Flynn and grab his arms firmly. He doesn't fight them as they jerk him to his knees. His wavy black hair is disheveled, those unruly strands dangling over his forehead in rebellion. I hate the way the guards are touching him, like he's nothing to them when he's everything to me.

"No!" I scream, fighting with everything that I am to get out of King Dolian's grasp. To get to the man kneeling in front of me bleeding out. *I can save him. I can save him.* My mind taunts me with those four words, because while I can save him, I need to be able to touch him to do so.

"It's going to be okay. Rhea, look at me."

My eyes scan him in a frenzy, but I can't focus. My blood pounds in my ears, and all I can picture is Alexi's cold, dead body in my lap. All I can see are his lifeless eyes. All I can feel is his blood going cold and thickening on my hands. I can't do it again. *I can't. I can't.*

"A traitor *and* a liar," King Dolian growls.

"Sunshine, I promise you that we are going to get out of this. Keep your eyes on me." Flynn's voice is steady, even as a guard kicks him brutally in the side to get him to stop talking.

I jerk against my uncle as Flynn growls, trying to hunch over but unable to because of the guards' hold. It's all so reminiscent of how Alexi died. It's history repeating itself, and I'm at the center of it all. *Again.* The king wraps his arms around me so tightly that I can't breathe—the heat from his body causing my own to revolt. Tears cloud my vision as I kick and scream.

"Another death to add to your collection, my darling. You and I might not be as different as you like to believe." His lips graze my shoulder as he inhales deeply, his beard tickling my skin when he moves closer to my neck.

I still—my fight temporarily leaving me because what if he's *right*? Even if we somehow escape, Flynn will never be safe as long as I'm with him. And if he brings me back to his family? They'll be in danger too. A new idea forms in my mind, my heart beating furiously as I do the one thing that will damn me but save him.

"You will die for touching her," Flynn vows, jaw clenched in anger.

"It is not *I* who will die on this day." The king chuckles darkly as he speaks, his breath cascading down my ear and cheek. His hand wraps around my chin as he jerks my gaze away from Flynn and towards him.

"What about a deal?" I beg, staring into his unforgiving hazel eyes. They narrow as he tilts his head to the side, his chestnut hair staying perfectly coiffed with the movement. Even in the face of chaos, he is regal and poised. "I want to make a deal for his life," I repeat.

"Go on," King Dolian answers, his fingers still abusively gripping my face.

Flynn starts to protest, calling out my name, but I block him out as I seal my fate. "I will go with you willingly. I will marry you and do so without any sort of fight. I will—" I swallow, fear clenching my throat like a tightened necklace, but I force out the next words even though it's the final drive of a dagger into my soul. "I will serve you in any way you'd like, but you *must* let Flynn go. You *must* let him leave and go home to his family."

"Rhea, no," Flynn growls, but I keep my gaze on the monster holding me hostage. I said I would rather die than let him touch me in that way, and I meant it. But for Flynn—for him—I would sacrifice everything. Even the last broken piece of my heart. It wasn't mine anymore anyways—it was his. So for him, I will do whatever it takes.

"Please," I beg while a tear rolls down my cheek. A King's Guardsman stands behind my uncle, his hand drawing my attention when he moves to grab his sword.

"You must care about him," King Dolian sneers as my eyes go back to his.

Immediately, I know I've made a mistake. Knowing I care about Flynn is a weakness to him—for him to use against me. *Oh gods, what have I done?*

"Rhea, you must believe I am the type of man willing to bargain. A man willing to make deals for traitors who believe that they can have what is mine. What has *always* been mine." He leans in even closer, his breath tickling my lips. "I will kill him because I *want* to. I will marry you because I *want* to. Those things are a mere truth because *I* am the king, and therefore, I can do what I please," he rumbles, moving closer until our noses touch. "I can also bed whom I please." Without warning, his lips push down on mine, the act causing bile to rise and my blood to boil. "Kill him," he says against me, his gaze penetrating mine before he lets go of my chin and I swing my head back to Flynn.

A desperate sob breaks out of me as I watch one of the guards begin to lift his weapon, the other two tightening their grip on his arms—keeping him from escaping.

In the darkness of the fallen night, with only the silvery light of the moon and stars, I see the gold sword draw back. Shadows drift around us in the pockets of pitch black, lapping around the guards' ankles and Flynn's knees. My eyes connect with his—always with his. I swear he *glows* like a midnight flame, the only thing in focus when the rest of the torturous world is blurred out. Words dangle on the tip of my tongue, but my mouth is frozen in shock. My breath squeezes out of me as I prepare to watch another person who truly saw me and did not back away die. Because of me.

Chapter Thirty-Five

RHEA

A LOW, FAMILIAR GROWL suddenly slices through the darkness before the king screams behind me, jolting from an impact that causes him to drop his hold on me. I freeze for all of a second before scrambling away, already knowing it's Bella. She's here, and she's finally getting to attack the king.

The guard whose sword was drawn—ready to kill Flynn—runs past me to help King Dolian. Using the distraction, Flynn twists his body and jerks out of the guards' hold on him, grimacing as the movement pulls at his wound. Rolling onto his back, he kicks a leg out and knocks one of the guards at his side down while the other stumbles towards him—tripping over something in the darkness. Grabbing his sheathed sword from the ground as he rolls to a stand, he narrowly dodges the swinging arc of a golden blade, gritting his teeth as he clutches his wound with one hand. Both the guards advance on him as he rights himself and begins to walk backwards, sliding the sword quickly from its scabbard. I start to take a step in Flynn's direction, unsure of how I can help but knowing I just need to get to him.

"Rhea, you need to run," he grits out, blocking a swing of the guard's golden weapon with his own, the clashing metal vibrating in the night air.

"I'm not leaving you!" I scream as a hand grips my arm and jerks me back forcefully. Gold armor glows on the arms of my newest captor as the nearly full moon casts its ethereal light, finally fully risen in the night sky.

Bella growls as she snaps her jaws at King Dolian again, nearly close enough to bite his hand. The fourth guard swings his sword in Bella's direction, but she easily dodges it and again darts towards the king. The guard holding me has his full attention on Bella, so I use every bit of strength I can to push him away, watching as he stumbles and lets go of me to catch himself as he falls.

"What's going on down there?" a new guard shouts out from the bridge as he looks down at the field.

"The king is under attack! Assemble the rest of the King's Guard!" one of the king's trusted yells. The guard on the bridge turns and runs, shouting something I can't make out as he crosses the long bridge to the castle.

I hear Flynn curse under his breath at whatever is being said. My eyes then move to the king and his guard as they still fight a quick and ruthless Bella. She manages to crunch down on my uncle's leg before she lets go to dodge the guard's sword. Closer to me, the man I had pushed is now scrambling back to his feet. He glares at me as he straightens to his full height, but then the king gives another shout of pain and he turns his attention back to him. The entire scene around me is pure chaos, and my feet feel frozen to the ground. I turn my head to look at Flynn, watching as one guard circles him while the other he was fighting lays motionless in the grass.

"Sunshine, run. I'll catch up to you. Please," Flynn's voice sounds so wrong, so devoid of the usual cheer and confidence emanating from him. "Please," he begs again as he fights the guard, holding his sword with one hand. Even injured, his moves are graceful and impressive, but I'm worried it won't be enough. I have to do something to help him.

"I am not leaving without you," I repeat. My magic pushes against the barrier of my skin, the sensation both warm and cold.

I move to Flynn's right as he kicks the guard he is fighting in the chest. The man stumbles back, falling down into the shadows cast by the moonlight on the grass. Flynn acts quickly, bending down to pick something up before grabbing my hand, leading me as we run towards the forest outlined across the field of flowers. Bella's name is a call on my lips as I turn my head to look for her, but Flynn stumbles and takes us both down before I can find where she is.

"Flynn!" I shriek, crawling over to his body where he lays in the wildflowers. The sweet fragrance and the delicate, colorful blooms around us mock me, hiding in their shadows the blood and death that is waiting behind us.

"It's okay. I just need a minute to focus, and then we can get back up again," he says on a grunt, bringing his hand to his stomach, but I'm not waiting any longer.

"I can heal you," I plead, averting my gaze from his and all the questions that I'm sure are dancing in his eyes.

"Rhea, no, you don't have to—"

"Stop it," I whisper, removing his bloody hand and placing my own over his wound. "I can't lose you too. I won't." I hear voices, and when I quickly glance behind me, two of the king's trusted guards are running in our direction. My eyes go back to Flynn's wound, closing as I inhale and gradually blow the air back out. *I will save him.*

"Sunshine, listen to me, I only need—" But the rest of his voice is drowned out as I focus on calling my magic to the surface as quickly as possible. It answers—faster than it did with Bella or Alexi—the shimmery white light glowing even through the darkness of my shut eyelids. My hands tingle with warmth, my heart pounding madly as I focus everything I have on healing Flynn. In my mind, I picture my magic flooding into him, reconnecting veins and muscles. It stitches together his beautiful tanned skin until no mark remains, until there is no evidence that anyone hurt him. It feels so right to use my magic on him, and I swear I feel something inside of him answer in response. It's like a recognition or a bone-deep knowing. It calls to my magic, to me, and I swiftly answer.

A rough hand lands on my shoulder, and my eyes fly open as I scream my frustration at being interrupted. Penetrating cold flows through my skin temporarily, my vision swimming in darkness. The hand disappears instantly, and I focus back on Flynn. Warmth replaces the bitter cold, my vision becoming clear again. His eyes are wide as he looks at me. My fear that this may be the last straw for him comes roaring to the surface. He didn't know I had magic; he didn't know I've been lying to him this whole time. Will he understand? Will he still look at me like I'm the only person in the room? Or will this betrayal disgust him to the point that he realizes I'm not worth the trouble?

The light of my magic reflects in his dark irises. His face softens immediately, the corners of his full lips reaching up towards his eyes. The skin along his handsome jaw glows with my magic but also with health—with life now. He is radiant against the backdrop of the night sky, a beckoning star guiding me to him from the very beginning.

"Rhea, I'm okay," he says, but I have to make sure. I can't stop until I know he is totally healed, fully whole again. "Sunshine, look at me." He sits up easily, but I keep my hands pushing on his stomach, my magic flowing into him and filling his torso with white light. I don't know how the guards haven't stopped us yet, and I'm tempted to look behind me, but Flynn's hand cups the side of my face.

"I can't lose you," I breathe the words—my voice a frayed, panicked plea through the tears falling down my cheeks. I hope he can feel the truth of it, of just how much he means to me.

"I'm right here. I'm not going anywhere. Nothing in this realm or any other could get me to leave you. Nothing," he promises quietly, placing affectionate kisses on my cheeks and the tip of my nose and sealing the promise of his words with his lips. "Call your magic back," he whispers over my mouth, his hand moving from my cheek to cup the back of my head. He pushes our foreheads together tenderly—his eyes never leaving mine. Flecks of silver are reflected there, commanding me to get lost in them. Somehow forcing the delirium of watching him get hurt to calm. "Call it back, Rhea."

There is no anger or disappointment or fear on his face or in his voice like I expect, so I obey his gentle command and let my hands ease up on him. Like when I healed Bella, I imagine the magic slowly coming back into my body to settle in again. It moves like water trickling into a lake, like it's slowly arriving home. Returning back to its source. The glowing that I hadn't realized was around us dulls, our surroundings coming back into focus. Noises of men grunting and faraway footsteps pounding on stone rend through the air, rushing back into me like they were waiting just beyond a barrier. As if a shield was around us.

"Don't look back," he says as unease slithers inside me, wrapping around my heart. Holding my hand, he quickly stands and helps me up, grabbing his sword from where it lays amongst the flowers. It's now that I notice he was able to snag both satchels before we ran. He puts them on, the straps crossing over his muscular chest.

"Bella!" I yell, trying to look back, but Flynn just pulls me closer to him as we run towards the woods.

"Just a little farther," he urges, tugging me another few steps until we are nearly halfway through the field. He finally stops, turning us around but making sure that I am a step behind him. His sword is drawn in front of him, his stance wide, as we both try to find Bella in the dark. In the distance on the bridge, I can hear the rhythmic pounding on the stones get louder.

"What is that?" I ask Flynn, my hand gripping onto the back of his tunic.

"More of the King's Guard. We need to get Bella and leave now before they have the chance to surround us," he urges, his free hand running through his hair.

"Bella!" I shout, as I swing my head from side to side, frantically searching for the glow of her white fur in the moonlight. The early summer air is warm though no breeze rustles the trees or makes the flowers dance. It's as if the universe, or maybe even the gods themselves, are hushed at this moment. Flynn's head snaps forward as two tall figures emerge from the shadows only twenty feet away. But it isn't the two guards who I saw before.

"How long have you had magic, Rhea?" My uncle's voice is cold and strident, while his face is a painting of pure fury. Silver light pours over him from above as he limps closer.

He knows. He knows. He knows.

The silence carries a heavy weight as King Dolian and one of his trusted guards stand across from us, both wielding swords. Both ready to drag me back to that prison. "How long have you—"

"Shut. The. Fuck. Up." The severity of Flynn's snarled words startles me, my fingers gripping the fabric of his shirt even more tightly.

"You *dare* talk to your king like that?" the guard shouts, his teeth bared in a menacing half smile.

"He is not my king." Flynn's answering growl threatens the space separating us from them. His sword lifts higher as he draws his right leg back in a fighting stance that I notice is different from the guard posed across from us. King Dolian's eyes are calculating as he studies Flynn. My own gaze is drawn to the glints of gold on the bridge behind them. Row after row of King's Guardsmen descend from the castle. They near a small staircase that connects the bridge to the grasses below. There are so many of them that my breath hitches in my throat, pure fear making my hair stand on end.

"You are free to go— Flynn, was it?" King Dolian asks, taking a step forward and lowering his sword. The guard standing next to him looks over from the corner of his eye and matches the king's step until he's next to him again. "I give you your freedom, and in exchange, you leave Rhea here."

Flynn laughs, the sound rough and menacing and so godsdamn *deep*. "How about instead, I cut your head off?"

The king takes another step forward, his eyes gleaming with rage. Behind him, the new batch of King's Guardsmen begin to pour off of the steps, like molten metal leaking onto the earth below.

"Flynn," I whisper, tugging on his shirt to make sure he sees what I'm seeing. The king is stalling, and we can't wait here any longer. *Where is Bella?* Flynn lowers his sword and steps back so that he is in line with me.

A look of triumph twists the king's features as he moves another step closer to us and extends his hand out in front of him. "Do you see, Rhea? No one cares about you as I do. No one else can make you a queen as I can. That's all I have ever wanted for you," he says, reaching his hand out farther. "To be safe, by my side. As mine. I do not even care that you possess the very magic that I would kill others for having."

"I am not *your* queen," I shout, my hands balling into fists at my side. That darkness inside of me sings in approval as iciness coats my veins, my skin, my *soul*. "Not today. Not tomorrow. *Not ever*."

King Dolian's eyes narrow as his body tenses, his arm dropping back down to his side. He watches as Flynn intertwines his fingers with mine, giving them a reassuring squeeze from where he stands next to me. Not in front of me, but beside me.

"I see," my uncle says, his gaze lingering on our joined hands. Those hazel eyes flick back up to mine, intense anger swimming in their depths. "This is your destiny, Rhea. You cannot escape it. You cannot escape me. You may run and hide, but I will always find you. And when I do, I will make sure you never leave again."

"You will die before you ever get anywhere near her," Flynn assures before tugging my hand and leading us in a run to the woods.

The trees are pitch black, their outline somehow darker than the landscape around them. The moon lights a path for us as we run through the flowers, a small part of me hating that such beauty will be trampled over and destroyed because of me. Flynn tugs my hand hard, willing me to push my body to keep up with his. Movement draws my attention to my right, and I see a bundle of white fur and pointed ears keeping pace with us as we sprint to reach the safety of the trees. *Bella.* I nearly scream with relief.

I hear shouting behind us, and so many sets of large booted feet are pounding into the earth that I can feel the rattling of it under my own. I glance one last time over my shoulder as we near the edge of the treeline. The king isn't chasing us like I expected. He stands eerily still, his sword pointing down at the ground by his side. He's too far away to make out the expression on his face, but his posture is relaxed, and that sends a chill through me. His trusted guard chases after us, and I wonder where the other remaining two I saw as I was healing Flynn are—assuming that Flynn *incapacitated* the fourth and Xander is still tied up. Perhaps they were busy trying to capture Bella before she managed to escape them.

My final view is that of my tower. The gray stone looming high into the sky comes to a pointed tip as it glows under the starlight. I stare at it for a few seconds, marveling at the fact that I'll never see the inside of it again. How many times had I looked out onto this land from the balcony and imagined dragging my hands along the wildflower petals? How many times had I seen the forest in the distance and wondered what might lay beyond it? I suppose it is only fitting that the king would ruin my first experience outside of that prison.

Turning back forward, my feet move faster, my free arm pumping by my side as I grip onto Flynn's hand with my other. The scent of the trees begins to roll towards us, tugging on my brain in familiarity. I breathe it in deeply, my chest heaving with the effort of running. I do not think I could have kept up with Flynn in any capacity if Alexi had not made me exercise. Even now, my lungs and legs burn with exertion. About ten feet separate us from the forest, the trees so thickly woven together at the top that no light from the moon and stars pierces through their canopies.

Something whizzes by my head, and Flynn jerks me to him quickly. "Shit," he curses as we finally reach the forest and cut in between the trees.

"What was that?" I gasp, stumbling while we run in near darkness. I keep tripping on roots, but Flynn somehow keeps me from hitting the ground. I can hear Bella's panting breaths on my other side, and relief washes over me that we made it. That we are all here together.

"An arrow. They shot an arrow at us." He slows our pace down slightly. I can still hear the footfalls of the guards behind us as they also enter the forest, their armor and weaponry clanging together with their movements. Flynn somehow navigates through the near pitch black, until a small pocket of moonlight comes into view ahead.

"How do you know where to go?" I whisper, afraid to let go of his hand for fear I'll fall into the abyss of darkness and be lost forever in the woods.

"I've made this journey a few times, so I know the general direction we need to go in," he huffs while keeping his voice low. "Though I usually don't leave in the middle of the night when it's this dark and I normally enter the forest near the capital." There's a hint of uncertainty in his voice that puts me on edge. It feels like we keep to our jogging pace for hours. My back is drenched in sweat, and my feet feel swollen and tight in my boots.

"Flynn, I need a break," I admit from where he's practically dragging me behind him. Even Bella's panting is loud next to me from the pace we've kept. Without another word, he brings us to a large tree, the outline of the trunk against the black night barely visible as he guides me to sit on one of the hard, exposed roots. Bella flops down next to me, laying on her side as she breathes heavily. Flynn stays standing, his sword drawn as he surveys the area around us.

The forest is quiet, the voices and banging of the metal armor lost a ways back as we ran. I lean my head back against the bark of the tree, closing my eyes briefly. But when I do, all I can see is Flynn's blood pooling around him in that field. Flashes of the night Alexi died get interwoven with the thought, a reminder that I almost lost Flynn too. My eyes open and go straight to him. *He's here, and he's whole.* Questions that I know we don't have time to answer right now push against my lips as I watch him.

"I have magic." My voice is a tiny whisper, both out of fear of the guards that may still be coming and out of insecurity that Flynn may be upset. I don't know why I say it. He obviously knows the truth of those words by this point without me having to speak them.

"You do," he acknowledges with equal softness. Prickling awareness causes goosebumps to break out over my skin as I sense his gaze on me.

"Are you upset with me? For hiding it?" I still feel it was the right thing to do. The less people that know about me having magic, the safer I am, but I can't help but feel nervous that he won't feel the same way. That he'll wonder if I didn't trust him with this secret. I suppose that, in a way, I didn't. At least, not when I thought he had the magic of the blood oath binding him to the king. I hear—more than see—him take a step to me and lower down to one knee. Fallen leaves from the surrounding trees crinkle under his boots, the smell of the decayed foliage—as well as something more earthy—stirring up from the motion.

"No, I am not upset," he says firmly, his voice low. His fingers gently touch the back of my hand, letting me know that he is there before they slowly travel up my arm and shoulder. I shiver as he trails them to my neck until he cups the side of my face entirely. A breath shudders from me under his touch, my shoulders relaxing vaguely from the invisible weight of worry that was sitting on them. We're not out of the woods yet, literally, but knowing that I'm here with him—that we're here together—settles me. His thumb caresses my cheek, and he whispers, "I understand why you wouldn't have told me. How long have you known you've had magic?"

My hand follows the line of his arm up to his shoulder, taking my time to feel the warm skin on his neck. "Since I was seventeen. I accidentally used it to save Bella from dying. I didn't know that I had it before then." I hear him take a deep breath, but he stays still as I bring my other hand to his face. "Thank you," I say, moving myself closer to him at that achingly slow pace he always uses with me. Giving him time to move away if this isn't what he wants. It's not the right time—here in the forest while we run from the King's Guard—but the fact that I nearly lost him has me feeling desperate. Desperate for his touch, for his safety, just for *him*.

He moves willingly with my hands as I pull him to me steadily until our noses brush. "For what?" he asks, his breath an airy brush against my lips.

"For not being upset with me." I slide one hand up to his hair where I know a few of the strands will be hanging over his forehead. My fingers push them back, but the strands immediately flop back in place. I don't know why I love that so much, why his hair has always been this irresistible part of him that I've yearned to touch and run my fingers through. "For making me feel less alone. For risking everything to help me leave." I move the hand in his hair down his chest until I feel the beating of his heart beneath my palm as I murmur each statement. "For seeing me as more than a princess locked in a tower."

His hand moves to tangle in my hair. Our lips barely touch, but I can tell he is smiling against mine. My magic starts to hum inside of me, the warm feeling moving slowly up my torso and down my arms to my hands. They begin to glow faintly, the magic pulsing to the beat of my heart. The angles of Flynn's face are illuminated by the mild white light between us, his smile causing that throbbing to go faster. My eyes flutter closed as his lips finally seal over mine, his hand tightening slightly in my hair. It's a more delicate kiss, our lips moving like we're mapping out unexplored territory for the first time. I'm lost in the passion of it, every nerve ending on edge while my mind is a quiet calm.

Perhaps Flynn is just as distracted, and that's why neither of us hear the crunching of the leaves or realize that Bella is growling until it's too late and a searing pain flares to life in my thigh.

Chapter Thirty-Six

RHEA

I scream as my hands, still alight with my magic, move to where the pain is radiating in the side of my thigh. I can feel the warm trickle of blood trailing down my leg from the arrow—an *actual* arrow—protruding there. Flynn wraps an arm around my waist and hauls me to the opposite side of the tree from where the arrow came. Though how he can tell in the pitch black, I don't know. Bella flanks my other side as I breathe through the pain in my leg, not wanting to make too much noise. My magic slowly fades from my hands as I focus on calling it back inside me and letting the darkness come into place around us again.

"Fuck, Rhea, it's going to be okay," he promises, his large hand covering mine while his other holds the sword up. "I can pull the arrow out, and you can heal it—"

"We don't have time," I say, gasping for breath as I grip Flynn's forearm tightly. The pain is unlike anything I've ever felt before; it's a radiating burn that feels like it's coming from deep within the bone in my leg. "We need to get away from them." Memories of the night Bella nearly died remind me of how much blood she lost when she was shot by an arrow. I've never healed myself from an injury like this before. What if it takes more time than we have and something happens to Flynn? My palms grow clammy as I force myself to push away from the trunk of the tree, gasping for breath.

"Rhea—"

"You know we can't stay still here," I whisper, grateful for the darkness as I wince and grit my teeth together. Gods, the pain reverberates in a searing heat down my entire leg and up to my hip. My stomach lurches as a bout of nausea and dizziness washes over me. In between Flynn and the tree, I try to stand, using them to hold myself up.

"And you know I can't bear to see you in pain. Let me take it out now. *Please.*"

My heart beats furiously, and my breath gets stuck in my chest. Tears roll down my cheeks; that piercing pain exacerbates with every second that passes. Flynn moves us a little farther into the trees, leaning me up against a large trunk. He places my hand on his shoulder, both of his now slowly traveling up my injured leg. His muscles tense as he gets closer to where the arrow is in my thigh.

"Rhea, please. Just a few seconds of pain, and then you can start to heal it."

"Alright," I whisper, bringing my other hand to cover my mouth as I heave air in and out of my nose.

"On the count of three," he says quietly. I squeeze my eyes shut, my fingernails digging into the muscles of his shoulders in a way that must be painful for him. "One. Two—" He starts to tug on the arrow as I scream into my palm. Suddenly, his hands are gone and he is on the ground in front of me, cursing into the darkness.

"Flynn?" I cry out as I try to drop to my knees, aware that my voice is ricocheting off of the trees and likely revealing our position.

"I've been shot," he hisses as panic ices my veins. Bella growls low at something behind us, and I don't have time to react before Flynn hauls the side of me that isn't bleeding closer to him. His arm squeezes around my waist, nearly lifting me off the ground with his strength. He says nothing as he starts to lead us through the forest at a faster pace which I know we won't be able to keep up, injured as we are.

I want to ask him where he was shot, but words are too hard to form. Tears leak from my eyes with each step we take as we run. I bite down on my lower lip to keep the building screams trapped in my throat as a metallic taste blankets my tongue. When I take a particularly jarring step on the uneven forest floor, a small sob escapes from me as the pain nearly causes me to black out—my vision, even in the darkness, blurs.

"Just a little farther, Sunshine. You can do it," he encourages, his steps never faltering as we move as quickly as possible between the trees. Leaves rustle around us, and it's hard to tell if it's from the noise *we* are making or if it's from the guards. I wonder momentarily if the king eventually followed his men out here and is hunting us down as well.

Small patches of moonlight dot the ground ahead of us, providing us with some much-needed guidance as we make our escape. Suddenly, Bella—who keeps pace a few feet ahead of us—stops, her paws skidding in the leaves from the abruptness. Flynn hauls me even closer to him, my arms already gripped around his torso for support. Bella's ears twitch from side to side as she slowly surveys the area in front of us. I stand completely still, feeling the skin around the arrow throb with each beat of my heart. My boot feels slick and warm, and the thought of that much blood pooling in it nearly causes me to vomit. Flynn steps back from me, his arm unwrapping from its place on my shoulders. I watch in the small amount of silver light streaming in above us as he reaches across his chest to his other arm and—gritting his teeth together—yanks something out with a sickening sound. He tosses what I see now is an arrow to the ground, exhaling a breath before running his uninjured hand through his hair.

"We need to get yours out next," he says softly.

I take a step towards him, my hands reaching out to heal the wound on his arm first. There's nothing to prepare me for when a second arrow enters the back of my shoulder, the force of it pushing me into Flynn. I can't help how one of the screams I've been holding back releases of its own accord.

"Oy! We are supposed to bring her back to him alive!" a voice shouts from in front of us.

"It's not my fault she moved in front of him right when I loosed the arrow!" another responds back.

Flynn is ripped from my grasp when someone tackles him from behind as large arms wrap around me from the side, pulling me into a chest covered with golden armor. The arrow sticking out of my thigh gets bumped in the scuffle, and the pain that shoots through me causes me to freeze as I scream out again.

"I have her," my captor yells.

Beyond the little bit of silvery light, I can just make out Flynn battling with two more guards. One is in front of him, the other behind, but his movements are graceful as he blocks and counters each of their attacks. He looks like an avenging god from the fairy tales I've read, even with his injured arm. His eyes flick to mine, and for a brief moment, our connection is undeniable. It's a tangible thread linking us—being pulled taut. Our souls connect for a breathless fragment in time.

"Your little escape attempt has failed, *bitch*. It's time to go back to where you belong." The guard's voice grates in my ears as he starts dragging me away with him. I fight to dig my feet into the earth, but my dizziness is winning and the leaves scattered everywhere keep causing my boots to slip.

"Flynn!" I scream, my consciousness beginning to fade. I'm doing everything I can to stay awake because I know that if I don't fight, then I will wake up back in that tower. Or, it hits me as I let out another frustrated scream, there is somewhere worse for me to end up—in the king's bed as his betrothed. I would rather make them kill me right here and now than go back to that. Back to him.

Bella growls from somewhere behind me as I kick and twist in the guard's hold, but it's no use. I'm completely helpless against him. My sobs turn to wails, my body growing weaker with each attempt I make. In my flailing, I connect a fisted hand with his face, causing the guard to hiss and loosen his grip on me. I jerk free and haltingly, painfully, run back towards Flynn and Bella. I make it four steps, adrenaline flooding my body as I try to get away, but a sharp yank of my hair pulls me backwards.

"No!" I scream, but the guard wraps my hair around his fist until my shoulder crashes into his chest. He pulls on my hair, forcing my face to tilt up as his other hand grips onto my outer hip harshly.

"If it wasn't a death wish, I would shut you up with my cock right now," he growls as his beady eyes bore into me. He squeezes me to his side as he begins to walk, his arm knocking into the arrow still penetrating my shoulder with each step. Tears and blood loss cause my eyes to blur, but through my weariness and hysteria, I start to feel a warm sensation—familiar and bright. I look down and see the glow of my magic in my palms. They grow brighter the longer I stare, and the guard sucks in a breath.

"What does your magic do?" he asks warily, bringing us to a halt. "Put it away!"

I thrust a luminescent hand into his eyes, hoping the light blinds him in the near darkness. He releases me immediately, screaming in terror as his hands rub his eyes. I waste no time turning around and hobbling in the direction where I last saw Flynn, trying to find that small bit of silver light to guide my way. My steps are filled with pain, my body beginning to fail after using up all of its adrenaline. I slow my steps down, each thud of my boots causing an all-consuming acidic fire to radiate from each wound throughout my entire body. I stop to breathe through the pain, my chest heaving as I push away sweaty strands of hair from my face. The forest is now silent. There is no clashing of swords or shuffling of leaves under feet. There are no harsh breaths or whimpers of pain except for my own. I'm alone, Flynn and Bella nowhere to be seen.

I force myself to keep moving, but I've lost all sense of direction. My shaky hand reaches up to the arrow sticking out from my shoulder, my muscles flaring in pain from the movement. It entered from the back, and

I gasp as I feel the tip of it just underneath the skin near my collarbone. A noise comes from my left—where I ran from the guard that tried to take me. Panic threatens to immobilize me, but I cross through the small clearing of trees to the other side and drop to my hands and knees behind a large trunk. The sound of leaves being stepped on echoes loudly throughout the forest. *Crinkle.* Pause. *Crinkle.* Pause. Like the ticking of a death clock, I hear whoever it is come closer and closer. My body is moving faster than my brain, and when I lean up against the tree, I'm quickly reminded of the trauma to my back. White hot pain sears my shoulder and arm as a renewed trickle of warm blood flows down to my fingers. I try to force air into my lungs, but the agony is too much. There's a pounding in my head and ears as I collapse onto my side, one hand gripping the earth in front of me. Blackness creeps into my vision, like one of the swirling galaxies from the Middle, and slowly begins to consume it.

A pair of black boots stepping before me is the last thing I see before darkness descends.

The scent of the forest wraps around me as my body is faintly jostled from side to side. My limbs feel heavy as they just hang there unusable. I try to move an arm, but I'm met with a fiery ache in my shoulder that halts my attempt.

A small whimper leaves me as more and more pain starts to filter into my consciousness. It radiates from my shoulder and my thigh until I'm gritting my teeth and hissing out breaths between them. Memories start flooding back into me: the ambush of guards, Flynn and Bella missing, footsteps nearing as I... *Oh gods.* What if I'm being carried back to the king? My fingers start to tingle, the sensation working its way up my arms and to my shoulders before draping back down my body like a warm ray of the sun—reminiscent of the mind cleanser exercises Alexi taught me. Just his name in my thoughts chills some of that warmth, that *other* feeling twisting inside of me like a snake poising to strike.

"Rhea, are you awake? Open your eyes."

Flynn. My panic immediately calms, the warm richness of his voice soothing my fear. It takes all of my effort to force my eyelids to open, to obey his simple command. When they do, it's too blurry to make anything out. This continues on for another few moments as I try to clear out what feels like a haze surrounding me. Finally, my eyes adjust, and even in the inky darkness, they find his. They always do.

"There you are, Sunshine. Stars above, I've been so worried about you," he rasps. My head is leaning on his chest, his arms holding me remarkably stable as he steps over jagged roots and pointed rocks on the forest floor. I turn to lean my head further into him, to bury myself into the safety of his hold, as his scent—that autumnal changing-of-the-leaves scent that is just so uniquely him—invades my lungs. "We need to get these arrows out of you. There's a small stream up ahead that should muffle—" He interrupts himself, breathing in deeply before continuing, "It should muffle the sounds when I pull them out."

My screams. He's talking about my screams of pain when he removes the arrows. I tilt my head away from his chest to look up at him. I can only make out the cut of his strong jaw and those incredible cheekbones. If I had to guess, I'd wager a few strands of his wavy hair are hanging over his forehead. Even in the shadowed darkness that surrounds us and through the waves of pain that keep hitting me, I am still so drawn to him. Like a moth to a flame, all I can see—all I can think about—is the mortal guard who risked everything to save me. Words fueled by the overwhelming emotions winding inside of me stack one on top of the other in my mouth, trying to break past my lips, but I swallow them down and instead focus on our surroundings. My eyes adjust to the dark, noticing how it all looks the same as it did when we entered the forest: trees for miles. I look down and see Bella walking a few feet ahead of us.

"How long was I out for?" I ask, trying to hold my head up but failing to do so for more than a few breaths.

"I don't know exactly. Maybe an hour."

My head swings back to him, trying to see his eyes but failing. "Have you been carrying me this whole time?"

"Yes," he says quietly before leaping over something sticking out of the ground. I barely move in the process, his bicep muscles bulging with the effort.

"I can walk. You must be exhausted from holding me." I move to wiggle out of his grip and let out a yelp of pain which only causes Flynn to lift me farther up his chest, his arms tightening as if he believes I possess the strength to actually get away right now.

"Do I appear weak to you, Sunshine?" he teases. But there's a tension there too, his words marginally more clipped than how they would normally sound. It hits me then that I can decipher his voice and cadence, even in just our few short months together. I feel like I don't know very many *things* about him but I have a decent grasp on *who* he is.

"What? No," I answer honestly. "Your body is built like you could carry ten of me, but it doesn't mean that you should have to. *Or* that it doesn't get tiresome."

"Hmm, tell me what else you've noticed about my body," he says, his voice low in a way that makes me feel very inappropriate things at a very inappropriate time. As if sensing the direction of my thoughts, Flynn chuckles before giving me a chaste kiss on my forehead. *This* is what is actually appropriate at this moment, but I wish someone would tell that to my body. Flynn grumbles out a "finally," and I'm confused at first until I start to hear the gentle trickling of water. We must be nearing the stream.

"Are you okay?" I ask tentatively. I want to touch his face but my good arm is pinned to his chest by the way he is holding me and my other arm is left immobile by the arrow.

"I will be. The sooner we get these arrows out of you, the faster and farther away we can get from the king." His fingers flex tightly where he's holding me, his anger and frustration palpable as we clear a few large rocks and start to descend down to the water. The closer we get to the stream, the colder I begin to feel—like the cool air off the water is poking holes in the warm humidity around us. At least, I hope it's the water that's causing an icy shiver to wrack my body. The trees begin to thin out as Flynn follows Bella's guidance. She leads us along the bank of a stream until a small piece of flat land comes into view, just below the bank and near the water. Flynn descends the bank swiftly, carefully. "When I lay you down, do you think that you can call your magic up to the surface so we have some more light?" he asks, his voice now more raw than it was a minute ago.

"Yes." My magic hums in answer as well. Through the larger gaps in the canopy, I can see the glittering moon—its presence welcoming.

Flynn gets down on one knee and gently lays me on the ground on my good side, moving a few leaves away so they aren't completely surrounding my face. I lay my head on the ground as I extend my arm out in front of me, palm up. I suppose that if there is an upside to being shot by two arrows, it's that they hit on the same side of my body. Bella lays down where I can see her, providing silent support as I prepare myself mentally for what's coming. I focus on calling my magic to my palm, trying to angle it awkwardly towards where Flynn is kneeling in front of me. It moves more slowly than the last time I tried, and I wonder if it's because of how injured I am. My magic has healed me while I've slept and fought to get free when I've been in danger, and it has heeded my calls, to either use or suppress it, every time I've tried. To feel it move so sluggishly causes a tightness in my throat. I may not understand how I have magic or why, but I've become used to the way it feels, the way its presence is almost separate from my own and always *there*.

When the mellow white glow finally illuminates our space, Flynn carefully begins to peel back the torn pieces of my trousers surrounding where the arrow sticks out. He curses soundly under his breath, and were this any other time, I might actually laugh. But the concerned look on his face has me working to swallow my fear.

"What's wrong?" My voice comes out shaky and uneven as the terror I'm repressing finds its way into my voice.

"Did you summon your magic to heal your wounds?" he asks while I lay my hand down on the ground.

I shake my head in response before saying, "I don't think so anyway."

He eyes me for another moment before dropping his gaze back down to my leg, a crease forming between his brows. "I've never—" He pauses, clearing his throat and running a hand through his hair. "We're going to have to re-injure you as we pull the arrows out." His voice is so gravelly that it sounds like it has been dragged over shards of rock. He adds more tenderly, "It's going to fucking hurt."

"It's okay," I murmur, holding his gaze. "I'm used to pain. I can handle it." His body goes completely still, like he has suddenly become made of stone. I survey him in confusion. "Flynn? What's wrong?"

"I will kill him, Rhea. I promise you." His dark eyes dance with rage as he looks just beyond me at the water.

To anyone else, he would be downright terrifying right now, and maybe even a month ago, I might have shrunk backwards at the way his body is radiating such lethal anger. But I know Flynn won't hurt me. I know his rage for the king isn't misplaced. And while I hate to admit that I have a tight feeling in my chest at the thought of him murdering *anybody*, I'm not naive enough anymore to assume there is a place far enough away from the king that he will stop looking for me. His death may be the only way I stay free, and I don't know why that thought makes me sick to my stomach. There's also the not-so-small detail that King Dolian knows I have magic now, and based on his obvious hatred for mages, I don't know if that affects his plans for me. I know that I'll never go back there willingly. He'll have to drag me back while I'm either unconscious or dead.

"Which arrow do you want me to take out first?" Flynn asks, bringing my thoughts back to the present.

Right, two arrows are protruding from my body. Despite my best attempts to keep calm, I can't stop the racing of my heart. "Surprise me." I try to joke, but the tremble in my voice gives away my true feelings.

The hand holding my shining magic starts to shake as well, causing the light to bounce everywhere but where Flynn needs it. His entire body eases when his gaze meets mine, like an exhale that's finally been released after being held for too long. He shifts up towards my chest, so I assume that means he's going with the shoulder arrow first. But he leans down instead, his nose grazing mine as his hair tickles my forehead.

"Do you remember what I said to you yesterday?" he asks, one hand coming to cup the side of my face while the other lazily slides up and down my back.

"Yes," I whisper, my body locking up tightly in anticipation.

"Tell me. Tell me what I said," he commands. And even though I know he's just trying to distract me, and I have enough fear running through my veins to drown me, I can't deny him.

"You said," I start, my voice quivering as he slides his hand slowly up again, "that you couldn't wait until we were safe." That hand pauses somewhere on my upper back, though where exactly I can't tell since my wound pulsates waves of pain across its entirety.

"And then what did I say?" His voice is guttural, the roughness drawing all of my attention. "I want to hear you say every single word." I watch his eyes dart over to my shoulder for a second before returning to mine. The dark depths of them call to me, luring me into them like a fish to water.

"You said you couldn't wait to explore every part of me," I rasp, feeling a sudden pressure surrounding the entry point at my shoulder. "And I said that I wanted that too."

"I can't fucking wait," he chokes out, his voice a subdued declaration. "Close your eyes."

I do as he says, hearing metal scrape against leather before a quick and searing flash of pain erupts on my chest. I hear the sound of wood breaking before I *feel* the arrow moving through me. My eyes shoot open, and I look down at the metal tip fully protruding from my front now, blood leaking across my chest and dripping onto the ground. A scream rips from my throat as I force my eyes to close again. I feel Flynn's hand move to where the tip of the arrow is, and with a jerk, the pressure of it being inside of me is removed.

"It's out," he says, his lips finding my forehead as I force air into my lungs and let hot tears leak down my cheeks. "We need to clean it to prevent infection before you heal yourself."

"I have soap in the satchel you're carrying," I grit out between ragged breaths. I hear him shuffle around in one of the bags, tearing a piece of fabric, before he steps up to the stream behind me. Within a few seconds he's back at my side, carefully dabbing a cold, wet cloth around the wound on my shoulder. I hiss at the contact, curling in on myself a little as he lightly wipes at my skin.

"Okay, call your magic up."

I release my hold on the magic, trusting that it will do what it needs to. I'm exhausted already, my head feeling dizzy and my eyelids heavy. I hear Flynn move back to the water before coming back into view and kneeling at my legs.

"Rhea, this one..." He trails off, a hand bracketing either side of the arrow sticking out of my thigh. "It's more complex—going through more muscle and maybe even hitting the bone. I'll have to try and reopen the wound so that the arrowhead doesn't shred your leg."

I swallow down the bile creeping up my throat. My magic, in trying to save me from losing too much blood, ended up damning me. I wonder if this is payback for not using it all those times it begged to be let out. I nearly snort at the thought. My breathing picks up again even though the pain in my shoulder has finally eased and is replaced with just a mild tenderness. I twist my upper body until my back is flush against the ground with my hips still stacked on top of each other. My lungs struggle to take enough air in, my mind whirling and vision swirling. The hand that's supposed to be providing light just grabs onto Flynn's leg.

"Flynn," I whisper, my voice drawing his eyes from my leg to my face, "I can't do this."

"Sunshine." He leans down, clearing the hair from my face and planting a soft kiss on my lips. "You can. You're so strong, despite what he's tried to mold you into. Despite everything, you're so incredibly fierce," he says each word while kissing the tip of my nose. "And so fucking beautiful."

I cough out a laugh, my wet lashes blinking away a few more tears as, despite it all, I find myself offering a small smile. Flynn gives me one final kiss and then kneels down by my thighs again. My eyes find the moon; it's nearly full with the Summer Solstice happening in just a few days. Bella moves closer to me, one of her massive paws laying gently on my uninjured shoulder. I know it must be my exhaustion and blood loss, but a part of me swears the moon pulsates in time with my heart. The stars wave their hello as well, bringing me comfort. It makes me feel braver. That cold curled up inside of me perks up for just a moment, but then it dies back down.

"Do it, Flynn." I breathe as he nods, brandishing a small dagger. My hand reaches up to grip Bella's paw while I keep my gaze on the sky above me and exhale slowly.

"Do you want to know why your nickname is 'Sunshine'?" he asks, but before I can respond, pain bursts to life in my thigh—unbridled and unrelenting. I cry out, the sound echoing out into the forest. I squeeze Bella's paw and try to steady my other hand as my magic flares brighter in my palm. My mouth gapes open as I try to gulp in air, my body begging me to breathe, but the pain is too piercing. I lift my head to look, but Flynn stops me.

"Don't look." He glances at me, his eyes focused and unyielding, and I wonder if this is hard for him to do. To be the one that is causing me pain like this. I also know that the arrow isn't out yet. My own eyes blur, my breaths moving quickly in and out through my mouth. Warm blood leaks down my leg, and I have the delirious thought that this entire outfit is totally ruined. Then I remember Flynn's question.

"Why did you pick 'Sunshine'?" The words are slurred through my sobs, and I don't know if he can even understand them. In my incoherence, I see the moon glow imperceptibly brighter right as Flynn begins to speak. Unfortunately, he also begins to *move* the arrow, and I don't hear a single thing he says before I pass out.

Chapter Thirty-Seven

BAHIRA

THE SUN POURS IN through the windows of my room and blinds me where I lay on my bed, my head pounding from the alcohol consumed the night before. A bottle lays on the green and gold ornate rug, the smell of hard liquor permeating the air—my stomach roils in response. Huffing out a breath, I roll slowly onto my back, a forearm resting over my eyes.

This is a new feeling for me. Well, that's not exactly true. The feeling of being a failure—of not amounting to anything—has simmered beneath the surface of my false bravado for a little while now. Each failed experiment and derogatory comment only added fuel to the fire that I tried desperately to keep extinguished. Today however, it burns brightly within me, creating a warmth that sends bile up my throat and trepidation through my body. Or maybe that is the alcohol trying to escape. Despite not wanting to reminisce at all about magic or experiments or journals, my brain has always worked too scientifically—too logically. Even half drowned in inebriation, it's still trying to sort through any data that can be gained from my latest failure. *You could try—*

"No," I respond to myself, halting the train of thought.

Another rush of nausea barrels through me, and I bolt from the bed, running to the bathroom and kneeling before the toilet just in time. I gather as much of my thick hair back as I can, vomiting so hard that I begin to see stars from the force of it. When the urge to expel my insides finally dies down, I collapse onto the cold stone of the floor. Tears already leak from my eyes, but I can't be sure if it's from being sick or if it's because of the crushing weight of defeat sitting on top of me. Squeezing them shut, I focus on my breathing to try and stop the swirling thoughts of "what if" and "what about." *It doesn't matter anymore.*

A gentle knock sounds on my door, as if the person somehow knows that my skull feels as though it might crack if the noise is any louder.

"Your Highness, are you awake?" a sweet voice asks. It's Sarai, one of the ladies-in-waiting for both my mother and I.

"I am," I shout back, immediately wincing at the slicing pain in my head that my volume causes. Fuck, how am I going to get through this hangover and attend the Summer Solstice celebration tonight?

"It is nearly time to join your family for the celebration, Your Highness, are you ready to get dressed?" Her much quieter voice doesn't feel like needles pushing into my brain, but the realization that I slept the entire day proves that I still do in fact have enough in my stomach to throw up again. I swallow the sensation down, truly feeling like I've hit rock bottom with the action.

"Sarai," I say, my throat burning and voice hoarse, "I need to shower, and then I will be ready to get dressed. Can you also send food up? And I will need—" I pause, swallowing again before forcing the words out of me. "I will need a healer. I'm not feeling well."

"Of course. Everything will be ready out here for you by the time you are done with your shower."

"Thank you," I rasp and wait to hear the door close before slowly sitting up and reaching over to turn on the faucet above the tub. I make it as cold as possible before undressing and practically slinking in like a snake. The water sprinkles down on me from the spout overhead, but all I can manage for a while is to stay seated and let the freezing drops slowly begin to clear my mind and calm my stomach.

For so long, I truly thought I was capable of doing the impossible. Magic in our world appears to be sentient—a living thing that allows the beings of Olymazi to wield it. The mages' connection with it is less *specific* than any other kingdom's. The fae use it to bond with their dragons. The sirens are given their seductive song and ability to live under water. The shifters can take two forms—one beast and one mortal. But the mages can manipulate the magic. They can spell it onto items and use it to control the elements around them. They can use it to heal and to hurt, in small degrees. And I just want that same connection. It is like I am standing on the outside looking in at my own world. Mortals may not directly have magic, but they can at least access the Continent's magic through blood. I have mage blood flowing through my veins. I *am* mage!

But then, maybe I'm not. What separates mages from mortals is nothing more than a slightly longer lifespan and the ability to wield magic. My mother had said that magic is secondary to the person wielding it, but that can't be true. I am not mortal, but I am not truly mage either. And that means I am adrift in the ocean between two worlds—one that I am desperate to be connected to and one that I am more a part of than I ever want to be.

Forcing out a breath, I slowly stand, feeling marginally better than I had when I first woke up. Tilting my head up towards the water, a sharp feeling of unease hits my gut as I remember what is happening tomorrow.

Kai Vaea, King of the Shifter Kingdom, will arrive at our border with the intent of taking a mage back to his island. I am still unsure what he expects someone to do about the supposed blight he believes to be affecting the magic there, but I put the thought aside as I have no room to talk about retaining the hope of fixing defective magic.

After washing my hair and body, I finally step out of the shower, feeling a bit more like myself again. A beautiful dress fit for the celebration tonight lays on the bed, as well as a meal of buttery rolls, carved ham, and zucchini. I reach for the food first, eating my fill and finally settling the bitter waves that have been plaguing my stomach. Sarai enters the room shortly after, helping me dress and styling my hair before an older mage, the official palace healer, steps in.

"Happy Solstice, Your Highness," he begins, his dark green robe with silver embroidery swallowing his frail frame. His long gray hair is braided back from his face, wrinkles inset in his dark skin near his eyes and forehead.

"And same to you, Galen. Thank you for coming on such short notice." I force a gentle smile to my face as he lays his hands on the top of my head. "I am not feeling one hundred percent today and wouldn't want to miss any of the festivities tonight."

He nods his head in agreement, a knowing glint showing in his eyes before he closes them to focus. "It is an honor to help you, Bahira. It is not often you have called on me, so it is a rare Summer Solstice present indeed."

His magic glows a brilliant green as it pours over me—the pain in my head ceasing immediately, as does the remaining sour feeling in my stomach. I take a true deep breath for the first time this morning. I watch in the mirror of the vanity as Galen's hands tremble from the effort of healing me. The man is in his sixth decade of life. His magic should be just as strong as it was in his second decade, and yet, I can tell from the strain on his face that he is struggling with just healing my hangover symptoms. And that angers me. It angers me that this man is losing his magic and, thus, losing his ability to help serve the people of the kingdom he loves. When his eyes open, I replace the look of concern that had painted my face with one of genuine warmth.

"Thank you, Galen. I am now feeling ready for revelry and raucous behavior," I tease. His responding raspy laugh sparks a true beaming smile from me this time as he pats my shoulder fondly and makes his way out the door. Sarai returns to her spot behind me, finishing up the last details of my hair before stepping back and interlacing her fingers in front of her.

"You look beautiful, Princess."

I stand to walk towards the mirror in the corner of my room and am remiss if I don't say I agree with her. My fingers roam over the light blue tulle of my skirt, the fabric gathering at my waist before flaring out. The top half of the dress is white and has a bodice with a deep v-cut in the middle and beads of glistening silver and black sewn into shapes of flowers and small suns. Creamy white silk fabric drapes delicately at my shoulders, contrasting brightly against my tan skin and the blue of the skirt. Sarai has made several small braids around my head, gathering them into one large plait that works its way to hang over one shoulder. I look regal and royal and like everything I don't actually feel at the moment but will have to fake at the celebration.

"You've outdone yourself, Sarai," I agree. "Thank you."

She smiles brightly, dipping her chin before leaving the room. I sit on the edge of my bed, wrapping the silver ribbons of my sandals up my ankles and part of my calves. Once they are laced, I take one last look at myself before leaving my room and walking down the stairs. While I have no idea what I will now do going forward—something that leaves me feeling unmoored—I know one thing for sure that will be resolved tonight whether I want it to or not. I haven't spoken to Daje since my fight with Gosston, when Daje stepped in and used his magic against him. I know he meant well, and I know he did it because he truly thought he was helping me. Looking back, I can even admit that I probably acted too severely in my response to him that day. I just wish he would have at least listened to me. That he would *trust* me. My heart beats heavily in my chest as I force down any lingering thoughts about magic and my place in this kingdom, choosing to instead put on the mask of a carefree princess. The warm summer air lays thick around me as I lift my dress and step into a waiting carriage.

Independent of the heat, sweat gathers at the base of my neck from my nerves. Nothing has changed for me save my own acceptance of my shortcomings, but it somehow feels like everyone will know that I am struggling when I step foot out of this carriage and into the midst of the celebration. Separate from my own spiraling, what will people think about the shifter king arriving in two days time? My father has already sent word that a strong mage will be chosen to go live for a few months on the shifter isle, but I wonder if it will dampen the mood at all.

I ponder this as I watch the trees whizz by as the horses pull the carriage down the stone pathway. The setting sun gilds everything with its soft glow, making flowers shimmer and leaves gleam. I am the last one to leave the palace, which undoubtedly means all attention will be on me when I finally arrive. *Fucking fantastic.*

Despite everything, my irritating brain can't help but contemplate the chart I have been developing from the information gathered out of the mage journals. Small symbols that represent every time a mage has commented on a change in magic throughout the kingdom lay out on a timeline in my mind. My lips purse together as I debate internally whether or not I should keep going with this research. It is like I have a person sitting on each shoulder shouting out opposing thoughts to sway me either way.

You love to read. What is this research but just reading?

You're reading with the intent to pull data, and so far all the data you've tried to utilize has been fruitless. Pointless.

There is no harm in simply charting out information.

There is harm when it gives you false hope that you might still find a solution.

Back and forth my thoughts go, a new headache forming from tension. The jostling of the carriage coming to a stop finally pulls me from my own personal hell as the door opens. I gather the tulle of my skirt into my hands, lifting it out of the way of my feet as I carefully step out, my eyes widening at the display of lights and decorations set up before me.

Every Solstice celebration is held in the middle of an old amphitheater that is now used more as a recreational area for various gatherings—both big and small. Deep, sweeping semicircular terraces are inlaid with a set of wide stone steps that lead down to a large, open grassy area at the center, the space large enough to fit everyone on this side of the kingdom. Arches of draping wisteria flowers in pinks and purples dot the pathway to the steps interspersed with spelled flames in glass bowls hanging from metal hooks every few feet. In the thick trees that surround the back of the open space below and the edges of the deep tiers, I can see flames dancing in glass balls, spelled to stay suspended in the air. The thick, twisting banya and pirang trees were originally only lightly grown throughout the tiered seating area to provide shade and improve acoustics for mages watching the performances below. Now, they grow every few feet along the steps down, creating a thicker interwoven canopy above. The large grassy center is left completely open to view the night sky, except for three large evenly-spaced arches overhead that span from one side of the oval amphitheater to the other. Each one has pink and yellow wisteria flowers and large vines of heart ivy in every variation of white and green draping down just over the heads of the party goers below. More spelled flames dot in between the arches, floating on a wind of magic.

Carefully, I make my way down the steps, noticing grass and small yellow flowers growing in the cracks of the laid stone. The center of the large space is entirely covered in short grass, the variety a thick, dark green that cushions each of my steps as I look around to find my parents. Wooden tables filled with food and drink stretch along the entire length of the open field on one side while a band of mages playing different musical instruments are placed on the other. Most are of the string variety, the light and melodious sounds beautifully fitting for a summer party. Sure enough, the eyes of the party-going mages find me, I politely nod and smile in their direction, ignoring the scream that's attempting to work its way up my throat.

I find my parents, dancing together right in the center of the celebration amidst the people they both love dearly, and make my way over to them. My father hugs me tightly to him, somehow a look of sympathy and understanding keenly shining in his eyes. My mother squeezes my hands lightly, commenting on the beauty of my hair and dress before leading me over to grab refreshments.

"How are you, my rose?" she asks, taking a small bite of a sun-shaped sugar cookie.

I don't like lying, especially to her, but I also don't feel like hashing out what the last twenty-four hours of my life has been like. So, I smile and take a sip of my water before answering with a generic "good." I know that she can tell it isn't quite the truth, but before she has the chance to ask further, a familiar voice sounds behind me.

"Would you like to dance, Bahira?"

I grimace slightly as I slowly turn to face Daje, not missing the amused glint in my mother's eyes. My gaze roams over him as his does the same to me. Where mine merely assesses what he is wearing out of simple curiosity—brown trousers tucked into black boots, a black long-sleeved jacket embroidered in deep red with gold buttons running up the middle—his devours me, a spark of heat appearing as he lingers over the exposed skin on my upper chest. I clear my throat, feeling uncomfortable under his stare. He is my friend but he wants so much more from me than I can give him—than what I can *be* for him. Or at least, that is what I previously thought. His gaze holds mine and I feel my barriers beginning to crack further.

Maybe a life with him is all that should be left for me to focus on now. All this fighting, all this reluctance to accept what is—it has been pointless. So why shouldn't I entertain the idea that maybe a life with him could be better?

Chapter Thirty-Eight

BAHIRA

I PLACE MY HAND in his outstretched one, letting Daje lead me out into a vacant space on the grass near where the musicians are playing. We face each other, our joined hands out to the side while my other hand lays on his shoulder, just the tips of my fingers touching him there. His large palm rests on my lower back, and I search for an inkling of heat—of desire or lust—within me at our close proximity, but I feel nothing of the sort.

"You've been avoiding me," he says, diving right into the conversation I know we need to have.

I shrug my shoulders as we move, our feet mirroring each step of the waltz that I learned as a child. My gaze is hooked over his shoulder on the other dancing couples behind us as I counter, "The same could be said of you."

He blows out a breath, the movement tickling the ends of hair by my ear. "I didn't know if I should reach out," he says slowly. "I—I know that you would have preferred that I had not intervened... But, Bahira, I couldn't simply watch him do that to you."

Adrenaline trickles into my veins, a fight or flight response building despite the fact that I'm not in danger. "I know," I respond thickly as I swallow down the sarcastic retort on the tip of my tongue. Tension clouds around us, my breathing quickening the longer the silence goes on. My mouth opens to say something to ease it, but Daje interrupts before I can.

"Haylee told me about what happened in your workshop yesterday." His voice is quiet, conscious of the few people who are dancing around us.

My body tenses as my steps falter. *Damn it, Haylee.* "I don't want to talk about that," I grit out as my frustration and embarrassment cause a heat to work its way up my neck and cheeks. My gaze meets his, those blue eyes vigilant as they watch me. Shouldn't it make me feel *something* to have him look at me like that?

"Come on," he whispers, turning to guide us to the edges of the trees surrounding the base of the amphitheater. We walk just past the treeline into the near darkness. Daje calls over a spelled flame, the yellow glow of his magic surrounding it as he holds it above us.

My mind feels like the normally well-oiled gears are colliding, chunks breaking off and clogging the ones below, continuing until everything reaches a standstill. His thumb rubs the back of my hand as he holds it, dragging his other hand over the top of his closely cut dark brown hair. He looks nervous, and I have to swallow down my own anxiety about what he is going to say.

"Bahira, you must know how I feel about you. I have held back, fighting with myself on either being content with just being your friend or begging you to take me as more." It's hard to breathe as we stare at each other, words I can't voice sitting at the base of my throat. "I have been in love with you since we were kids," he proclaims, and *fuck*, I should feel my heart flip at that. "But I hate the thought of you being alone purely based on principle."

My eyebrows draw together as I look at him. "I'm not alone on principle, Daje," I correct firmly. My hand pulls from his, and I cross my arms over my chest. "I am *alone* because I've been focusing on other things, and I don't want to just se—"

"And now?" he interjects, taking another step towards me.

"And now, what?"

"Do you have the time now? Are you still focusing on those things *now?*"

The implication in his tone settles heavily on me, harsh and suffocating. Am I ready to settle down *now* that I have another set of failed experiments under my belt? *Now* that I've hit a rock bottom that I previously hadn't?

I shake my head and huff out a breath, as I keep my gaze locked on his and answer, "That is unfair of you to ask, and you know it."

Bugs in the forest behind us buzz loudly, the revelry from the party mixing in to create a jarring noise that represents how chaotic I'm feeling on the inside. I honestly thought I knew the answer to this question already. Yes, I have the time now. Yes, I'm ready to stop and settle down. But I can't force myself to say it. For some reason, my instinct is to say no, I'm *not* done. No, I *still* have work to do. No, I *don't* want to settle down with you. But I can't say that either because I don't know if it's the fucking truth.

Daje sighs when my silence drags on, taking a small step back. "I need to be honest with you, Bahira." His chest rises with a deep inhale before he slowly blows it out. "I want to marry you. I want to be able to protect you without fear it's going to cause you to bite my head off. I want to see you happy and thriving and not so focused on fixing something that isn't your job to fix." Each word is meant to be a declaration of love by a caring man asking me to be his, but they hit me like he's throwing invisible, jagged knives at my heart instead. "Marry me, Bahira. Marry me, and let me make you happy. Let me show you what a life of being cared for by me is like. Because I can't do this anymore." His hands gesture between us, like the sum of all of our time together is coming down to this moment.

"You can't do what anymore?" All I can do is speak in three or four word sentences now as my mind tries to play catch up with everything Daje is saying. It's funny how his version of me happy has never *once* included asking me what *I'd* like to do. He wants permission from me to let him be the center of my world.

"I can't continue to watch you sneak off and bed other men, thinking I don't know. I can't continue to watch you lose more of yourself on this quest to fix magic." My breath catches in my throat at his words. They aren't exactly mean but they hit their mark in me all the same. "If you can't marry me—if a life with me isn't what you want—then we can't..." He trails off, looking back towards the celebration before releasing a sigh and meeting my eyes again. "Then it would be best if we go our separate ways."

My head rears back, my jaw falling open as I gape at him in surprise. "You are giving me an ultimatum? Marry you, or lose you as a friend?" I blurt out, confused and indignant.

"I'm asking you to marry me and gain something more than a friend," he corrects.

My heart beats hard and fast in my chest. Daje is one of my oldest friends, and though things have started to change as we got older and his feelings for me began to morph into something *more*, I never imagined it would come to this. "Daje, please don't ask this of me," I breathe, my fingers curling into fists. "Why can't our friendship be enough?"

According to him, us marrying would be the solution to all of the problems in my life. A week ago—hell, two days ago—I would have scoffed in his face. I might have told him to fuck off and marched back into the celebration with my head held high and a deep belief that what I was doing held purpose. That it held value. Now however, I am so lost and confused, and I just don't know if I can handle losing something I thought would be a constant in my life.

"Do you think I haven't tried? To push these feelings I have for you so far down that I hope they disappear? Only to have them come rushing back to the surface every time I see you smile?" His blue eyes shine with silver as he stares at me. "I have tried to let it be enough, Bahira. I have begged and pleaded with any gods that might listen to let me just be happy with what you will give me. But I can't—" He hesitates, his head dropping for a few breaths before he looks back up to me. "I can't keep sacrificing my heart in the hope that one day you might catch up and see me the same way I see you. If you care about me at all, if there's even a *tiny* chance that your heart calls for me like mine does for you, then it's worth it to try."

My lips purse as I contemplate his words. I don't love Daje in that way now, but could I learn to? If I allowed him to change the parameters of our relationship into ones he sets the rules for, maybe I *could* find happiness. Maybe I could settle down and feel fulfilled by it. I have never been in a long-term relationship, by my own choice, but maybe there has been a solution right in front of me all this time.

"When do you need an answer?" I question, to both his shock and my own. His eyes move between mine as if he's trying to figure out if I am being serious.

"In two days," he answers. "I will be at the palace for the council meeting after the shifter king leaves. You can tell me then." It's a strategic move, and a smart one, on his part: either I have to reject him in my own home, possibly even while his father is there, or accept his proposal in front of the council, in front of my father. He swallows, a nervous but hopeful look flashing briefly in his eyes.

"Okay. I will give you an answer then." A feeling of unease settles inside me as I agree to his terms.

Daje nods, moving to take a step before pausing. "I would do anything for you, Bahira. I just want to make you happy."

My throat feels like it's being squeezed in a tight vice. I watch him walk back to the party, taking the spelled flame with him and leaving me alone in the darkness.

367

I take the steps back up from the center of the amphitheater slowly, the ringing in my ears blocking everything else out. The entire carriage ride home, Daje's words replay in my mind, and that sinking feeling grows. My brain begins running through the possibilities of what my life would be like if I were married to Daje. And each time I picture that future scenario, there are no butterflies in my stomach, no fluttering of my heart. There are no happy wedding day smiles nor tangled bodies in the sheets later that night. There's nothing but that sinking feeling, the pit of my stomach aching with something that feels an awful lot like dread.

"Fuck," I whisper, feeling like I can't breathe. The carriage finally comes to a stop in front of the palace, the guards opening the door and helping me out. I stop at the bottom of the stone steps, my gaze tilting up to stare at my home. In two days, it will be the place where I mete out an undetermined judgment on my own future. My hands grip the fabric of my dress, my breaths coming faster and faster.

"Your Highness, is everything alright?" one of the guards to my side asks, but my brain feels like it's spiraling out of control.

It feels like the very essence of who I am is being ripped out of me in one harsh yank, and I don't know where that will leave me after. I have never felt so unsure, so defeated. I need to go anywhere else, *anywhere* but here. I turn and start running down the stone path, the guards calling out behind me, but I don't stop. I run, my dress rustling with each step, and the only other sound is that of the wildlife around me. It takes a few minutes, but I end up at my destination with sweat dripping down my brow. When I step into my workshop, I exhale heavily. I would have gone to the library, but everyone else is down at the celebration, meaning it is locked.

I need to work this out logically, but when it comes to love and relationships, it isn't that simple. There is no way to write out Daje and I as an equation to find a true singular solution. He's in love with the *idea* of what I could be for him, and I care about him only as a friend. Those two things cannot mix, and yet I don't want to lose him from my life. He stood up for me when I was picked on and isolated from the other kids for being magicless. He listened quietly as I told him about my theories on magic and my latest experiments. He had sparred with me and attended boring council meetings and been someone for me to vent my worries to about Nox being gone. And now, he wants to be even more or he wants to be nothing at all.

Spelled flames hang from glass bowls on either side of the space, giving the room a calming ambience. It feels ridiculous to be wearing such a fancy dress in this space where literal sweat—and now, I suppose, blood—has been spilled. I walk over to the desk at the front of the room and sigh as I take a seat and hold my head in my hands. Haylee's poems and stories are stacked on one side, while the other has two mage journals that I accidentally left a few days prior. I had stopped in to make sure everything was clean and ready for my experiments the following day. I snort at how pointless that ended up being. My eyes dart over to the journals, those two voices once again on my shoulders: one begging to read them and one pointing out that it doesn't matter anymore. But I need something to ground me or, at the very least, distract me enough to calm my spiraling mind. My fingers brush against the soft leather cover of the top journal before I grab it and slide it towards me. Flipping it over, I bark out a crazed laugh at whose journal it is: Kallin Keria, Daje's father. *Of course.* There must definitely be a god out there just laughing at my plight.

"Might as well," I mutter before opening the journal to the first page. The date on this one is from two years ago. The beginning is mostly notes about various council meetings and decisions they've made that bear no interest to me, what with my data collection being focused on tracking magical discrepancies. About halfway through the book, Councilman Kallin mentions an incident with magic in another small town. Concordia has about three hundred residents, and is situated right on this side of the border with the Mortal Kingdom. According to Kallin's notes, older mages in their eighth decade of life are completely magicless now, or at least unable to wield any magic they may retain. That correlates with what Councilman Arav wrote about the mages living in his small town that bordered the Fae Kingdom. Searching through Haylee's papers, I find a blank one to tear a corner off of and bookmark the page so that I can add the information to my data chart in my own journal. I spend another hour or so reading and bookmarking before the words start to blur on the page. Exhaling, I lean back in the chair and stretch my arms overhead while closing my eyes. Rolling my head side to side, I work out the tension in the muscles there as I think.

While I still have no idea what I'm going to do regarding Daje, at least I am now calm enough to go home and try to sleep. I roll my head once more to the left, holding the stretch there as my hands come to rest on the table. My eyes open as I stretch to the right and look over at the table where my experiments are performed. All of the glass bottles are pushed to one corner from my hasty clean up after Haylee left. I gaze over them, my nails digging into the desk as I remember the moments when I could see the magic fading from the leaves. When they started to turn brown again and return to their decayed—

My eyes catch on one of the containers. I blink twice, my brows drawing up, before I push up from the desk and hasten over to the table, nearly tripping on my skirt as I do so. Slowly, with trembling hands, I slide it closer to me. My breath catches as I stare at the contents, my heart beating riotously in my chest. I pull the other two bottles used in the experiment forward and line them up next to each other. One is still full of dead, brown leaves, and it could be either Haylee's or Erick's. One bottle contains the leaves affected by my father's magic, and the leaves are vibrant green and sprouting a few roots, but not any further along than where I had left them yesterday. But in the third bottle, not only are the previously dead leaves teeming with life, but roots and new buds have blossomed from more leaves than any other jar.

I stare for what feels like an eternity at each jar, trying to figure out how this could have possibly happened. There was obviously some sort of delayed reaction with either Haylee's or Erick's magic, and I'll have to look at the plants more closely under a magnifier tomorrow, but it worked. Something quantifiable and tangible and *new* happened. My smile lifts my cheeks as I feel a warm tear fall. *It worked.* A sob breaks loose, an overwhelming feeling of exhilaration causing me to fall to my knees in front of the table. More tears descend as my eyes burn and my chest heaves in relief and excitement.

I know there are still so many questions and this may be yet another dead end, but I can't help but feel like maybe the timing of it is no coincidence. Like maybe this is a sign that I am not meant to settle.

Chapter Thirty-Nine

RHEA

Heat envelopes me from all sides, the soft thumping of my heartbeat slowly pulling me out of sleep. *No, not my heart.* In the distance, water trickles in a tranquil song, the hushed rustling of leaves in the wind adding to its melody. *His* scent is right under my nose, so I snuggle in a little closer until it's all I can breathe.

Images of golden armor, arrows, and blood—so much *blood*—beat against my shut eyelids. With my heart pounding faster, I force my eyes open and focus on the forest around me, the trees stretching up and their branches intertwining in the canopies. The sun must be just starting to peek above the horizon from what I can see through gaps of the leaves above. The dark blue sky is a combination of the first rays of day mixing with the lingering black of night—a meeting in the middle between two worlds. My eyes drag back down to where I see Bella sitting guard near my feet—our feet. Her eyes meet mine, her head slowly tilting to the side. We don't need words to be spoken for me to know what she's feeling and vice versa. My gratitude and love for her is reflected back at me.

I sit up slowly, bracing myself for pain, but there is only a slight ache—which might have more to do with sleeping on the hard forest floor than my healed wounds. Flynn's arm stays wrapped around my hips, his other tucked beneath his head. The position pulls the sleeve of his tunic tight around his bicep, which I shamelessly trace the outline of with my eyes. Other than the slight muss of his hair, he looks remarkably put together after a night of running and fighting. And tending to me. My heart beats funny against the walls of my chest as I contemplate dragging my fingers through his hair.

"You're staring at me." His sleep roughened voice brushes against my skin like a calloused caress, and I can't stop the shivers and goosebumps that happen as a result.

"Just admiring," I say, my tone joking even if I'm not. His lips kick up into a grin, and my heart does that little dance again.

"You can admit it. I'm the most attractive person you've ever seen."

"Yes, but to be fair," I start, biting back my own smile, "I haven't seen very many people." His answering squeeze of my hips makes me laugh as his eyes sedately open.

"That hurt more than getting stabbed did," he jests. Though his words, and the memory that accompanies them, sober the moment. My hand rests on his chest, his heart beating steadily under it. A reminder that he is *here*. That he is alright. "I'm sorry, that was probably too soon to say," he admits. I snort but don't move my hand. A few quiet moments pass before he asks, "How are you feeling?"

I nod, exhaling slowly as I force a small smile to my face. "Good. I'm good."

Flynn watches me for a moment before he swiftly sits up, catching my hand as I move to pull it off his chest. "You can tell me the truth," he says, interlacing our fingers and laying them on his thigh.

"I'm sorry." The words come out in a whisper as I drop my gaze from his. For so long, I've been alone with my feelings. Yes, I had Alexi, but while I always knew I could vent and talk to him about anything, our time together was too short to focus on my emotions for long. I didn't want to weigh him down with how *heavy* I was feeling at times when I'd rather just enjoy his company. And while Bella has always comforted me when I needed it, it's not the same as talking with someone and getting their advice. The majority of my life has been me tucking hurts—small and large—into boxes in my mind, locking their lids and throwing the key away into a dark abyss. And after Alexi died, it was easier to solidify those locks and build a fortress around my heart with layer upon layer of ice so thick, no one could break through. No one *should* have been able to break through.

"Don't apologize." His fingers tilt my chin up to meet his gaze again. Even with just the smallest hint of the growing morning light, the silver flecks in them sparkle. "Talk to me. Let me help you."

A knot grows in my throat at those four words. I try to speak, try to work past the emotions trapped there, but I can't form words. It's like my body is so used to bottling everything up that it doesn't know how to react when someone is begging me to let it all out. I look around the forest instead and remember that we're supposed to be on the run. We don't exactly have time for me to sift through everything here. And though I know Flynn would give me the space to do it, we're risking our lives the longer we sit here. I've caused plenty of that already. So I close my eyes and take a steadying breath, clenching my free hand into a fist until that lump in my throat disappears.

"We can talk when we are farther away from the king," I say finally, opening my eyes and giving him a small smile. He studies me, his too-observant gaze roaming my face, before he nods and then stands in one fluid motion, pulling me up with him. He hands me my boots, and I realize that he has cleaned out the one that was soaked in my blood. I quickly wash off the remnants of dried blood that is on my hands and feet before we brush our teeth, and I start asking Flynn questions about the previous night. "How long were we sleeping?"

He returns the toothbrushes and mint leaf paste before grabbing the two satchels and crisscrossing the straps as he places one on each shoulder. "I carried you for about three hours before I needed to stop and rest. So based on the sun now, I would guess that we've been in this spot for nearly the same amount of time." He says it casually, as if carrying someone for that long is to be expected. Meanwhile, my jaw is practically unhinged as I stare at him. "What?"

"You carried me for three hours." I confirm, shock drawing my eyebrows high on my forehead. "After pulling the arrows out? In the dark?"

"Yes," he responds. His head moves up and down in a slow nod as Bella comes to stand at his side, nudging her head into his hip. He doesn't break eye contact with me as he gently scratches her neck.

"How are you not more tired?" I blurt. He stretches his arms over his head, craning his neck side to side as he does so. His tunic rises with the movement, showing me just the smallest sliver of tanned skin over the black waistband of his trousers. I swallow and avert my gaze so that I'm not caught ogling him. Again.

"I'm used to not getting very much sleep," he says before grabbing my hand and starting to walk.

What does that mean? Blinking, I notice that he has turned us in a direction that *isn't* towards the rising sun. I tuck my mess of hair behind my ears, suddenly feeling more self-conscious as I ask, "Shouldn't we be going east?" It's half pulled back in a ponytail, half just a wild knot of tangles. Bella trots ahead of us, her steps quick and light as her ears flick side to side—listening for danger.

"If memory serves me correctly, we'll have to follow this stream north a little bit more before it converges with the Vida River. Then we can follow that east pretty much the entire way," he answers. "Let's get as far as we can before the sun starts to set, and then we can wash up in the river and change."

I nod my head, looking down at the mess of my clothes. They are torn and stained with dried blood, as well as covered with dirt. One of my boots still has drops of crimson on its side. I stare absent-mindedly at my foot as it comes into view every other step. Blood. And just like that, I'm back with Bella bleeding out onto the gray rug of the tower. My fear over losing her causing me to use magic for the first time that I didn't even know was there. The memory shimmers in my mind like the rippling of a rock dropped into still water. Now, I'm kneeling in a pool of blood with Alexi's head on my lap. His hand cups my face, his last breaths a declaration of love. The ripples move again, and it's Flynn in the field near the wildflowers. His dull eyes pleading with me to run as blood leaks out around him.

So much blood has surrounded me that wasn't my own, that *I* was a direct cause of. Well, I suppose I *have* finally lost a good amount of my own as well, if my clothes and boots are any indication. I keep my gaze down at my feet, lost in thought but trying not to trip over anything, as we traverse the uneven ground of the woods. Each step farther from the tower is freeing in a way that I couldn't have imagined, and yet... I don't feel like I thought I would. Is it because we are being hunted? I knew that my uncle wouldn't let me go without a fight, but so much happened during our escape that I wonder if it just exacerbated the vile feelings he has about me. If it just made him more desperate.

A short while later, Flynn points out where the small stream we are following joins the much larger Vida River. I have never seen a river in person before, and I marvel at how on the surface it looks so calm, so smooth. The blue waters contrast against the dark green and brown of the trees and fallen leaves surrounding it. But beneath the surface, the underwater grass and plants are bent from the force of the moving current. It is so unassuming, so deceptive. Is that what I am doing to Flynn? He has seen me cry, he has seen me after being abused by my uncle, and he has seen me use my secret magic. But he doesn't know about the dark well of thoughts that reside in my mind. He isn't aware of all of the locked away feelings that I still feel the pressure of every single day. He doesn't know of the cold, ancient *otherness* that is part of my magic. And what will happen when he finds out? He may call me "Sunshine," but I often feel like the cold shadows the sun casts.

"Are you hungry?" he asks, the weight of his gaze heavy on the side of my face. I nod, feeling a bit lightheaded from my lack of food or the loss of blood or maybe from the use of my magic. I'm not sure. Was it only yesterday that everything had happened? Not even a full day has passed of me being out of the tower, and we have all nearly died, with the exception of Bella.

He leads us to a tree, the twisting limbs of which grow in every direction as they sprout from all over the trunk. Flynn passes me an apple and some nuts, placing a pile of freshly picked leaves on the ground to put some dried meat for Bella onto. She is famished though, eating her food quickly and giving Flynn what he calls "sad eyes" in order to get more food. Of course, he doesn't object at all. When I voice my concern about running out of food for her, he just laughs. "She's a wild animal," he says and shrugs as he meets my gaze over his shoulder. "If she runs out of what we brought, then she can hunt for more food for herself."

"She's been in the tower with me for nearly five years. What if she doesn't know *how* to anymore? She's practically more mortal than fox now," I point out. Bella's head lifts from where she is eating, her golden eyes staring as she tilts her head. "No offense?" I add on. Bella huffs, but goes back to her food.

"I still can't believe you trained her to use the toilet." Flynn walks over to where I sit on one of the tree's twisting branches, legs dangling underneath. He leans a shoulder against the thick trunk, folding his arms over his broad chest.

"I wish I could take credit for it," I sigh, "but the truth is that I merely showed her where the toilet was and she figured it out herself." Finishing the last of my food, I start to slide off of the limb, but Flynn steps in front of me, his large physique taking up my view. "Shouldn't we head out?" I ask. Though I'm sitting a few feet above the ground, he is so tall that I still need to look up at him.

"You've been quiet and lost in your thoughts," he says, the heat from his body radiating to me. My shoulders draw up to my ears on instinct as I prepare to wall up my defenses again. I can't have this conversation right now. "And if I need to say this a hundred times, I will. I want to be here with you. I want to help you. All you have to do is let me." His hand reaches out for mine, gently brushing his fingers against my skin.

I suck in a breath, somehow feeling both weightless and weighed down by his words. Speaking is beyond me at the moment, but I manage a nod.

He leans towards me a little more, his hand trailing up my arm slowly as he does. "There's something I need to tell—" His voice cuts off as something catches his eye behind me. I watch as his gaze narrows, his brows drawing together in concentration. Bella moves as well, lifting her head up and focusing her gaze on the same place Flynn is. "We need to go. Now!"

He hauls me off the branch, carefully setting me down on the ground before quickly putting both of our bags on his shoulders with his sword sheathed down his back beneath them. Grabbing my hand, we start running along the edge of the river. I struggle to keep up with Flynn, my body still so exhausted. Bella runs just ahead of us, her pace a bit faster than ours.

"What did you see?" I ask, gasping for breath, but I don't need Flynn to answer because I see it then too. Reflecting the light from a now fully risen sun are glints and gleams of golden armor. The King's Guard isn't only coming from behind us. A line of them is parallel to the river we are following. "Oh gods," I whisper. The gold glitters far ahead within the trees. It's an entire battalion, just for the three of us.

"We need to get in the river. They won't jump in to follow us with all of their armor on." He huffs, eyeing the water next to us. "There." He points to a spot up ahead where the bank goes up a hill, the river many feet below it. The water is also less calm on the surface and more indicative of the strength of the current I saw earlier.

"Flynn, I can't swim," I state obviously. My eyes wide as we start to make our ascent. My legs protest fiercely at the climb—my entire body does.

"I won't let go of your hand when we jump. Hold on to me as tight as you can," he says in between heavy breaths. "And when we're in the water, you'll get on my back and wrap your legs around my waist. Okay?"

I nod because I'm so out of breath that I can't do much else. The hill starts to level out, Flynn never breaking pace but practically dragging me behind him. I hear the *zing* in the air only a moment before an arrow lands in the ground at my side, narrowly missing my foot. A scream gets caught in my throat. We're completely exposed out here, an *actual* moving target, and judging by what happened yesterday, all they need is one small opportunity to land a shot on one of us, and our escape will be that much more difficult. Flynn can't make another hike while carrying my dead weight—or maybe he can—but I definitely don't want to have another arrow taken out of me.

"We're going to jump on the count of three. Keep running, and *do not*," he emphasizes each word pointedly, "let go of my hand." I hold his stare, seeing the determination there—and the fear.

"I won't."

"One." Another arrow rushes by his head, way too close. My heart beats frantically, my hand squeezing his as tightly as I can. "Two," he calls out, checking to make sure the straps of the satchels are tight around him so that they don't get lost in the water. We're a handful of steps from cresting the top of the hill, my feet aching each time they pound on the forest floor. There's a ringing in my ears, my magic right under my skin like it's going to burst through. "Three," Flynn shouts, and we make an abrupt turn to leap off the highest point of the hill.

But I falter as my gaze catches briefly on an entire line of golden guards who stand at the base of the hill, their swords drawn as they wait for us to descend the other side. They would have had us completely surrounded if we had stayed on land. My hesitation means I jump a fraction of a second later than Flynn does, and his hand is suddenly ripped from mine. I scream as my legs kick in the open air, the water below no longer blue but more gray from the agitation of the faster moving current. Time feels suspended for a moment as I watch Flynn and Bella fall, but then the river is rushing up towards me, and the dark glow of something black catches my eye before I'm abruptly submerged. The water is astonishingly cold, especially for it being summer. My eyes open under the surface, though the dirt makes it impossible to see anything but the light shining above me. My fingers go to tighten around Flynn's, to wait for him to pull me up, but instead, my fist closes in on itself.

Terror causes me to thrash under the water as I try to kick and move my arms in a way that will bring me closer to the surface, but I don't move upwards. No, instead, I keep falling deeper and deeper. The urge to open my mouth and take a breath of air that isn't there is relentless. The current pushes me forward, but I sink farther from the surface. My cheeks burn from how I'm fighting to hold my breath in and keep my mouth closed against my body's instincts. I should have timed it better and inhaled deeply before hitting the water, but I didn't think. I just assumed that Flynn would be here to help me. My back scrapes along something in the water, the pain instinctively causing me to scream, and that's all it takes. The last of my air is now gone, the bitterly cold river water replacing it instead.

Despite being freezing, the water burns my lungs as my body thrashes and pain erupts all over. The beating of my heart starts to slow, more time growing between each pulse. My body stops its jerky movements, my limbs growing numb while my mouth moves as though it's still trying to get air in, but there is none. *Thud.* My eyelids grow heavy, so I let them close, all fight leaving my tired body and weary soul. *Thud.* Warmth floods my chest, a shimmering white light flaring as I feel my magic start to hum, but I still can't take a breath. I picture Flynn and Bella in my mind. I hope they stick together and make it back to Flynn's home safely. My only regret—*thud*—is that I dragged them into this.

T h u d.

Chapter Forty

RHEA

"I*T IS NOT SUPPOSED to be her time yet!" The voice sounds shrill, panicked.*

My eyes flutter open, and I immediately know where I am, the familiarity of it relaxing my anxious state. The air cradles me as I float weightlessly, caressing me on all sides. I can't help but smile as I find solace in the fact that maybe I can finally rest here. Maybe I can even visit one of the many swirling galaxies overhead. The purple one straight above me glows brightly, surrounded by a hundred—no, a thousand—stars. She said that they were other worlds, and I'm curious to know what they look like. Perhaps now, I'll have the chance to find out.

"You are not staying," she says, her voice calmer but still laced with worry.

"She cannot fight death," another voice insists. Where the familiar woman's cadence is silvery and ethereal, this new one is deep and robust. Where hers dances past me in small particles of stardust, his embraces me like I'm wrapped in the finest silk. "Especially without—"

"She is not dead yet," she hisses, the stars and galaxies above flickering with her anger.

I try to sit up, coming to my elbows as I look around. In all directions, the sky of purple and black and blue and every other color imaginable is lit up by billions of stars. Galaxies dot nearly every square inch as well. It's so overwhelmingly beautiful.

"Rhea, it is not your time. You must make your way back," she pleads, her desperation palpable as I swear that I can see the words drift towards me on a floral-scented breeze. "Try to cough the water up," she commands, but I don't feel the need to cough. I don't feel anything at all. "Rhea, listen to me. He needs you. They need you." A sharp punch of air hits my back, causing something to sputter inside of me. "It is not," she grits out as another harsh gust lands on my back, spurring the urge to cough. "Your." Another hits me until I feel something cold move up my throat. "Time," she shouts.

I cough, and something wet dribbles down my chin. The wind starts to whip around me, my long hair unbound and wild as I sense myself getting heavier and heavier. But I want to stay. I say those words in my mind since I know that she can hear me. There is a ghost of a touch on my cheeks, shimmery stardust swirling around me.

"I know," she whispers, "but they need you more, Rhea." The stars and galaxies flicker all around as my soul slams into my body layer by layer, and then, darkness and calm descend into chaos.

Water squeezes out of my lungs forcefully as strong hands roll me to my side and pound on my back. My chest heaves and my throat strains to get all of it out between the small gasps of air my body is trying to take. The tingling sensation that always appears after a *visit* to the Middle hurts this time as feeling comes rushing back into my limbs.

"That's it, Sunshine," Flynn says with a sigh of relief. He waits until my breaths are steady before picking me up off the ground and cradling me to his chest from where he's kneeling. "I really need you to stop almost dying," he rasps, bringing his forehead to mine.

"Maybe King Dolian was right. Maybe I truly am safer in the tower," I joke. My throat is sore, talking nothing more than a painful rasp.

"That's not funny," he replies, squeezing me more tightly to him. I shut my eyes to focus on simply breathing. My chest burns from the water that had filled it only moments before. I wonder how close I was to death and why only moments of duress get me to the Middle.

"Neither was the sword joke you made earlier," I counter, clutching onto his tunic to anchor me as I breathe him in with big gulps of air.

"Do not," he whispers, "do that again."

My responding laugh is strained because I absolutely agree with him—drowning is not the sort of experience that I want to repeat. His eyelashes lower, his gaze laden with the unspoken words of a man terrified to lose something important to him. Terrified to lose *me*. And it ravages my already devastated heart because I put him through this pain.

"I'm alright," I say, and it's partially true. I'm alive and in his arms, in a pocket of safety here. I leave out how I went to a magical place where I could see other worlds and how a spirit woman basically saved me from death—or at least worked in tandem with him. My gaze holds his as I watch him pick apart my words. He's always seen right through me, seen what no one else ever bothered to look for, but even he can't discern the darkness within me. A muscle in his jaw flexes as I watch water bead from his wet hair to trail down his temple and cheek, traveling further down his neck and under his wet tunic. My body stills, anticipation coiling at the base of my spine. The tautness in the air feels sticky and thick, like honey dripping onto a petal.

"It would be alright if you weren't okay, Rhea," he murmurs. His lips are so achingly close to mine—the perfect distraction. I lean in, needing to feel their softness and warmth. Wondering how long it has been since we've kissed, and then remembering that it has only been a few hours. But Flynn pulls back before I can feel him. My eyes flick up to his, hurt and disappointment dragging like rocks against my chest. "No kisses until you tell me how you're really feeling." His smile is a pointed thing, double-edged with his own desire and his care for me.

"Flynn, I'm fine," I urge, unable to hide the slight bit of frustration from my voice. His determination doesn't waver, but I'm not ready to discuss what is lurking in my own shadows, so I change the subject. "Where is Bella?"

"Still so terrible at being subtle. She's right there." He smirks as he points to the side with a jerk of his chin. My gaze falls from his as I look to Bella; her head rests over her crossed paws, her wet body rising and falling with her breaths as she rests. The river is at our backs, the water flowing more quickly like it had been where we jumped.

"How far away from them are we?" I ask, forcing my body to sit up.

The forest looks the same as it did when we first entered it, so other than following the river, I don't know how anyone could traverse these woods without getting lost. I wish I had more time to appreciate my surroundings. I had always imagined what walking amongst the trees might look and feel like from afar, but my only experience with them now has been linked with fear and pain. It seems like that may be the only way I'm allowed to live.

"I'm not sure. We were in the water for longer than I would have liked," Flynn answers. "The current was moving so quickly that I couldn't get us to the bank for several minutes," he exhales, sounding completely drained. We're both soaking wet, and I assume the items in the satchels are as well. "Are you okay to start walking? We shouldn't stay in one place for too long."

"Yes," I reply but make no effort to move, and neither does he. My hand cups his cheek gently, my touch lessening some of the tension in his body. He leans into it as he watches me, so many emotions flashing in his eyes. "Thank you for saving me. I'm afraid that it might be a full-time job for you if we stick together," I say quietly with a small smile. My light tone masks the fear I hold of the truth in those words. How many times can I make him choose me over everything else? When will he realize that I'm not worth the trouble?

He turns slowly and plants a tender kiss on my palm, lingering there for just a moment before facing me fully again. In a smooth voice, he says, "While I'd rather not have to rescue you from literal death, I'd do it every day." My eyes dip to his lips and back up, watching as he does the same. "I have told you so many truths, Rhea," he says, dropping his voice lower, "and I meant them all. I am yours to command. I will fight for you, kill for you, and rescue you as many times as you need."

Tightness squeezes me, begging me to reply with something—*any-thing*—but what is there to say? My magic dances inside of me, an anxious feeling to it that leaves my stomach in knots.

He gives me an easy smile before helping me up to stand, my stiff limbs needing support from him for a few steps. Bella stretches from where she is laying before she gets up as well. I walk over to her, scratching down her neck and on the top of her head. Flynn puts both of our bags back over his shoulders, his sword still strapped down his back, before holding my hand and leading us back into the thick trees. We're on the other side of the river now, so I hope that means we'll have an easier time escaping if the King's Guard shows up again. Our pace is brisk and quiet, neither of us wanting to waste breath on talking. Still, I can feel Flynn's sideways glances towards me every so often, his concern for me a cloak of reassurance wrapped around my shoulders.

What's wrong with me? He has stated over and *over* that he just wants to help, but I can't find it in myself to open up to him. I want him, the need going beyond just a physical ache and more like an insatiable feeling—a rightness that is begging to be fulfilled. Yet I can't stop the immense guilt I feel over it. *It's because you know you don't deserve him.* Tears well in my eyes as I try to fight them off. Deep down, I know it's the truth. He's already risked so much—*given* so much—and what has he gotten in return? What could I possibly give him but a life of being hunted by the madman who happens to rule our kingdom? Who has unlimited resources to try and get me back? A man who has already shown me that he'll kill anyone who gets in his way? Nowhere will be safe for him. Flynn's given me care and compassion and friendship, but I've gotten him stabbed, forced him to go on the run, and risked his home and family in the process. I'm selfish—so stupidly selfish—just like I was with Alexi. Just like I was with Bella.

It's almost instantaneous, how those thoughts lead to a void that I thought I was long past. It's laughable how easy it is to pretend like I don't have this icy darkness lying beneath the surface, waiting to completely pull me under. And as the hours pass and the moon begins to rise, I wonder to myself how much longer I'm willing to put him at risk while I chase a freedom that might not exist.

⸎⸎⸎ ⸎⸎⸎

We finally stop to rest when Flynn spots a small sandy bank on the edge of the river. The waterway has widened quite a bit since we started following it, the trees on the other side barely visible in the moonlight past the water's edge. We haven't spoken in hours, and as I chew on some mint leaves that Flynn found for us on our trek, I wonder if the tension between us is imagined or not. The cooling taste of the mint wears off as Flynn slows our pace down.

"We can wash up here and then move a little farther into the woods to sleep for a few hours before we need to get moving again," he says, taking off our bags and laying them up against a tree.

"How much farther do we have to go?" I ask. My eyes are on him as he sets up a little area for Bella to finish off the food we brought for her. With all of the walking we've done, I know she'll have to hunt for additional food to sate her hunger.

"We should hit a small town tomorrow in the late afternoon if we can walk a good portion of the night. We can sleep at an inn there for a few hours, and then it will take us another day and a half to get to our final destination." He walks over to my satchel, picking it up from the ground and handing it to me. "Why don't you wash up first? I'll be waiting on the other side of the trees here to give you some privacy."

My hand brushes his as I grab the bag, our eyes lingering for a moment before he turns to walk away. I watch him move towards a bigger tree on the edge of the bank, his back to me the entire time before he sinks down and leans against the trunk. I'd be lying if I said I didn't want to call him back, to ask him to come with me into the water. The offer is on the tip of my tongue, burning to get past my lips, but it appears as if Flynn doesn't want that. Could I blame him if that were true? Thorny vines constrict my throat, but I force a swallow down and ignore the feeling.

I set the satchel down at my feet, digging under the food within to grab my hair and tooth brushes, soap, and the mint leaf paste for my teeth. I take out my clean clothing and set them on top before walking to the edge of the water. The river curves here, the current appearing more calm at the wide bend. Sitting down, I remove my boots. My feet don't ache nearly as badly as I know they could, and I'm sure that I have my magic to thank for that. Once the boots are off, I stand up and peer around me. This area of the forest is dark, but the moon is right overhead, its glowing light illuminating enough of the water that I can see a few feet ahead of me. I look back over my shoulder to where Flynn is sitting, and a small flare of disappointment hits when I see his back is still to me.

I shouldn't be surprised, he doesn't strike me as the type of man that would sneak looks at me. I sigh, exasperated with myself before I untuck what remains of Alexi's shirt and lift it over my head. Sadness washes over me as I stare at the dirty and bloodied fabric that belonged to him. My throat constricts, my emotions feeling too volatile—too wild—as I reverently fold the destroyed shirt and lay it carefully on the ground. The rest of my clothing comes off in a more hasty manner before I grab the soap and tiptoe into the water. It's cold enough that goosebumps break out over my skin causing me to suck in a breath. I continue on until the water comes up to my shoulders, the iciness of it temporarily numbing my feelings. Scrubbing meticulously at my scalp first, I run my fingers through my hair with the shampoo lather, working out as many knots as I can. While I wash my body, I search for scars on my shoulders and thigh but find only smooth skin. I shouldn't be surprised that my body holds no sign of injury, but the pain that I felt as Flynn removed the arrows made me wonder if there is a threshold to what my magic can heal. If there is, I apparently haven't found it yet.

Once I'm washed and rinsed, I walk back to the shore, squeezing out the water from my hair as best I can. I get dressed in my undergarments, the light blue cottony material becoming damp from being unable to dry myself off first. I hold the mint paste out and realize I don't exactly want to use the river water to wash my mouth out.

"Do we have any more water left?" I shout out to Flynn, picking up my toothbrush. He brought two full waterskins with him in his pack that hopefully aren't ruined from our detour into the river.

When my question goes unanswered, I look up to where Flynn should be sitting against the trunk of the tree. Instead, I find him standing—waterskin in hand—gaze locked on me. His chest rises and falls harshly, and even across the small distance that's blanketed in shadowy moonlight, there is no mistaking the wild look in his eyes. Despite the air being warm, my body shivers under his undivided attention. I don't know what he can see, and as my heart races, a small voice from the corner of my mind confesses that I don't care. The thought should be jarring, as this is the first time I've ever been in less than a modest nightdress in front of a man before, but I make no move to cover myself because this isn't just *some man*. It's Flynn, and while I may not feel like I'm worthy of his affection, I yearn for him all the same. I still want him in ways that are primitive and fierce. It's a demand that blazes within and shuts all other emotions out. Inside, I feel reckless, but outside, I just want to feel *him*. My body craves his touch as though it is a different kind of sustenance.

He doesn't move to me though, his grip on the waterskin so tight that I'm afraid it will burst. His body is all rigid tension and held-back desire, but his eyes devour me in hungry licks over my skin. I take a step to him—then another and another—until our chests are merely a hand-width apart. Flynn's gaze stays pinned on me, dipping to look at my body before quickly coming back up. His throat bobs, and his fist tightens even more on the waterskin. My lips part, a whisper of breath rushing in and out of me as I tilt my head up to look at him. Neither of us moves for a moment, the only sound that of the owls hooting in the distance and the gentle movement of water behind me.

Finally, Flynn drags his hand up my arm slowly, his fingertips leaving goosebumps as they make their way to my shoulder. There, he caresses my skin for a moment, his breath quickening before his hand moves up higher on my neck until he is resting his thumb just underneath my jaw. His fingers wrap around to the back of my neck, tangling in my hair, as he just holds me there. I wait for the burning desire I can see aflame in those pools of smoky slate to overtake him—to overtake *me.*

"You are *everything,*" he breathes as his eyes flare with all-encompassing want. A look that I know mirrors my own.

"So are you," I whisper. Unable to hold back any longer, I reach up to wrap my arms around his neck, my fingers brushing the silken ends of his hair. Lifting onto my toes, I press my body against his, though I don't close the distance between our lips. *Home.* I nearly gasp out loud at the quiet word that tumbles through my mind. At how *right* it feels.

"Fuck," he growls, the word scraping along my mouth and flooding my body with heat.

Like the merging of two summer storms, lightning sparks as our lips find each other in a frenzy. The waterskin falls to the ground, his hand now flat against the bare skin of my lower back. My soft answering moan is the only sound competing with the forest animals as I hold onto him. His taste is that of mint and something so uniquely *him.* I need more, my fingers digging fully into his wavy strands. He presses me in even closer, my front completely molded to his, as my mind falls blissfully quiet. My mouth moves against his, our tongues so closely entangled that it's a wonder I can still *breathe.* Kissing him is like feeling every flickering star in the sky burn through me. It leaves me full yet desperate for more at the same time.

A calloused hand slides down to my hip slowly, the sensation driving me to a precipice I've never felt before. He grips my hair gently, a groan vibrating in his chest and sending chills throughout my body. I want more, and I never want him to stop touching me like this. It is a *relief*—the desire that he causes within me burns too brightly to let my darkest thoughts surface. I revel in it, one of my hands sliding down from his hair to his chest and then more slowly towards his firm abdomen. My heart beats in my ears, every part of me on fire as I near exactly what I want to feel. What I've never felt before. Until, suddenly, Flynn stops. He unseals our lips to stare down at me, his gaze starving. Our chests heave in tandem, my hand frozen near his waistband, while he slowly begins to release his grip on me. *No.*

"What is it?" I ask with a lust-induced slur to my words.

His forehead rests against mine, our breaths mixing together as his eyes fall closed.

"I need you to please get dressed. *Please,*" he finally answers, though the words seem painful for him to say. He releases me fully as I step back, dropping my gaze to my body and wondering if he finds something lacking. When I look back up, he's already walking back to the tree he was at before. My heart sinks as I grab the waterskin off of the ground and walk over to my dress, pulling it on before stepping back near the edge of the water to brush my teeth. When I'm finished, I leave the soap and paste out for him and grab my boots and hairbrush, making my way barefoot to the edge of the tree line.

"Your turn," I say quietly, taking a seat on a thick exposed root. Flynn stands, studying me silently for a few seconds before he makes his way onto the bank. Bella trots out from the deeper part of the forest before me, hauling something very dead that I'd rather not look at in her mouth. "Please do not eat that by me," I caution, fighting off the urge to gag. She moves a few trees down before laying her kill on the ground and digging in. It's definitely not far enough away, as I hear the crunching of bones and tearing of flesh. To keep myself from vomiting, I focus entirely on brushing out my long hair, starting at the tips and slowly moving up. I'm nearly finished by the time Flynn reappears. He has changed as well, wearing a dark blue tighter-fitting tunic over black trousers tucked into his calf-high boots. I notice his sword isn't on him nor anywhere near the tree. "Where is your sword?" I ask, keeping my gaze on the pile of fallen leaves ahead of me.

"I'm going to leave it here. It's better that we enter the small town without it," he answers before falling quiet again. I move to grab a ribbon from my satchel leaning against the tree next to us, feeling hyper-aware of his stare on me the whole time. "Can I—" Flynn starts before clearing his throat as my eyes flick to his. "Can I braid your hair?" The moonlight doesn't fully make it all the way to where we are, tucked into the edge of the trees, but it's enough to see the slight blush on his cheeks. The faint color is at odds with the dark stubble now growing in on the lower half of his face.

"You know how?" I query, digging through my satchel to find the hair ribbon.

"I do," he answers. "My mother taught me as a boy." His admission brings a small smile to my face, his words invoking the image of a younger version of him practicing at his mother's behest. But then my smile fades, his actions earlier making me tense again in response.

"You seemed mad at me," I say. When his eyebrows draw together, I explain further. "Earlier, when we were together."

"Ah," he sighs as he reaches a hand out for me. I step forward, placing mine in his and meeting his softened gaze. "It wasn't anger, Sunshine. It was self-preservation."

My head cants to the side in question, watching him place a gentle kiss on the back of my hand before he gestures for me to sit. I take a seat in the middle of his legs, hugging my knees to my chest as he begins to run his fingers through my hair. My eyes close from the feeling of being cared for, a yawn quietly escaping me. If I exclude the time that Tienne and Erica did my hair, the last occurrence was when I was a small girl, before Alexi came into my life.

"I could teach you how," he offers, "if you want."

"Okay," I sleepily respond, the day swiftly catching up to me as I relax under Flynn's touch. He moves slowly, never once pulling or yanking as he works down the length of my hair. In my weary state, I let a question slip through my lips that I don't mean to ask out loud. "How many girls' hair have you braided?"

Flynn is quiet for a moment before reaching for the ribbon and tying the braid off. "Besides you?" he clarifies, pulling me to him so my back rests against his chest. "Only one." He presses a tender kiss on my temple as I snuggle back against him, my exhaustion nearly pulling me under before his words register.

Only one.

Chapter Forty-One

RHEA

AFTER SLEEPING FOR A few hours, Flynn wakes me with another barely there kiss on the top of my head, and I can't help the pang of disappointment I feel at that. We both eat a snack of dried meat and nuts while Bella splashes and swims in the water. The moon is high overhead, its silver light blanketing everything that isn't blocked by the canopy of the tall trees. The warm summer air carries the earthy smell of the forest and the water as a gentle breeze rustles a few strands of hair that came loose from my braid while I slept. I play with the ends of my hair as I sit cross-legged on the sandy bank. Flynn sits a few feet away—leaning back on his hands, his long legs extended out in front of him.

Only one. It shouldn't bother me as much as it does. Just because I have lived my life in seclusion in a tower, stuck in time, doesn't mean that other people have. Flynn is extremely handsome and kind and funny. I'm sure he could—and did—have his pick of women wherever he went. And maybe that's why his choice of me is so ludicrous, because I'm not like any of the other women he might have come across. It just solidifies the thought in my mind that I can never be what he needs, what he *truly* wants. I wonder if he is beginning to realize that too and that's why he doesn't want things to go too far between us. Surely kissing isn't as big of a deal to him as it is to me.

We pack up and begin our trek quietly, moving in a single-file line with me in the middle of Flynn and Bella. It's like I am surrounded by a cloud of melancholy, unable to enjoy or even process anything I am seeing. A lot of what I *am* seeing is a first for me, but I can't find it in myself to truly care. The sun has risen overhead, and I hardly notice. Even my magic lies dormant inside of me. All this time I have desperately clung to the hope that if my circumstances were different, then I would be different too. But here I am, getting farther and farther away from that tower with each step that I take, and yet nothing else about me has changed. I am still broken, still in jagged pieces no matter how much I want to force them to fit together. Despite wanting to give the illusion that I am anything but.

Lost in the turmoil of my mind, I don't notice that the outskirts of a town have come into view. Flynn stops walking, taking a long sip from the waterskin before handing it to me. "What is this place?" I ask before taking a drink, hoping that it will help me swallow down the imaginary rocks in my throat.

"Celatum," he answers as he runs a hand through his hair and looks down at me. His gaze is heavy and I sense that he has something more to say.

"Is this where you're from?"

"It's close, but no. This is just my last stop on my way home," he answers. His hand reaches out for mine, and though I know there is quite a lot left unspoken between us, I take it. And stars above, just that small touch quiets some of the screaming thoughts that have taken root in my mind.

The town is built right in the middle of the forest, and as we get closer, I notice small homes made from familiar gray stones. Though here, there is a blending of stone and wood in the structures that takes away from the cold feeling that exuded from my tower. The path we walk on is worn down, the ground bare except for a small scattering of fallen leaves. Smoke billows out of chimneys as the noise from what must be the town's square starts to trickle in. There are a few people outside of their homes tending to gardens and chatting with each other, each of them giving a dip of their chin as Flynn passes them. I squeeze his hand tighter as I lean in closer.

"Will these people know who I am?" I whisper, trying to keep the panic off of my face as we near the center of the town.

"I doubt it, but stay close to me. The king may have hidden you away, but here, your beauty is going to make you stand out." My eyes widen as I turn to look at him, a blush crawling up my neck and cheeks. Flynn smirks, and that damn curve of his lips leaves me feeling more breathless than running for our lives did.

More stone homes dot each side of the path we walk down, the trees even taller here than the rest of the forest that we had just traveled through. They reach towards the sky like they hope to touch the very sun that gives them life. The path looks to run directly through the town, and within a few more steps, we're surrounded by people walking and chatting. Wooden carriages carrying piles of goods and being pulled by horses move past us at a leisurely pace. My eyes don't know where to focus as I try to take in the buildings on both sides. The smell of something savory cooking permeates the air, spices I can't name making my mouth water. I don't even realize that I've stopped walking until Flynn wraps an arm around my shoulders.

"Are you okay?" he asks me, but all I can do is shake my head.

My breath catches at the colorful awnings and flags that hang in the middle of each structure and crisscross over our heads. The names of the taverns and shops are in large cursive script on wooden signs hanging from the front of each establishment. But what really sends my mind reeling, what absolutely makes me tighten my grip on Flynn as I take it in, is all of the *people*. I have never seen so many people at once. Men wearing tunics and trousers of every color walk confidently to stores or gather in small groups to chat with each other. Women in skirts and flowy dresses haul babies on their hips as they shop. And the children—so many children—laugh and scream as they run around people, chasing each other while their hair flows freely in the breeze. This is what life could have been like for me. Had my parents not died, this would have been my existence. Instead, I spent it locked inside a gray prison, beaten and belittled and broken.

My chest rises and falls quickly as men and women pass, and I feel like the eyes of every one of them are on me. Do they recognize how much I stand out? Do they know that I don't belong here? Music coming from somewhere slices through the voices of people talking, but it all starts to become discordant as my brain tries to comprehend everything I'm seeing. The words of each shop name start to blur together as my head grows dizzy. My throat closes, and a cold sweat breaks out on my palms and neck.

I can't breathe. I can't breathe. I can't breathe. Distantly, I'm aware that I'm being moved to the side of the road and between two of the shops, out of view of the townspeople and into the shade. Flynn angles his body so that I'm completely hidden by it as he hovers over me.

"Rhea, what's wrong?"

"I don't know," I choke out. I have no idea why the trees are closing in on me. I can't explain why I'm out in the open but my mind thinks I'm trapped within those stone walls again. "I don't know," I repeat while gasping for breath. There is a quiver to my voice as tears line my eyes. My chest tightens like it's being crushed by the weight of an invisible force. And I hate it. I absolutely hate that this is happening right now and that I'm powerless to stop it. *What is wrong with me?*

Large, warm hands frame my face as Flynn bends down to be on my eye level. "You're okay, Sunshine. Try to take a deep breath with me," he coaxes, inhaling deeply through his nose and exhaling out of his mouth. I try to do it with him, but a mountain is sitting on my lungs.

"I can't. I'm sorry, I can't." The words rush out of me on a shaky breath. *Broken, so hopelessly broken.*

"Rhea." His voice commands my attention, breaking through the thick fog of panic coating my mind. "Breathe with me." His tone is firm, but there isn't a hint of anger or frustration. His eyes search mine in fear, and maybe this instruction is just as much for him as it is for me. I keep my gaze on him as I force a slow breath in and out—over and over again until the ringing in my ears stops. My hands grip his wrists as Bella rubs her body up against my hip. It takes far too long, but I finally begin to feel the weight ease off of my chest. Flynn notices the moment it happens and drops his forehead to mine, letting out a long exhale.

"I'm sorry," I murmur as I squeeze my eyes shut to hide from him.

"Don't apologize to me. Not now, not ever, okay?" he demands softly, though his tone leaves no room for argument. I nod, leaning away from him and back against the cool stone wall of the shop. "Let's go somewhere quiet."

He waits for me to nod my head again before stepping back and reaching for my hand. Our fingers interlace, and then Flynn guides me to the edge of the square, closer to the shops on one side and away from the chaos in the middle of the wide road. We walk to a large white stone structure where a bright green awning hangs off the front. My eyes travel to the sign by the wooden front door that reads "Immie's Inn" as Flynn ushers me in with his hand gently placed on my lower back.

The inside is bright, the sun shining directly into the windows from between the trees as if they built this place knowing exactly where the rays would hit. It smells of lavender and lemon, the scent achingly familiar but also *different.* Flynn keeps his hand on me as he guides us across the dark wood floors to a large desk where a few papers and a small silver dome sits. He reaches out and taps the dome, a high-pitched chime ringing out into the small space. I study the interior of the inn, looking behind the desk at the wall of keys to the left and a set of stairs leading to a second floor to our right. Directly in front of us, a long hallway with doors on either side stretches towards the back of the inn. One of those doors opens, and an older woman walks out, her silver hair pulled back in a tight bun at the base of her neck. She walks with a slight limp as she comes closer, eyes lighting up as soon as she sees Flynn.

"Well, it's about time you show your handsome face around here again, boy!" She laughs as she rounds the desk and moves right to Flynn, who she pulls in for a hug. He towers over her but receives the embrace with a smile on his face. "And who do we have here?" she asks, tilting her head my way.

"A friend I'm bringing home," he answers after a few seconds. *A friend.*

She studies me as my mind starts to spiral once again until I notice how her eyes slowly begin to widen. The smile on her face morphs into something else as her jaw falls slack. She gawks at me, her hands gripping her dress tightly as her gaze roves over every part of me and lingers longest on my eyes. I look like a complete mess after traversing through the forest, but she scrutinizes me like she can't accept what she is seeing. The tense silence goes on until even Bella is disturbed by it and comes to sit by my side.

"Do you have a room for me?" Flynn inquires, cutting through the haze that this woman seems to be in.

She shakes her head as if to clear her thoughts and rounds the desk, grabbing a key off of the wall and handing it over to him. "Your usual room upstairs is ready. Everything you've asked for is there as well." Confusion wrinkles my face as I look up at Flynn. How did she know we would be coming?

"Thank you, Immie." He says her name with a fondness that I don't understand. "How's the gang since the last time I stopped by?"

"Din was taken by the Cruel Death last week," she rumbles quietly, a solemn frown pulling at her lips.

"I'm sorry to hear that. He was a good man," Flynn says. He moves around the desk to place a hand on her shoulder in comfort.

"Each week, more and more are falling ill. All so young too. It makes you wonder why… Anyway, why don't you two go get settled." Flynn nods his head in agreement, a grim weight heavy on his brows, as she waves her hands in front of her as if to physically clear the air of any sadness. Immie gives him a knowing look and a small smirk before she shoos us to the stairs. "Food will be brought up momentarily. Does your fox want to go rest in the gardens outside? I can make sure she eats as well," she says, pointedly looking at Bella. I tense, feeling uneasy at being separated from her.

"She is safe here. We all are," Flynn assures, tucking a piece of hair behind my ear. I turn towards Bella, her golden eyes piercing mine as she tilts her head to the side. Walking to her, I give her a tight hug before letting go and watching her and Immie walk out the front door. "I promise, she'll be alright. The only danger is the children who may want to play with her." He smiles and reaches for my hand again before leading me up the stairs.

At the top is another hallway, the doors spaced out on either side. Windows are cut every few feet into the ceiling, letting light filter in and illuminate the way as Flynn walks us to a door at the very end and places the key into the lock. Everything about the inn so far has appeared small and compact, but it's because all of the space is given to the rooms. Our room is large, my eyes drawing up to the high ceiling as the sun shines in through a wall of windows directly across from us. An intricately patterned dark blue and gold square rug lies in the center of the room between the largest bed I have ever seen and a small wooden table and chairs. It's simple in its layout—in the decor that adorns the space—but it somehow is still infinitely more welcoming than the stone tower. Flynn steps over to the table, taking the satchels off of his broad frame, but my attention again goes to the four-poster bed. Sheer white gossamer crisscrosses above it, connecting to each corner post and then draping down to the floor. A bright white comforter is pulled taut across the bed, and if I wasn't so filthy from our journey, I would crawl on top of it and attempt to sleep.

I step farther into the room and notice a door off to the side. "That is the bathroom," Flynn supplies, stepping back up to my side. "Do you want to shower? Immie should have left us a few days worth of clothes to choose from."

"How did she know we would be coming?" I ask as that small seedling of doubt takes root again.

"I sent her a message about a week ago," he states simply while turning to step in front of me.

I shake my head, my brows drawing together. "But, we didn't leave until a few days ago," I'm puzzled at how he could have possibly known to send her a message that long ago.

"Yes, but I have been planning on helping you escape for a while," he replies, his gaze earnest as he looks into my eyes. "Ever since you said you wanted to leave. It's why I was so upset when you attempted to do it on your own." His hand cups the side of my face, his thumb gently stroking my cheek.

"You had been planning?" I ask, laying my hand on top of his. He nods, black strands of his wavy hair hanging loosely over his forehead. I don't know what to say. Every feeling and thought is battling for dominance inside of me, and it is exhausting. I am just so *exhausted*.

So instead, I slip away from his touch and walk over to the table, sorting through what I assume to be clothes for me. I find a pair of slim black trousers and a slightly oversized but lightweight cream-colored undershirt—similar to the one that was Alexi's. There are also what look like brand-new undergarments, more lacy than the cotton ones I am used to, and though Flynn doesn't see them, I blush all the same. I gather the clothing and then let Flynn show me how to use the shower. Water coming from a spout in the ceiling is incredible, and I should be more awed by it, but I'm just tired. Like even something as instinctual as breathing takes more effort than it should.

Water sprays onto my skin, though the warmth of it doesn't begin to touch the bitter cold that settles inside of me again. I still don't understand why everything has to be such a struggle. Why can't I just be happy and grateful to be out of that tower? Why does it still feel like I am caged behind guards of gold and walls of stone, unable to find a way out? Deep within, a weakened and dark part of me wonders quietly if it is just easier to not exist at all. If constantly fighting against these thoughts and feelings is worth the effort.

If *I* am worth the effort.

Chapter Forty-Two

BAHIRA

L AST NIGHT AFTER MY discovery of the new plant life in either Haylee's or Erick's bottle, I cried on the floor of my workshop for a long while. It wasn't the first time tears had fallen there, but they were the first tears not born of frustration. Going from the lowest of lows to the mountaintop of highs had left me feeling emotionally spent. When I awoke this morning, I found a rose waiting for me outside of my bedroom door with a note from Daje, and reality came crashing back into me. It wasn't even important, just a few words about how beautiful I looked last night, but I'm frustrated that I can't even get the time he allotted to consider his ultimatum without getting input from him. *Probably not a good feeling to have for a man I'm considering marrying.*

I groan internally, the weight of this decision stealing all of my focus. There is a different kind of safety in marrying him, one that pulls on my heart a little stronger than anything else. I won't ever have to question if he is choosing me because he truly loves me or because he can get something else out of it: status, recognition, bragging rights. Or any other myriad of reasons that may make a male decide that being a magicless princess' consort is worth it. With Daje, we grew up together and his father is already on the council. He wouldn't have anything to gain except for *me*. I know that his feelings for me are true and born of something that began while we were children. It is *my* side of the relationship that is a struggle.

There is also a chance he might get chosen as the mage to go to the shifter isle, and my stomach twists unexpectedly at that. Perhaps that would provide a loophole to this ultimatum. Unlikely, but not impossible. It would certainly give me more time to figure out what I want and what I am willing to lose. My lips flutter as I blow out an exasperated breath and return my attention back to the magnifier.

I click the next glass lens into place, adjusting one of the knobs on the side to clarify the enlarged image before I peer down with one eye through the scope. When I look at the dead leaf laying on the slide, it takes two more levels of magnification before I can see them on a cellular level. The cells of the brown leaves have no movement, the normally hexagonal shape of the cell walls crumbled and shriveled in. Sliding my journal and spelled pen over, I write the magnification level and descriptions down, and then replace the slide with one of a freshly picked healthy leaf *not* treated by magic. The cell walls are plump and bright green, the healthy chloroplasts moving within. Jotting down that observation, I then grab the slide containing a leaf that is spelled with my father's magic. It has been two days since the experiment, but looking down through the scope, I watch as the chloroplasts move with strength. My eyebrows furrow as I click another lens into place, zooming farther in. Yes, the chloroplasts are thick and *alive,* but there are *so* many of them that they push on the cell walls. The normally straight lines of the hexagon cells are bowed and crooked.

My eye strains again as I increase the magnification even further. *There.* In the center of the overfilled cell, squished between two healthy chloroplasts is a decayed, crumpled one. I slide the tray over just a bit and the new part of the leaf shows the same thing. There are still plenty of healthy chloroplasts, but some have started to break down—the weak, brown crumbling cells speckle throughout the healthy ones. There are not enough yet to change the outward appearance of the leaf to the naked eye, but there *are* enough that it shows the magic is wearing off within the cells. I write down my examinations and then place the final slide on the magnifier—the one spelled with either Haylee or Erick's magic.

When I stare down into the scope, it takes a second for my eye to adjust to the intense magnification of the leaf. I observe the bursting cell walls, similar to the ones I saw feeding off of my father's magic. The chloroplasts inside are moving and wiggling, like they have more vigor. Like they aren't just wiggling side to side, but they are purposefully moving to *create life.* I slide the plate a little to the side to look at a new portion of the leaf. More cells, more healthy cell walls, more moving chloroplasts and mo— A small gasp escapes me. *What in the gods above is that?* I force my eye closer to the scope as I stare at something that definitely should not be there. Mixed in with the wiggling chloroplasts of the plant are little circles of red. They are smaller than the chloroplasts, easily slipping into spaces between them— No, wait. They are *attached* to them. As if the chloroplasts are somehow feeding off of them. Or being fed off of.

"What the hell am I looking at?" I whisper as I click the very last magnification lens into place. After focusing the image, it indeed confirms what I am seeing.

The circular red organelles are attached to the chloroplasts. I watch them move for a long time, sliding the tray to the left and to the right. My mind whirls with more questions as I study whether these plump red organelles act the same throughout. And they do. Quickly, I grab the pen and my journal and draw everything that I see, listing out their descriptions and all of the observations that I make. I don't know what it means. I don't even know what I am looking at, but it doesn't stop the flutter of excitement that bursts free in my chest. These leaves are *different,* and I have proof of it. I will have to ask Haylee and Erick to come back to test their magic again. This time, I will wait here in the workshop until I see the change happen myself. Carefully, I put the small glass slides with the leaf samples on a wooden plank, labeling each one and placing it carefully on the back counter behind me.

My hands tremble slightly with excitement before I pull my long, curly hair over one shoulder and start to loosely braid it as I leave my workshop. Those little red organelles consume my thoughts for the entire walk back to the palace, my journal tucked safely under my arm. This is the first time that I have found something new to work with in all of the years that I have spent researching. I sort through all of the data stored in my mind, everything that might possibly explain how this could have happened or what it means. But it's like trying to put the pieces of an imageless puzzle together—I need more information.

The sun has nearly set by the time I greet the palace guards and walk up the steps to the massive double doors. My father had asked that I join him and my mother for dinner tonight, and I only agreed on the condition that it just be our family. Normally, dinners in the palace are open to any of the council members and their families to attend, but I want time alone with my own to discuss what will be happening with the arrival of the shifter king tomorrow.

After a quick shower, I change into a sleeveless white top and a flowing green skirt and walk downstairs to the queen's dining hall. There are two dining spaces in the palace, the queen's being the smaller and more intimate. The throne room is where larger gatherings take place, as it has enough room for over a hundred people to not only eat but to mingle and dance as well. I pull open a large door, the image of our family sigil burned into the wood, before walking into the dining space where a long table made to fit twelve holds three place settings. Two large chandeliers hang above, each with three tiers of spelled flames held within glass orbs. The table itself has been in the palace for as long as anyone can recall, the center of the ancient wood carved with the celestial sigil of the first-ever queen of Void Magic. The shining black stone floor is covered by dark green and ocean blue rugs. On the white stone walls, twinkling under the light of the spelled flames, are portraits of our family. My favorite being the most recent one, where Nox was forced to sit on a chair for hours while the palace artist gushed about how handsome his jawline was. The thought now tugs my lips into a smile as I greet my parents and take my place at the table.

"You look lovely, my rose," my mother says, her hand holding my father's.

"Thank you, Mother. How late did you guys stay at the celebration?" I ask as I reach forward and scoop some salad onto my plate.

"Long enough to tire out your father," my mother responds with a laugh and pats his hand.

"I wasn't that tired if you remember," he purrs back. My father reaches his hand out and gently drags a knuckle down the side of my mother's face.

"That is gross." I set my fork down on my plate, suddenly without an appetite, as I grimace and stare at both of them.

My parents laugh, the cheerful sound echoing in the room. Despite the fact that I now wish I could turn back time and avoid hearing them talk about last night, I do love how happy they are together. How they complete each other without forcing one another to become something they aren't. Without making them settle into being someone new. It makes me shift uncomfortably in my seat because of my own predicament.

"Are you ready for King Kai's visit tomorrow?" I inquire. My stomach grumbles with enough hunger that I'm willing to forget the aforementioned coupling of my parents, though it doesn't stop the shudder that moves through my body.

The reddish-gold light in the room is enough to make out the tense lines on my father's face as he thinks my question over. Though smiling, there is no mistaking his nervous energy as he taps my mother's hand with a finger. Leaning back in his chair, he finally answers, "We are. We are going to tell him that we will only agree to the deal if there is a time limit on how long our mage is required to be there. Whoever the magic chooses shouldn't have to put their life on hold indefinitely."

"Any guesses on who might be chosen?" I know that there are still a few powerful older mages, but none of them compare to Nox—not even my father. Daje and his friend Arin—as well as my instructor, Dilan—are the next strongest of the mages in our kingdom.

"It's hard to say. It all depends on how King Kai chooses to word the contract before it's bound in blood," my father answers as he looks at my mother and gives her hand a small squeeze.

I chew on my salad as I think over what the shifter king had said when we spoke with him through the Mirror. He believed that there was some sort of blight affecting their magic, causing it to act *strangely*. I'm not familiar with what shifter magic entails besides the obvious ability to change them into a wild animal. A part of me does feel a small kernel of jealousy at whoever is going to be chosen to go. That envy also sparks my desire again for finding answers in *this* kingdom, for my own loss of magic.

Swallowing down the bite of food, I look up at my parents and tell them what I discovered today. I explain the difference in the cells of each leaf and the shocking discovery of some sort of symbiotic *organelle* that had grown or appeared at some point after I had left my workshop—when I thought the experiment failed.

"Is it possible that the experiment was tainted?" my father asks. He eyes me curiously from above where his chin rests on his now-interlaced fingers.

I tilt my head in thought before answering, "I suppose it's a possibility, as with any experiment. There could be something in the air, or someone could have snuck into my workshop. Though the physical appearance of the leaves themselves didn't seem tampered with. So if they were, someone would have to have these organelles already separated enough and infused with adhesion molecules to drop into the cells of the leaves." And that is nearly impossible to do. Also, what else besides magic could cause leaves to sprout new life and be *fed* like the ones I saw?

My parents nod in thought—my father genuinely looks like he is trying to solve the theoretical question posed, while my mother has a different sort of glint in her eye. I know that look, and I tense in preparation.

"Daje looked extremely handsome at the celebration. You two made quite the pair as you danced," she prompts, the sweet tone of her voice making the frustration rising in me settle some.

"He looked like Daje." I shrug at her as I push the remaining food around on my plate with my fork. The stress of the past two days and the addition of the exciting new discovery has left my stomach more in knots than anything else.

"And have you given his proposal thought?"

I drop my fork with a start—the metal echoing sharply in the room—as I stare at her. To her side, my father releases a long sigh, looking over at my mother. They communicate silently for a moment before both turning to look back at me. Cautiously, I ask, "How do you know about that?"

"Bahira," my mother says breezily, leaning forward to rest her elbows on the table. "I have known Daje as long as you have. He is like a second son to me. I recognized the look of elation on his face the moment he walked away from your private discussion at the edge of the trees."

Fucking Daje. A scoff leaves my mouth as I force myself back in my chair. "He did propose," I say hesitantly, deciding how much information to give my parents. "I have to answer him by tomorrow after King Kai leaves." I leave out the part about his ultimatum, about how turning him down means losing him forever.

"And how do you *feel* about his proposal?" my father asks. His gray eyes are contemplative as he looks at me, studying my face.

I don't answer for a few moments, my heart beating loudly in my ears. "I know he is a good man, and I know he would treat me well. *And* he has been my best friend since we were children." Swallowing, I keep my gaze focused on the sigil in the middle of the table. "But we are different people in a lot of ways. And I know you have practically had our wedding planned since we were children, Mother, but it isn't as simple as *willing* our friendship to be something *more*."

"Oh, Bahira," my mother whispers.

"Bahi, you can't force these things. Your mother and I were lucky to have found love in an arranged situation, but that is not something that you have to do," my father says.

"I just want you to be happy, my rose, and I had thought that perhaps you returned Daje's affections. I thought that you were just waiting for him to act on them." My eyes flick up to hers, the gray in them gleaming slightly under the spelled flames. "I should have made sure that was the case instead of assuming. You should never have to settle for anything other than what *you* want, and no one—myself included—should try to take that power away from you."

A knot forms in my throat as silence settles in the room. The permission that I didn't realize I needed to hear until right then makes my chest feel less tight as I blow out a slow breath. Dwelling on this anymore tonight, however, is something I'm too fucking tired for.

"I assume you haven't heard anything else from Nox?" I wonder aloud, not so subtly changing the subject as I sip some water.

"Nothing new, I'm afraid," my father sighs as he taps his finger on the edge of the table. My mother smiles slightly, her body tensing in concern.

"I'm sure he's alright," I say quietly, though I also have my own anxiety over where he is and what he's doing at the forefront of my mind. My father nods in agreement before shifting the conversation again. We chat about the upcoming Equinox Competition and the past few Flame Ceremonies before I inhale a rather large yawn, which has my parents practically begging me to go to bed.

Once I get to my room, I open the balcony doors, letting in the warm summer breeze as I wash up and change for bed. Sliding into my cool sheets, my head is heavy as it sinks into my pillow. It feels like my future is dangling in front of me but I have two different threads to pull on. One will bring me a certain type of security, and happiness to Daje—one of the very few people I truly care about—but it will be at a personal sacrifice. The other will leave me the most fulfilled, but it will mean that I'm alone in that satisfaction.

My eyes drift closed, and the last thought that crosses my mind is how much easier this would all be if I could just make progress on my experiments. If I could find something tangible to fix what is broken, then perhaps everything else would fall into place.

Chapter Forty-Three

RHEA

B Y THE TIME I finish with my shower, Immie has brought food to the room and confirmed with Flynn that Bella is thriving in the gardens, enjoying the attention of a few children. I sit on the edge of the perfectly made bed with crisp white linens, staring out the window at the people who look to be setting up for a celebration. Today is the Summer Solstice, I realize with a jolt. My finger drags along the gold bracelet that Alexi gave me so many years ago. I remember the night he gifted it to me in exquisite detail, a small smile pulling on my lips. But as I watch the townspeople outside of my window, my mind starts to wander. Edging in are my uncle's words about how he wanted to spend my birthday this year, and I can't help but squeeze my fists in response. He is so vile and foul, to expect that sort of relationship with me—from me.

I sit in silence, lost in my thoughts, until Flynn comes out from his shower a short while later. He's changed his clothing—though they still resemble his guard uniform. The black-on-black ensemble might have made anyone else look morose or drained of color, but he manages to glow against the dark color of his short-sleeve tunic and form-fitting pants. My eyes are immediately drawn to his tan arms, the muscles there impeccably well-defined. Silence builds—like a stone wall going up brick by quiet brick as he sits down next to me.

"We need to talk," he says at my side. His fingers trail lightly through my wet hair, just barely brushing against me. I turn and face him fully, our knees grazing. "I need to tell you something, and all I ask is that you believe me when I say that I haven't lied about anything that I've said to you." He reaches out his hand to hold mine, our fingers interlacing.

"Okay..." I hesitate, an imaginary fist tightening around my heart.

"My home and my family are in the Mage Kingdom." His eyes stay locked on mine, his hold on my hand tight in anticipation of my reaction.

When my mind finally catches up, air rushes out of my lungs as I gape at him. My heart skips a beat as my thoughts start crashing into each other, a tangled web of confusion and questions—and hurt. I finally stammer, "You're—you're mage?"

He nods slowly as his eyes soften and he continues, "It's why I was able to avoid the blood oath. I healed the wound with my magic before I said the binding words."

The blood oath didn't take. It's what he had told me, and I suppose that wasn't *technically* a lie. I remember the feeling of doubt that had risen within me at those words, but with everything that happened after, I had completely forgotten to bring it up to him again. I should have trusted my instincts and made it a priority to have him explain. I never thought he would lie, about *anything,* and that naivety was coming back to haunt me— *Wait, he* healed *the wound?*

"Your magic can heal too?" I ask incredulously. I had practically *begged* him to let me save him, to use my magic to stop his bleeding so that he would live. And he was *hiding* his ability to heal himself the whole time? Why would he lie about that? My stomach feels like it's twisting in on itself with his revelation. Was he *using* me for something?

"I can use it to heal"—realizing how that sounds, his eyes widen—"every mage can, but I need to be able to concentrate fully for a few seconds in order to wield it. I was so focused on you and getting you away from there—away from him—that I was only able to start partially healing the wound."

I think back on that moment, how my magic mended him *and then some,* more quickly than it had with Bella. *Because he was already healing.* I feel panic start to build within me, betrayal trying to curl its way around my mind. I pull my hand from his as my body starts shaking.

"What do you want to know, Rhea? Please ask me, and I'll tell you anything—everything," he begs, moving closer to me on the bed.

My thoughts tumble inside of me, but I don't know where to begin. He's been lying to me this whole time, and that realization *hurts.* It makes me question every word—every declaration he made in that tower. If lying about something so huge was so *easy* for him, were the smaller private moments between us easy to fake as well? I struggle to sift through everything I want to ask and instead just blurt out, "Why are you in the King's Guard for the Mortal Kingdom if you are mage?"

"I did it for my family. That wasn't a lie. They needed me to join, so I did." His words are sincere, but I don't know if he's lying to me. Or I suppose, I don't know if he is telling me the entire truth. He reaches his hand back out to reclaim one of my own, but I keep them fisted in my lap. He swallows roughly, dropping the outstretched hand to the bed. "What else?"

"Have you used magic around me?" And if he did, was it obvious? Did I completely miss the signs?

"Yes," he replies with a small nod of his head. "The biggest thing I did was heal your back after the king hurt you." My mind is so muddled by my racing thoughts that I have a hard time recalling the memory that he's speaking of. "But more recently was when we went into the river. I protected the bags so the items inside wouldn't get wet."

My eyes widen. I hadn't even questioned the items being dry later that night. I just— I didn't think. I was so preoccupied with my own feelings and thoughts that I didn't see what was right in front of me.

"And I also used it to help you when I pulled your unconscious body from the water. You were passed out for this, but I healed my arrow wound as well," he adds on.

My gods, the arrow. A little bit of guilt bleeds into my unease at the thought that I had forgotten he had *also* been hit with an arrow.

"Why? Why didn't you tell me sooner? Why are you telling me now?" I ask as I study his expression, my frustration growing with each word.

"Fear," he answers honestly, running the hand that had reached out for me through his hair and holding the strands there. "At first, I was afraid that you would tell the king. I didn't know you or the truth of your relationship with him that well yet. You know how he feels about those from the Mage Kingdom." And I did; it's part of the reason why I never told him about my own magic. "Then I was afraid that telling you would mean that I'd lose you. That you'd be so angry with me for lying that you'd want me to leave." He hangs his head, his hand dropping from his hair as he looks up at me. Even with his hair ruffled and his expression solemn, he is still the most beautiful man I've ever seen.

"And why are you telling me *now*?" I ask again, appeased slightly by the sincerity in his words. "There were quiet moments on our trek here where you could have told me, Flynn."

"Because I knew you were hurting and I didn't want to add to that. You wouldn't talk with me about what you were feeling, and I didn't want to push it. I also wanted to give you the choice," he confides. His voice is low, but his assumption that I have a choice only causes my emotions to heat again. "If you continue on with me, we will pass through the Spell and cross over into the Mage Kingdom. But if you would rather not, you can stay here. I trust this town and Immie to help keep you safe and settle into a new life." My heart drops into my stomach at the thought. "And as much as it would kill me to leave you, I would honor your wishes. I want you to know that. When I said that you have total power over me, that includes if it leads to my own destruction. *Whatever* you want, I will do it."

"What I *want*?" I whisper, staring at him. All my emotions, ones brought on by his confessions and ones I've kept buried beneath the surface for too long, begin to rise until I feel like I'm going to burst. A hoarse laugh scrapes up my throat though there's nothing funny about this moment. "You *lied* to me. You *pretended* to be somebody else, what, to lead me out of the Mortal Kingdom?"

My hands dive into my hair, and I find a kernel of calm in the storm swirling through my mind at the familiar way I grip the strands right at the root. Flynn tries to speak, but it's like a buzzing in my ears.

"And now you want to pretend like I have a *choice?* What choice do I have? I can go *nowhere else!*" I shout as I stand from the bed, and that heavy pressure builds behind my eyes. I had never been anywhere but the tower. I wasn't even sure I could *survive* on my own. I needed Flynn, I—

"Rhea, I'm *sorry.* I'm *so* fucking sorry," he pleads, reaching for me but stopping short when I flinch away.

His hand drops down to his side, his defeat something that perhaps hurts me more than the actual lies. It makes me feel queasy, like I'm swinging back and forth on a vine unable to find purchase. A tear slips from my eye, Flynn tracking the movement as it falls down my cheek. And I see it then in his gaze, his realization that he caused that tear. That he's the reason I'm hurting. His eyes flick back up to mine, and they shatter completely. Dejectedly, he walks to the door, placing his hand on the knob before turning back to look at me from over his shoulder.

"I'm sorry, Rhea. Truly. I wasn't— I didn't want to hurt you." The door clicks shut quietly behind him, and maybe it's foolish, but I wish he hadn't left.

The look of devastation that completely filled the depths of his eyes was genuine. He wasn't faking the way his fingers trembled on the doorknob. Yet I can't help the way that *I* feel. So I lay on the bed, curling up on my side as I face the window. It reminds me of the many times I crawled into the comfort of my bed in my tower, but I never thought that these feelings of sadness and anger would trouble me again, let alone because of Flynn. I let the tears fall, my mind settling into complete numbness as cold darkness prods its way in. And I remember what it is to find relief in boxing everything up until nothing remains.

The bed dips at my side, the warmth of someone foreign caressing my arm and thigh. My stomach tightens, air squeezing from my lungs. Something is very wrong.

"Flynn?" I call out into the darkness. I try to pry my eyes open, but my lids won't pull up. Panic rushes up my throat, a silent scream— No, a hand on my mouth muffling me.

A royal voice whispers in my ear, "You are mine, *Rhea."*

My body tenses, and his hand squeezes. His lips graze my shoulder and then my neck, hot breath rustling the fine hairs at my temple.

"You've always been mine, not his."

I choke on my fear, but it has nowhere to go. I can't move, I can't scream, I can't—

"Rhea, wake up." His soft voice and warm hand caress my cheek, and I relax into the way he makes me feel *safe*. My eyes open as I gulp in air, my vision slightly blurry but still able to see the outline of Flynn. Able to see his concerned expression—the tightness of his mouth mixed with the incredible sadness in his eyes. "Were you having a nightmare?"

I nod my head as I try to wake myself up further. The nightmare, while horrific, provides a clarity I wish I would have seen sooner. "You're here," I gasp in relief. His expression eases as his thumb continues brushing soothing strokes along my cheek. I sit up slowly and watch him freeze, unsure of what he should do—of what I will *allow*. And it breaks me because, while I hate that he lied by omission and can acknowledge that it hurts to learn that he did so, isn't that what I did to him as well? Did I not hide a giant piece of myself out of fear?

When I said that you have total power over me, that includes if it leads to my own destruction. Whatever you want, I will do it, he had said. He had given me the truth when he didn't have to and then given me the ability to make a choice. An option that I had been deprived of for my entire life thus far. Somehow, I knew that he had meant every word. That if I told him I wanted to stay here, he would leave me even if it broke him to do so.

So what do I want? The answer is simple, and yet it still hits me like a bag of stones. It overwhelms me the same as when I succumbed to the cold waters of the lake. I want *him*. In all forms and in all versions, and in whatever ways I can take him. Only and always him.

My eyes stay locked onto his, but this time, *I* reach out to him. He doesn't hesitate as he slides his hand into mine, though he holds his breath like the moment might disappear otherwise. "I'm sorry," I try to say steadily, but it comes out as nothing more than a harsh whisper.

"Sunshine, what did I tell you about apologizing? Never to me," he rushes out, lifting my hand to his lips. The tender, tentative moment sinks beneath my skin as my eyes roam to take in the room. I notice it is lit with the glow of the sunset, golden light twinkling through the window. My mouth opens to speak again, but I can't decide which words I need to let out first. Which feelings I'll allow him to see. He must see the torment on my face because he continues, pleading, "Just talk to me. I promise whatever you're thinking, whatever has you stuck in your head, I can take it. I *want* to take it, Rhea."

Pressure builds behind my eyes, and I avoid bringing my gaze to his. *Remember his truths,* a small voice whispers, and I do. I can clearly picture the way he poured his heart out to me as he declared the way he felt in the moments after my failed attempt to escape. But, he hasn't really seen all of my truths—how *ugly* they are—how *ruined* I am. I'm a walking mirage. On the outside, I appear to be one thing, but the closer people get—the closer *he* gets, the more he'll see just how *broken* I am.

The way his eyes implore me, however, to let him in—to *let him help me...* What would that be like? To not have to carry this internal turmoil in the dark by myself anymore. To have someone continually by my side and not just for small pockets of time. I've been so caged in every aspect of my life, but this? This could be a step towards true freedom.

"I'm feeling scared," I finally admit. "I'm scared that we won't make it to your home, that you will get hurt—*again*—because of me. I'm scared that you'll realize just how much of a mess I am. That you'll see all of the ugly, broken pieces of me that I know I won't ever be able to put back together again." I whisper the words as I hold back the tears that line my eyes. "And I'm terrified that, even if I somehow managed to become *whole*, it still won't be enough. That I won't *ever* be enough for you—for what you deserve—and I'll have to watch you walk away because of it." My chest feels tight, my throat somehow hoarse. Speaking these things to him, they feel almost like a release, as if a bright light is shining into that inner obsidian.

He grasps my chin gently and turns my head to face him again.

"Rhea, I see every part of who you are. And the more time we spend together, the more moments when you offer another glimpse of yourself to me, it doesn't make me want you any less," he says softly, his heavy gaze cementing his words. "If you're in pieces, then I want every fucking one of them. I want you—in any way you can give me. No scenario changes that."

I shake my head, my lips trembling and eyelashes growing wet. Memories from the last three months together flash in my mind in rapid succession. Flynn was my guard, then my friend, and now—now he felt like my home. "I *need* you," I breathe, feeling the force of that need bearing down on me. "Like nothing I've ever felt before. It's an ache that stirs in the deepest parts of me and curls out until it's soaked into my bones. It's the way that the stars need the night and the moon needs the sun. It's relentless and bottomless and like free-falling all at once."

Flynn's chest rises and falls in quick motions, his lips parting like he's trying to inhale my words. He leans in, his hand coming to cup my cheek, but I am the one to close the distance, my mouth suddenly on his. He wastes no time sweeping his tongue inside in decadent strokes—the feel of it is a claiming that I eagerly return. My arms wrap around his neck as he pulls me onto his lap, my knees straddling his powerful thighs. His arms band around me, those large hands laying flat on my back as he squeezes me flush against him. I remember the feeling of wrapping my legs around him for our first kiss, and my thighs strain to clench together at the thought.

"Is this alright?" he asks, pulling back to look into my eyes.

"Yes," I nod as I slide my fingers into the still-damp waves of his raven hair, gripping them gently.

He swallows roughly, holding my gaze as he takes a deep breath, and moves in close again. "I need you too, but more than that, I *crave* you. You feed my soul in a way nothing else ever has before. You've altered my very being by the way you've carved yourself into my heart," he murmurs against my lips. His words are like kindling to a flame, and I want nothing more than to be consumed by them.

When he deepens our kiss, I find that I'm desperate to taste every bit of him, to know his body better than I know my own. His responding groan rumbles down his chest and travels directly to my core. He kisses down my jaw and neck while his tongue dips out to taste each inch of me like there's nothing sweeter. My hips roll in response, the seam on the thin fabric of my pants creating an incredible friction at the apex of my thighs. The sensation of the heat of his mouth, as his teeth tug lightly on my earlobe, causes shivers to roll down my arching back as I gasp. I didn't understand what it was to be so undone by desire until I kissed Flynn.

I moan his name, holding his head to me as he grazes his teeth down my neck to where it meets my shoulder. His touch creates an insatiable longing—a brightly lit inferno—that causes something reckless to rise within me. I don't know what I'm doing, but I let my base desire control my movements as I abruptly push him down on the bed. His eyes grow wide for a moment before my lips meet his again. The strands of my hair fall to either side of our faces, cocooning us in our own honey-colored world where it's just him and me and this all-consuming force. It's a madness that I'd happily lose myself to for eternity. From this position, the bulge of his erection rubs right at my center, and gods help me, I may die from it. His hands rest on my hips, and I can feel his restraint beginning to waiver as he guides them back and forth, that grip tightening just a little more.

"Rhea, I—"

My mouth stops his words as my tongue follows the movements of my body, and I can't help but smile at the way his breath stutters in response. He then emits what can only be described as a growl of pleasure, the noise so carnal that it causes me to whimper in response. Stars above, is it normal to feel this way? To be so undone by simply melding your body to someone like this? To want their scent branded into your lungs and their taste to be a permanent pleasure on your lips?

Flynn slowly slides an arm up and around my waist. The world tilts, and suddenly I'm underneath him, his hips sinking into the middle of my widened legs.

"You like being in control?" he taunts me from above with a provocative smirk.

"Do... you like that?" I ask, vulnerability somewhat cooling me down as I stare into his darkened eyes.

They soften for just a moment before he leans down and presses a sweet kiss to my mouth. "I like anything you do," he breathes against my lips as he slowly drags his hand down my side. I can hear the pounding of my heart in my ears, my skin tingling under his touch. My breath catches at the feel of him—of how hard and ready he is for *me*—and I can feel how wet I am for him as my body conforms to his above me, my hands roaming his back. "But I especially like *that*."

He braces his weight on one forearm by my head as he kisses me again, somehow deeper and harder than before. His other hand finds purchase on my hip, pinning me in place with a tenderness that lets me know I can move at any time. I don't want to stop him though. No, I need more. I want all of him—with nothing between us. And I'll give him whatever he wants, whatever he'll take of me—it's all his. *I'm* his, and maybe that's why I let the words slip out.

"Explore me," I whisper, recalling how he said he'd do that very thing once we were safe. And that's all I have ever felt with Flynn—safe. From the very first interaction, he has always made me feel at ease. I trust him with every part of me, including my body. His hips sink further into me, his cock straining against his trousers as he lines up perfectly with where I need more of that sweet friction.

"You have no idea how badly I want to," he rasps. His rough voice is a pleasurable scrape along my body as his teeth gently pull on my lower lip. My fingers skim up his sides, nails dragging along his skin as I lift his shirt higher and higher. "You can tell me 'no,' and I will stop at any time, you know that right?"

"Don't stop." My voice is unrecognizable to my own ears, and when his hips roll in response, I descend further into our chaos—everything else becoming a distant fragment outside my reality.

My magic starts humming inside of me, warmth and white light pushing on the confines of my body as I moan at every new sensation. For once, the only thing I feel is desire; it devours me from within, setting every nerve ending alight with need. My hips lift, and I rock against him until I'm left panting. The hand on my hip travels slowly underneath my shirt, his fingers moving closer to my breast as his mouth continues to devour mine. He kisses me thoroughly, soundly, in a way that makes me feel powerful.

All I know is this pleasure and the intoxicating grip it has on my senses. My hands roam down his back and lower, until they are dipping under the waistband of his pants. The muscles of his backside flex as he grinds into me, and just that sensation has tension beginning to coil at the base of my spine, my toes curling into the bed.

"You're so fucking perfect," he murmurs as his lips start traveling down my jaw and neck again. When the tip of his thumb grazes under my bralette, I gasp and arch my back, wanting to give him more. And wanting to take everything in return.

But the moment is interrupted by three knocks on the door.

Chapter Forty-Four

RHEA

FLYNN AND I FREEZE, our hands placed precariously on each other's bodies. I take in his wide pupils and the way his tan skin is flushed. When another set of knocks sounds, followed by the grumbles of an older woman, Flynn drops his forehead to mine and sighs. "It is better that we stop anyway," he whispers, much to my chagrin. Flynn laughs as his eyes close for a moment, the hand under my shirt sliding back down to my hip.

The weight of his body on top of me is a comfort, a feeling of security. Of home. And of love. My heart flips for a moment at the thought of that word and what it means. *Love.* I think I love him. I repeat the words in my head, and each time, the truth of them becomes more and more clear. *I love him.*

Like he can hear my thoughts, Flynn's eyes open and he pulls his head back to look at me. Our gazes lock, and something flashes there quicker than I can read before he kisses the tip of my nose and sits up, taking a slow deep breath.

"Do you not want to—" I bite my still-tingling lip, blushing under the weight of his gaze despite how we just writhed together until I was nearly brought to an orgasm.

"Of course I want to," he answers my unfinished question.

"But the night at the lake... You said it was self-preservation. What did you mean?" I ask quietly, finally meeting his gaze.

His lips draw into a slow, devastating smile. "It means that I was trying to restrain myself." His eyebrows draw down slightly before he leans over and brings his thumb up to my lip—which is once again trapped between my teeth—and gently frees it. "I'm sorry if I made you feel otherwise. That was never my intention."

"And why is it better that we stop now?" I question.

Another knock shakes the door, but he ignores it as he pulls me up to sit as well, his hands then framing my face. "Don't mistake my preference not to fuck you in an inn or in the woods as me not having the desire at all," he declares. His voice is deep and sharp as it drags along my skin, causing goosebumps to raise in its wake. "You deserve to be somewhere we can take our time, where we can explore every inch of each other—as promised—without worrying about someone hearing our moans of pleasure or interrupting us."

"Gods," I whisper before our lips meet again. The kiss is both how I always hoped it would feel to share myself with another and still nothing like how I imagined it could be. And maybe that's because I never allowed myself to think about a scenario where the man kissing me was someone like Flynn. With a deep groan, he finally lets go of me and stands, walking over to the door.

"Immie, what is all of this?" he asks, stepping out of the way as the older woman walks in holding a small cake, a black bag, and a glass bottle with a cork in it.

"I assumed you two would want some privacy and wouldn't be attending the town festivities for Summer Solstice." She huffs out a breath as she walks over to the table. "Plus, it isn't a birthday unless you have cake."

I halt my steps towards her as my gaze swings over to Flynn's. He tilts his head to the side as he looks at Immie, crossing his arms over his chest.

"And whose birthday are we celebrating exactly?" he asks cautiously.

"Oh, don't play dumb with me boy," she chides, turning to face us and pinning me under her stare. "I would recognize those green eyes anywhere." Her lips curve to the side, her hand going to a small pendant hanging from a silver chain around her neck. I bite back the urge to ask her what she means by that. She limps to me, wrapping my hand in hers. "Anyway, your secret is safe with me. Flynn here can attest to that. You made the right choice, leaving with him. He's a good boy, even if his hair could use a cut and his style is a bit bland."

"I'm right here," Flynn mumbles as I bite back a laugh.

"Happy birthday, Your Highness," she says, smiling and patting my hand twice before heading to Flynn. He gives her a hug and walks her to the door.

"We'll be gone before the sun rises," he murmurs quietly as she steps out into the hall.

"I'll pack some more food for you to take with you on the road. Be safe," she says before leaning over to look at me. "Both of you."

I nod at her, returning her smile before she turns and heads down the hallway. "She knows you're mage?" I ask as I follow him to the table.

"She does," he answers, opening the black bag and taking out two forks and two glasses. I take one from him, holding it up as I study its design. It's tall and skinny in shape, with a stem like a flower coming down and flattening out at the bottom. "It's a flute glass." He grabs the bottle and uncorks it slowly, a fizzing sound coming from within it. "And I'm betting this is the Mortal Kingdom's version of sampanie."

"Is it alcohol?" I wonder aloud, watching how it bubbles when Flynn pours it into the glass.

He nods his head and hands me one before pouring one for himself. He watches as I take a tentative sip, the bubbly golden liquid dancing along my tongue.

"It's sweet!" I am completely surprised by the sugary aftertaste. Alexi had told me that he found all alcohol to be disgusting, not enjoying the *earthy harshness* of its taste. I guess he had never tried sampanie. The memory of his face forms in my mind, and my heart skips a beat in response.

Flynn watches me, his smile affectionate as he guides me to the window with a hand on my back. "The floating lanterns should start any minute," he comments before leaving for a moment while I stare out at the rapidly approaching night sky. The sun is only another moment away from setting fully.

"Does every kingdom light lanterns on the Summer Solstice?" I ask when he steps up to my side again. Excitement bubbles up inside of me, rivaling the sweetness of the drink, as I stare out the open window.

"I think it's more of a Mortal Kingdom thing to light them," he answers, rubbing a hand up and down my back. I love the way he desires my touch as much as I crave his. We'll get to do this as often as we want, *whenever* we want, without the limitations of a tower or the worry of being caught. I can't stop my widening smile at the thought. "In the Mage Kingdom, there is a celebration. You dance and eat the entire night, and then when the sun rises—if you're still awake—everyone stands still and lets the orange and pink rays of the first summer sun pour over them. It's supposed to bring you good luck."

I ponder over the image of that, of how beautiful it sounds. "I can't wait to experience it next year," I confess before looking up at him. "With you. Though you'll have to make sure you teach me more dance moves because I—" He halts my words with a kiss, his soft lips coaxing a quiet moan from me until I'm left feeling dizzy when he pulls away. "What was that for?" I ask, hopelessly breathless. His eyes hold mine, those molten pewter depths beckoning me to get lost in them.

"I'm just happy to be here with you," he replies. And though his smile is bright, there's something that clouds his expression. I start to question him about it, but he speaks again before I can. "I have something for you," he says, holding out what looks like a skinny book. The smooth leather of it is pure black with a gold floral pattern embossing the edges, and on the bottom right corner, in cursive script, is my full name: Rhea Maxwell.

"What is this?" I gasp while running a finger along the lettering, my heart playing a strange staccato in my chest.

"It's a journal," he answers reverently, drawing my eyes up to his. "I thought it might be nice for you to have something to document all the new experiences you're sure to have now that you're free." A swell of emotion tightens my chest and creeps up my throat as tears well in my eyes. "I'm going to go check on Bella, but I wrote you something on the first page." He steps closer to me, his hand cupping my cheek as he whispers, "Happy birthday, Sunshine."

Sweetly kissing my forehead, he steps back and heads towards the door, slipping his boots on before quietly shutting it behind him. I sit on the edge of the bed, my breath shaky as I open the journal up to the first page.

Sunshine,

Writing this reminds me of all the letters we passed back and forth to each other in the tower. While I am particularly fond of those memories, I am much happier to have you outside of those stone walls. There are so many things I could write, so many things I want to say to you, but I haven't found the courage. So I'll start with a truth that I know you're eagerly waiting for: why do I call you "Sunshine"?

It all started the moment I begged you to step out from the wall you were hiding behind. My breath caught in my throat—although to be fair, that could have been because you startled me. You moved to the railing of your loft, and the sunlight shining in from the window hit your hair in such a way that it appeared to be glowing. You looked like a true goddess, and when your eyes held mine—and that golden hue of your hair glimmered around you—an unshakable truth settled deeply within me.

You were the answer to a question I hadn't known to ask until then. I had spent years feeling suffocated, unsure if what I was doing actually mattered, and then you were suddenly there. Like the first rays of sunshine after a thunderstorm, you radiated light against the dark. As I found ways to spend time with you, to bribe you with sweets in order to get to know you, it became clear to me why I was led to the Mortal Kingdom. It was because of you.

You're everything I never knew I wanted and certainly never thought I'd find. I said I only want what you can give me, whatever capacity that is, and I meant it. No matter what happens going forward, you will never be alone again. I will always be here with you. To stand by you. To fight for you. To remind you how strong and incredible you are. You need only to let me.

Happy birthday, my Rhea. May you never forget how brightly you shine.

Adamantly yours,

Flynn

I close the journal and hold it to my heart as warm tears trickle down my cheeks. Happy tears this time because I know the truth of his words in my heart and in my soul. I bask in the way they pour into me like the sweetest nectar, melting me and filling those often dark and cold spaces with warmth and devotion. And when the boxes that I've kept so tightly locked in the chasm of my mind rattle, I let them. I don't fight it when I can feel some of the sadness and guilt that so often plagues my heart, especially since Alexi's death, well up inside of me. Instead of burying them back down, I imagine those feelings filtering out with my tears, letting each drop carry the weight of a burden I don't need to hold onto anymore.

When the door opens and Flynn steps through, it's like seeing him for the first time all over again. No—even better—because I know who he is now. I *see* all that he is, and I *feel* how much I love him, and I'm not afraid anymore. Our eyes meet, my heart pounding wildly in my chest, and I stand to go to him, but he's already moving to me. He holds me tightly while I cry tears of joy and tears of that long-held sadness—of longing and of deeply buried sorrow—because I believe him when he says that he'll be there for me always. When my tears start to slow, his thumbs gently wiping them away, he walks us over to the window where we watch the light of the floating lanterns begin to dot the sky, now black with night. My eyes widen when he holds out a lantern to me, the paper beacon adorned with a golden outline of a roaring lion—the Mortal Kingdom's sigil. He strikes a match, lighting the small candle held within. While we wait for the air inside the lantern to get hot enough to float, our eyes meet over its glow, and I can't help the smile that breaks across my face. It's wide and bright and brimming with triumphant *happiness*.

"Did you know that I absolutely love your eyes and your smile? The way you look at me?" he says softly. His voice is deeply mellifluous, like a melody meant only for me. I'm about to respond when the lantern begins to pull at our fingertips, ready to be let loose. Sticking our arms out the window, we release it and watch as it floats up, joining what must be hundreds of others in the dark. I'm lost momentarily in observing the way they move when Flynn gently grips my chin, turning me to face him. "I love you."

Everything freezes. Time and space and happiness and heartache all pause because of those three words. They do something to me, beginning to heal parts of my soul that were left shredded. They fill darkness with light and guilt with reprieve. Those words burn away the bitter and vile actions of another, and in the ashes, something incredible and beautiful rises.

Flynn slides his hand up my jaw to reverently hold the side of my face and repeats, "I love you." His words are laced with precious adoration as his voice slightly shakes. "Wholly. Inexorably. In a way that exhilarates as much as it frightens me. With everything that I am or could ever possibly hope to be, I love you. I don't want to know an existence without you in it. You don't have to say it back, and it's probably too soon— "

"Flynn," I whisper, my hands cupping his face as I pull him down to me. "I love you too." My eyes hold his, stars swirling in them as I wonder if perhaps I'm dreaming. If I am, then I don't ever want to wake. My thumbs caress his cheekbones, the overwhelming sense of rightness pulling words from me easily. "You saved me in ways I can't explain yet, in ways that I never thought possible. When I think of *home,* I picture you. My heart has never felt so full, despite its many losses. I *love* you."

The words are barely past my lips before his are there—a demanding and desperate kiss to seal them between us. To make sure that no matter what happens in the future, there will always be this moment cemented in both of our minds—an unbreakable truth for two people who chose each other despite the challenges of doing so. When we break apart, I swear that the room glows brighter, the silver in Flynn's eyes glinting, but when I look behind me to find the source of the light, there is nothing there. Flynn doesn't seem to see it as he stares intently at me, so I don't say anything before he turns me to look back out at the lanterns. Standing behind me, he wraps his arms around me protectively while I sink back against him.

When I'm too tired to stay standing, he crawls onto the bed and pulls me with him, my head laying on his chest as the beat of his heart lulls me into sleep. The last thought I have on the brink of consciousness is that I know without a doubt that the day Flynn entered my life, it was forever changed.

Chapter Forty-Five

BAHIRA

T HE SUN WARMS MY skin from overhead as I watch the shifter king's ship ride the waves in the distance. We stand on our side of the Spell, the glittering wall reflecting its iridescence in the sunlight. As with all land that borders the ocean, the Spell allows a few feet of beach as a neutral ground for beings to meet on. Our shipping docks and ports are built into these neutral zones, and I imagine it was a safeguard of sorts when the Void Magic user originally cast the Spell.

My mother had suggested that we wear our more traditional mage dresses for this meeting, reminding me that it is the first known in-person meeting of leaders since the Spell was put into place. I chose a dark blue quarter-sleeve dress made of linen. The fabric of the bodice wraps tightly across my breasts and stomach before the dress flows out towards my feet in a relaxed skirt. I added a gold and silver chain belt around my waist, the pattern of a petalum flower twisted into the metal. My hair blows behind me in the ocean breeze, the scent of salt and sea permeating the air.

A large gathering of people has begun to form behind us on the beach, including the members of the council and Daje. My father sent out missives to every resident in the kingdom a few days ago, asking them to send their strongest magic user to the beach for this meeting. He assured them that even if the magic chose them, they would have the choice to decline going to the shifter isle. It is the only way he will make the deal with King Kai and a perfect way to strong-arm him into agreeing. Since the shifter king has already spent time sailing here, he won't want to sail back home empty-handed. My father will also make sure that there is a time limit to how long the chosen mage will be required to stay in the foreign kingdom. It all sounds reasonable enough to me, and yet nerves burrow into my stomach at the thought that King Kai won't agree.

My fingers curl by my sides as I watch a small rowboat depart from the ship and head in our direction. The island king was arrogant and unsympathetic in our previous meeting, and I pity whoever it is that will get stuck working with him.

My parents stand next to me as we watch the king and what looks like his advisor, Tua, row the small wooden boat near. My mother has chosen a similar style of dress to mine but in a light pink, while my father wears his traditional blue and silver mage robe over simple brown trousers and a white tunic. It had jolted me a bit when I met them in the foyer of the palace earlier because he was wearing one of the traditional diadems of our kingdom. The chosen crown has three pointed tips at the front, each one topped with a round yellow diamond surrounded with golden flares. The one in the middle is the largest, roughly four inches in diameter, and rests atop a crescent moon made of black diamond, the points tipped up. Woven around the golden circumference are emeralds in the shape of leaves in all different sizes with small diamonds layered throughout. I always thought they looked like stars sprinkled into the foliage.

"Are you ready, My King?" my mother asks, looking over at my father. He is one of the most unflappable men I have ever known, but the pressure and secrecy of Nox's mission has begun to wear on him. His finger taps on her hand, his nervous tick drawing my attention.

"This is the right decision," he responds as he gives her a small smile. "There is no kingdom without its people, and this deal will ensure that ours will be safe if a threat indeed presents itself." My mother smiles fondly at him, leaning in to press a kiss to his cheek.

My heart pounds in my chest as the row boat hits the sand and the king of the shifter isle steps out. He is even larger in person than the Mirror made him appear. His dark brown hair is cut short on the sides and longer on top, the slightly wavy strands pushed back from his face. He's dressed in a sleeveless green tunic, the missing material showing off the enormity of his arms. I try to make out the design of the black tattoo scrolling down his right limb, but it's a pattern that I can't decipher even now that we are in person. He is massive—the muscles of his chest and back flaring out enough that I imagine even if I put two Daje's side by side, it still wouldn't be as wide as he is. His legs flex even through the light material of his black trousers as he walks through the sand with ease. He isn't wearing a crown of his own, which I find odd. It also pains me to admit that, even through the slight distortion as he nears the wall of the Spell, he is the most stunning man I have ever seen. His build and coloring are completely unique to the island he comes from and his shifter blood. He smirks when our eyes meet, making mine narrow in response as I cross my arms over my chest. *Arrogant ass.* Tua follows behind him, struggling to keep up with the large steps of his ruler.

"Welcome, King Kai. I hope your journey here was easy and uneventful," my father says, his voice resonant.

The island king's face is that of stone as he subtly gives a nod of his head. "Only one interruption by the sirens that was dealt with quickly," he responds, his deep voice reverberating over the sound of the gentle waves.

My eyes widen at the mention of the beings who live under the water, their beautiful and supposedly eerie song usually a death trap to any who are caught in its chorus. Though I had, obviously, never heard it.

"Shall we begin, King Sadryn?" King Kai asks, gesturing to the space in front of him. Together, my mother and father step through the Spell, their figures blurring for a quick second before they appear on the other side. From where I stand, I hear the sharp inhale of a few of the council members.

"We have conditions we would like to discuss before any blood is bound," my father announces firmly. King Kai towers over him by about four inches, his domineering presence met by my father's stoic calm. My mother grips his hand fiercely, her eyes never wavering from their observation of the island king. I watch as his gaze travels down to their joined hands and back up again—his lips softening into what might have been described as a small grin, if it weren't for the harshness of the rest of his features.

"Queen Alexandria, it is a pleasure to see you again. What are your conditions?"

A flicker of surprise sparks inside of me at the respect shown to my mother. It's not that all men believe themselves to be above women, it's just that—other than the siren queen and our last Void Magic queen—there aren't women ruling in any of the other kingdoms. While traditionally our kingdom has always acknowledged one ruler, my father includes my mother in all major decisions—and not just behind closed doors. He has never taken kindly to being questioned about it either by some of the council members. In his words, "A king is only as wise as his queen pushes him to be."

"We think it would be fair to allow the mage chosen by the magic to deny the opportunity to go, should they prefer," he responds confidently. "The magic may choose as many mages as it takes until one agrees to go with you."

King Kai's demeanor doesn't change, his unyielding face betraying no emotion of how he may feel about this concession. Time drips by slowly as his advisor leans in close and whispers something to him. *Accept, damn it.*

The shifter king takes a deep breath, his large chest rising with the movement before he dips his chin in agreement. "I accept." A collective exhale of relief sounds on our side of the Spell. "Anything else? I assume that can't be all," he says, a dark brow raising slightly.

His attitude causes an involuntary scoff to leave my mouth. His eyes flick to mine, that brow raising impossibly higher as he studies me. The sun hits the angles of his square jaw, its glare highlighting his sculpted cheekbones and strong brow. And for some reason, which I don't have the time to examine, a quick flash of desire roils through me before I clear my throat. As if knowing that I've been betrayed by my body, King Kai kicks up his smirk into something that can only be described as a wolfish grin. It's a move that turns whatever idiotic yearning I might have felt into the more appropriate feeling of irritation.

My father breaks through my musing as he continues speaking, "We believe that there should be an expressed limit of time that the mage is expected to stay on your isle—to be determined by you and the chosen mage."

"And what happens if, at the end of that time limit, your mage hasn't been able to figure out our issue?" King Kai asks, the only tell of his frustration the slight flex of his bicep. "Our end of the bargain will only be upheld for as long as there is a mage actively working with us on the magic, or a solution has been discovered."

Of course he would bargain with the safety of our people for his own kingdom's gain.

"I would humbly request, one ruler to another, that you consider the lives of the innocents when you threaten us." A proud smile curls my lips at my father's words as the shifter king clenches his jaw again, a muscle fluttering in his cheek while he considers.

"I will not tell another kingdom about your ability to pass through the Spell, no matter the outcome of your mage's efforts. However, I will only agree to offer refuge for as long as a mage is in my kingdom. After that time is up, so is our offer of protection."

433

If I am ever left alone with that foreign king, I will absolutely punch him in the face.

"That is fair, King Kai. Let us bind the words in blood." My father steps forward, only releasing my mother's hand in order to grab a familiar dagger from its sheath on his belt—the black stone hilt stark in the daylight. Blood rushes in my ears as I watch them, King Kai stepping up past his advisor and extending his opposite hand forward. "Speak the words as we've discussed them, and then our joined blood will soak into the Continent—the magic of it binding our words and this deal."

"I, King Kai of the Shifter Kingdom, ask that—in exchange for moving the people of the Mage Kingdom to our island should they fall under attack—the best mage be chosen to help us fix the blight that has been plaguing our magic. He or she chosen will have the opportunity to decline, and thus, another will be nominated to take their place until one has agreed. A time limit, as specified between myself and the appointed mage, will be put into place. Our protection of the people of this kingdom is only applicable for as long as there is a mage working with us or a reason for the blight has been found. I will also keep your Spell *abilities* secret."

My father wastes no time slicing into his palm and doing the same to King Kai, who peers questioningly at him when the spelled dagger drags across his skin. Without another word, the two kings grasp hands and hold them together, until their intermingled blood drips down into the sand. A shimmering glow, like that of the Spell, lights up the sand where the blood has gathered. The outlines of my father and the shifter king briefly glimmer as well before the men release their hands.

"And now we see who the magic has chosen," my father says quietly, looking out onto the gathered crowd. Seconds tick by as I search the collection of people as well. My eyes find Arin, then Dilan, and finally Daje, but none of them look any different. Suddenly, someone gasps, followed by another, and a low murmuring breaks out amongst the mages. I scan the crowd, trying to figure out who the magic has chosen, when Daje's panicked voice snags my attention.

"Holy gods, Bahira," he blurts out as my gaze finds him and he takes a step closer to me. "It's you."

"What?" I ask, glancing down. My normally tan skin shimmers with that white, iridescent light of the Spell. My heart beats frantically in my chest as I stare at myself in a state of shock.

"It has made a mistake," Daje shouts, walking up to my side. "The magic chose the wrong person." My head wrenches around until I can see him, my eyes narrowing in annoyance. Seeing the look on my face, Daje's shoulders rise as his throat works to swallow. "You know what I mean, Bahira. You don't eve—"

"Are you claiming to know more than the ancient magic that runs through this very world?" King Kai asks, his voice rumbling through the tension in the air.

"Of course not, it's just that Bahira doesn't have the right tools to help you. She—"

"Maybe instead of speaking *for* her, we should let the *princess* decide if she would like to accept being chosen." His tone is one of boredom, but when I look at the shifter king's face, his eyes burn with a type of fury that seems too intense for this situation. It's a predatory kind of glint, one that is a precursor to an impending attack. I can't decipher if he's mad at me being chosen or at Daje's words or at something else entirely.

"Bahi, why don't you come over on this side," my father suggests.

"Bahira..." Daje starts, but I ignore him as I turn and walk towards the Spell.

I've stepped through the glimmering wall only twice before: once to see what it felt like to step through and once because I wanted to feel the cool water of the ocean for the first time. I had let the waves lap at my toes for a few moments before turning right back around and stepping through the thin boundary. It feels just as I remembered, like walking through the softest, thinnest silk. When the distortion clears and I'm instantly face to face with the unfamiliar king, my traitorous stomach clenches.

"Princess," he drawls, his gaze holding mine as Tua to his right subtly shifts his weight between his feet.

"You know you have the choice to stay here," my father reminds me.

My eyes bounce from his back to the island king's as my mind fights to make a choice. My answer should be obvious, but much like the choices

I've been given lately, nothing is quite as easy as it should be. I'm a magicless mage, and yet the magic of the very Continent *chose me* as the best option. How can I deny the way that I feel at being recognized like this? How could I not, at the very least, *consider* going?

My shoulders roll back as I lift my chin and steel my gaze towards King Kai. "How long?"

"Bahira, no!" Daje yells out from behind me. My father holds his hand up, halting what I assume must have been Daje's attempt to come through the Spell to get to me.

King Kai tilts his head down to me, a roguish grin growing as he contemplates his answer. "I *am* curious as to why it picked you, Princess. You don't strike me as the type with experience in these matters."

My lips lift into a sneer, "*Now,* who is claiming to know more than the ancient magic of our world? Even *your* small brain must recognize that I was chosen for a reason." My mother gasps, and my father quickly brings the back of his hand to his mouth, stifling a laugh. But I'm too focused on the haughty male in front of me to care. "You would be lucky to have me spend even one month of my time on your little *island.*"

"Even my supposedly small brain acknowledges that one month isn't enough time for anyone," he counters, taking a small step towards me and making me strain my neck backwards even farther to hold his gaze. "Six months."

I throw my hands out to the side as I stare at him. *Six months? No fucking way.* "Six weeks."

"I don't think you understand how bargaining works."

"And *I'd* argue that *you* think too highly of yourself," I grit out through my teeth, my chest rising and falling with quickened breaths as my hands brace on my hips.

"One might say the same thing about you," he replies, dropping his voice even lower. He leans into me, his eyes burning with irritation. "Five months."

"Two."

"Bahira, this is madness. You can't do this!" Daje demands from behind me.

I turn to glare at him, to remind him that this isn't *his* choice, but movement just beyond him catches my attention. A tall familiar figure stands in front of the crowd, his black hair longer than it had been the last time I saw him.

"Nox?" I breathe, as Daje's father grips his shoulder, but my brother's attention is on that of the petite woman in front of him. Her golden blonde hair glows in the sunlight, the strands of her loose braid billowing in the breeze.

"You're not the right person for this," Daje says again, gently this time, from the other side of the Spell. My gaze is then drawn to his hand as he reaches out to me, anger twisting in my gut. I lift my eyes back to his, the pleading look in them begging me to turn down this opportunity. Fervently beseeching me to stay here, with him.

"Three months, Princess. Final offer. Accept it, or we'll choose someone new," King Kai barks in annoyance from behind me.

Silence descends on my mind as the weight of this decision coats me like a thick mist. In front of me is the life I've always known, one that may hold certain comforts but only at the sacrifice of a part of myself. One that, even with my newest discovery, has been laced with disappointment and often a feeling of being incomplete. Behind me—an ocean away—lies a new opportunity, a new experience. While solving their blight with magic, I might in turn find an answer to our own problem. Two different worlds, two unlikely choices, and yet I was chosen by an ancient, powerful, unseen force. I was chosen because it found me *worthy*.

"Bahira," Daje rumbles again, his fingers stretching even farther to me.

"Deal," I say firmly, keeping my gaze pinned on his but speaking my answer to the looming shifter king behind me. "Three months."

Chapter Forty-Six

RHEA

WE WAKE UP JUST before the sun has risen the next morning to begin the final leg of our journey to his home, although I suppose it is my home now too. He offers to braid my hair again, which I quickly accept, and then we go to find Bella in the gardens. Immie has indeed given us an incredible amount of food as well as refilled our waterskins. I look back at the small town one last time as we walk away, now quiet as the people who celebrated late into the night sleep peacefully.

Our journey through the woods is mostly uneventful, with the exception of running into a small pack of black bears. My heart beats wildly at seeing them up close, but Flynn insists that we keep our distance despite my protests. We continue following the winding Vida River, staying just inside the treeline. Bella has grown comfortable walking far ahead of us, just the sway of her fluffy white tail visible between the trees from where we follow behind her.

Flynn and I walk hand in hand, keeping our pace brisk. For the first time in perhaps forever, but certainly since we had left the tower, I don't feel bogged down by the swirling thoughts in my head.

I am anxious but also so excited to explore Flynn's home. To see where he has grown up and meet his family and friends. My past has been a series of sorrows and torments, but now with my twenty-second birthday behind me, it feels like my life is finally beginning. We lay down in a small clearing of trees that night, Flynn offering to stay awake so Bella can cuddle up next to me. My hand runs down her side, my heart swelling with love and gratitude for my oldest friend. For the fact that we have been able to stay together through everything that has happened, that we both get to truly *live* now.

"The moon may have the stars, but I'll always have you," I whisper against her head before falling asleep.

***

"We're nearly at the border," Flynn says as we climb a small hill the next day, stepping over exposed roots and under winding tree branches.

Trees still blanket the area heavily, though the limbs are more twisting and dense than they were closer to the Mortal Kingdom. It's like each trunk is stretching out to the neighboring tree so that they can interlock and form a barrier. I'm grateful for how dense it is, as it gives us shade from the summer sun, but I'm reminded yet again that, even though I did exercises in the tower, I certainly am not fit enough to spend days on end traversing through the woods. We crest the hill after a few more steps, my legs crying out for me to take a break as breath huffs in and out of my chest.

"There." Flynn points, but I don't need his guidance to make out what must be the border. I stare with wide eyes and parted lips at the shimmering, iridescent *wall* that starts on the ground and rises as far as the eye can see into the sky. Speckles of sunlight breaking through the gaps in the canopy of trees cast an illustrious shimmer on the Spell, reflecting every single color of the rainbow. My hand goes to my chest as my magic immediately starts coiling and writhing within me, moving like it is trying to reach out towards the Spell.

"Oh my gods," I state in shock as he leads us closer to it. Bella walks ahead, trotting happily to the barrier, but *I* have to swallow down my nerves as I squeeze Flynn's hand. "Are you sure it's okay for me to walk through it?"

I know what happens to those from other kingdoms who pass through the Spell—they lose their magic in whatever capacity they possess it. And those from the Mortal Kingdom lose their youth. Flynn had explained to me on our walk here that the Spell recognizes those with mage magic and allows them to pass through without any repercussions. It had been a shock to learn that, and I am still feeling uneasy about the risk of crossing the border .

"I've lived in the Mortal Kingdom my entire life, what if I go through and it makes me old on the other side?" I whisper, somehow afraid that the Spell is going to hear me and enact that very scenario.

"From what we understand, the magic reacts to how you present, so to speak," he explains, as we descend the hill. "You have *raw* magic, which means that you are not mortal. Plus, you are now the age when mage magic hits its peak strength. Because of that, the Spell should recognize you as mage. At least," he teases, looking down at me with a smirk, "that has always been the case in the past."

"Very reassuring," I mumble as his chuckle suffuses the otherwise-quiet woods. "Well, you're the one who will be stuck with an old lady if that happens, so you better have meant what you said about taking whatever I can give you."

He brings our joined hands to his lips, softly kissing the back of mine. "That won't happen—even if it did, you'd still be mine. But the Spell kills whoever crosses through it within a few days."

I squeak out a noise of shocked surprise while he leans in to kiss my forehead. "You're joking right?"

"Don't worry, I wouldn't let you cross if I didn't think you would be safe." I start to question him again, but Flynn suddenly halts my steps, his head moving slowly from side to side. "Where is Bella?" he asks as a chill scrapes down my spine.

"Maybe she already walked through the barrier?" I answer, stepping closer to him as my eyes search intently for her. The wall of the Spell is thin, easily translucent enough to see through to the other side, though the image is slightly distorted. It's what I imagine looking through a bubble would be like.

The forest is frozen, not even a rustling of leaves on the branches as it watches us. I feel the heavy gaze of something or *someone* bearing down on my skin. My magic—already at attention because of our proximity to the Spell—moves down my arms and into my palms, a glimmering white emitting from them. I begin to question why it always does this, but then I'm distracted when I see Flynn's magic glowing in his palm as well—the darkest purple, nearly black, illuminates his entire hand. It's as beautiful as it is deadly looking, and I can't believe I didn't ask him to show me what it looked like before now.

"Call your magic back, or we kill the fox," a stentorian voice splinters through the air. A flash of gold steps out from behind a tree followed by another and another until we are completely surrounded in a crescent shape, only the barrier of the Spell behind us not lined with guards. A tenuous hush claims the air, interrupted only by the harsh pounding of my heart in my ears. Two men step forward, each of them holding the end of a rope in their hands. My eyes follow the ropes down as Bella is dragged between them. The two ropes wrap around her neck in a noose-like fashion, and the sight of it makes my heart drop into my stomach.

"Bella," I whimper, moving to take a step towards her. The guards yank the ropes hard, causing Bella to whine—the noise piercing my heart like a spear. All around us, guards draw their swords, the scrape of metal being unsheathed an ominous ballad to our demise.

"Call your magic back *now*," the guard on the right of Bella snarls out. "Or so help me, I will have her killed." His blonde hair falls just above his eyes, giving him more of a boyish appearance, but there is no mistaking the pure hatred that seeps from him. He jerks his head to the right, and another guard in full armor steps up with an arrow drawn taut on his bow. It's pointing directly at Bella.

"Flynn," I whisper as panic seizes me. A tingling sensation starts at my scalp and works its way down to my toes.

"It's going to be okay," he replies, though the way it comes out from between his gritted teeth tells me that he doesn't quite believe that. "Take a deep breath, and call your magic back inside of you."

I do as he says because what choice do I have? I can't lose Bella. As our magic fades from our hands—my chest tightening in response—each guard around us steps forward, boxing us in even further.

"Here is what's going to happen," the blonde guard says, his jaw clenching as he speaks. His knuckles turn white from how tightly he grips onto the rope, and bile crawls up my throat as Bella struggles to find purchase with her paws. "You," he says, looking directly at me, "are going to come with us. If you do so peacefully, your fox will return home with you as approved by His Majesty." Flynn steps closer to me, though there is no way he can protect me from every single guard. *He doesn't even have a sword.*

"*You*," he says as he points to Flynn, "will be allowed to live so long as you go through the Spell." Flynn *growls* in response, the sound vibrating on my back from where it's pushed up against his chest. "You already have two guards' deaths on your hands, Princess. Do you want to add your fox and your *friend* to that tally as well?"

Two? My hands clench at my sides as my chest rises and falls quickly. The other guard holding Bella yanks on his rope, causing her to yelp loudly. "Please, stop!" I cry, moving to step towards her again, but I'm halted when Flynn wraps an arm around me. "I have to go! They are going to kill her," I shriek while my fingers dig into his forearm. "Flynn, let me go!"

"Rhea, I'm not giving you to him," he warns, turning me around so that we're facing each other. Alarm flashes through his eyes as he surveys me, but what can we do? My life isn't worth the loss of both of theirs.

"You promised me that you would do whatever I wanted. Even if it destroyed you," I say tearfully, gasping for air. "You promised."

"I did," he agrees quietly. His thumbs brush my shoulders as he looks behind me towards Bella. It's just a few seconds—a breath's worth—before his gaze finds mine again, and it's agony staring back at me, an unrelenting agony that threatens to take me to my knees. "But I'm not willing to let you destroy yourself."

My eyes go wide, but in two quick movements, he hauls me up against his chest and starts backing up towards the Spell, his dark magic glowing powerfully around us. My gaze flies to Bella, where a glowing ball of Flynn's magic hits one of the guards holding her. I watch as she turns and snaps her jaw around the hand of the blonde guard. His blood-curdling scream pierces through the air, the rope falling from his hand. Terror locks my limbs as Flynn continues to move us farther away from Bella, though he sends another ball of magic at the guard holding the bow and arrow and knocks it out of his hands.

The other guards dodge around the trees as they descend on us like a sea of shiny gold, their swords lifted high in the air. Time stills as everything around us blurs. The only things I see is Bella and the unrelenting love that I can somehow decipher within her eyes. She darts in our direction, only making it a few feet, before she's yanked back—a different guard standing on the ropes that are still bound around her neck. I scream until my voice gives out and I have to force air back into my lungs. She darts around to the guards she can reach, snapping at any exposed flesh not covered by their armor. She's giving us the chance to escape. And I hate it. I hate it with everything that I am.

"Bella, no!" I scream, trying to pry myself away from Flynn. "Don't do this!"

My feet kick in the air from how I'm being held, Flynn's strength overpowering any of my attempts to escape. The guards are pushing on the barrier made from the dark radiance of his magic that he has up to shield us from them.

"Flynn, please stop." My words ride a ragged wave of despair, filling the distance that separates Bella and I.

She dodges the sword of a guard, his blade missing its mark but severing the ropes that are keeping her in place. Immediately, she turns and rounds a tree as she starts to sprint to us. Flynn sends another glowing bolt of magic into the closest guard chasing her, their back slamming into the forest floor from the impact. I can *feel* the humming of the Spell right at our backs, the opalescent glimmer of a foreboding wall separating kingdoms. The guards can't come after us if we go through it, but Bella needs to make it through as well. Her paws kick up dirt and fallen leaves as she weaves around trees, the distance separating us closing quickly. The brush of something powerful, ancient and familiar, blankets my skin and soaks into me as Flynn pulls me through the Spell. I sharply inhale, and in my mind's eye a series of images flash by too quickly for me to make out what they are.

And then we're on the other side, the sensation indeed like going through a bubble. Because the Spell is nearly crystalline, I can still see Bella running in our direction. My hand reaches out towards her—only four more strides, and she'll be on this side. Blood rushes in my ears while my heart beats hard in my chest, the pace matching the pounding of her paws on the forest floor. I stretch my arm out, fighting to wiggle free of Flynn's hold. My eyes meet hers through the distorted barrier, and then she collapses, her body sliding to a stop as a sharp, brutal howl rends the air. An arrow sticks out of her hip, blood already spilling onto her white fur.

"No!" I roar as I drop to my knees and Flynn falls down behind me, an arrow whizzing overhead. I try to crawl to her, my magic alight in my palms ready to heal as soon as I reach her, but Flynn is there, pulling me backwards. The guards—gods, there must be forty or fifty of them—line the Spell and surround Bella. The dark swirling glow of Flynn's magic rests on one palm, slowly seeping down into his body again until it disappears—my hope along with it. "Let me go!" I yell, pushing my hands against his chest.

"I'm sorry, Rhea," he rasps, holding my wild gaze with a silver-lined one of his own, "I can't."

I spin around to look at Bella again, her chest lifting up and down with the heavy panting of her breaths. Through the Spell, I watch her pick her head up, the guards coming in from all directions to surround her. And in her eyes, I see it—her desperation for me to go. Her silent pleading for me to be safe, and with a mortal-like nod of her head, her permission for me to leave her behind.

An arrow flies through the Spell, nearly hitting me before Flynn drags me to the side. "We need to go," he begs, hauling me up to stand, but my legs give out almost immediately. An arm reaches under my knees, the other around my shoulders as he scoops me up and starts to run, another arrow landing precariously close behind us. I watch as the guards completely encircle Bella, cutting off my view of her. And as Flynn rounds a corner of the path, before my eyes completely blur from the tears gathering there, a flicker of light blue briefly shines at the center between the guards before dying out.

And then, Bella is gone.

❧❧❧❧ ❧❧❧❧❧

"I'm sorry, Rhea." It's the fourth or fifth time that he's said it as we walk, his glances burning into the side of my head.

I don't know what to say though. A familiar numbness blankets my body, my mind, my *soul*. I understand why he pulled me away. I know that we were in a difficult position. I'm even aware that Bella sacrificed herself so that we could get across the Spell. I comprehend all of this, and yet I can't stop the way that my heart aches like it's been pierced with a sword. An invisible weight sits square on my chest making each breath nearly impossible. And Flynn... I know he was doing what he thought was right, but he chose me over her, and I can't help but feel like he chose wrong.

We spend hours following a well-worn path of gray stones that cut through the most beautiful and lush scenery I could imagine. Trees surround us in all directions as we walk, and I notice that there is a variety I've never seen before. The trunk of this one is absolutely massive as it stretches high into the sky, no branches growing from it until the very top. There, a thick canopy spans out in all directions. There is so much *color* everywhere I look that it's almost as if I can't comprehend that this place is real. To go from being confined by gray stone to unbound in a brilliant forest of color is too good to be true.

I breathe in more deeply, the scenery helping to calm me. A familiar smell tugs on my memory as we continue walking. *Flynn.* His scent has an underlying note of something unique to him, but without a doubt, he smells of this forest—of his home. Even though I know that the sun is high in the sky, the treetops are so tightly woven above us that the light only trickles in where there are small gaps. It's beautiful, enchanting even, and I sigh deeply because I can't enjoy it. I can't allow myself to when the only reason that I'm here is because of the sacrifice of someone else—someone who mattered *more*. That is the sum of my existence—either I suffer alone and in a cage, or I have to watch as the people and beings I love are forced to give up everything so that I can have a modicum of freedom. It isn't fair, and it isn't right.

"Rhea," Flynn says, his hand brushing against my arm. I halt my steps, finally turning to look at him. His face is like a heartbroken plea for me to talk to him. "Let me help you."

"You can't," I mutter. The sound is barely audible.

"Talk to me. I know you just lost someone—"

"I didn't just lose *someone*," I snap, taking a step closer until we're nearly chest to chest. "I lost *everyone*. My parents, Alexi, now Bella. Let's not forget about the nearly twenty-two years I spent inside a fucking tower and everything I lost because of that! I lost my freedom, the possibility of ever having friends, even the ability to choose a meal for myself."

My hands shove into my hair, pulling at the strands as I step back from him. Flynn's panicked gaze follows me, moving from where my hands rip at my hair and then back down to my eyes.

"Don't pretend that you know anything about what I'm going through right now or how you could possibly help me, because you don't.

You can't!" I scream as my hands slide down to cover my face. "No one can. I'm completely alone."

"You're right," he concedes. Gently, his hands cover mine and pull them away from my face, holding them safely in his as he steps closer. "I don't know what to say right now. I don't know how to help. But you are not alone anymore." He enunciates each word sharply, imploring me to feel the truth in them. Begging me to not walk this path of grief and sadness and anger by myself any longer, and to let him take some of the impossible pressure that burdens my heart and soul for himself.

You are not alone anymore. Let me help you. You need only to let me. Each declaration from him washes over and through me like a phantom wind. And I may not know anything about love—about *being* in love—but I know that the way I feel about Flynn is stronger than any other emotion whirling inside of me, and maybe that means I need to surrender to it. To him.

"Okay," I whisper, crashing my body into his as I weep. I weep and weep until my eyes burn and my throat is hoarse. Until I have nothing left and have hit rock bottom. "I feel so broken." I murmur the words into his chest, unsure if he can even hear me.

But he does—of course he does.

"You need to break in order to heal, Rhea," he says quietly while he rubs my back. "And I will be here the whole time. You can fall apart piece by piece until you feel like you have nothing left to give. I will be here picking up your pieces and holding them for you until you're strong enough to put them back together." His hands slide up to cup my face as he steps back, his beautiful gray eyes engulfing me in compassion and love. "Because you *are* strong enough, but until you're ready, I will hold you together."

Another sob is pulled out of me, nearly painful in the way it scratches up my throat. "She died because of me," I heave out, gripping onto his wrists.

"She *lived* because of you, and then she chose for you to do the same. You saw the same look in her eyes that I did, Rhea. She chose *you* in her final moments because she loved you," he proclaims quietly, his thumbs wiping away my tears.

We stay enveloped in our own world for a few moments longer, and I allow myself to give some of that turmoil to him. It's so terrifying to do so, and it doesn't make the pain go away, but it liberates me. It frees me from not having to pull more mental boxes out to shove my feelings into. To not have to pretend that I am okay or put another shield around my heart. Though maybe there is a different, softer one there now, formed by the man by my side—to guard what is already his. One that isn't meant to keep anything out, but instead is there to remind me that I'm not alone. And while I may not know what this new life is going to look like now that Bella isn't with me, I cling to the only truth that I can right now: I love Flynn and he loves me.

We walk for another few hours, Flynn giving me space to grieve but holding onto my hand tightly. Occasionally, he points out homes and other small shops as we walk, the sight of them incredible because of how they almost blend into the forest. Every structure has flowers growing around it *and* on it. I've never seen so many shades of green, and I have certainly never seen so many different flowers.

There aren't very many people out, I notice. The few that do walk on the path near us stare at Flynn keenly for a few seconds before giving him a large smile or a respectful nod of their head. Flynn is polite—returning their greetings—but he also dips his head as if he's trying to hide. My mind is hazy as I focus on putting one foot in front of the other when I hear what sounds like scuffing on the stone ahead of us. Through the foliage, a man that looks to be about Flynn's age appears. Flynn moves his head forward, squinting his eyes slightly before he smiles broadly.

"Cass!" he yells at the man and picks up our pace to a fast walk. The man freezes in place, his hand reaching for what appears to be a sword strapped to his back before recognition lights his eyes and his hand drops back down.

"No fucking way! You're back." He laughs as he jogs the rest of the way to us and nearly tackles Flynn with the intensity of his hug. Flynn lets go of my hand to embrace the man, patting his back vigorously as they laugh and start talking too fast for me to understand.

After a few moments, Flynn clears his throat and reaches for me, his hand finding the small of my back. "Rhea, this is Cassius, my best friend."

Cassius steps forward, dipping his head respectfully as he looks me over. His dark skin crinkles around his light blue eyes as he smiles, his white-blonde hair long and tied back from his face. He stands nearly as tall as Flynn, though his build is less muscular.

"Rhea? That's a beautiful name. And *you* are a beautiful woman," he all but purrs, adding a wink. His grin grows even wider when he sees the narrowing of Flynn's eyes. I notice that his cheek forms a tiny indent on one side when he smiles, and I can't help but give him a weak smile of my own. Even if my heart feels like it has been trampled on.

"Are my parents home?" Flynn asks as we amble back down the path. Cassius leads the way in front of us, and although he has a long sword strapped down his back, he wears no metal armor. He's dressed in thick leathers in different shades of brown that belt and buckle in such a way that I wonder how long it takes him to get dressed.

"Holy shit! Oh my gods, that's right. You don't know," Cassius says, swinging around to look at Flynn as he walks backwards now over the stone. My amusement grows as I wonder how he knows where to step while not looking. His eyes bounce excitedly between us, and it's then that I notice he has a small scar on one temple that runs from his hairline to right underneath his eye.

"I don't know what?" Flynn asks curiously, concern tightening the corners of his eyes.

My lips purse in response as I wonder if we are in any kind of danger. If perhaps King Dolian somehow knew that we were coming here and sent an army to get me back. *They can't get through the Spell.* I breathe out a little sigh at that.

"Your father made a deal with the shifter king. He arrived a little bit ago, and everyone is at the beach now. I'll get a carriage ready, and we can head there." He runs backwards for a few feet, waiting until Flynn nods at him, and then turns around to sprint away.

"The shifter king?" I question, gazing up at Flynn. He tugs on my hand until we're in a jog as well. Who is Flynn's father that he can make a deal with a king from another kingdom?

"I guess so," he says warily. Our footsteps echo out against the trees, my gaze down so that I don't accidentally trip on anything. It isn't until Flynn slows our jog that I look up again, gasping at the sight up on a hill in front of me.

The most beautiful structure built between four of the largest trees I've ever seen towers over me on my left as we walk. Stone, wood, vines, and flowers make up the building materials of this large... house? Castle? It looks palatial in its appearance though different from anything in the Mortal Kingdom. Each of the three levels has a wrap-around porch with portions of it covered by an awning made of flowers and vines. It's the most breathtaking thing I've ever seen. As we near, I see mages dressed in the same way that Cassius is step in front of us on the path. Their eyes roam over us, only hesitating for a moment before they step off to the side. When we pass them, I watch as one of them stares at Flynn with a surprised look on his face. His gray eyes are glued to the man at my side.

A light wooden carriage adorned in vines and colorful flowers rolls up in front of us pulled by two large black horses, their coats shiny and thick. Cassius opens the door and extends a hand for me, which I take as I step up into it. Two deep green velvet benches line either side, but what draws my attention right away is the fact that the top of the carriage is completely missing. I take a forward-facing seat close to a small window, Flynn sitting next to me. Cassius shuts the carriage door, and I hear him climb onto the front before there is a snapping sound. Then we begin to move, the motion jarring. I let myself sink back into the seat, and Flynn extends his long legs out to the other side, his heels resting on the bench there. For a moment it's silent as I look out the window, watching as the trees pass quickly by.

"After we see what is going on at the beach, I will introduce you to my parents and—" Flynn hesitates, waiting for me to look over at him. He brings a finger under my chin, gently tipping it up even higher. His lips kiss mine, just a trace of sensation, before he pulls back again. "And we can talk more."

There's a certain penitence to his voice, but before I have the chance to comment on it, the carriage is already slowing to a stop. I hear the soft murmuring of something in the air, and a scent I've never smelled before stings my nostrils. I look at Flynn in question, and without having to voice a single word, he smiles and nods his head.

"It's the ocean," he says softly, tucking a strand of hair behind my ear.

The carriage door opens as Cassius pops his head in, his eyes dancing with delight as he looks from Flynn to me. "You two lovers ready?" He grins, laughing when Flynn shoves him back outside.

I step out of the carriage, and it takes a moment for my eyes to adjust to the scene ahead of me. A large gathering of people lines the entire beach in both directions. Flynn holds my hand tightly as Cassius leads us through the crowd, many of the people taking a double look at Flynn as he passes. I notice how their eyes grow wide before they all dip their chins at him, their gazes then going to where his hand holds mine. This repeats with nearly every single person we pass as we trudge through the sand. While Flynn is graceful in his movements, my shorter legs struggle to keep up with him as sand gets in my boots, flying everywhere with each step that I take. We finally break through the crowd, and Flynn halts our movements. I see the same iridescence of the Spell that I saw in the forest. The shimmering wall moves into the sky and over the water as far as the eye can see.

I can't stop the small step I take forward, tugging on Flynn's hand as I stare out at the expanse of water ahead of me. My heart beats wildly, as if it can pump fast enough to spread the tiny inkling of *excitement* I'm feeling through my otherwise-depressed state. The ocean is enormous; the bright blue waters, glimmering under the Spell, seem to go on forever. It's similar to the lake I grew up looking at every day, but it's also *so much more.* In the distance, a large ship bobs on the waves while a smaller row boat is pulled up onto the sandy shore. On the other side of the Spell, I can see a small group of people, three men and two women.

"Does the Spell work the same here as it did in the forest?" I ask Flynn quietly, chewing on my bottom lip.

His eyes stay locked on the people standing there as he answers, "No, there is a small section from the water to where the border officially begins that is like a neutral ground." His hand squeezes mine tighter as we take another few steps closer.

The sun beats down on us, and I notice that no trees grow on the beach to block it out. Closest to the water is the largest man that I've ever seen, his height towering over those standing before him. His light golden brown skin and dark brown hair gleam under the bright daytime sun, only broken up by black swirls of some sort that go down the length of one arm. Standing directly in front of him is a woman. Her hands are on her hips as she leans forward, almost appearing as if she is yelling at him.

The breeze blows her dark blue dress and her curly brown hair behind her as she continues her conversation with the large man. To her side are an older man and woman holding hands. The woman has the same style of dress on, though hers is in a pink color, and her curly brown hair is tied up, but there is no denying that it's the same hair as the woman in the blue dress. The man next to her looks to be about Flynn's height, half of his longer black hair pulled back. He wears a style of clothing that isn't quite a dress but goes down to his feet and is open in the middle—the dark blue and silver color of it contrasting against the light brown, almost white, color of the sand. And upon his head, glinting under the sun, is a golden crown.

Flynn tenses when the man with the crown looks over in our direction. He stares for an eternity, like his eyes can't believe what they are seeing. Then they move on to me, where my hand holds Flynn's, and a look I can't decipher crosses his face through the slight malformation of the Spell. His gaze goes back to Flynn's, and he moves to step forward when my view of him is blocked by an older man.

"Nox! Your Highness, it is so good to have you back safe and sound!" he says, planting a hand on Flynn's shoulder. "And perfect timing as well. Tell me, was your mission in the Mortal Kingdom..." He trails off, eyes flicking my way for a moment before he continues, "successful?"

My heart pounds in my chest as my brows draw together in confusion. *Nox? Mission?* I must have misheard. I *had* to have misheard. My hand begins to tremble—or perhaps that is Flynn's—as my gaze meets his, and I know. Even in this, he doesn't hide his expression.

His dark gray eyes practically bleed with remorse, his lips parting as he takes a sharp inhale. "Rhea," he breathes, moving in front of me to cup the side of my cheek, but I step back from his touch, dropping his hand from mine.

And in this moment, on a beach in the Mage Kingdom under the afternoon sun, I realize that the man I love—the man that I thought I could trust with my heart—is more of a liar than I ever thought possible.

Epilogue

T HE ORANGE AND PINK light on the horizon cradles the setting sun, its last golden rays casting out and permeating the cold ocean water. The glimmer of a choice made two hundred years ago moves with the waves, the sparkling Spell extending from the surface and down into the water a few feet, permanently separating those on land from those below it. From *us*.

Swimming against the current, my tail fin undulates with my lower body as I propel myself closer to the black mass ahead of me, my anxiety feeling as large as the depths of the sea itself. Beneath me, spindly multi-colored coral and silky green sea kelp begin to gleam faintly, their full luminescence waiting to peak until the moon lifts itself high into the sky. Water glides past, my gills taking in the oxygen I need to breathe.

A bloom of iridescent jellyfish—their long, delicate tentacles fluttering in the current—part for me as I flow past, my chin dipping in thanks. Finally reaching the sea stack, I lift myself up onto the black jagged rock, my tightly coiled ruby-red braids clinging to my face and body as my breathing automatically switches from my gills to my lungs—to my mortal form. The waning sunlight reflects off of the shiny gradient scales of my tail—blending from red to yellow and then into green—creating small reflective flares on the dark, craggy mass on which I'm perched. I blow out a breath, not from exertion, but from steeling myself for what is about to happen. For what I have to do.

In the distance, a ship sails the waters on its way to deliver goods, but I know that they won't be making it to their destination. Their fate is now in the hands of me and my *kind*. My heart beats in anticipation—or in fear—as an ancient song tickles the base of my throat. Beside me in the water, another appears, drawing my attention.

"Are you ready?" my sister asks, the ends of her short light amethyst braids brushing the tops of her dark shoulders.

I sigh, pulling my gaze from her and looking back out over the water, as the taloned end of my finger taps the rock gently. "Do we have to kill them?" I whisper only loud enough for her to hear. For if the others heard such a thing, my life would be forfeit. It's silent for a moment as I watch the ship draw nearer, but I already know what she's going to say.

"You know that we do," Lyre answers back quietly. The water ripples as another siren breaks through the surface, and another, until fifteen gather around the rock. Nearly all of them gaze at the ship with malice and hunger, their jewel-toned hair haloed with the last remaining glow of the sunset—our beauty just one of our weapons. Just one of the ways we are set apart from everyone else.

"I get the captain," Allegra sneers from her place at the front of the group before she turns to look at me with her deep blue eyes. "You better not hesitate this time, or I *will* tell the queen," she adds with unbridled disgust. "Let's go."

The troop of sirens dip back into the water and begin to swim towards the vessel, their excitement at the hunt palpable.

"We must go, Aria," my sister pleads, lowering into the water so that only her lavender eyes remain above.

I nod, taking one last look at the ship against the fading sunset sky before I dive off of the rock and back into the cool ocean. My heart cracks with each oscillating movement of my tail fin that brings me closer to the unsuspecting men. This feels cruel and ruthless to me, but then again it always has. I wonder briefly if perhaps I can swim away before Allegra notices, but the thought washes away before it's fully formed. I know that more than just one pair of eyes are watching me, making sure I do what is expected of me. So with immense regret, I follow my fellow sirens, grateful that the sea hides the saltwater tears that spill from my eyes.

Allegra swims out to intercept the ship. Though many ships are fast enough to get away from us, all it takes is the whisper of our alluring song on the wind to ensnare them to our will. A group of sirens trail behind the ship while the rest split up to move to either side. Lyre and I stick together on one side, her ombre purple to dark green tail rolling with the movements of her hips as we swim faster. A low whistle sounds in the water, our sign from Allegra to swim up to the surface. My clawed fingers twitch with nervous energy as I guide myself up higher and higher until the warm summer air meets my skin. Immediately, our eerie song fills the air, the entire ship's crew surrounded by the melodic lilt of their impending death.

My throat tingles as our voices, a blend of bass and soprano and everything in between rains down on the men. Sounds coming from the ship clash with our song, but it's too late. If they can hear us, they are already under our spell. The ship doesn't slow down, however, and continues to barrel towards Allegra. Her sapphire blue hair covers most of her face, just her glacial gaze set in the stark brown of her skin stands out against the water as she watches the vessel near. Suddenly, those sharp eyes narrow, and she stops singing, a loud curse filling the air instead.

"Fucking shifters! Abandon the ship!" she growls, her teeth glinting in the now-silver moonlight before she dives back under the water. My eyes widen as I stop swimming, sculling above the water with Lyre by my side.

"Hide your relief, sister," she whispers before slipping under the surface. I school my face into one of practiced indifference, but the truth is that I want to scream in elation.

A ship full of shifters—immune to our song when in their animal form—was the best thing that could have happened. It will be a short-lived reprieve, but I'll take anything I can get. Any moment where I don't have to take an innocent life is worth celebrating. The ship continues sailing away, the crew safe and unharmed.

Shifters... What incredible luck.

My head tilts back to look up at the now-darkened sky, a few stars winking into place as the moon shines on the opposite horizon. With another deep breath, I slowly sink below, opening my eyes as the coral and sea plants glow neon and phosphorescent. When I see I'm alone, the rest of the sirens already making their way back to Lumen, I let a smile upturn my lips as I slowly start following along behind.

And, though it would make the siren queen furious, I thank the stars above that I was spared from having to kill.

THE END
Rhea, Bahira, and Aria's stories will continue in
book two of The Five Realms series.
Coming Fall of 2024

Acknowledgements

HOSAM may have come from my brain, but it wasn't at all able to become the book it is today without the help of many along the way. Allie and Brea, this book does not exist without you two. I know you hate it when I say that, but guess what? It's permanently in the book now. I win. Without your constant support, your editing, your willingness to bounce ideas and flush plot holes out, the world Olymazi would have existed solely in my head as a partially thought out wish and dream. There are not enough words to properly say thank you, so you'll have deal with this shitty paragraph instead. I love you both so much! I'm so happy that we were brought together and I'm sorry, but you are stuck with me now because we have three more books to write!

Leia and Isla, though only ten and six, you both understood that mommy was doing something important. Your excitement over my reels and character art in turn made me more excited. When you said you would tell all your friends that your mom wrote a book, I cried in the bathroom. I love you both so much and I'm so grateful to be your mom.

Joe, without your willingness to let the house slide into chaos while I spent late nights writing and then editing, and then editing more and then formatting, this book would also not exist. You never once batted an eye when I said I needed to purchase something and though I've never told you the full cost of what it took to bring this book into peoples hands, I hope that one day, I can put ten times that back into our account because of it. This was a dream that I didn't know I wanted, but one that was only made possible by you. I love you!

To Lauren over at @bookshelftees, without you posting about your love of reading and your own business creation because of it, I never would have turned to reading as a hobby to try out. I never would have started a bookstagram, which lead me to meeting some incredible people, and I never would have written a book. So thank you for always being so kind, and for having truly one of the best book merch shops.

To my alpha readers, Sheila, Lindsey, and Reenie. The way I had a panic attack the night I sent you the book will probably haunt my husband's nightmares for a long time, but it was so worth it to get your reactions. You were the first set of eyes on this baby after myself, and my editors, and I can't say thank you enough for the dedicated way you read the story and gave me truly helpful feedback. You ladies are the best!

To my bookstagram friends: the way you guys shared every post and reel with feral excitement will never cease to amaze me. Any hype this book gets is solely thanks to you, and I will never stop being grateful for it.

To my author friends Frankie Diane Mallis, Lauren Greene, and Madeline Eliot, thank you for answering all my MANY questions on how to navigate this space as an indie author.

Thank you Taylor Swift and Pedro Pascal. I don't really think I need to say anything else, you guys get it.

And finally, thank you to you, the reader, for taking a chance on this book. For hopefully loving Rhea and Bahira and wanting to continue their stories. I hope that if you take anything away from HOSAM it's that heroine FMC's don't have to all be one way. We can value and find strength in someone who is soft and beautifully raw and tragic just as much as we can value someone who is hard and wonderfully flawed, with a penchant for violence. HOSAM is a different type of fantasy story, one that I hope will resonate with people looking for something new. I can't wait for you guys to see what is in store next!

About the Author

Jenessa Ren loved reading romantic fantasy so much, she created her own series! When she isn't causing chaos for the world of Olymazi, she's hanging out on bookstagram. You can follow along on Instagram at @jenessalikes and Tiktok @jenessaren